PATCHWORK GIRLS

PATCHWORK GIRLS

RACHEL C. HYDE

PATCHWORK GIRLS
Paperback ISBN: 978-1-915129-53-6

Published by Two Trees Books
An imprint of Chartus.X LTD
www.chartusx.org

Copyright © Rachel C. Hyde
Edited by Xyvah Okoye
Cover design by Elyon from thebookcoverdesigner.com
Illustrations by Holly Raddy

The moral rights of the author and artists have been asserted.

*To all the girls who are jigsaws,
you make a beautiful picture.*

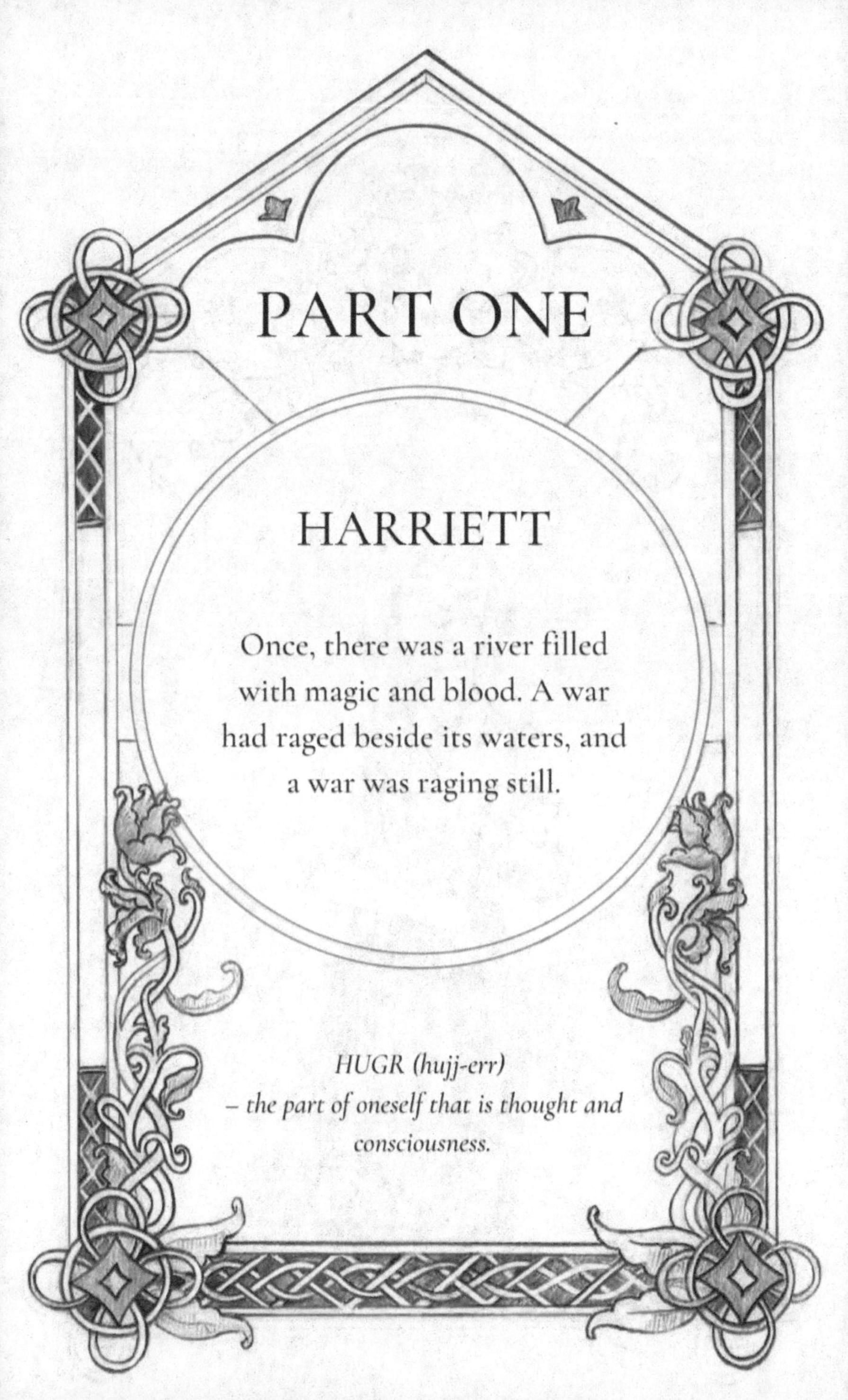

PART ONE

HARRIETT

Once, there was a river filled with magic and blood. A war had raged beside its waters, and a war was raging still.

HUGR (hujj-err)
– the part of oneself that is thought and consciousness.

Chapter One

THE END OF SUMMER

She had never been to a funeral before. Her mother had bought her a dress specifically for the occasion. It was black lace, modest and stifling hot. Harriett could feel the sweat drip down her neck and slide down her back—it was all sorts of uncomfortable. She wanted to adjust the damn thing or better yet, take out some tissues and dab her neck dry. But she didn't. She didn't want to give people more reasons to stare at her.

The chapel itself was quite large but made small by the amount of people crammed inside it. Harriett and her family sat in the front row while her friends; Ruby, Emily, and Sarah sat directly behind her. She looked around the hall until her eyes lingered on Hayley's friends. They sat in the pews a bit further to the back, their makeup smudged and holding onto each other's hands tightly.

Ruby leaned forward in her seat so that her lips almost brushed Harriett's ear.

'How you holdin' up, Sinclair?' she whispered.

Harriett tilted her head back slightly; she wasn't one to tell a lie. 'I'm not,' she replied.

The service had been long and in truth, she hadn't listened to most of it. She didn't want to witness as her sister's life was squashed down into a few measly paragraphs.

So instead, Harriett remembered the last few moments they had shared. It was a memory that had been playing on repeat in her mind since the police had discovered Hayley's death.

They'd been in their bedroom and Hayley had been rummaging through the bedside table for lipstick, which she had then applied in a smooth, precise motion. Harriett had always envied Hayley of that knack - the knack to make even the smallest gesture seem somehow graceful. Her blonde hair had hung loose, a black headband pushing the fringe away from her face.

She had been wearing her favourite summer dress, a navy-blue number with daisies dotted across it. Harriett had been watching her intently. The sisters were similar in all ways but one—Hayley laughed more often and with far more ease. She did so then.

'What are you staring at Hattie?' she'd asked.

'Where are you going?'

Hayley had smiled a sly smile, 'Out.'

Harriett had continued to frown, which only made Hayley laugh more.

'Don't worry!' she'd exclaimed, 'I'll do a Cinderella.'

'You'll be back by midnight?' Harriett said, trying her best not to smile.

Hayley had simply winked and then kissed her sister jokingly on the cheek. 'You know it.'

Then she'd left the room skipping, leaving nothing but a red lipstick mark on Harriett's skin.

But she hadn't returned at midnight and now Harriett was staring at her coffin. With every passing second, she found herself increasingly unnerved by just how *small* it seemed. As though it couldn't possibly be large enough to hold all of whom Hayley was.

When Harriett thought of her sister, she thought of bright smiles and grand plans, of orange nail-varnish and handfuls of daisies. She remembered them playing hide-and-seek with Henry and of late-night chats where Hayley would whisper her dreams for the future. Now she was gone, and Harriett was facing all that was left.

How was it possible that seventeen years of life and laughter could be packaged away so neatly into a box?

The service ended and music played across the room but to Harriett it was all an empty, noiseless sound. She just kept staring, staring, staring at the coffin until it no longer looked like a thing anymore.

The curtains closed and it was gone.

Tears clung to her eyelashes and her throat felt suddenly dry and raw. A hand clasped around hers and she turned to see her brother—he was crying too. She couldn't bring herself to even look at their parents. She thought if she did that the world might break.

They all filed out of the church in silence, vaguely she could feel her friends guide her toward the door and then the summer heat hit her in the face like a slap. The sky was a deep, burning red and the cemetery stretched on for a mile.

'It was a lovely service,' Emily whispered once they were all outside.

Harriett gave a terse nod. She watched as Hayley's friends gathered around her parents to offer their sympathies and condolences. Hayley had acquired friends wherever she went, she collected them the way other people might collect books or stamps. It had been one of her superpowers.

'Are you okay?' Sarah asked bluntly, taking hold of her hand. She opened her mouth to say more but Ruby silenced her with a look.

'We're here,' Ruby said, placing a thin hand on Harriett's arm. 'Whatever you need.'

Harriett gave them a weak smile. She knew her friends were looking to her for guidance on what to say or how to help, but for once she wasn't exactly sure how to give it. All that mattered, all that ever mattered, was that they were there.

'Thank you,' she said.

Leaning forward, Harriett rested her forehead on Ruby's shoulder, then Emily and Sarah huddled in as well so that together they formed an awkward four-way hug. The familiar vanilla smell of Sarah's perfume filled her up and for a moment—just a moment—she could imagine that they were somewhere, *anywhere* else. In the back of Emily's garden, picking flowers and playing pretend; at their favourite coffeeshop, or even sitting in Sarah's room, watching a film.

Sometimes, she forgot exactly how or when she'd met them. Her friends were like a song she knew all the lyrics to but couldn't quite recall learning. They had simply always been there. And they were now, their arms wrapped gently around her, shielding her from the world.

Harriett didn't want to think anymore, she had spent far too much time thinking and remembering and feeling. She was exhausted from feeling. Now she just wanted to wait as the blurs of black suits and black dresses passed her by until it was time for her family to go home. She wanted it to be over, she wanted it to be done.

As she stared at the crowds of people passing them by, she found her eyes drawn to a figure lounging against a tree about twenty yards away. Tall, blonde, and slim, it almost seemed as though the figure was watching them. Faintly, Harriett realised that she should be angry at the person gawking at their grief, but instead found she was too numb to care. It wasn't until she noticed what the figure was wearing that the numbness ceased, only to be replaced by an intense sudden urgency.

Even from where she stood, she recognised the dress. *The dress.* Navy blue and, if she was not mistaken—which Harriett rarely ever was—dotted with daisies.

'Hayley?' Harriett breathed.

Instinctively she jerked away from the embrace of her friends, ready to sprint forward. But before she could move even a few feet, the figure tilted its head to one side, turned away and *evaporated*.

Harriett dropped to the ground.

And that was the end of summer.

Chapter Two

A PLACE OF NO CONSEQUENCE

Hayley and Harriett were bright girls in a bleak town. Hayley Sinclair had had the ability to laugh at anything. Even herself. She was smart, confident, liked by everyone. There was no part of her that was not colourful, not even her hair, which was yellow like the sun.

Harriett Sinclair took after her sister in more ways than one. If it were not for the fact that Hayley was almost two years older, they could have easily passed for twins. Harriett shared her sister's intellect and confidence and she was equally amiable, though less outgoing. It was also fair to say that she laughed a little less, that there was a seriousness to her that her sister sorely lacked. But if anything, that made her smile even more brilliant—more *luminous.*

Woolington-on-Sea was not a place of "brightness" as a rule. It was a small town of absolutely no consequence, and it was grey in the way that only English seaside towns can be grey. It almost always smelt like rain. Wooly's was home to the very young, their parents, and the very old. No hip twenty-somethings lived there. It was boring as every small town, with nothing but an old cinema and an abandoned car park, can't help but be. Nothing, nothing, *nothing* ever happened there.

And then something did.

Overnight Woolington-on-Sea found itself swallowed by a mystery both curious and grim. A girl was dead, and no one was sure how or why.

It was the first rain of summer the night that Hayley Sinclair died, and to Harriett, it felt as though it had been raining ever since.

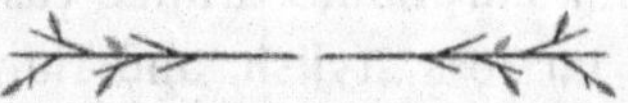

WHISPERS FOLLOWED HER as she walked through the school gates. The other girls did not even try to hide it. They whispered loudly with their hands over their mouths. Whispered with their backs turned to her. Whispers on top of whispers until all Harriett could hear was a faint hissing in the air.

'Do you want me to boot anyone?'

Harriett turned to the girl walking beside her, except for the funeral she hadn't seen her best friend all over the summer, yet on St Catherine's grounds it seemed as though nothing had changed. Ruby was as unkempt as usual; her school shirt was untucked, and her tie was wrapped around her wrist like a bandana.

Everything about this girl was a warning; hair dyed to the colour of soot, skin white as paper and an expression not dissimilar to that of a shark that had just sniffed out blood. Ruby Coleville was a tornado wrapped inside a girl, ready to blow up everything in her path.

'Definitely not!' Harriett said sternly.

Ruby's eyes narrowed. 'One swift kick and suddenly they're all talking about something else. I don't mind, honest.'

Harriett smiled ruefully. 'I know you don't—*that's* what worries me.'

They had reached the main building, the Watts Building, its faded red brick inviting them in. Harriett had never been so relieved to be back at school.

'Guys! Guys wait up!'

Two girls headed toward them; they both wore the long black skirts of St Catherine's along with the burgundy jumper with the olive branch logo emblazoned on their chests. The similarities between the two girls ended there.

Sarah wore the uniform as though she were on a catwalk, her trademark pink earphones draped casually around her neck. Emily was far less stylish, and Harriett noticed the graphite smudges on her nose and fingers, no doubt the remnants of her most recent drawing.

'For a minute I thought we'd missed you,' Sarah said, grinning broadly.

She had inherited an awful lot from her mother; money, confidence and a smile made for compliments.

'Hey,' Harriett said. 'Good summer?'

Sarah faltered, eyeing Harriett from beneath thick, curled lashes. After a moment's hesitation, she gave an enthusiastic nod and casually flicked her hair over her shoulder.

'The best! The parents and I went to *Rome*, thank you very much! It's, like, ridiculously pretty over there.'

Harriett forced a smile. Every summer Sarah would jet off with her parents to travel around different parts of Europe. She always came back tanned, taller and with fascinating stories of all the places she had been. And, usually, of all the boys she had kissed.

'So, you and Anthony are still together?' Harriett asked.

Sarah nodded eagerly. 'Of course! I think he might be *the one,* you know?'

Ruby scoffed and Sarah narrowed her eyes at the sound.

Brusquely turning to Emily, Harriett asked; 'And how was your summer, Em?'

They all knew the answer to this question, but Harriett had asked it anyway.

Emily looked down at her feet.

She was the eldest of five children. Every year her parents scrambled together what little money they had to take them all to a campsite that was barely five miles away from Woolington.

'Busy,' Emily said. 'We went camping.'

'Sounds fun.'

Emily shrugged. 'It wasn't.'

A silence passed over them. Emily had a habit of doing that, inducing the quiet.

The bell rang, causing the four of them to jump, and all around them, St Catherine's Girls hurried inside.

Sarah ignored the movement. Clearing her throat, she said; 'And I suppose you two just spent all your time at the Neville and the Cornerhouse?'

Ruby averted her gaze.

'No,' Harriett replied simply. 'We didn't.'

Sarah wasn't wrong to assume this; it was how the pair usually spent their summer. And yet Ruby had vanished over the last few weeks. It wasn't as though Harriett hadn't *tried* to see her; she had passed by Ruby's house many times, only to find it strangely empty. Strangest of all was that Ruby hadn't told her why.

Harriett followed Ruby's fixated gaze to the gold-painted words above the entrance doors.

'I guess that makes sense,' Sarah said. 'I mean, you did have a lot going on...'

The shrill, high-pitched ringing of the school bell cut through the awkwardness once more, signalling for them all to get to class.

Sarah let out a sigh of relief and adjusted her bag so that it sat higher on her shoulder. 'Well, see you at lunch, *Head Girl*.'

Harriett flushed and made to touch the badge that was pinned onto her jumper as Sarah disappeared inside with Emily following closely behind her. Only Ruby hesitated.

'Look,' she said quietly. 'I need you to know, I wasn't ignoring you.'

Harriett paused, thinking of how to respond. 'That's what it felt like.'

'Well, I wasn't. I wanted to be there for you, trust me I really did...' Ruby gently scuffed the floor with the tip of her shoe. 'I just couldn't... okay?'

Harriett regarded her carefully.

'Okay.'

Frowning, Ruby let out a soft breath. 'I know you said not to ask but how have you been feeling? Y'know, since the graveyard?'

Harriett grimaced. She had only told the three of them about Hayley's ghost, but to be fair she hadn't had much of a choice. After all, they had been there to witness the entire mortifying scene.

Harriett let out a little laugh. 'You mean since that time I hallucinated the form of my dead sister at her funeral?'

Ruby shrugged. 'It's understandable. It's a lot... you're going through a lot.'

Harriett met Ruby's gaze and Ruby stared back unblinkingly. Ruby could be cold, abrasive and incredibly rude but somehow, she always, *always* knew exactly what Harriett needed. And right then, with tears brimming in her eyes and school about to start, Harriett desperately needed to be left alone.

Ruby gave her the briefest of nods and then walked away, leaving her standing on the spot; hurriedly she rubbed her eyes clear as one more group of girls rushed indoors. She tapped a finger on the *Head Girl* badge and continued to gaze up at the words that Ruby had appeared so transfixed by.

Scientia sit potential.

She did not know exactly how long those words had been inscribed upon the school walls, only that she had spent the last three years gazing at them, memorising them and occasionally repeating them to herself when she felt... unravelled. *Knowledge is power.* Harriett used to think this was undeniably true.

That knowledge was a currency. That knowledge was the ability to speak and have people listen to every word spoken. Now... she didn't *know* anything. She felt as though the carpet had been tugged from beneath her. It was like dancing the cha-cha to a waltz or watching a film being played backwards.

Everything felt wrong. *She* felt wrong.

Before, St Catherine's High School for Girls had been the backdrop for all her dreams and aspirations. Now, it was simply where life made the vaguest bit of sense again. Home was complicated; home was the land of unspoken feelings and empty spaces. School was just school; straightforward and predictable. Here she knew where to be and what to do and how to behave.

At home, she was Hayley's younger sister, the grieving daughter. Here, she could be *anything.*

Scientia sit potential...

If knowledge was indeed power, then Harriett Sinclair intended on becoming very powerful indeed.

Resolute, she straightened her tie and pushed open the doors to the school.

Chapter Three

RED RIVERS, BLACK COFFEE

When Harriett arrived home from school, she found a stray cat sitting on her doorstep. It was black as coal, or at least she thought it was black. Its fur was so matted and covered with grime that it was impossible to tell where the colour of filth ended, and the colour of its coat began. It was thin—skeletal even—and as it stared at her from its upright position, with its brilliant blue eyes, Harriett had only one thought.

Must. Pet. The cat.

'Hey kitty, kitty...' Harriett cooed, bending down and gently offering out her hand. 'Are you hungry? Would you like some food?'

The cat tilted its head in what almost looked like a refusal and then sprinted away into the bushes.

Deflated, Harriett stood back up.

A voice laughed from behind her, she didn't bother turning to see who it was.

Harriett's younger brother was almost a foot taller than her, just as blonde and, on occasion, ludicrously charming. Sarah had once joked that if Henry was just a year older, she would be tempted to go out with him herself. A statement which had forced both Harriett and Ruby to pretend-vomit into the air for approximately ten minutes.

'Hello to you too,' Harriett said glumly.

Henry sidled up next to her and they both stared at the front door to their house in silence. Neither of them made a move to step inside.

'So,' Henry said. 'I take it your day was as shit as mine?'

'Don't swear.'

Henry rolled his eyes. 'Was it though?'

Harriett sighed. 'Yes. It was awful.'

They continued to stare at the door.

'All people wanted to do was ask me about her and even if they didn't, I could tell they wanted to...' Henry said quietly. 'Do you think... Do you think we'll ever *know* what happened? Mum and Dad won't...' he trailed off.

Harriett felt her lips thin. 'I don't know.'

They stood for a moment longer before Harriett, aware that she couldn't stand on the front step forever, opened the door.

Inside their mother was ironing clothes in front of the television, their father was not yet back from work.

'Hello darlings,' she said, not looking up. 'How was school?'

'Kind of crap, actually,' Henry said. He made his way to the computer desk on the other side of the room, effectively dismissing himself from any further conversation.

Harriett glared at him. 'It was okay. How about you? How are you, Mum?'

'Oh, I'm alright.' Her mother smiled faintly. 'Keeping busy.'

Harriett regarded the piles of laundry that were stacked across the living room floor and then looked to her mother. Julie Sinclair's hair was piled messily onto the top of her head and she appeared to be wearing the same shirt that she had the day before... and the day before that.

'Mum, are you ironing socks?' Harriett asked incredulously.

Her mother nodded. From across the room, she saw her

brother glance up from the computer screen, and they shared that universal look between siblings, the one that usually occurs right before or after a parent does something ridiculous.

'Socks don't *need* ironing,' Harriett finally said.

But Mrs Sinclair either didn't hear or merely chose not to answer, Harriett looked over to Henry who shrugged and returned his focus back to the computer.

'I'm going upstairs to do homework,' Harriett mumbled.

'Oh, that's good,' Julie said, still not pulling her gaze away from her ironing. 'Staying focused is good; you have so much potential...'

Harriett's heart squeezed painfully in her chest. 'Thanks Mum,' she said quietly. Then she wandered upstairs, dragging her heavy bag of books behind her.

Harriett's room was the biggest in the house, but this was only because she had once shared it with Hayley as well. Now it seemed obscenely large for her alone. Hayley's bed had been removed and Harriett's had been dragged slightly further into the centre of the room. Hayley's cupboard was gone, and in its place, there now stood a grand, full-length mirror. Every trace of Hayley had been erased, swept away in the fierce purge of her mother's creating mere weeks before.

Harriett had managed to salvage two things; the first was Hayley's patchwork doll. Which was kept tucked safely inside the folds of her pillowcase, only to be retrieved when she felt the loss of her sister most strongly.

The second was a box of photographs that had been stashed at the bottom of her wardrobe which she had not yet had the courage to open.

She sat down on her bed and rummaged for the doll. It was threadbare and worn, and one of its button-eyes had long since gone missing. Harriett had always thought of the doll as hideously ugly; it had never made much sense to her for a doll to be made up of quite so many clashing colours and fabrics.

Slowly, Harriett folded her legs under herself so that she was curled up on the bed. Despite everything, it was still *their* room. The faded flower-wallpaper had not been changed, the frilly white curtains had remained the same and there was still a blotch of orange smudged into the carpet from where Hayley had once spilled her nail varnish.

The space around her was somehow both emptied of, and yet full of Hayley. Harriett closed her eyes.

Staying focused is good; you have so much potential.

How could she, though? When her mind felt so messy these days. Cluttered full of projects that needed to be finished and tasks that hadn't been started yet. Hayley's death had slammed the stop-button on her life, and yet now more than ever it seemed to her that there was so much wasted time, wasted life… wasted potential.

Teachers always used to say that Hayley had 'so much potential' and that she was 'going places, that girl,' though they never specified exactly where. They would say the same about Harriett, but from now on it would always be tinged with pity and sadness and followed up with the inevitable comparison; 'so much like her sister'.

She wondered what happened with all of Hayley's potential after she died. Did it float around in the atmosphere somewhere, just waiting to be used up by some other hopeful dreamer? Or was it snuffed out immediately? Disappearing along with Hayley herself…

Uneasily Harriett sat back up on her bed. She had to *be* someone or *do* something. She didn't want her own potential to simply sit there, gathering up dust like forgotten books on the highest shelf. She did not want to forever be competing with the memory of a girl who never had the opportunity to truly live.

Harriett shook her head. Her thoughts had become entangled again, she needed to iron them out smooth and lay them out flat where she could see them.

Sighing, she retrieved some work from her school bag and opened a practice paper.

The British Monarchy is nothing but a powerless figurehead in the present day. Discuss.

And so, Harriett Sinclair, girl-wonder and all-around bright spark, rubbed her eyes and started to write.

THE WATER WAS a dull, dark red. That was how she knew she was dreaming.

The river was wide and long, spanning for miles and miles before disappearing into the horizon.

The sky was a deep, blushing pink.

Harriett thought that the scene was vaguely familiar, like maybe she'd seen a photo of it on the back of a postcard or a painting of it in a museum. It was jarringly and hauntingly beautiful, yet it did not hold her attention for long once she saw the figure standing at the water's edge.

She made to walk toward her, but she found that she didn't need to move, the dream moved around her so that she was suddenly standing by her sister's side.

'Hayley...' she whispered.

Hayley smiled, her red lipstick just as bright as she remembered, she looked exactly as she had the last time Harriett had seen her.

'Hattie,' Hayley breathed, but her voice was too loud— unnaturally so—it filled the air to bursting.

It was most definitely a dream.

'What is this place?' Harriett asked.

Hayley looked out over the river and frowned. 'Hmmm. I thought *you* would know.'

Harriett inspected her surroundings more closely; there were no birds to be seen or heard, no insects or clouds. The blood in the river did not move the way that water would have, everything was perfectly, ominously still.

She shook her head. 'I've never been here before.'

The two sisters faced each other; green eyes met green. They were so very alike.

'I miss you,' Harriett said, unsure of what else to say to the dream-sister. Then she let out a little chuckle. 'I mean, I suppose this is just my subconscious trying to get me to... I don't know, confront my feelings? So, here it goes. I miss you Hayley. I miss you a lot.'

'Why?' Hayley asked brightly, her eyes wide. 'I've not gone anywhere. I was *supposed* to go... but I didn't. And now I'm stuck.'

The dream flickered; the scenery vanished around them and then reappeared in a blink. In the dream Harriett felt her heart beat faster.

'What do you mean?' Harriett asked quickly. 'Why are you stuck?'

'I had something to tell you,' Hayley said thoughtfully. 'But now... now I can't remember what it was. It's on the edges of my mind... I can feel it.'

Harriett could feel the fabric of the dream slipping away as the river glimmered in and out of focus. Frustration and panic were beginning to bubble up inside her and for a moment she had to remind herself that none of it was real. She took a deep breath.

'There must be a reason?'

'You look different here. Older...' Hayley murmured. She reached out to give Harriett's side-plait a gentle tug.

'I'm the same as I've always been,' Harriett said.

Hayley stared at Harriett a little more intently. 'You might be right,' she said simply. 'It might be me that's different.'

The dream shifted, the sky was now draped in black and suddenly there was sound. The river began to rush, insects began to hiss into the air and then there was *rasping*. Or rather the echo of a rasp creeping closer and closer—

Hayley grabbed her arm, her nails digging into Harriett's skin. 'It's coming after you!' she croaked, and the sudden change of tone in her voice was alarming.

Hayley's grip was still firm on Harriett's arm, Harriett leaned forward. 'What is?'

'I remember now! I came to warn you, to tell you that *it* is coming after *you*,' Hayley smiled, clearly pleased with herself for successfully passing the message on.

'I—I don't understand,' Harriett said.

The smile wiped itself off from Hayley's lips, like lipstick being smeared away. Now she was frowning, her expression both confused and serious. She was just a little closer to the sister that Harriett remembered.

'Neither do I,' Hayley said. Then she let her arm go and Harriett was lurched backwards into the dream

into blackness

into nothing

All the while she heard her sister's voice rattling around in her head, saying just one word over and over.

Run.

HARRIETT AWOKE TO find herself lying on the bedroom floor. Her alarm clock was blaring, and Ruby sat on the end of her bed.

'So, was the bed just too comfortable?' she said, grinning.

Harriett sat up and looked frantically around the room. Her head was pounding viscously, and the last fragments of the dream still lingered in her mind.

'I must have rolled off the... hang on, what are you doing here?'

'Your brother let me in. I got up early and thought I'd grab us some coffee.' She handed Harriett a paper cup. Harriett reached out to take it and Ruby froze. 'Sinclair, *what* is on your arm?'

Harriett glanced down to see four angry, red lines etched into her forearm. Scratch marks.

'Must have happened in my sleep,' she murmured. Then she took off the lid of the coffee and inhaled; black Americano with two sugars. She forced a smile, but her mind was still reeling.

'You know me so well.'

'That I do,' Ruby agreed. She headed over to Harriett's wardrobe and started yanking out school clothes, chucking them haphazardly onto the bed. Harriett noted that Ruby did not seem to have a coffee herself.

'I missed you this summer,' Harriett said quietly.

Ruby's body stiffened as she started rummaging for Harriett's shoes. Slowly, she picked up a pair of black loafers and sat back on the end of the bed. There were dark circles pressed under her eyes and a definite gauntness to her face that Harriett was certain had not been there before.

'I missed you too.'

Harriett crawled onto the bed next to her, mind whirring from her nightmare and the impossible fingernail marks. 'Ruby, are you sure you're alright?' she asked.

Ruby plastered on a grin. 'I'm dandy. Now c'mon, school's waiting. St Catherine's girls are never late!'

'St Catherine's girls are never tardy,' Harriett finished. She took a deep drink from her coffee, letting the bitterness and sugar warm her up. She pulled on her uniform and organised her book bag, brushed her hair and plaited it to the side as she always did—all the while Ruby stood waiting.

Finally, Harriett went to check her appearance in the mirror, signifying the end to her morning ritual. Everything was as she expected, there was not a single crease in her clothes nor a single strand of hair out of place and yet... as she stood in front of her own reflection, she found that she no longer recognised herself. Her face was all wrong, her cheekbones too high and her eyebrows too thin. For a fraction of a second, she saw *someone else* gazing back at her.

Ruby placed a hand on her shoulder. 'You okay?'

Suddenly the world returned, only an unsettling feeling of *disremembering* lingered on her being. A sense that she had forgotten something, and that the truth was skirting somewhere nearby, only just out of view.

First, the dream. Now this.

Run.

'I'm fine,' she said, flexing her fingers as if to make sure they still moved at her command. She picked up her coffee and swallowed the last dregs. 'Let's go.'

Chapter Four

TROUBLES AND MISFORTUNES
OF SAINT SINCLAIR

As they made their way to school Harriett found her mind to be everywhere and nowhere all at once. She rolled up her sleeve and saw that the scratches still shone pink and raised on her skin. She checked the time on her watch; they still had twenty minutes until the first bell.

Abruptly, Harriett changed direction.

Ruby followed.

Methven's was the tiny coffee shop that sat perfectly nestled between St Catherine's School for Girls and St David's School for Boys. It was a hipster's paradise, decorated just shabbily enough to be considered chic. It was filled with lamps that had no lampshades, mismatched tablecloths, and twee patterned mugs.

It was a known fact that Methven's served the strongest coffee in all Wooly's and—in Harriett's modest opinion—that made it the best.

When they reached the coffee shop's front door, they found Sarah leaning against the wall waiting for them. She smirked as they approached.

'So, tell me, how many will it be this morning?'

'This will be her second,' Ruby said, before Harriett could answer.

Sarah scoffed. 'You have a problem.'

'With what?'

'With coffee.'

Harriett gasped, mock-shocked and relieved to play a part in a normal conversation. Dream-rivers and warnings were trivial asides when faced with the warm smell of hot beverages and the smile of a friend.

See? She thought to herself. *Nothing's changed, not really.*

'How dare you!' Harriett exclaimed. 'I do not have a problem with coffee, I love coffee and coffee loves me. We have a symbiotic relationship.'

'*Symbiotic relationship*? Do you even hear yourself when you speak?' Sarah rolled her eyes and laughed. 'And it's not a relationship, it's an addiction.'

'You're just jealous. Coffee cares for me and coffee would never force me to watch it play football on a Saturday morning.'

The three of them queued up behind a boy in a green blazer.

'What's this about football?' Ruby demanded.

Sarah waved a hand dismissively. 'I've been watching some of Anthony's Saturday league games, that's all.'

Ruby stared at her incredulously as Harriett ordered her drink. Ruby had perfected two looks over the course of her short life. The first was a knife-like grin that was more unsettling than it was endearing, the second was a withering, dialogue-stopping stare that said; *I refuse to dignify that statement with any further conversation.*

'So, where's Emily?' Harriett asked.

'I told her that we'd meet her by the bike sheds, I wanted to speak to you guys alone first. It's about her birthday. I looked into the prices like you said, and I got this quote,' Sarah pulled out a pink slip from her bra and passed it over.

Ruby pulled a face at her. 'Have you seriously had that in there this whole time?'

Sarah shrugged. 'Why not? It's where I keep everything else; my phone, my hairbands, any loose change…'

The two of them descended into habitual bickering while Harriett took the slip from Sarah's hand, guilt washing over her. After everything that had happened over the summer, she'd completely forgotten about Emily's birthday.

It seemed almost impossible that amongst all the madness ordinary events such as birthdays still existed. Life went on, however, and they had traditions to uphold.

'That looks about right. £15 each seems reasonable,' she said. The waitress passed her the coffee from over the counter.

Sarah smiled. 'Excellent. If you both give me the money tomorrow, then I'll order it for the weekend.'

'That's fine,' Harriett said, and it was. Mr and Mrs Sinclair gave their youngest daughter a small allowance at the end of each month and had done so since she was ten. Harriett, being the sensible girl that she was, saved most of it.

'Yeah, I can't do that,' Ruby said, fidgeting with the frayed edges of her jumper sleeve.

Sarah's silken voice sharpened. 'Why not? Do you not want to wish Emily a very happy birthday?'

'No, it's not that,' Ruby said. She raised a hand and scratched her nose, then folded her arms and unfolded them again. 'I just don't have any money.'

Harriett frowned. 'What about your paper round?'

'I quit.'

Both Harriett and Sarah exchanged glances. 'Why?' they asked in unison.

'Does it matter?' Ruby practically growled at them, her pale skin flushing red. 'C'mon, we're gonna be late.'

Then she stalked off.

Harriett sighed. 'Is it just me or is Ruby acting strange?'

'She's always strange, you're only just noticing,' Sarah said.

Harriett rubbed her temple. It wouldn't be fair to not pay for Emily's surprise, but at the same time she wasn't really in the mood to force Ruby into doing something she didn't want to do.

'I'll pay for Ruby's share,' she said.

Sarah threw back her head and laughed, it was a tinkling, jovial sound. Her hair rippled down her back and she smiled knowingly back at Harriett. It really was impressive how astonishingly beautiful Sarah could be with such little effort.

'I assumed you would,' Sarah said, and then they headed to school.

HARRIETT SINCLAIR HAD a mountain of problems, one stacked neatly on top of the next. It always seemed to her that as soon as one problem was solved another would scurry along to take its place. Yet there was one persistent problem that Harriett had never *quite* succeeded in fixing.

And that was Ruby.

Harriett could never remember exactly how she became friends with Ruby Coleville. She thought that she might have known Ruby first, before Emily and Sarah came along, but she couldn't quite be sure. On the whole Ruby was an excellent friend to have; she was loyal and fierce and honest even when lies were easier.

The issue was that being friends with Ruby was rather like being friends with a human kettle. There was an anger always simmering just below Ruby's surface, weeks could go by and they could almost forget that it was there, until one day she'd spill over. It was an occupational hazard of simply being near her that they might get splashed. It was by mere habit alone that Harriett found herself constantly cleaning up the mess.

Ruby had always been quick to anger, slow to solutions. It was simply her way. Ruby was most herself when running on a track, swinging a racket or, unfortunately for those around her, throwing a punch. It was only when Ruby was pushing her body to its limits that the outbursts could be kept at bay. Harriett knew the pattern well enough and she knew Ruby would be at her worst at the beginning of the school term, the lack of activity in the summer having driven her to boiling point.

Harriett had theorised the many different reasons why Ruby might be how she was. Maybe it was a temper she had inherited from her mother. Maybe it was the absence of a father. Maybe it was just who she was and there was no explaining it, like asking why Sarah was so tall or why Emily was so damn quiet all the time.

Regardless, Harriett was not surprised when that Tuesday lunchtime, Ruby snapped again.

They were sitting at a table in the food hall for a change and Harriett had spread out a pile of books in front of them. She had spent most of the morning break organising school clubs with the other prefects, already her homework diary had notes upon notes of jobs that needed finishing. She had to start recruiting students to create the yearbook, she had to ask the Deputy Head for permission to continue the chess club *and* she had to organise the prefect hallway rota.

She had also surreptitiously snuck a leaflet into her diary, a leaflet full of testimonies and advice on the five main ways to get into Oxford or Cambridge Universities.

It was three years before she could apply but still... it couldn't hurt to look.

'I had an odd dream last night...' Emily said pensively.

Harriett's head shot up from her diary. 'You did? What was it about?'

Emily poked a hole absentmindedly through her cheese sandwich. 'A castle, I think. I didn't like it...'

Harriett's pulse slowed. She wasn't sure what she had been thinking, that Emily would have had the same dream as her? That was ridiculous. Emily seemed as calm and as serene as ever, her mass of hair standing on end in the magnificent way that it always did. She glanced at Sarah.

'Who are you texting?' she asked.

'Anthony. He's going to meet me after school today.'

Emily didn't say anything to that, choosing instead to poke more holes into her sandwich.

Then a voice, loud and grating, shouted over to them. 'OI, COLEVILLE!'

Suddenly, Harriett remembered with a sharp, ugly clarity why they didn't usually sit in the food hall.

Sophie Grimely was a beast of a girl with beetle eyes and a mouth that didn't smile so much as it *curled*. It often seemed to Harriett that Sophie came to school for only two reasons, the first was to smoke behind the bike sheds with her motley-crew, and the second was to start fights with Ruby.

Not that Ruby needed any encouragement. Theirs was a feud that had begun back in first school; Sophie had tried to steal Ruby's lunch and in return Ruby had bitten the back of her hand until she drew blood.

Rumour was she still had the scar.

Both Sophie and Ruby had dutifully carried their hatred for one another from primary school into secondary; their loathing for one another was as much a matter of principle now as it was an actual feeling.

'I didn't see you this summer, Coleville. You hidin' from me or something?'

'Please. Hiding from you would mean acknowledging your existence,' Ruby leaned back in her chair and let out a short, bark-like laugh. 'We both know how much I'd *hate* to do that,' she said the word *hate* as though she relished the sound of it on her tongue. It stretched out languorously in the sentence until it was the only word worth noticing.

Sophie and her crew stood at the end of the table now, dangerously close. Sophie eyed Ruby carefully.

'Y'know, I don't think it's fair to fight ya. You've gone skinny on me Coleville, what's that all about? Your mum can't afford to feed you no more?'

Ruby's eyes flashed, a smile cracked across her face.

'Oh honey...' Ruby crooned. 'Don't hurt yourself worrying about me. Your whole goddamn head might explode.'

It was a well-known fact that the angrier Ruby was, the more she smiled, and right now she was positively beaming.

'I'm gonna beat that damn smile off your face,' Sophie hissed.

'Ruby...' Harriett warned, but Ruby wasn't listening.

'Come near me and I'll shove your head so far up your arse it'll come out your mouth,' she said sweetly, all the while wearing her knife-like grin.

Harriett buried her head in hands, knowing all too well what was going to happen next.

Sophie charged at the table just as Ruby slid over it and the two girls slammed into each other.

Immediately everyone in the lunch hall stopped to watch, crowds of girls formed a ring around them. It was rather like watching a modern-day gladiator fight, two people circling each other while hordes of girls gathered around them, shouting and chanting—an audience eager for blood.

Again, and again the two girls launched themselves at one another, punching and pushing to the sound of *ooohs* and *aahhs.*

There was one glaring difference between the two girls. Sophie was angry; every muscle in her body was tense and coiled ready to pounce. Whereas Ruby was *smooth*, her arms hung loosely by her side, there was an almost jaunty rhythm to how she moved. This was as easy as dancing to her.

'It's like watching a cat play with a mouse, isn't it?' Sarah whispered, disgusted.

Harriett fixed her gaze on Ruby. It struck her then that Ruby had kept herself calm the past few days for Harriett's sake and Harriett's sake alone. Now the mask had slipped, and she was a monstrous thing once more; restless and wild.

Sophie threw another punch but again Ruby dodged it, the grin on her face widened.

'Come on then!' she sang. 'Hit me.'

Sophie slammed her hand into the side of Ruby's face and the sickening sound of the smack echoed across the hall. Ruby's hair fell in front of her eyes, her expression temporarily obscured, but then she tossed her head back and the mess of black hair was gone, revealing a terrifying sneer.

Sophie must have seen it too for she charged at Ruby, in a move that could only be described as bull-like, she aimed head-first for her stomach. Harriett watched in horror, fearing that at any moment her friend was going to be knocked to the ground like a human bowling pin.

And then, something incredible happened. Ruby *jumped*. She sprung upward over Sophie's head just as the collision was imminent. Sophie stumbled and as she did Ruby grabbed her by the collar of her shirt, yanked her backwards and sent her crashing into the ground.

There was a collective gasp from all the onlookers, Ruby herself seemed perplexed and the sound of shouting suddenly ceased; all the frantic energy sucked from the room.

'Get up,' Ruby whispered.

Sophie sat, her nose was bleeding and though she met Ruby's gaze with a sneer, she didn't move.

'You wanted a fight,' Ruby said. 'Get up.'

'Stop her,' a voice said.

Harriett spun around to see that Emily had appeared directly behind her, or perhaps she had been there all along. Her dark face and dark eyes bored into Harriett's; the dreamy expression she usually wore noticeably absent.

Harriett stepped forward. 'Come on Ruby, that's enough.'

Ruby ignored her. 'Get up!' she said again.

Seeing Ruby stand there, a brutal combination of violence and recklessness, Harriett snapped.

'Stop this, *now*.'

It was barely a whisper and yet her voice rang out loud and clear. Her words were a tremor that rippled through the hall and every girl in a ten-foot radius held their breath. Ruby slowly closed her eyes and then, like a puppet on a string, took three steps back. She glared at Harriett as Sophie scrambled from the ground.

Sophie faced Harriett, her broad face coloured crimson. 'You're such a good little girl ain't ya, Saint Sinclair? Always keepin' your pet outta trouble.'

Then she spat at Ruby's feet. Ruby didn't even flinch.

An awkward silence followed as Sophie marched out of the hall, her friends scampering along behind her.

The other students were watching Ruby and Harriett intently.

'Please leave,' Harriett said.

Students looked from one to another, there was the sound of hushed voices and muffled footsteps. Just like that the four of them were alone; Harriet, Ruby, Sarah and Emily.

Harriett pinched the bridge of her nose and turned to Ruby. 'What is wrong with you?' she paused hesitantly. 'This anger problem is—'

'I don't have a fucking anger problem,' Ruby snapped.

Harriett crossed her arms over her chest. 'Yes, well *now* I'm convinced.'

'Ruby went off into a torrent of unintelligible swear words until finally Harriett held up her hands in finality.

'*Enough.*'

Ruby stopped mid 'Fu-' her mouth slamming shut and her breathing heavy. An eerie silence passed over them.

It was a strange gift that Harriett Sinclair possessed, the gift of giving out orders and having them followed. She did not have to raise her voice or threaten or bribe. She simply had to say what she wanted and truly *mean* it.

Ruby ran a hand through her short, spiky black hair. There was a thin layer of sweat across her brow—but she said nothing. Instead she seemed to be studying Harriett, looking her up and down.

'Ruby, I mean it, this has to stop. Don't we have enough to get on with? This is the final year of school; do you really want to get expelled?'

'They're not going to expel me,' Ruby sniggered.

Harriett gaped at her. 'If you keep this up, of course they will! What makes you think they wouldn't?'

'Look, I never asked you to fight my battles for me. So, do me a favour and stop acting like you've got to! You can be *Saint* Sinclair for somebody else.'

Harriett froze; Saint Sinclair was the name that was exclusively used by the likes of Sophie Grimely and her ilk. She had always found it amusing coming from them, but from Ruby it was a word dipped in malice, and she had no words to return to her.

Sarah, however, did; 'Hey! Stop acting like such a bitch. It's embarrassing.'

Ruby snorted. 'Not for me it ain't.'

Then she spun on her heel and walked away.

Harriett watched her leave. She knew that if she called Ruby back, she would come. She knew that if she told Ruby to apologise, she would. She simply couldn't bring herself to open her lips and speak.

The hall was empty but for the three of them, yet as Harriett stared at the ground, she saw a fourth shadow stretched out forebodingly across on the floor. This shadow seemed somehow darker than the others, longer—less human. Harriett blinked, and then it was gone.

Sarah wrapped an arm around Harriett's shoulders. 'Are you alright?'

'No,' Harriett said. She rubbed the spot on her arm where the dream-Hayley had left nail marks. It was still sore. Her breathing was uneven now as fear and panic, panic, panic filled her up to bursting. She was most definitely *not* alright.

In fact, she rather thought she was going mad.

Chapter Five

GIRL FIGHT CLUB

Hayley in the graveyard... Hayley in the dream... The shadow.

Over and over Harriett went through the list in her head, trying to make sense of it all. And over and over she reasoned with herself that it was just her imagination. That what she was experiencing must be some form of grief; her mind playing cruel tricks on her. Hayley's ghost most certainly had not visited her and there had been no fourth shadow on the floor.

Still, there was a gnawing in the pit of her stomach that wouldn't go away, and still there was the warning.

It is coming after you.

Run.

When the final bell rang at the end of the day, Harriett breathed a huge sigh of relief and practically fled the classroom to get outside. When she reached the bike sheds, she found Emily already waiting.

'Shall we wait for the others?' Emily asked.

Harriett nodded, she wasn't entirely convinced that Ruby hadn't already left, but Sarah would still want them to wait. As they stood there, she allowed her eyes to dart across the field. She knew it was insane and ridiculous and a thousand other stupid things—but she kept thinking that any minute now she would catch another glimpse of the shadow or (just maybe) her sister.

Emily squinted and cocked her head to the side in a bird-like manner.

'You can talk to me, you know. Whatever it is, you can talk to me.'

'It's nothing,' Harriett said quickly.

Emily nodded, but they both knew it wasn't nothing. 'Nothing' rarely ever was.

It was then that Ruby and Sarah made their way towards them from across the field. Ruby's eyes were fixed determinedly ahead, and Harriett noticed she was carrying a takeaway cup. When they reached them Ruby practically thrust the cup over to her.

'Girl Fight Club?' Ruby said gruffly.

Harriett regarded the cup and then Ruby. It wasn't an apology, but it was close enough.

'Girl Fight Club,' she agreed.

Sarah rolled her eyes in Emily's direction. 'Really? This again? I thought we'd finished with that ages ago.'

Harriett couldn't help it, she smiled. Girl Fight Club was a title Ruby had been using for them since Sarah went through her Brad Pitt phase. Together they'd watched all his movies right up until *Fight Club*.

Then Ruby had ruined it by constantly quoting from the damn thing, ending almost every conversation with a casual; *'First rule of Fight Club: you do not talk about Fight Club!'* Sarah had eventually gotten so annoyed by it that she labelled the movie 'depressing as hell' and declared that she had always preferred Leonardo DiCaprio anyway.

Still smiling, the four of them made their way down the path toward the school gates, where swarms of St Catherine's girls were alreadly cloistered in groups and giggling on the streets outside. Ruby shook her head despairingly.

'Pathetic,' she grumbled.

It was a well-known fact that ten minutes around the corner from St Catherine's High School for Girls was St David's High School for Boys. It was also a well-known fact that while the girls at St Catherine's had an hour lunch break the boys at St David's only had forty minutes, the result being their school day finished twenty minutes earlier. So, at the end of every day, as the girls of St Catherine's were leaving school there would already be St David's boys clustered about, just waiting to catch their eye.

'I wish these uniforms weren't so damn unflattering,' Sarah said, pulling up her skirt so that it stopped skidding along the floor.

The four girls had almost reached the gate and sure enough they were met by a flurry of green blazers.

'Who are you trying to impress?' Harriett asked.

Sarah scowled at her. 'You know who.'

A large group of St David's boys sauntered towards them, and at their front was a tall, muscular boy with blonde hair that was just scruffy enough to be stylish. He grinned broadly when he saw Sarah. Harriet, Ruby and Emily dropped behind as Sarah and Anthony kissed each other.

Ruby made a gagging sound, Emily blushed and Harriett... Well, Harriett was fascinated. Boys were still a mystery to her, their purpose still undiscovered. She had seen the movies; she knew what was *supposed* to happen. Boy and girl meet, sparks fly, they share a kiss and then BOOM! They're in love.

Harriett had been kissed before. Once. Messily, and by a boy who tasted faintly of oranges. She was in no great rush to go through the ordeal again.

But Sarah believed in soulmates and wasn't shy about the search for hers. Harriett didn't believe in it much, the idea of finding one person destined for you in a world of seven billion people seemed a little far fetched. Especially as so many people discovered their 'soulmates' right next door.

Still, the word had a nice ring to it.

Sarah and Anthony pulled apart, he whispered something in her ear and Sarah giggled, her hand pressed coyly to her mouth and her eyes fluttering girlishly.

'Gross,' Ruby said under her breath.

'Ruby…' Harriett said warningly. 'It's not gross.'

Ruby pulled a face. 'Are you sure we're looking at the same thing?'

Anthony waved at them and they wandered over to where Sarah, Anthony and the rest of his crowd were standing.

'I was just telling Sarah that I'm having a party at my house for my sixteenth,' Anthony said. 'I'd love for you all to come.'

Ruby scoffed. It was true that in the entire time he and Sarah had been dating, Anthony had barely exchanged more than two words with them.

'We'd love to go,' Harriett said.

Both Ruby and Emily turned to her in astonishment. It was no secret that Harriett wasn't the biggest fan of parties, and she liked them even less during school term. But Sarah was their friend, and Anthony was important to her. They were a pack, the four of them, where one went, they all followed.

Anthony grinned. 'Excellent! It's on the 29th, you can bring your own booze and my house is down Romulus Road, number eighteen.'

Harriett gave Sarah an incredulous look, she grimaced and placed a hand on Anthony's chest.

'Babe, Harriett lives literally three doors down from you. I thought you knew that?'

Anthony frowned. 'Really?' he laughed. 'I guess you won't be late then!'

Sarah grinned, and Anthony wrapped an arm around her shoulder. For a moment the five of them stood there in silence, regarding each other awkwardly.

'So, I'll see you all tomorrow,' Sarah said brightly.

She waved from over her shoulder as Anthony and his group led her away, his voice booming down the street, discussing football and penalties and other sports-related things.

'We need to save Sarah,' Ruby said as soon as they were out of earshot.

'Why?' Harriett asked.

Ruby looked back at her solemnly 'Because I think there's a really good chance that he's going to bore her to death.'

'He's harmless,' Harriett said.

'He's *dull*,' Ruby replied. 'Not to mention so, *so* stupid. What does she even see in him anyway?'

Harriett shrugged. Sarah's reel of boyfriends had always been rather interchangeable to her, though she had to admit Anthony did seem to be lasting longer than most.

'She says when they kiss her insides twirl,' Emily said vaguely.

Harriett and Ruby gaped at her, but she wasn't paying attention, she was too preoccupied curling a strand of her frizzy hair around her pinkie finger.

Ruby looked to Harriett once more.

'Gross,' she said again.

Emily bit her lip. 'I think it's kind of nice...' Then she turned and walked away in the direction of her home. 'See you later,' she called.

Harriett watched as Emily wandered further into the distance, her silhouette blocking the sun and her wild curly hair flowing behind her. She had always been effortlessly graceful, her lithe body almost danced instead of walked. As Harriett watched, the air around Emily seemed to shift, and Harriett found herself trapped inside the moment.

Time slowed... and slowed... and then it stopped. Emily's body remained suspended mid-walk, caught frozen within the time between seconds. Harriett's eyes continued to stare at her, and as she stared, she was filled with that familiar feeling of *wrongness*. That the world was on a balancing scale and it was tipping frighteningly off kilter.

She stared at Emily and found her image distorted.

Time clicked back into place.

Harriett blinked, and Emily continued to walk. She walked until she reached the house at the end of the road, then turned the corner and out of sight.

'Erm, Sinclair. Your bag is leaking.'

Harriett spun around, surprised to see Ruby still standing behind her.

'What?' she said thickly.

'Your bag, it's leaking,' Ruby said. She pointed to the school bag that hung on Harriett's back. Without thinking Harriett shrugged it off so that it was on the floor, noticing how much heavier it felt as she did.

It wasn't just leaking; it was soaking wet.

'You don't have any water bottles in there, do you?' Ruby asked, kneeling to get a better look.

Harriett shook her head, and she kneeled as well. She glanced around them, the crowds of students had long since dispersed—it was just the two of them now.

Hands trembling Harriett reached out and unzipped the bag. As soon as it opened water spilled from it like a tide—brown grimy water. It spattered over their skirts and spooled out onto the pavement around them. Ruby swore and fell backwards as Harriett, heart and head thrumming wildly, picked up the backpack and tipped it upside down so that its contents emptied onto the floor.

Sodden, water-drenched books landed onto the ground with a smack, and then lastly... something oval and solid hit the pavement with a sickening clap and rolled a few feet away.

The two girls stared at it.

'Is that... is that what I think it is?' Ruby whispered.

Harriett's mouth dropped open. Blood pounded in her ears, a horrendous rushing sound that would not go away.

She closed her eyes, hoping against all hope that when she opened them it wouldn't still be there. That maybe she really was losing her mind after all.

She opened her eyes to see it still laying there in a puddle of water, both horrifying and harrowing all at once. It was cracked and yellowed, with chipped teeth and hollowed eye sockets that nonetheless seemed to be staring right at them, judging them.

A skull.

A god-damn, solid as anything, beyond impossible, human-fricking-*skull*.

WHEN HARRIETT ARRIVED home, she did not say hello to her family, she did not stop to tell them how her day had been or pause to get some food from the kitchen. She simply ran upstairs and shut her bedroom door carefully behind her, without uttering a single word she dropped her bag to the floor and opened her wardrobe to retrieve a box.

It was her box of forbidden things, of secrets that she didn't want her family to see—photo albums of her sister.

Slowly and carefully, she took the skull out of her bag and held it as far away from herself as possible, as though it were a bomb that might go off at any moment. Then she hurriedly placed it in the box, pushed the box back inside the wardrobe and slammed the door shut.

Breathing heavily, Harriett collapsed against the wardrobe door, her mind reeling and her entire body shaking.

All the way home she had batted away the questions that kept flying through her head. How had it got in her bag? Who put it there? Who did it *belong* to? Was it even real? But above all the *why's* and *who's* and *how's*, there was one question that shouted louder than all the rest.

What do I do?

From inside her shirt pocket she felt her mobile vibrate. Still shaking, Harriett pulled out the phone to see a text flash across the screen.

DON'T WORRY, I WON'T TELL ANYONE.
GIRL FIGHT CLUB. – RC

Harriett let out a strangled sob, of relief or frustration or panic she didn't know. She sat there for a long while, eyes stinging as the room swam around her. Everything felt as though it was spinning nowadays, and she didn't know how to make it still.

Chapter Six

A LITTLE MORE
SIXTEEN CUPCAKES

It had been a while since Harriett had last visited Emily's house. The Walters lived in a tall, narrow terraced building down Oakchurch Way, right next to Charles Park. The house was painted entirely white with a bright green front door. Inside, there were bundles of dried flowers dangling from the ceilings and incense sticks poking out from various corners. Emily's father was an artist, so there was always an assortment of paint pallets dotted around in odd places; on bookcases, coffee tables or by the kitchen sink.

Canvases decorated every wall, and each painting told an absurd and beautiful story. A small canvas next to the front door showed a dancer trapped inside a silken web. Another in the kitchen depicting a boat floating lazily in the middle of a vast ocean. But the most hypnotising of all, was the family portrait that had pride-of-place on the living room wall.

Emily's parents stood as trees: Her mother, blonde and pale, wrapped in cherry blossoms; her father, dark skinned and strong, in maple leaves. In front of them knelt all five of their children. Emily, the eldest, wore a crown of sunflowers. The twins, Heather and Daisy, stood beside her, draped in their namesakes, while Violet wore a dress of purple.

Oakley, the only boy, knelt in a cape of oak leaves, clutching acorns in his hands. Harriett always stopped to stare at it.

Somehow Mr Walters had managed to capture the serene gleam in Emily's eyes and the wistful curve of her mouth. No detail had been missed, not even the small scar that ran through the edge of her left eyebrow. Harriett always thought that, while all the characters in the portrait were beautiful, the image of Emily was the most striking.

Perhaps she was biased, perhaps she only saw those things in the portrait because she knew they should be there.

It was, in Harriett's opinion, exactly what a home should be; warm and comforting. It was where all her fondest childhood memories had taken place.

The day was Saturday, and Harriett sat on the countertop in the Walter's kitchen. The sun shone through the window and outside the garden was overgrown and unkempt—the perfect backdrop for a child's imagination. In front of her, Emily hummed as she added generous amounts of chocolate powder to the milk boiling in a pot.

'It's nice that they've let you have the house today,' Harried said.

Emily grinned, revealing big, white teeth. 'It's not every day a girl turns sixteen.'

Harriett felt her mouth tug into a broad smile. 'Do you remember when we used to play dress-up in the garden?' Harriett asked. 'Sarah always had to be a princess; she had that god-awful pink gown she wore everywhere.'

'Yes.' Emily smiled. 'Ruby was always a soldier, or a warrior...'

Harriett laughed. 'I think that was mainly so she could beat up the rest of us with sticks.'

The sticks were, of course, the only logical substitute for a sword. Harriett delved further into those childhood memories. 'You were the witch, right?'

Emily looked thoughtful for a moment and then nodded, her hair bouncing as she did. 'And you were the queen.'

Harriett remembered. Even back then it had been unsettlingly easy to tell people what to do, and even more thrilling to see her instructions followed. She thought of Ruby pulling herself away from Sophie. There was no doubt in Harriett's mind that had she not been there, nobody else would have been able to stop her friend.

Emily glanced at her. She was standing only a foot away from her but the distance between them was palpable. Emily was a bit like that with everyone—unreachable.

Harriett thought back to that moment outside the school gates, before she and Ruby had found the skull. The moment when Emily hadn't seemed like Emily at all. 'When was the last time we did this?' Harriett asked, shaking away the thought. 'Hot chocolate and a sleepover, I mean.'

'About a year ago. Before GCSEs' started.'

'That long? I miss it.'

As children, they'd always been together, tucked so neatly inside each other's pockets. As young women, they were still close, but it was beginning to feel as though they were drifting apart; inch by inch each day.

The chocolate milk bubbled merrily in the pan.

Emily sighed. 'Mum didn't want people over after Oakley was born. There just wasn't enough space.'

That made sense. Harriett couldn't imagine living with six other people under one roof.

Sarah and Ruby arrived in the kitchen just as the hot chocolate was being poured into large grey mugs. Sarah carried a large box proudly in her arms and beamed when she saw them.

'Garden?' she asked, without even saying hello.

Harriett looked out the kitchen window; the edges of Woolington were beginning to bleed pink as the sun sank lower into the night.

'Garden,' Harriett agreed.

Sixteen sweet cupcakes for Emily's sweet sixteen. It was a cheesy idea, but also somewhat of a long-standing tradition between the four of them. Every birthday was commemorated in this way. For Harriett's fifteen birthday, they had bought her fifteen glazed doughnuts, and for Sarah's fourteenth, they had bought fourteen helium balloons, and so on and so forth.

The four of them grabbed some blankets from the living room and sat outside, mugs of hot chocolate in their hands and a large box of cupcakes resting between them. The twisted tree stood in front of them, its old branches hanging several feet above, its twigs criss-crossing over one another to create a cobwebbed canopy.

'These look lovely,' Emily said, gingerly picking up a cupcake. The bright pink icing stood at almost an inch tall and was decorated with fine white sugar, Harriett grabbed one eagerly while Sarah had already taken a big bite into hers.

'They should, we got them from that fancy bakery at the end of Montpelier,' Sarah said. Harriett could tell that she was on the verge of telling Emily just how expensive they were.

'I strongly believe that cake is one of life's greatest pleasures,' she went on, then she turned to Ruby. 'Are you not having one?'

Ruby shook her head. 'Do you know how much sugar is in the damn things?'

'Exactly the right amount,' Sarah replied with her mouth full.

Ruby pulled a face. 'Either way, it's not my thing.'

She didn't seem to be drinking the chocolate either, simply holding the cup in her hands. Harriett regarded Ruby carefully; with the absence of the long school skirt, she could see clearly just how twig-like Ruby's legs had become.

She had always been a girl of sharp cheekbones and harsh edges but now Harriett feared that if she were to touch Ruby's shoulder, she might leave a hand-shaped bruise. Ruby wasn't just skinny anymore, she was *bony*.

As though feeling the heat of Harriett's gaze Ruby took a large swing from the flask that she'd brought with her. Harriett decided against asking her what it contained.

'Do you feel any different? Now that you're sixteen,' she asked, turning to Emily.

'Different how?' Emily frowned.

Sarah grinned. 'Older, wiser, *sexier*.'

'I don't know about sexier...' Emily blushed.

'C'mon you're the eldest!' Sarah exclaimed. 'Shock us with your superior knowledge and womanly ways.'

Emily spluttered and shook her head so hard that her hair fell messily over face. Then she shovelled another cupcake into her mouth, until there was nothing but a dot of pink icing on the tip of her nose.

Ruby snorted. 'Smooth.'

The four of them sat there for a few moments laughing as Emily wiped her face clean. It was the first time Harriett had really, truly laughed since her sister's death... The laughter quietened and somewhere in the distance a bird sang. Harriett pulled one of the blankets more tightly around her and surveyed the group. Torn between the want to laugh again, and the sharp stab of guilt that had accompanied it.

'It is crazy though, isn't it?' Sarah said. 'Soon we'll all be sixteen, and then we'll be in college, and then we'll be adults.'

'C'mon, Sinclair practically walked out her mother's womb with the mental age of a thirty-five-year-old,' Ruby said, shrugging. 'It won't be that different.'

Harriett scowled. 'I am not middle-aged.'

Sarah and Ruby both raised their eyebrows and smirked to one another.

'Let's see… You can't start the day unless you've had a cup of coffee. You're always telling us not to swear. You actually write down stuff in your calendar and…' Ruby faltered then looked to Sarah for assistance.

Sarah's eyes widened. 'Ooh, ooh! You always have hand gel in your bag!'

Harriett could feel her cheeks getting warmer, 'So, I like to keep my hands clean! Em, can you help me out here?'

Emily shook her head and smiled sweetly. 'I can't. They're right. You're like an old lady.'

Ruby winked at her and took another sip from her flask, then wrinkled her nose in disgust.

'What is in that thing, Rubes?' Harriett finally asked.

'Protein shake,' she said without missing a beat. 'Okay so let's play this out. Sinclair, tell us what you want to do when we finish school, and don't tell me you haven't thought about it, 'cos I know you have.'

The question caught Harriett off guard, her mind flashed to the university leaflets she'd stuffed in her bag, now lying in a bin somewhere after being soaked through with water. She pictured the skull currently hidden in the back of her cupboard and hastily blinked the image away.

Ruby wasn't wrong. Harriett *had* thought about the future—she'd thought about it a lot. It was only that lately she found it difficult to differentiate between her future, and the future that should have been Hayley's.

In many ways Harriett *did* know what she wanted. She wanted to carve a small piece of the world out for herself. She wanted her name, who she was, to mean something. To be blazed into the memory of everyone whose life so much as brushed against her own… To make an impact. To leave a mark. It was a wanting that engulfed her and swallowed her whole. But it was a dangerous thing to go on wanting and never get.

Besides, it wasn't exactly a job description.

'I don't know, a lawyer maybe?'

'So, something high powered and neurotic?' Ruby said. 'Sounds standard. I mean boring as all hell, but predictable. How 'bout you Acton, Walters?'

Sarah remained silent making it clear that Emily was to go first.

'I want to be an arborist,' Emily said.

'A what?' said Ruby and Sarah together.

'An arborist,' Emily repeated. 'A tree surgeon. It's all about healing plants and cultivating and preserving all types of trees.'

'Where on earth did you come up with that idea?' Sarah asked.

Emily twirled a piece of hair around her index finger. 'Well, I was walking toward my house and I thought to myself; "hey, where did all the trees go?" and then I thought; "hey, how do we bring them back?" So, I looked it up online and discovered arborists.'

Harriett blinked. A part of her was surprised to learn that Emily didn't want to be an artist. She always had paint stains on her clothes and hands. And yet... now that she'd said it, it made perfect sense. It was so simple, so absurd, and so unusually fitting. It was also one of the rare instances where Emily spoke for longer than a couple of seconds.

Emily really was a marvellously odd creature.

'Well, I don't want to be anything,' Sarah said blithely. 'I did think maybe a model or a singer, but none of it really matters, does it? All I want is to be happy, like my Mum and Dad. They're always together, I want what they have. I want to be happy and in love.'

Sarah said it all so casually. As though it was the easiest

thing in the world. Harriett raised her eyebrow, trying to think of the politest way of pointing out to her that even if she fell madly in love straight out of college, she'd probably still have to *do* something.

Ruby had no such tact. 'Hang on a sec. So, your whole goal in life is to *find* someone who has goals in life?'

Silence.

Followed by raucous laughter.

'You can laugh all you want Ruby Coleville, but it's not a *bad* thing to be loved!' Sarah glared at her then crossed her arms over her chest fiercely. 'It doesn't make you weak, sometimes it even makes you strong.'

Both Harriett and Emily had been watching quietly as their little spat unfurled. But now Emily's eyes were fixed solely on Sarah. She was looking at her as though she was a complex problem that desperately needed solving. Then she pulled her gaze from Sarah and turned to Ruby.

'She's right you know,' she whispered.

'Go on then Ruby, tell us your grand plans if they're so damn fantastic,' Sarah demanded, loudly. 'What do *you* want to be in the future?'

Ruby took another swig from her flask. 'Alive,' she said it bluntly and with her sly, trade-mark grin.

Sarah threw up her hands in defeat, let out at an exasperated groan and then finally smiled, bemused. As though it was just Ruby being Ruby. Harriett alone had the unnerving feeling that she might not be entirely joking.

From inside the house behind them they all heard a loud, girlish cackle, followed by the sound of thumping upstairs.

Emily smiled. 'The twins are back from ballet.'

One by one the windows to the house lit up, and more noise and laughter erupted from inside. Harriett felt a twinge of something that was not-quite sadness in her chest. Her own home was so quiet now, it was comforting to know that other families were still reliably chaotic.

She took a sip of her hot chocolate and let the warm sweetness run through her. Above them the stars were beginning to spill out into the sky like sugar across a countertop.

From beside her Sarah lifted her mug in a salute to the night. 'To Emily.'

'To Walters,' Ruby said, grinning and raising her own cup. 'May this coming year make you older, wiser and – of course - *sexier.*'

Harriett raised her mug and laughed, 'Happy birthday Emily.'

Emily buried her face in her hands, a small chuckle managing to escape from in-between her fingers, and then all of them were smiling.

Harriett's cheeks ached from it.

And her heart hurt from the strange feeling that was swelling, swelling, swelling inside her chest.

Not quite-sadness, not quite-happiness.

She had *missed* them. She had missed the comfort that being with her friends, laughing with them, sharing secrets and cupcakes with them, inevitably brought.

It was at times like this, sitting in Emily's back garden, with only the stars watching them and the feel of cool grass pressing between her toes, that she experienced a contentedness she did not feel anywhere else. The world seemed bigger; the universe more infinite.

It was just the four of them and the rest of the galaxy.

She felt small, but not insignificant.

Harriett curled her fingers around the hot mug. Beside her she could hear the calming breaths of Ruby, Sarah and Emily, and the gentle rippling of wind through leaves. It was a good moment to stay trapped in

Chapter Seven

A LITTLE LESS HAUNT ME

That night they slept in the Walter's living room, where two mattresses had been placed on the floor for them. Their chatter turned into watching movies, and watching movies turned into snuggling under the blankets until one by one they each dozed off to sleep. Ruby and Harriett shared one mattress, Emily and Sarah shared the other.

The last thing Harriett heard was the gentle rhythm of Ruby's snores and the rustle of blankets, then she closed her eyes and let sleep claim her.

Harriett dreamed.

She dreamed of the games they played when they were little. In her dream, Ruby brandished her make-believe sword and Sarah wore a crown made of yellow thistles. A young Emily watched her through heavy lidded eyes and spoke in a language that was familiar to her, but that she couldn't quite understand.

Then, abruptly, she woke.

It was not a gentle stirring of awake-ness that pulled her coaxingly back into the world. It was as though someone had slammed shut a door in her mind, cutting her off from the realm of sleep and forcing her to open her eyes. She sat up; and was acutely aware of the feeling that she was being watched.

The smell of melted chocolate lingered in the air, half-drunk cups and empty cupcake cases littered the floor. Ruby slept peacefully beside her. On the opposite mattress Emily and Sarah had curled up beside one another their noses mere inches away from touching.

For a brief shining moment, the uneasiness subsided, and she felt as though she had been *found* despite never having been lost.

And then there it was. The Shadow.

Only it was clearer this time, it's dark and ethereal form stretched out across Emily's living room wall. It was obvious to her now that the Shadow took the form of a man; standing upright, broad and tall. Though the room was coated with the dark blue of night she knew that it was staring right at her. A scream curdled in the hollow of her throat, but she swallowed it down.

The Shadow tilted its phantom head, glided toward the living room door and *opened* it with long, spindly fingers. The door creaked and the Shadow continued to stare at her.

It was waiting.

Whenever she watched horror movies Harriett was always the first to yell at the TV screen for the main character to NOT GO IN THE BASEMENT or to NOT FOLLOW THAT VAMPIRE.

And yet...

She knew in her bones that she had to follow it. The Shadow's energy was magnetic, it crackled through the air, dragging her toward it. Without hesitating Harriett pulled the blanket off and stood shakily to her feet.

The Shadow flickered from one wall to the next, it's movements as fast as blinking. Finally, it hovered in the doorframe and then flitted away. Harriett sped after it, only vaguely aware that the others were stirring around her.

'Sinclair—?' a voice croaked.

But Harriett ignored them. She scrambled after the Shadow, only just catching a glimpse of it as it slipped underneath the Walter's front door and onto the streets outside.

Without thinking she fumbled for the keys, which hung on a hook next to the lock, and haphazardly shoved them into the lock. She could feel the presence of the others now, standing behind her, unsure and confused as to what she was doing.

The key clicked, and the door opened with a creak.

There, underneath the flickering orange glow of the streetlamps stood the Shadow. Except it wasn't standing, it was hovering, a foot or so from the ground. And it was so black... darker than black. Looking into the Shadow was like looking deep into a void or an abyss.

It was like looking into *nothing*.

Somehow it was more than mist and yet far, far less than human. A dangerous cocktail of smoke and vapour, spirit and menace.

Every fibre in her being screamed that the Shadow was a threat—an enemy—and yet there was something tying them together—a force hooked fiercely around her waist, pulling her toward it.

Slowly she drew closer, closer, closer to it and as she did, she was overcome by the smell of rot and dirt and damp. She continued forward only halting when she stood an arm's length away.

'What do you want from me?' she asked.

The Shadow leaned forward, and the smell of rot grew stronger, filling her nostrils and clogging her throat. She stared into its empty face and for a split second thought she saw the flash of a man.

She couldn't see the Shadow's mouth move but she heard the voice; clear and loud and rasping.

Remember me.

It wasn't a question. It was an order.

The Shadow lifted a smoky hand to her cheek and Harriett fell backwards. Afraid to feel its touch, if she even could.

From behind her Sarah screamed.

The Shadow turned and for a moment Harriett feared it had fixated on Sarah instead. Then it floated upward, disappearing into the inky blackness that existed between the stars until there was no evidence that it had ever been there at all. Harriett remained on the gravel, gaping upward as a blend of different emotions swam through her.

Fear, curiosity, awe.

Then Ruby was in front of her, waving a hand frantically in the spot where the Shadow had once been.

'You saw that right?' Harriett whispered, 'I'm not crazy, am I?'

Ruby grimaced and ran a shaky hand through her hair, then she held out a hand for Harriett. 'You're not crazy.'

Harriett grabbed Ruby's hand and squeezed as she was pulled up from the ground. The four of them stood under the watchful eye of the pale moon, the orange glimmer of streetlamps casting an ominous shade over their faces, and the wind whispering in their ears'.

Remember me. Remember me. Remember me.

It was Ruby who spoke first, her voice shaking.

'What the actual fuck was that?'

HARRIETT SINCLAIR WAS a sensible girl. As such she only believed in sensible things; timetables, colourful pencil cases, cookery books and coffee. She was not the sort of person who believed in fairy tales or ghost stories. Yet there they were, four girls standing under a star-spattered sky, dishevelled and tired but wide, wide-awake. Living out a nightmare.

'Harriett, what was that?' Sarah breathed.

'I don't know,' she said.

'Why were you following it?' Emily asked, she stood far away from the three of them, close to her house as if she were guarding it.

'I don't know.'

'Did you see what was on its head?' Sarah said.

'I don't—wait, what?'

Harriett spun around so that she could see Sarah, standing barefoot on the street, her hair scrunched up into a messy bun and wearing her pale pink nightie.

'On its head...' Sarah said, her voice shaking. 'I thought I saw a shape, kind of pointy, like maybe, I don't know a crown or something?'

Harriett frowned; she hadn't seen any such thing. But then, she had been preoccupied staring *into* it rather than at it.

'This is insane,' Ruby said, 'first the skull, now this...'

'Skull?' Emily asked, her voice unnervingly calm.

Ruby looked to Harriett, as if asking for permission, Harriett gave the slightest of nods and Ruby began to explain. As she did, Harriett wandered a little further down the street. In-between the lampposts, hidden in the black, for a moment she thought she saw a flash of blue. And—though she couldn't be certain—the curling of a tail.

She reached the spot but just like the Shadow, whatever it was had disappeared.

'Come on,' Harriett said quietly, wrapping her arms around herself. 'We can't just stand here all night.'

Obediently they all followed her back inside and into the living room. It was still warm, and it still smelt faintly of chocolate, only the room seemed somehow darker now—

smaller. Every rustle of wind from outside made Harriett's skin tingle, every creak of the floorboards set her teeth on edge. A question loomed menacingly in her mind.

How can we hide from the dark?

She wiggled under the blankets on the mattress and Ruby lay down beside her.

Minutes ticked by.

'What are we going to do?' Ruby asked in a hushed voice. On the other mattress Emily and Sarah appeared to already be asleep but Harriett knew that they were listening.

'I have no idea.'

Harriett could feel Ruby's frown rather than see it. But what could they say and who would believe them? Her mind whirred with unanswerable, impossible questions and she kept coming back to the same solution.

'We've got to find out what that thing is.'

She felt Ruby nod and heard Sarah groan quietly, if Emily had a reaction, she kept it to herself. Harriett pulled the blanket closer to her neck and allowed her gaze to wander to the window. Outside, she could see the outlines of the trees and all the other houses that occupied the lane, blissfully unaware of their midnight haunting.

She rolled over and closed her eyes and knew she would not sleep again that night.

Chapter Eight

A HOUSE MADE OF GHOSTS

Two weeks passed without a glimpse of the Shadow. While Harriett fiercely wanted to discover what happened that night, the others seemed to want to forget the ordeal. And then there was Ruby, who had pulled an almighty vanishing act and disappeared from school altogether.

Harriett busied herself with work for the most part, occupying her time with homework and prefect duties, while spending every spare moment she had at the library. She read up on everything she could about Shadows. Every myth and legend, she devoured, determined to find an explanation no matter how bizarre it might be. She read about poltergeists and ghouls, banshees and ghosts. Harriett even learned about Shades, the dead that 'lived in the shadows.' It was all interesting and horrifying in equal measure, but none of it came close to describing the aching, desperate blackness she had seen.

There were moments where time became a labyrinth and swallowed her, only to spit her back out again. She would enter a room and forget how she got there, she would be speaking with someone, and they would disappear only to suddenly rematerialize a second later. It was as though something was cutting away minutes of her life, like a friend borrowing a book only to return it with pages missing. Over the days her face became increasingly stranger to her, she found herself examining her features before bed, without knowing what she was inspecting them for.

Harriett was certain she was not alone in this *other*ness. In history class, Sarah had stared vacantly into the distance for an entire three minutes as the teacher repeatedly called her name, when she finally jolted from her reverie, she had seemed *puzzled.* Harriett could also have sworn that when asking for the dinner lady to give her some pasta Emily had spoken in a completely different language, though she claimed to have no recollection of it after.

As for Ruby, well it was difficult to tell whether Ruby was acting strange or not. She was coming into school less and less, and whenever she did deign to turn up, she looked a little thinner, a little paler – a little less like Ruby.

At night Harriett would lay in bed staring up at the ceiling or into the vacant space where her sister once slept as she tried to organise her thoughts. As she tried to find even a crumb of sense that would help her understand but every time her mind came up hideously blank.

She felt as though reality was slipping...

Slipping...

Slipping away....

And she did not know how to get it back.

It was the Friday evening before Anthony's big party and Harriett was sitting at home on the sofa, watching silently as her brother played computer. Their parents were out, supposedly "shopping." It hadn't escaped Harriett's attention that they went "shopping" every Friday evening and that they returned home with very little. Harriett gazed at the clock, it was six thirty and she'd finished all her homework, tidied her room and made dinner for both her and Henry. Now she found herself in the undesirable position of being alone with her thoughts.

She was just considering whether it was worth making a short trip to the library when suddenly Henry spoke.

'I reckon it's either counselling or they're meeting with a private investigator,' he said, not looking away from the computer screen.

'Huh?'

'Mum and Dad. They're either seeing some sort of counsellor, or they've hired a detective.'

Harriett regarded her brother carefully. His eyes remained fixated on the screen; he had not even bothered to change out of the St David's uniform. He looked older, his blonde hair seemed to have turned a shade darker and his round face didn't seem quite so round anymore. He was growing up... and she was missing it.

She had tried to talk to him, back when *it* happened. But neither of them had known what to say and so the silence had won out - they hadn't had a real conversation in weeks.

Harriett had always assumed they were seeing a counsellor; it had never occurred to her that their Friday evenings were being spent somewhere else.

'What makes you think they'd get a detective?' she asked.

Henry swivelled in his chair so that he faced her. 'Mum doesn't believe that Hayley's death was an accident, and the police closed the investigation. It's the next logical step.'

Harriett nodded, impressed.

'Yes,' she said quietly, 'I suppose it is.'

The mystery of Hayley Sinclair's death had long since been declared unsolvable. There had been no wounds, no signs of murder, nor had there been any signs of aneurysms or any other health-induced fatalities. The police and doctors were all stumped. It was part of what kept the people of Woolington so fascinated by the Sinclair's misfortune.

'Dad reckons that Mum needs to let it go and accept that there are some things in life we just don't know the answers to. He thinks that they should focus on being here for us rather than obsessing over something they can't change. I heard them arguing about it the other night. Mum was crying, Dad was crying... it was horrible.'

Harriett's mouth dropped open. 'Where was I?'

Henry's eyes narrowed. 'You were here. Or at least your body was. I don't know where your head is at these days, but it certainly isn't with us,' he stared at her; a frown etched upon his face.

Harriett could feel her eyes start to sting. 'That's not fair.'

Henry shrugged. 'Don't worry, none of us are really *here* anymore, it's like living in a house of ghosts.'

The space that stretched out between them seemed never ending, then Henry turned back to his computer screen. Blood thrummed in Harriett's ears as his words imprinted onto her brain.

It's like living in a house of ghosts.

It was the truth. Hayley might have been a ghost in the traditional sense of the word, but the rest of Harriett's family had become ghosts as well. Each of them floating through the house silently and aimlessly, disconnected from everything and everyone around them.

'There's one thing that really bothers me though.'

Harriett looked up. 'Hmm?'

The screen of the computer illuminated Henry's face so that his eyes and skin shone unnaturally bright.

'Just say it wasn't some sort of freak accident, just suppose Mum's right... and Hayley *was* murdered, then who killed her?' he paused, breath shaky. 'Who would want to?'

With every word her brother spoke it felt as though someone was sucking all the oxygen from the room and squeezing the breath right out of her lungs.

How had she ever been so stupid?

How had she not made the connection?

There had been too much going on. Her world had been slowly turning inside out and she hadn't noticed...

She hadn't thought to link the dots.

The Shadow.

It's coming after you.

What if it had gone for Hayley first?

'Harriett? What's wrong?' Henry was staring at her, his eyes wide with concern.

'I just... I've got to go check something,' she practically choked on the words, and then she fled from the room.

It had been the mystery that enveloped the town. *How* had Hayley Sinclair died? For Harriett, it had been hard enough to think of her lying on the side of the pavement. Alone and pale, her hair splayed out behind her and her blue daisy dress spattered with dirt from the rain. She hadn't even tried to discover the truth, after all if the professionals couldn't figure it out, what hope did she have? She'd even thought that perhaps not knowing was for the best. After all, knowing the *how* and the *why* wouldn't change anything, except perhaps to make them all feel a little worse.

She ran up the stairs, into her room and positioned herself in front of the floor length mirror where Hayley's cupboard used to be. For the first time, Harriett allowed herself to really think about the events that had led to her sister's death that night. The moment that their lives had been twisted in knots.

Hayley had been walking home, Harriett knew that much, though where she had been walking from was hard to say. And then, to all intents and purposes, she'd simply dropped dead in the rain, only to be found four hours later by an early morning jogger.

How?

Before Harriett had assumed that it was some underlying health condition the doctors simply couldn't detect. The police had thought so too, and that's why they had closed the case. It was only now, with a skull sitting inside her cupboard and a midnight haunting under her belt, that Harriett thought the answer was all too obvious.

She had been murdered.

She could see it so clearly... Hayley walking home, the rain emptying from the heavens in a gentle steady mist. Then darkness, the Shadow filling up the sky until there was nothing. Hayley Sinclair, crumbling to the floor wide-eyed but no longer awake.

Harriett found her body trembling, the reflection in her mirror showed a red-faced girl, side plait in disarray and tears spilling freely down her cheeks.

It wasn't sadness that she was feeling any more...not really. It was an emptiness. A black hole that seemed to grow larger inside her each day. It was a vastness that crept into her bones and soul, until everything was grey and scraped bare of life.

And in the empty space where her sister once was, there was now only chaos. Chaos and Shadows and nightmares.

'Hayley...' she whispered to the air, 'I don't know what to do.'

She stared at her reflection, waiting for the answers to come. Waiting for some sort of sign that she wasn't going mad and that somehow everything, everything would be alright.

Then her reflection smiled.

Harriett clapped her hand over her mouth, her insides turning to ice. The reflection's hand remained fixed on the floor.

It was wearing a blue daisy dress.

A sob shuddered through Harriett.

It was wearing a *blue daisy dress.*

Leaning forward, Harriett reached for the mirror. It was Hayley. It had to be. Harriett wanted to touch the mirror, to try and pull her sister out of the smooth surface. She wanted to smash it to pieces, to shatter it with her bare fists.

The girl in the mirror shook her head and pointed to the right of her.

Harriett's sobs stuck in her throat. Her eyes were blurry, and her cheeks were wet but now she was afraid too. She followed to where Hayley was pointing.

It was Harriett's wardrobe, or rather what lay hidden inside it.

Harriett made her way across the room, noticing that as she did so Hayley's image vanished from inside the mirror. Biting back more tears Harriett opened the cupboard and the box that contained her sister's memories...and the skull.

It seemed an impossible thing, a skull in her wardrobe. So strange and so abstract that Harriett could almost convince herself she was dreaming.

But it *wasn't* a dream.

When she reached out to hold the skull, she found it cold to the touch. Too cold, as though it had been stored in a freezer rather than kept in a box at the bottom of a wardrobe. She shivered and turned it around in her hands so that she was looking directly into deep, round eye sockets. She stared into it and for a single, horrifying moment it occurred to her that perhaps the skull was Hayley's, but the thought soon vanished from her mind. She simply knew that it wasn't, though she wasn't sure how...

She continued to stare at the skull, and it continued to look blankly back.

It was so old, she thought, ancient even.

Old and ancient and—

'Cursed,' a voice said.

Harriett looked up to see Hayley standing in front of her.

Hayley looked at her pensively, her head tilted to one side and a pitying expression casting a dull light on her face.

The hairs on the back of Harriett's neck stood upright and the atmosphere in the room grew tighter, colder. She wanted to scream. She wanted to scream and never stop. The room was spinning, spinning, spinning and as it spun a torrent of images and feelings flooded through her.

She had been emptied and now she was being filled.

Her fingers slipped, and the skull fell to the ground.

Jewels on her fingers, the smell of fire in the air.
A river and a cheering crowd.
A child's cry.
Blood.
A name whispered in the dark, low and deep.
'Gwendolen...'

Chapter Nine

A FEELING OF FORGETTING

Harriett Sinclair was forgetting something. Something important.

She had spent the entirety of her Saturday morning trying to remember *anything* from the strange, cracked moment when Hayley had stood beside her. She closed her eyes and desperately tried to recall the name that she had heard so clearly. She could feel it there on the edge of her mind, tantalising close and yet so far away she could not reach it.

Eventually she had resigned herself to the fact that she couldn't remember, and instead she had scrounged up an empty notebook and started writing notes and lists of everything she could. Jotting down dates that she thought might be important, trying to find a message in all the madness. If anything, her scribblings brought even more questions than answers:

Shadow Timeline

12th August – Hayley found dead.

26th August – Hayley's funeral, first ghost sighting.

3rd September – Cat on doorstep(relevant?) dream-Hayley warning.

4th September – First glimpse of Shadow. Skull and rocks in schoolbag.

15th/16th September – Shadow haunts sleepover. (Cat sighting again, maybe?)

29th September – mirror-Hayley. Hallucination???
Other Notes
** Short bursts of memory loss/nightly examinations of own face/friends also displaying odd behaviour.*
** Are the Shadow and the cat connected? Is the cat important at all? Who does the skull belong to? How did I come to get it? How is Hayley involved?*

Harriett made the notes as she would for any other subject. Detailed lists with clear headings, neat handwriting perfectly spaced about. She thought that by doing this she might declutter her head a little and see the truth more clearly. But as she read and re-read the list, the more infuriating it all seemed.

So, she made notes on her research, on the different legends of Shadow daemons she had discovered. She was just about to pull out her laptop to look up myths on black cats when suddenly her door opened.

'See? I told you she wouldn't have even started getting ready.'

She looked up to see Sarah, Emily and Ruby all standing bemused in her doorframe. Sarah, she noticed, was holding a small suitcase in front of her.

'Ready for what?' Harriett asked.

Ruby sniggered as Sarah let out a horrified little gasp. 'Anthony's party! We all agreed to get ready here, remember?'

'Erm...' Harriett had, of course, completely forgotten. Frantically she scrambled around, picking up the loose pieces of paper and shoving them inside the notebook.

'I guess I got preoccupied.'

Ruby sauntered across the room and grabbed the notebook from Harriett's hand.

'What you got here, Sinclair?' she grinned, but the grin slipped from her mouth when her eyes found the list.

'What is it?' Sarah asked, she was on the other side of the room. She had already started to unzip the suitcase.

Harriett met Ruby's eyes; she was determined not to blink. Determined not to show any form of embarrassment or shame. Then slowly, oh so slowly, Harriett shook her head.

Ruby shrugged and flung the notebook casually onto the bed. 'Just Sinclair being Sinclair,' she said.

Harriett grabbed the notebook and rammed it into the drawer of her bedside table. It was at this moment Sarah chose to unplug the headphones from her phone and blast her music throughout the room.

'This is my *"Get Fabulous"* playlist. Do you like it?'

Harriett nodded absent-mindedly. 'What time is it?' she asked.

'Half-five,' Emily answered. She had sat herself down by the cupboard, her arms wrapped around her knees and her chin resting on her arms, she was watching Harriett and Ruby closely, her expression curious.

Harriett turned to Ruby, with the intention of whispering a *'thank you'* to her, but instead froze when she saw what she was wearing.

'"*Skank*?" Really?'

Ruby's eyes glinted mischievously. 'Yeah.'

Sarah spun around and eyed up the offensive shirt in question, a baggy white number with the word SKANK written across it in bright red. 'Tell me you're not wearing that tonight.'

Ruby smiled wickedly. 'I could tell you that. But I'd be lying.'

Sarah let out a groan and then turned her attention to Harriett. 'What will you be wearing?'

'I hadn't thought about it,' Harriett said truthfully.

Sarah stood up gracefully, holding half a dozen outfits in her arms. 'Excellent, then you can try on some of these.'

She threw them on the bed. Harriett gaped at it all, it didn't seem wholly possible that so many sequins and neon colours could exist in so few pieces of fabric.

Ruby smirked. 'Bet you wish we weren't going now.'

Ruby was right, Harriett *did* wish they weren't going. But not because of the tightly fitting dress that Sarah was undoubtedly going to force her into. Harriett didn't want to go because she felt as though there was something *else*, they should be doing instead. Something that they were missing—that *she* was missing.

And she wanted nothing more than to find out exactly what it was.

Chapter Ten

ROMULUS ROAD

An hour later Harriett found herself standing on her street. As predicted, she had somehow been coerced into a tight-fitting orange dress, and she had also (for reasons unknown even to her) allowed Sarah to smear so much makeup across her face that her cheeks now felt cemented in place. The overall effect being that she now closely resembled a human traffic cone.

Ruby had not been persuaded to change from her SKANK t-shirt although she had consented to painting her eyes a charcoal black, which only seemed to add to her overall dishevelled appearance. Emily had happily slipped into the long white dress Sarah had picked out for her. Sarah had also taken it upon herself to apply a shimmering layer of gold eyeliner around Emily's eyes, the effect was somewhat startling.

Emily was beautiful. The kind of beautiful that only becomes more so the longer you look. Her skin was dark, her eyes a glittering, mesmerising black and her hair was frizzy and wild – simply looking at her was an adventure. Yet her habit of disappearing into the background meant that people often somehow *forgot* this. Emily was forgettable, but only because Emily *chose* to be so.

Then there was Sarah. She was almost loud to look at – wearing a deep green crop top with a matching high-waisted skirt and black boots that went up to her knees. Gold bracelets dangled loosely around her wrists. Her eyes were shadowed with silver and her lipstick was a sharp, enticing red. Her long hair fell to her waist.

What she had created was kind of like art; vivid and beautiful and feline. She was a siren, a temptress, a *seductress*. A young woman planning a night of stomach twirling kisses.

The four of them stood outside Anthony's house. Harriett felt uncomfortable and Ruby looked it. Emily appeared supremely unbothered by the entire event. Only one out of the four of them *wanted* to be there, and that was Sarah. The fact that they all stood in attendance was a demonstration of her persuasive abilities.

The ground vibrated beneath their feet and Harriett could see the silhouettes of figures jumping up and down through the front window.

'Are there any adults at this party?' Harriett asked, knowing the answer.

Sarah smiled her bright smile. 'Nope.'

Harriett bit down a groan and said; 'Let's get this over with.'

Together they headed inside and were immediately hit by noise and smoke and mess.

Anthony's house was identical to Harriett's, this wasn't a surprise as they both lived down Romulus Road. The four of them navigated their way through a narrow hallway and made their way into a spacious living room and diner.

The living room had two sofas and a coffee table that had been pushed to the side of the walls. Everything was a faded orange, it looked as though the place hadn't been redecorated in at least ten years. There was a patio door at the back just behind a table full of food.

'So, who's here tonight?' Harriett asked, adjusting her dress awkwardly.

'Erm I think it's just Anthony's football team, us four, Sophie Grimely and Lacey Greenfield,' Sarah said the last name as though it tasted funny in her mouth and Harriett couldn't help but smile. Lacey and Sarah were two sides of the same coin; they were both beautiful brunettes, they were both top of the year in music and they were both far more popular than either of them had any right to be.

Plus, they both hated each other with the passion of a thousand dying suns. Though neither admitted this fact openly.

Harriett saw Lacey and Sophie chatting animatedly with Anthony and a friend in the corner of the room. Sarah's eyes narrowed, and she spun around to face them while Ruby and Sophie sneered at each other from across the room.

'Tell me I look better than her tonight,' Sarah demanded.

'You look better than her tonight,' they chorused back.

'You're such bloody liars,' Sarah snapped, but then she breathed slowly and smiled. 'But it's fine. I'm just going to go over to Anthony and snog his face off until she gets bored of watching and leaves.'

Sarah stalked away with purpose in her step and as soon as she was gone Ruby and Emily both immediately turned to face Harriett.

'It's like they talk in a code or something,' Ruby said.

Harriett agreed.

As a rule, Harriett didn't generally enjoy parties and tonight she felt particularly on edge. So, it was unsurprising when - less than ten minutes later - Harriett, Ruby and Emily found themselves huddled by the food table. Watching as Sarah and Anthony attacked each other's faces from the other side of the room.

Harriett sighed, turned to the table of food and picked up

a plate of chicken wings then passed the plate to Ruby, who shook her head firmly.

'What are you too cool to even eat now?' Harriett demanded, exasperated.

Ruby pulled a face. 'Don't be thick. How many of these grubby little boys have touched these plates? I don't want whatever germs they're carrying thanks.'

Emily took a wing and nibbled on it. 'Do you think we should say hello to Anthony?'

The three of them looked over to where Anthony was sitting in the living room, Sarah was sprawled across his lap and practically glued to his face.

'I think he's a little preoccupied right now,' Harriett said.

Emily looked away.

Ruby made a vomiting sound and then cackled. 'Oh my God, look at Lacey's face.'

Harriett's eyes soon found Lacey standing on the other side of the room, hand on her hip and face glowering.

'What is it about Anthony that has the two of them so desperate to jump his bones?' Harriett asked.

Ruby stretched her arms and yawned. 'Oh *please*, Lacey only wants him because Sarah does, he's absolutely no different to any of the other gormless git-faced idiots here.'

Harriett glanced around the room, to Anthony and Sarah and their fierce game of tonsil tennis, to a group of boys trying and failing to start a game of beer pong, and to a young boy in the corner who was desperately trying to get Lacey's attention by dancing in awkwardly close proximity to her. She had to try and suppress a smile.

'Git-faced? Really?'

Ruby grinned her sharp, pointed grin. 'I just call it how I see it.'

'What do you think Emily? Can we in good conscience label all the boys here git-faced?'

But Emily and her piece of chicken had vanished.

'Where did she go?'

But Ruby wasn't paying attention, instead she was staring at the other side of the room.

Harriett followed her gaze. 'Who's that?'

In the far corner of the room, sitting just outside of Anthony's football group, was a boy. He sat stiffly in his chair, his hands folded in his lap and sitting so straight it looked as though a pole might be holding him into place. He had thick dark hair that was shaggy and unkempt, and he was pale and thin with thick-rimmed glasses that fell down his nose. Harriett thought he appeared almost delicate in how he was sitting. But what sparked her curiosity was the intensity of his stare, and how his gaze was most definitely fixed on Ruby.

'How the hell should I know,' Ruby snapped.

Harriett almost wanted to warn the poor boy to stay away. To inform him that Ruby, with her sharp cheekbones and piercing blue eyes, was only pretty from a safe distance and, much like a Venus flytrap, might eat you if you stray too close.

'Are you going to say hello?' Harriett asked half-heartedly, knowing the answer before the question was even really finished.

'I'd rather drag my face across hot gravel.'

Harriett rose an eyebrow. 'That's colourful. Ridiculous, but colourful.'

'I never said it wasn't ridiculous. I just mean I would rather drag my face across hot gravel than have a conversation with literally anyone here.'

'He could be nice.'

Ruby shrugged and averted her gaze. 'Or he could be king of the git-faces. Either way, I don't care enough to find out.'

Just then the boy made a face, as though he had decided on something. He stood up and made his way across the room until he halted clumsily in front of them.

'Uhm... hello,' he said.

Ruby responded by staring at him as though he were some sort of alien creature.

'Hi,' said Harriett brightly.

The boy continued to gaze at Ruby, confused, while she frowned back at him.

'I'm Alex,' he said to Harriett, his glasses slipping down his nose so that he had to hastily push them back up.

'That's nice,' Ruby said, then she turned abruptly back to Harriett. 'Do you think we should go find Emily?'

The boy's shoulders slumped and when it came clear that she would not be talking to him, he slunk away back into his seat on the other side of the room.

'Well,' Harriett said, 'that was painful.'

'For you and me both.'

Harriett fixed her attention back to the spot where Emily had been standing only moments before. It was eerie sometimes, her ability to melt into the background. She was always with them, but also not with them at the same time.

'Do you think Emily's a bit...odd?' she asked.

Ruby blinked at her. 'Aren't we all?'

Harriett took in Ruby's SKANK t-shirt, then glanced over at Sarah and Anthony who were now thoroughly tangled up in each other, finally she looked down at herself, standing out of place in an orange cocktail dress so clearly not meant for her.

She found she couldn't disagree.

In front of them one of Anthony's football friends decided to drink an entire beer in less than a minute. There was a chorus of applause and cheers from the other boys, and then he promptly sneezed half of it back up in an explosion of froth and coughing.

Ruby pulled a face and muttered something that sounded suspiciously like *"git-face."*

Chapter Eleven

DEAD BOYS DON'T PARTY

Fifteen minutes later and the room had grown sweaty, Harriett's hair was hanging loose for once and it was sticking horribly to the back of her neck. She missed her room and she missed the security of her plait.

She and Ruby remained loitering by the food table, not even attempting to mingle. Harriett allowed herself to watch the events of the room unfold around her. One boy accidentally stumbled and shattered a photo-frame. Lacey had evidently found someone suitable to snog in the corner. And the Alex boy was still sitting uncomfortably in his seat.

There were moments where Harriett would find her eyes straying to Anthony and Sarah's entwined shapes; she couldn't help but notice how comfortable Sarah was, sitting on his lap, her arms draped around his neck.

She shifted uncomfortably from one foot to another.

'Have you ever… you know, been interested in a boy?' she asked, turning to face Ruby, who groaned immediately.

'C'mon Sinclair, please don't tell me that you actually *like* one of these shitheads?'

'No!' she exclaimed, rolling her eyes. 'You know it's nothing like *that*."

'Then why the sudden interest?'

Harriett lowered her voice. 'It's just the other day I swear I heard a man's voice, *in my head*.'

Ruby regarded her cautiously. 'What did it say?'

'I don't know. No matter how hard I try, I can't remember,' Harriett said.

The two of them went back to people watching and silence passed over them.

'That list looked intense,' Ruby said eventually, not meeting her eyes.

Harriett ran a hand over her dress, attempting to smoothen the creases. 'I just needed to lay it all out on paper. To see if any of it links together.'

Ruby turned to her and Harriett could feel her gaze on her cheek. 'And does it?'

'I don't know.'

'Bummer,' Ruby sighed.

'Are you sure you didn't see where Emily went?' Harriett said, changing the subject and attempting to fan herself with a paper plate.

'Nope,' Ruby said, shaking her head. 'She might've gone outside.'

'Then that's where I'm going too, I can't handle this sweatbox anymore!'

Ruby nodded and moved in the opposite direction.

'You're going the wrong way,' Harriett said.

'No, I ain't. Sarah dragged us to this damn party, least she can do is spend a few minutes with us.'

Ruby strode over to where Sarah and Anthony were sitting, tapped her on the shoulder and pulled her away from him, all the while Harriett watched, both appalled and impressed by Ruby's audacity.

'Right,' Ruby said, rubbing her hands together. 'Let's go.'

WHEN THEY STEPPED into Anthony's garden, the crisp night air enveloped them. They walked into silence.

It was as though all sound had been snuffed out. They could no longer hear the shouting of adolescent boys and the thumping of too-loud music.

The garden itself was long and wild with the grass coming up to Harriett's shin. In the dark it appeared as a ghostly forest; ivy growing up the fences, weeds littering the earth and large scrubs blocking their path. All the trees were painted black with night.

'It's too quiet,' Sarah whispered.

It was true. Her words seemed too loud; their steps too noisy.

'I think we need to find Emily now,' Harriett said.

The three girls wandered further into the garden, through the twisted trees and past a garden bench.

'I don't remember it being this long before,' Sarah murmured.

'Shhhh!' Ruby hissed, and she pointed a finger ahead.

At the end of the garden there stood two figures. The first was Emily, angelic in her white dress. The other appeared to be a boy.

'Emily!' Sarah called, as they all walked toward her.

But Emily did not hear. She was transfixed by the boy in front of her—scared even. Harriett didn't understand it, he seemed normal enough, small and runty. Emily took a step toward him and let out a strangled cry.

Harriett's heart froze in her chest and once again she had that feeling of *otherness*. The notion that everything, everything was unravelling around her. Seconds on top of seconds, colliding and piling together. Then there was a spark; a memory of a place she had already been, a figure she already knew, an act already done.

Deja vu on loop.

It came out of the ground, slowly, slowly, slowly, oozing and spitting out thick like oil. Both the boy and Emily jumped back as it formed a puddle in the grass. Then it rose from the ground and twisted into a shape.

The shape of a man.

The Shadow glided closer to the boy, whose eyes widened with horror, paralyzed with fear and seemingly unable to move. The Shadow lifted itself aloft and dangled high above them. It remained there for a moment, suspended in the still black night. Its own dark so unfathomably deep that they could still see it even against the backdrop of night.

In a smooth quick motion, it plummeted downwards straight towards the boy, forcing itself into his mouth. He tried to scream but the sound was muffled, he scratched at his own throat, but the Shadow was gone, it was *inside* of him. Then he started to shake, violently and viscously.

Sarah shrieked.

Harriett ran forward.

Ruby made to stop her, but Harriett shook her off and grabbed the boy's arm—trying to help him or do *something*. He stopped shaking immediately, his head flopped to one side and he fixed her with a malicious, other-worldly stare.

'*Remember me,*' he breathed.

Harriett's mouth went dry.

'Who-?' but the question died on her tongue as the boy jumped on top of her, his hands wrapped tightly around her throat.

She couldn't scream, she could only stare into his face, his eyes were wide and filled with such a venom that it terrified her. He was heavy on top of her and she found she struggled to move, struggled to breathe.

Time suddenly crashed back into gear and she was filled with the overwhelming fear that she was running out of it.

Hayley.

Ruby peeled the boy off her by his shirt and threw him to the side. She went to run at him, but he toppled to the floor, not only shaking now but frothing at the mouth like a rabid dog. He coughed, and blood sprayed from his mouth in a fountain of red, spattering Ruby's shirt. Then his jaw went slack.

Smoky black tendrils glided out of the boy's open mouth, curling up, up, up into the air. Harriett scrambled backwards on the grass away from the body until she was next to Ruby, Emily and Sarah. The four of them stared, transfixed as the Shadow grew back into the silhouette of a man. A man wearing a crown, Harriett saw it now, and wondered how she hadn't seen it before. The Shadow hovered above them, surveying the scene. Watching them with its hollowed-out face.

*This is only the beginning. **Harriett...*** The Shadow hissed and then it *laughed,* as though her name was something amusing. For an instant Harriett felt herself go blank, her person wiped clean.

Useless.

Then, the Shadow grew wider and wider, stretching out until there was nothing but a fine mist curling out into thin wisps, brushing past each one of them. The touch of it on her neck made Harriett's bones go cold.

The Shadow was gone.

After a moment of tense, shocked silence, Emily turned around and stared at Harriett, meanwhile Ruby rushed over to the boy.

He was lying face up on the ground, his eyes staring at a sky that he could no longer see. Harriett wanted to vomit, she wanted to scream.

The silence that dangled over them broke, shattered to pieces, and the noise came rushing back. The sound of the music blaring from the house, the sound of the leaves rustling in the trees, and the manic, crazed voices of her friends desperately trying to mend what could not be mended.

Ruby knelt over the body, her pale, trembling hands pushing into the boy's ribcage. Once, twice, three times.

'Oh my god... oh my god, oh my god, oh my god!' Sarah dragged a hand frantically through her hair and then across her face - her eyes were smudged black with eyeliner and lipstick was smeared on her chin.

She did not look innocent.

'Will you shut up and help me?' Ruby snapped. She was leaning over the boy, pounding his chest desperately trying to perform CPR. Blood was splattered across her bright white shirt, a shirt that had the word SKANK written across it in a violent red.

She didn't look innocent either.

'Stop doing that, he's already dead!'

'Well at least I'm doing something!'

Harriett could hear what they were saying but she wasn't really listening. She just kept playing over the moment that he had died in her head. It had all happened so quickly. One moment he was there and then...

'No, no, no, no...' Sarah muttered under her breath, like she could turn back time if she only said it enough.

Ruby was still pressing her hands up and down into the boy's chest. *Up, down, up, down, up, down...*

Then there was Emily, knelt in the grass only a foot or so behind Ruby, her previously clean white dress now covered in grass stains and mud.

'Did you see it?' she said quietly, looking directly at Harriett. 'Did you see the Shadow?'

Harriett didn't answer, of course she had seen it. They all had.

'Harriett what do we do?' Sarah sobbed.

Up, down, up, down, up...

She rubbed her hands over her eyes. Trying to think as Ruby continued to try and frantically pump life back into a corpse.

'Harriett?'

Up, down, up, down...

She didn't want this. All she wanted was a moment to breathe.

Up, down, up...

All she wanted was to go back.

Up, down...

To before this whole nightmare had started.

Up...

...

...

'Harriett, what do we do?'

An idea. A plan. Anything.

She inhaled deeply; all three of them were watching her, waiting for their instructions. She crouched down and wiped her blood-stained palms on the grass. In her mind there was only one answer, and she hated herself for it.

'In a minute I'm going to go inside and scream. Then the police will come...' she paused, her lips and tongue were dry, and the words felt like bile in her mouth. Already she regretted the decision she was about to make. 'And then we're going to lie.'

Emily looked to Sarah who looked to Ruby who stared right back at her.

'Are... are you sure?' Ruby whispered.

No. Harriett was not sure.

Because Harriett Sinclair was haunted. She was haunted by who her sister was and who she could never be. She was haunted by all the decisions and the choices she had yet to make. She was a girl terrified by what her future might hold and by all that the past contained. Now she was haunted by a Shadow.

And nothing, *nothing* made sense anymore.

She took a deep breath.

'Yes.'

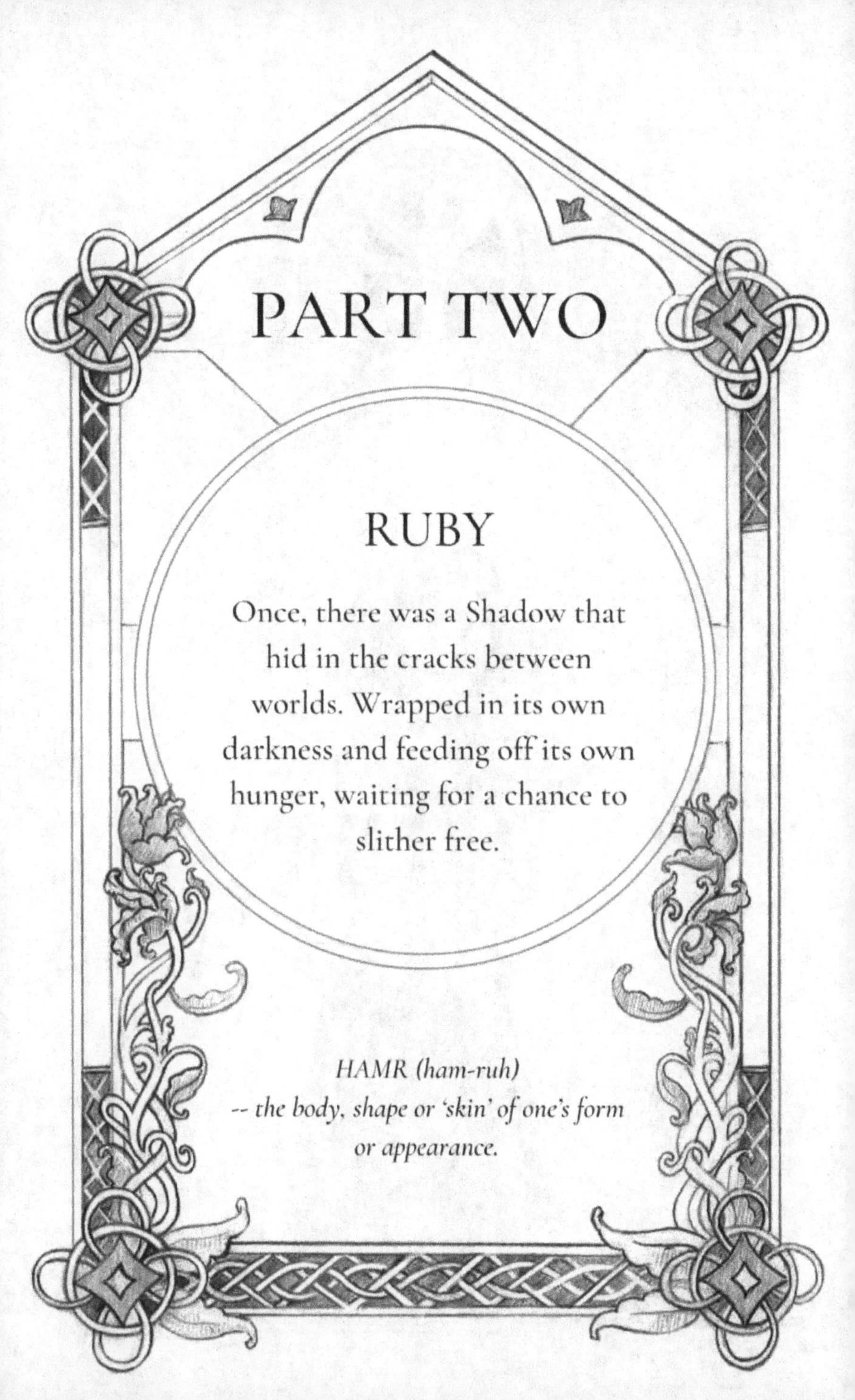

PART TWO

RUBY

Once, there was a Shadow that hid in the cracks between worlds. Wrapped in its own darkness and feeding off its own hunger, waiting for a chance to slither free.

HAMR (ham-ruh)
-- the body, shape or 'skin' of one's form
or appearance.

Chapter Twelve

SMALL TOWN SECRETS

It had been the end of summer and she'd been wearing a black dress.

She had been wandering along the seafront promenade toward the Cornerhouse, allowing her eyes to stray over the ocean. It had been barely visible in the dark, an aching blackness that stretched out into forever.

When she'd reached the cinema, she'd stopped outside and perched herself on the bus stop bench. Of all the places in Woolington, the old Cornerhouse cinema had always been her favourite. Ruby loved how old it was, as though it had been snatched out of another time.

She'd sighed and tilted her head back, then scratched her head, then shifted again. It had been three hours since Sinclair's sister's funeral, and she hadn't been able to stop thinking about the moment that Harriett had collapsed to the ground, sobbing over a figure no one else could see. She had never seen Sinclair so unhinged before. In the moment that it happened, Ruby had only one instinct. *To make sure no one else saw.*

But as she sat at the bus stop, she wondered whether that had been the right decision. After all, seeing ghosts wasn't exactly normal.

She folded her arms across her chest and stared as the large doors of the Cornerhouse opened with a creak. Ruby's breath hitched in her throat as a boy walked through. She watched as he leaned up to bolt the doors, and she watched as he fiddled with the keys with long, pale fingers. He was tall and elegant, a collection of finely drawn lines and delicate movements. He somehow even managed to make the Cornerhouse uniform look suave; right from the ridiculously blue waistcoat, to the bright orange nametag that was pinned to his chest.

He'd turned around and grinned when he saw her.

She could have *lived* in the crooked edges of that smile.

'You look good in a dress, Coleville,' the boy said.

'Shut up,' she'd replied.

Ruby grabbed the edges of her skirt and squeezed hard. She could feel her skin flush red, but the boy simply raised his hands in mock defeat. Then he smiled shyly and sat next to her. Her eyes flickered to the nametag; *Alex.*

'It was a slow day today,' Alex said conversationally.

Ruby snorted. 'I'll bet. Half the town was at the funeral.'

Alex raised his eyebrows and then closed his eyes, his face pulling into a grimace.

'Oh *shit*. I completely forgot that was today. How was it? Is your friend okay? Are you alright?'

Ruby ran a hand through her hair, then scratched at her palm. *How was he making this so difficult?*

She forced herself to look him in the eye. 'I can't see you anymore.'

Alex raised his eyebrows. 'O-kay... why?'

There were so many reasons. All of them bad. None of them really reasons at all.

'Sinclair needs me.'

Alex let out a small, disbelieving laugh. 'You know you can have more than one friend, don't you?'

'Sinclair needs me,' Ruby repeated, and then she stood up as if to end the matter.

She was painfully aware of Alex's eyes following her

movements. She'd made to walk away, then stopped, and spun around to face him.

Once again, she was struck by how *pretty* he was. There was no other word for it. Everything about him was entrancing.

Ruby had never been interested in boys before. Not as friends and certainly not as boyfriends, and Alex was...well, she wasn't sure what he was. She only knew that she had shared almost all her summer with him. She only knew that the sound of his laugh made her insides squirm, and that when he smiled, he always tilted his head to the left a little, and that he had a small scar on his chin from when he'd crashed his bike when he was six.

She bit down hard on her lip, pulling herself back into focus.

'You haven't told anyone, have you?' she asked quietly. 'About my... *problem*.'

Alex's mouth dropped open and his shoulder's slouched. 'Is that really what you think of me?'

She didn't think she'd imagined the hurt in his eyes.

When she left him, she'd hoped that she would never have to see that look on his face again.

She was wrong.

'MISS COLEVILLE, YOUR friends have all been very compliant with us, it would be beneficial for you to do the same and answer the question. What happened?'

Ruby leaned back in her chair. On one side of the desk there sat two understandably tired police officers. On the other side was Ruby and her mother, Janice Coleville, a nightmare of a woman tucked neatly inside a second-hand Gucci suit.

'Miss Coleville, what happened to Timothy Small?'

Timothy Small—that was his name. Had *been* his name.

It had been a long night. After Harriett's performance the police had arrived almost immediately. The scene that followed was a blur of flashing lights, loud noises and teenage hysteria. Parents were called, accusations were made. Until ultimately everyone at the party had been escorted to the police station where they each had to wait to be questioned.

We're going to lie.

Ruby had instead opted to maintain an impenetrable silence. She was neither willing to lie, nor eager to spill the truth. So, she simply sat there, quietly watching as the officers grew more and more agitated with her.

The entire time she couldn't shake the image of the boy lying flat on his back, nor the feel of his ribs beneath her hands—so fragile, so breakable.

'Miss Coleville, I will not ask you again. What happened?'

She was in so much pain, her stomach boiled hot. She looked down at her lap and then up again.

'He swallowed a Shadow,' she said flatly.

The two officers looked at each other, unnerved, while her mother let out a *tssk*. One of the officers reached for a pen and started to write something down on a clipboard. Harriett's voice echoed in her head:

Ruby, you are going to go along with the exact same story as the rest of us.

Her stomach was cramping, and she felt the familiar sensation of bile rising in her throat. She clutched at her stomach.

Girl Fight Club, remember?

She leaned forward and threw her hands up in what she hoped was a convincing show of resignation.

'Look, I don't know what to tell you. We were at a party. That's all. Emily went into the garden to get some fresh air and when we went out to find her, he—Timothy, I mean—was there. We went over to say hello and he collapsed. I tried performing CPR but... but he was already dead,' she said it all so bluntly. As if reciting a shopping list, but still – she said it.

Harriett's voice stopped whispering in her ear, but the pain in her stomach persisted. Slowly, she wrapped an arm around her stomach, instantly her mother stiffened beside her. One of the police officers leaned forward in his chair, staring her down. 'Are you sure that's what happened?'

The room was so white. White and dull and dreary.

'Yes,' she said. 'Can I go now?'

The policeman looked as though he was prepared to ask her more questions but at this point her mother stood up. 'Officers, my daughter is in a state of shock. I think it would be best if we left it here, she's told you all she knows.'

'Mrs Coleville—'

'*Ms*,' her mother corrected.

Ruby could see the officer restrain himself from rolling his eyes. '*Ms* Coleville, we really should ask a few more questions.'

Janice folded her arms over her chest. 'Can you legally keep us here?'

The policeman faltered. 'No but—'

Her mother smiled, a sickly sweet, venomous smile and Ruby couldn't help but smile too.

'Goodbye officers. You have my number if you need to get in touch.'

With that Janice Coleville hoisted Ruby up from her chair by her arm and swept out of the room with Ruby in tow.

Together they marched through the police station, where they were immediately met by crowds of concerned parents. It didn't take long for Ruby to spot Harriett and Emily, both sat huddled in the corner, their parents sitting on either side.

She gave them a curt nod.

Don't worry, Sinclair, I stuck to the party line.

Her mother steered her through the waiting room. All the while Ruby continued to scan the crowd for Sarah and—

Alex.

There he was. Sitting with his brother and his mum, his hands resting gently in his lap and his eyes firmly fixed on her. Without thinking she jerked her head instinctively in the other direction. She still couldn't believe he had been at the party. She still couldn't believe she had *ignored* him like that.

Heart pounding, her mother opened the exit door and Ruby found herself being practically dragged to the car and ushered hastily inside.

For a moment the two of them simply sat there. Her mother poised and thin-lipped, Ruby slouching and head turned to the side, her cheek pressed against the window.

'How long?'

Ruby stared out of the window, gazing into the now early morning Sunday sky. 'Just now.'

Her mother's eyes narrowed. 'Don't lie to me.'

Ruby bit her lip, she was so, so tired... 'A couple of hours.'

'Damn it, Ruby!' Janice thumped her hand down onto the dashboard.

Ruby flinched but said nothing else, in silence her mother switched on the car engine and began to drive.

Ruby continued to stare out of the window. She tried to focus on the houses that flashed by, or the orange glow that emanated from the evenly placed streetlamps. She tried to focus on anything—*anything, anything, anything*—but the memory of how hollow Timothy Small's chest had been.

Her phone vibrated in her hands and her heart juddered when she saw who the message was from.

> WE NEED TO TALK. I SAW EVERYTHING. - AM

It took everything inside her to stay still. To not scream or swear or throw the phone out the window. Her fingers trembled as she typed out the reply.

TELL ME WHEN. - RC

When the message had been sent, she almost wanted to laugh out loud. How did Sinclair really think they were going to convincingly lie about what happened to Timothy Small? How did *she*, Ruby, think she was going to keep her and Alex Mason's friendship a secret? How did she even think she was going to keep hiding her problem?

Small towns were breeding grounds for badly kept secrets, and Ruby Coleville had more than she cared to count.

And Woolington-on-Sea was a very small town.

Chapter Thirteen

A GODDAMN WARRIOR

Janice Coleville marched into the kitchen and slammed her bag onto the countertop. She muttered darkly under her breath as she opened the fridge door, revealing boxes and boxes of what looked like milkshakes. Then she rooted around until she held one of the small bottles in her hand and then she banged that onto the countertop too.

'You're not going to bed until you've had it,' her mother said sharply.

Sullenly Ruby picked up the bottle from the counter, peeled off the straw and jabbed it into the lid as aggressively as she could. She sipped at the shake, it was thick and horribly sweet, with a metallic aftertaste she still hadn't gotten used to—despite her mother's assurances.

'What were you thinking?' Ms Coleville demanded. 'Parties and all sorts! Did you ever stop to think what might happen if you were to collapse?'

Ruby shrugged. 'I figured someone would call you and you'd order me back to consciousness.'

Her mother's lips formed the thinnest of line and her nostrils were flaring larger than they ever had. Ruby had heard it said on numerous occasions that her mother was a "monster" of a woman. This was not a name bestowed due to her size or appearance, but on her sheer force of will alone. Janice Coleville was a woman made of steel, she had mastered the art of the scowl and had a stare so withering it had been known to push grown men to tears. She was a woman who loved her daughter and herself and that was it. Everybody else was just collateral damage.

'We've got an appointment with Dr Leigh first thing tomorrow,' her mother said.

Ruby took another sip. 'I know.'

'And an appointment with your dietician on Wednesday.'

Another sip. 'I know.'

Ms Coleville took a deep breath and Ruby knew what was coming next; 'Ruby, honey, I really don't think you should be going to school right now.'

Ruby swallowed the last of the shake and placed it down on the counter. 'I'm going to bed.'

'Don't you walk away from me young lady!' her mother snapped.

Ruby spun to face her. 'What? I'm not allowed to eat, I'm not allowed to do my post rounds, I'm not allowed to go to school, what next? Am I still allowed to see my friends?'

Her mother's posture slouched, if only a little. 'You know I'm not saying that darling, but your condition... you know you shouldn't be pushing yourself.'

Ruby had heard it all before, and she saw the sense in it. She just didn't want to give in, she viewed it as surrendering to enemy demands, and Ruby Coleville surrendered to no one.

No one.

Not even her own damn body.

'Can I just... can I just have one more week?' she asked, hating herself for sounding so whiny, like a child begging for five more minutes before bedtime. 'Please?'

Her mother sighed and began rummaging through her bag for a cigarette. She lit it and took a deep drag, the smoke curled around her, framing her face. When she met Ruby's gaze, her dark eyes seemed to be sizing her daughter up.

'One week. That's all, got it?'

Ruby let out a breath. 'Thanks Mum.'

They held each other's gaze for a moment longer, mother and daughter, each uncomfortable in their own way. Both knowing that when that week was up Ruby would beg for one more after that, and then another one, and then another...

'Last night...' her mother began slowly, 'what happened with that boy... Are you alright?'

Ruby thought back again to the moment when the boy swallowed the Shadow. He *swallowed* the *Shadow*.

'I don't know,' she said truthfully. Standing there in her kitchen, with her mother lecturing on doctors' appointments and an empty medical shake sitting in front of her, it all seemed an impossible blur.

But she only had to look down at herself and see the bloodstains crusted onto her t-shirt to know that the impossible had happened.

'Darling, come here.'

Ruby did as she was told and was immediately wrapped in a hug. She was overwhelmed by the bittersweet smell of smoke and sharp perfume. Ms Coleville rubbed a hand up and down her back in what would usually seem like a comforting gesture—only Ruby knew it was her mother's ham-fisted way of trying to see just how thin she was and whether she had lost any more weight in the past few days.

Ruby closed her eyes and let her mother hold her, after a few moments she hugged her in return.

RUBY PEELED OFF her dirt-blood-ridden clothes and collapsed onto her bed. Her room was a small, manic disorderly space—clothes were strewn across the floor, schoolbooks were piled messily in the corners and posters of her favourite bands were plastered haphazardly onto the walls and ceiling.

She wanted to play over the events of the night in her mind but found that she couldn't. Partly because she was so fatigued that her eyelids were fighting to stay open, and partly because the seething hot pain in the pit of her stomach had arrived once more.

She hadn't told any of her friends about her... *condition*. She hadn't wanted Sinclair to worry.

Over the summer Ruby had so desperately wanted to be by Harriett's side, comforting her through her grief. She couldn't even imagine what it had been like for Sinclair to lose her sister. But she thought it might feel like if Ruby had lost Sinclair...

While Sinclair mourned the loss of her sister, Ruby had been in London, and not for any of the glamorous or fun reasons that might make Sarah go. No, Ruby had been in hospitals having cameras rammed down her throat, she'd been shoved into MRI machines, jabbed with all types of needles, pumped full of drugs, and just generally having a rather miserable time all round.

After, when she came back from her nightmarish week, she'd buried herself in her room, switched off her phone and tried to come to terms with the fact that she wasn't healthy anymore.

That she was ill.

In a way—Ruby had been mourning as well.

Then she'd met Alex. Alex, who worked at the Cornerhouse most of the summer. Alex, who was understanding and easy to talk to. Alex, who was so far removed from her friends that she felt as though she could say the words out loud.

'I am ill. And I am never getting better.'

Now it transpired he wasn't as far removed as she'd thought.

She had convinced herself that she was going to tell them all the truth when school started again, but then she had gone to Hayley's funeral and found Sinclair so... broken. Ruby couldn't bear to let her know that she was broken too.

It wasn't the only reason. If she was being honest with herself—and Ruby almost always was – it was that she didn't want to admit the embarrassing, horrifying truth. She did not want people to look at her and see a weak, pitiful thing where previously they would have seen a devil of a girl.

So, she carried on as she had always carried on, creating chaos and mischief, and fighting anyone who wanted to fight. She grinned the smirk of a grin that she had spent so many years perfecting and laughed at anyone who called her a maniac for it.

She didn't know what else to do.

No, that wasn't right. She didn't know how else to *be*.

But the walls were closing in on her now, shadows and sickness were taking over her life. She could no longer distinguish between the pain in her body and the pain that was *everything else*.

Every day Ruby stepped into her devil's skin ready to fight the world, ready to show people only what she wanted them to see; Ruby Coleville, untouchable and fearless.

But now she was afraid.

She tried to convince herself that it didn't matter, if only she made up for it with everything that she *was*.

She was a force of nature.

She was dynamite made human.

She was a warrior.

Ruby rolled over onto her side as another wave of nausea hit, she clutched at her stomach as the cramping fire-hot pain began, then her eyes spotted the bucket her mother had discreetly left by her bed.

'I am a warrior,' she whispered to herself. 'I am a goddamn *warrior.*'

And she knew it to be true.

Then she reached for the bucket and threw up.

Chapter Fourteen

A TOUCH OF HYSTERIA

'How are we today?' Dr Leigh asked.

Ruby felt like slapping him. *Who me? I'm fine! I mean, my body's falling apart, and I watched a boy die two nights ago. But I'm just peachy thanks! Dickbag.*

'The same,' she mumbled.

Dr Leigh nodded sympathetically. He was a big man, with thick lips and fine, wispy white hair.

'Okay, let's get down to it shall we? Your recent tests show a slight improvement in your terminal ileum, possibly due to the infusions, but the disease in your right colon has spread which means we are now at risk of scarring or strictures. So, we have to decide what to do next.'

Ruby bit down on her lip. She hated the way he said "we," as though they were all ill and taking the drugs together, when really it was just her.

Just her.

'What do you recommend?' her mother asked, reaching out to hold her hand. Ruby glanced down at their entwined fingers, hers were so bony and fragile now.

'As Ruby has been non-responsive to immunosuppressant treatment, I think it's time to consider surgery.'

Ruby's mother frowned. '"Non-responsive," what does that mean?'

Dr Leigh leaned back in his chair. 'It just means that so far your daughter's disease appears drug resistant.'

'Oh, is that all?' Ruby said drily.

'Ruby...' her mother warned.

Ruby ignored her. 'What happens next?'

The doctor looked from Ruby's mother to Ruby, then he picked up his pen and placed it gently onto the desk, on top of her file.

'Well, we could continue with your drug treatment but...as it hasn't started working yet it's unlikely to do so now.'

There was a ringing in Ruby's ears. They had been warned it could come to this. 'Does that mean the surgery... do I *have* to have it now?'

Dr Leigh nodded. 'At this point, I would strongly recommend having surgery to remove the diseased part of your colon. This would prevent it from spreading further; Then we could revisit possible drug treatments after your recovery.'

Ruby blinked slowly, her mother's grip over her hand tightened.

'Do I have to stick with the liquid diet?'

'Yes.'

Ruby's throat felt dry. 'And will I... will I have a scar?'

He nodded again. 'If we go in laparoscopically, it should be minimal, but there's no guarantee that we won't have to open you up further.'

Her skin was cold and the fire in the pit of her stomach was burning. 'That's fine,' she said, shaking her head. 'Cool. I mean, what fifteen-year-old girl doesn't want to be knocked out, sliced open and scarred?' She laughed, the sound brittle, even to her.

'Ruby, honey, it is okay to be upset.'

'I'm not upset, Mum. I just said it's fine.'

Her mother opened her mouth, but Ruby turned to look at Dr Leigh; 'When would the surgery be?'

'I don't have a specific date for you yet, but given the nature of your condition I think I can make space within the next two months.'

Ruby had suspected for a while that she was running out of time. She wouldn't be able to keep her condition a secret for much longer. She wouldn't be able to bluff her way into disappearing from school for three whole months while she recovered. Besides, most of the teachers already knew anyway.

Soon, everyone else would, too.

Ruby let out a long, slow breath. 'Brilliant. Great. Book me in.'

THE JOURNEY HOME was silent, Ruby was afraid what might happen if she opened her mouth, she felt as though she might scream or yell... or worse, cry. So, she settled for nothing at all.

Her body felt like it was made of lead as she dragged herself from the car, the pain in her stomach ever present. Her joints ached. And there was this feeling she couldn't shake, a feeling of having a thin layer of mist over her vision. It had been months since she had felt truly, *truly* awake, the numbness such a part of her now that she saw the entire world through a dreary, miserable lens.

Crohn's Disease, she thought, *what a bitch.*

She kicked a stone across the gravel driveway and watched as it skipped along the pavement until it landed at the foot of a cat. Ruby froze. The cat looked up at her, blue eyes wide and watchful, then it sauntered away, its matted, crooked tail pointed high in the air while Ruby remained rooted to the spot. She remembered what she had seen in Harriett's notebook only a few days before.

Are the Shadow and the cat connected? Is the cat important at all?

'Honey, what's wrong?' her mother asked gently.

Suddenly, it was all so hysterical. In two months, she would be put to sleep and sliced apart. But only if a Shadow demon didn't kill her first.

Ruby, laughed; loudly, raucously, feverishly.

Chapter Fifteen

THE FACELESS MAN

In her sleep, she saw Timothy Small, lying on the ground with a sword protruding from his chest.

Her sword.

She pulled it out from him with a sickening *squelch,* and then she ran. Her body was bruised, her limbs heavy but she felt alive.

Alive, alive, alive.

Around her was nothing but noise. Shouts and screams and blood - her skin was painted with it. She could taste it; warm and metallic.

In the distance, there was the figure of a man. He was tall and broad, a silhouette against the horizon. He stood surveying the scene, above it all; a bruised sky and an open field, decorated with the bodies of slain warriors, their armours and shields glinting underneath the sun like jewels.

Ruby ran forward, sword in hand. There was no pain here, only the fight. A man in armour charged at her and she sliced through him like butter. Another man followed, and he too fell to the ground. Then another. And another.

On and on it went until she reached the figure. His face was cast in shadow and his features were distorted, yet somehow—*somehow*—Ruby knew him.

Suddenly, they were alone. No one else, no bodies. Nothing but her and the faceless man on the field.

Her sword slipped from her fingers as his hands curled around her throat. He lifted her into the air, and for a moment she thought she saw the flicker of brilliant amber eyes.

When he spoke, it was not the rasp that Ruby expected, but a voice, both smooth and deep.

'The world has changed, but you have not. You are still Gwendolen's *dog*.'

Ruby couldn't breathe. She grappled at his hands, scratching, but it only made him squeeze tighter. Then she stopped struggling, her body went limp, and she felt herself fading away…

REACH FOR YOUR KNIFE.

Ruby felt her right hand move down towards her thigh, felt her fingers curl around the hilt of a dagger. She pulled the dagger from its sheath and, in one clumsy movement, jabbed it into the faceless man's side.

She felt the hitch of the blade as it cut into him; heard his gasp of pain.

He released her, and she fell to the ground, still holding the knife.

The shadowed man staggered backwards, and she ran at him, she held the knife above her head and plunged it straight into the side of his neck.

'Long live the king,' she sneered, yanking the dagger ruthlessly out, only to shove it right back in.

It was then that the shadow fell from the man's face, revealing not a man at all but a boy.

Timothy Small.

Ruby threw the knife onto the ground. It skidded away and disappeared into the grass. She bent over Timothy, placed her hands on his chest and frantically tried to pump life back into his eyes. Only, her hands kept slipping, they were too slick with blood.

She was failing, he was dying, there was nothing she could do.

A laugh echoed around her and the Shadow rose from the ground, blotting out the sky with its vastness.

'I have not forgotten you, *little warrior*. And I do not forgive.'

Then the Shadow condensed into a slither of black and soared through the brilliant, purple sky, right into Ruby's open mouth.

She swallowed it whole.

RUBY AWOKE, PANTING and sweating.

She knew it was daylight, despite the curtains of her room being drawn. She couldn't remember when she had laid down to sleep, all she could see was the anguished look on Timothy Small's face. All she could feel was the blood on her fingers.

She glanced down at her hands and sighed with relief when she saw that they were clean.

Slowly she rolled over to check her phone, which was charging on the floor by her bed. It was flooded with texts.

> RUBY, YOU CAN'T KEEP SKIPPING SCHOOL LIKE THIS. – HS

> ARE YOU OKAY? – HS

> PLEASE JUST TEXT ME BACK. – HS

> OR DON'T. ENTIRELY UP TO YOU. – HS

> RUBY? – HS

> FOR GOD'S SAKE REPLY TO HARRIETT SHE'S
> ANNOYING THE HELL OUT OF ME. – SA

Ruby felt frustration bubble up and clenched the phone more tightly in her fist, it was already 3:00 pm. She had missed yet another day of school. She gritted her teeth, swore, and began to type.

> DON'T GET YOUR KNICKERS IN A TWIST,
> SINCLAIR. I'M FINE. SEE YOU SOON. – RC

She remembered now.

After the appointment with Dr Leigh her mother had ordered her to go upstairs and lay in bed for half an hour. She couldn't exactly have argued with her, not after her spectacular performance of the one-girl-cackling lunatic in the front garden. So, she had stomped off to bed with the intention of laying down for no longer than necessary and then marching off to school.

Instead, she'd slept through the whole damn day and had that weird, messed-up dream.

No, not a dream. A nightmare. And even though half of it didn't make any sense, she could still hear the deep baritone voice of the faceless man taunt her.

Gwendolen's dog.

'Well, joke's on him because I don't know any damn Gwendolen,' Ruby muttered, standing up and rolling her shoulders back. Ever since Timothy's death she had decided against pretending these strange occurrences were group hallucinations. She knew they were all real. But it didn't make it any less crazy.

In a foggy haze, Ruby made her way downstairs into the kitchen, trying to piece together what she could remember of the dream. She had been a soldier—no, a warrior—or at least someone who knew how to wield a sword; and there had been a battle, though she didn't know who it was between. It was rather like trying to put together a puzzle but with only half the pieces, frustrating and ultimately fruitless.

She reached the fridge only to find a note pinned onto its door in her mother's neat, spidery handwriting.

**Rest up. Don't go to school today. I'll
be back at 7. Remember you must
have six shakes.**

Ruby snorted, opened the fridge, and reached for a shake. She was starving, and somehow the banana flavoured drink didn't quite cut it. With every passing day her fantasies about food grew more and more vivid. She'd made a deal with herself that when she could eat again, she was going to get the biggest, greasiest burger she could find and eat it as impolitely as possible.

Over the course of the next twenty minutes Ruby forced herself to drink two bottles of the shake. Then she pottered aimlessly about, her body restless and her mind buzzing.

The Coleville's house was a small, narrow building. It had shelves filled with books, walls covered in photos, and a lingering scent of smoke. With no dining room, the Coleville women ate their dinners on the sofa facing the television, usually watching one of Ms Coleville's DVD's—of which there were many.

Ruby kneeled onto the floor, opened the wooden chest beside the television, and perused the DVD collection. Her fingers traced the spines of the DVD cases; *To Kill a Mockingbird, Cleopatra, Singin' in the Rain, Calamity Jane, The Audrey Hepburn Collection.*

Her fingers hovered over *Roman Holiday*. When she was younger her mother would put it on to make her feel better whenever she was ill, or when it was raining. It was an odd tradition. Now, whenever she watched the black and white scenery of Rome or heard the clipped, sharp tones of Mr Bradley, she always thought of winter afternoons; of her mother wrapping her in blankets and giving her a bottle of Lucozade to drink.

Ruby didn't think she'd ever live it down if Sarah were to discover her fondness for old-fashioned romance films. Sinclair knew, but then Sinclair knew almost everything.

Her phone flashed again.

WE NEED TO TALK. THE CORNERHOUSE,
THIRTY MINUTES. – AM

Ruby let out a long, slow groan. She made to pick up the movie again, but it was no good. The moment she'd received the text, she knew she was leaving. Besides, she didn't want to sit in her stuffy front room watching something she'd seen a hundred times before. She wanted to be out and *doing* things. She wanted to breathe air that her mother hadn't polluted with menthol cigarettes.

Her mind flew to the note plastered on the fridge. It had instructed her not to go to school. It had said nothing about going anywhere else.

<h2>Chapter Sixteen</h2>

THE BOY WITH
THICK-RIMMED GLASSES

The Cornerhouse Cinema was an old building made of large cream-coloured bricks and a turquoise domed roof. It had a balcony resting on tall pillars and a vintage tea shop that faced the sea.

Ruby had always loved everything about the Cornerhouse from its faded, red velvet chairs to its apparently-never-ever-been-cleaned chandelier. She loved the way it smelt of popcorn and how it almost felt like stepping into one of the old movies that she and her mum loved so much. It was a relic from another time, threadbare and glorious in its dusty beauty. Sinclair had never quite understood her fascination with the place, but like most of the teenagers in Woolington they'd spent many of their summers there, mostly because there was so little else to do. They would catch the odd film, eat ice creams in the teashop, and if it was hot enough, sometimes they'd wander over to the sea for a swim.

It was predictable and easy and oh-so quaint—but Ruby loved every second and inch of it.

Right then, however, she didn't have enough money to catch a film, and she couldn't order anything from the teashop. So, she simply stood there, a reedy figure against a smooth, blue ocean backdrop, draped in black and tapping her scuffed boot repetitively on the floor.

In her head she could practically see Harriett Sinclair rolling her eyes and saying, *'See?* This *is why you make a plan* before *you go charging off!'*

It didn't matter, any minute now he would arrive.

After a moment she crossed her arms and stomped inside the teashop.

'A bottle of water please.'

The young girl behind the counter chewed her gum, robotically pulling out a bottle from one of the shelves and handing it to her. 'Pound,' she grunted.

Wordlessly Ruby placed a pound on the counter.

The teashop was empty but for one very elderly lady reading in the corner. Ruby smiled awkwardly as she passed, and the woman smiled toothlessly back, finally she placed herself at the table closest to the window. For a while she simply gazed out at the sea, watching the light shine off the smooth surface. In the distance she could make out the silhouettes of the wind farm, the thin spires lazily spinning round and round and round.

Long live the king.

'Hey Rubes.'

Ruby jolted from her reverie and swore loudly. 'Jesus! You shouldn't jump out at people like that!'

Alex raised an eyebrow. 'How am I jumping out at you when we arranged to meet here?'

She looked up at him, she'd never seen him in the St David's uniform before, though it was hardly surprising to see him wearing it, most of the boys in Woolington did.

Alex pushed his glasses nervously up the bridge of his nose, then dropped his satchel onto the floor and reached for the seat next to her. As he pulled it from underneath the table the chair scraped against the floor in a dreadful shriek. Blushing a deep crimson, he sat down.

'I tried calling you a few times,' he said after a while.

'I know,' Ruby replied.

Her mind flashed back to when she had first met him over the summer. It was the evening she'd returned home from London. The same day they had told her she had one more drug to try. The same day that she had been sent home with boxes of liquid shakes and the instruction to not let another piece of food pass her lips.

Upon arriving home, she had stormed out of the car and marched to the Cornerhouse. Once there she had asked the boy behind the counter for a large popcorn, a large coke, a hot dog, and a bag of chocolate drops - just for the hell of it.

It had been the last of her paper round money.

Stupid, stupid, stupid.

He had raised an eyebrow at her then too. 'Hungry?'

'Ravenous,' she had snarled.

Then she took her tray of food and froze.

She'd looked at the tray, at all the things she could not eat, at all the food that would inevitably cause her pain, and her hands had started to shake.

Then she'd broken.

She'd hurdled the tray across the foyer and watched with grim satisfaction as the contents spilled across the floor.

'Damn,' the boy had said. 'I guess that popcorn really had it coming.'

She'd told him everything right then and there, she told him about the disease she had somehow got out of nowhere, she told him that none of her friends knew, she even told him about Harriett and how her sister had died only a week before.

Patiently, he had listened to her, all the while tidying up the mess she'd created. Then he'd *kept* listening to her, for the rest of summer. And to her endless surprise she had found herself listening to him too. He was a gentle sort of creature, nervous and steady all at once.

Now though he just looked hurt, his eyes regarding her carefully through his spectacles. The top button of his school shirt was undone. Ruby couldn't help but notice these small details about Alex, it was infuriating. She turned away.

'Are you alright?' he asked.

'Nope. You?'

'No. Not really.'

The seriousness in his voice startled her. She sat a little straighter.

'Come on then, tell me,' she said. 'What did you see?'

'I'm not really sure...' he said cautiously, then he lowered his voice. 'The other night when you went into the garden, I followed you.'

Ruby pictured it all so easily, the Shadow and Timothy's limp body lying in the grass and Alex standing at the other end of the garden, witness to the whole macabre bloody scene.

'You followed us?' she repeated, stunned.

Alex nodded grimly. 'I was angry, and I wanted to confront you, about pretending not to know me. I wanted to know if I embarrassed you or something. I wanted to...' He trailed off, his cheeks glowing red. 'I needed some fresh air anyway; it was really hot in that room and I—I followed you.'

He stared at her, waiting for her to answer his unspoken question. She was determined not to say a word, so she glowered right back; Taking in the shape of his eyes, the curve of his neck, the waves in his hair.

She swallowed, and placed her hand on the table, her skin was cold and behind Alex's head she could see the sun slowly begin to set. Finally, she could take the silence no longer. 'Just tell me what you saw, Alex.'

'That's the thing,' he whispered. 'I'm not really sure, when I got into the garden it was like... it was like all the air had been sucked out from space. It was dead quiet, y'know? I walked through the garden and that's when I saw you... and Timmy.' His voice wavered, and it occurred to her that perhaps the two of them had been friends. Her heart gave a little twinge.

'Did you know him?' she asked quietly.

'I knew him...' he said softly. 'I saw that girl, the one in the white dress, standing with him. And then, well I thought I was seeing things, because I could've sworn that some*thing* came out the *ground.*'

He said all this gazing directly at her, his deep brown eyes meeting her icy blues. It was as though he was waiting for her to react, for her smallest movement to give something away. Ruby stayed perfectly still.

On the other side of the teashop, the old woman with her book coughed violently, snapping the two of them back into reality.

'I'm not really sure what happened next,' Alex continued. 'It was dark, and I couldn't see properly. Next thing I knew Timmy was stumbling backwards and then he was on the ground and I—I ran back inside,' he cast his eyes downwards.

'You didn't really see what happened then,' Ruby said, relief flooding through her.

Alex shook his head. 'I did hear a voice from across the garden. It said; *"Did you see it? Did you see the Shadow?"*'

Ruby didn't say anything, but panic must have passed over her face, Alex's eyes widened.

'That's what it was, wasn't it?' Alex exclaimed, his voice rising. 'A Shadow was what came out the ground? A Shadow killed Timmy!'

'Keep your voice down, will you?' Ruby hissed, glancing around frantically, but the girl behind the counter had earphones in and the elderly woman appeared to be deeply immersed in her book.

Ruby tapped her fingers on the table. 'We don't know,

okay? But yeah, that's what it looked like.'

Alex's pale skin went, if possible, even paler. He leaned back in his chair and his shoulders slumped.

'That's mad, completely mad,' he breathed.

'Tell me something I don't know,' Ruby snapped.

Alex rubbed his eyes and let out a long breath, then he frowned. 'You don't seem all that startled by this.'

Ruby opened her mouth to make a sarcastic remark along the lines of; *Well, it turns out the novelty wears off after your first haunting.* But she held her tongue, unwilling to admit that she had seen the Shadow before.

Alex seemed to regard her more carefully, it was as though he was trying to find something in her expression; a hidden clue or a nugget of truth.

'How long has this been going on, Rubes?'

Ruby scowled. She knew there was a reason her mother advised her to stay away from boys. A couple of weeks spending time with her in the summer and somehow Alex had cracked the code on how to read her damn mind.

'Since Hayley's funeral,' she said stiffly. There seemed no point in hiding it now. He'd seen it, he knew about the Shadow.

How was she going to explain him to the girls?

'So, what are you all then? Witches?'

Ruby snorted and let out one short, loud, 'HA!'

'Well, isn't this the kind of stuff that normally happens to witches?' he asked.

She supposed it was.

'No, of course we're not!' But Harriett Sinclair's face swam to the forefront of her mind. She thought of the strange dream and the moments of forgetting. 'I don't know what we are...'

For a moment the two of them sat opposite one another, neither speaking, neither moving. Ruby thought he was trying not to stare at her, though rather unsuccessfully.

'You lied about it, didn't you?' Alex said.

Ruby didn't need to ask what he meant. Their interviews with the police had been splashed across all the town's newspapers;

ST CATHERINE'S GIRLS WITNESS SMALL'S SUDDEN DEATH, SUSPECTED NATURAL CAUSES.

'Do you think they would have believed us if we told the truth?' Ruby asked. 'You spoke to the police too; did *you* tell them what you saw?'

Alex opened his mouth, then closed it again.

'Didn't think so.'

'Well, at least I'm not crazy,' Alex said. 'For a moment there I really thought I was.'

Ruby froze. 'I wouldn't rule it out just yet.'

Alex followed her gaze, across the seafront there was an explosion of colour and noise.

Caravans, dozens and dozens of them.

Only Ruby hadn't seen them arrive and they *definitely* hadn't been there mere minutes before. It was as though the caravans had simply sprouted out from the ground, people and dogs in tow.

Slowly, Ruby rose from her seat and stumbled outside, Alex close behind her.

'You see them too, right?' Ruby whispered; it was always good to double check nowadays.

Alex nodded. 'They're kind of hard to miss.'

This was true. The sun had all but sunk into the sea and pink streaks had seeped into an otherwise clean blue sky. The ocean was a glittering deep blue velvet, and the caravans sat perched in front of it all. An enchanting wooden village. Even from the other side of the road Ruby could see that each caravan was painted in its own, unique and vibrant colour. It was like staring at a very bright and very colourful dream.

Vaguely, she could hear dogs barking and people singing.

'It's beautiful,' Alex said. Ruby found she couldn't disagree.

From behind her the door to the café swung open and the old lady with the book came pottering out.

She hobbled up to Ruby and smiled her toothless smile.

'Come see me,' she said, in a voice that sounded like the ripping of paper. 'And bring your friends with you.' Then she pressed a card into Ruby's hand and hobbled across the road. Ruby watched, dumbfounded, as the woman disappeared into one of the caravans.

Slowly she unfurled her fingers to read the card. It was a small black square with white tree-branches painted across it. In the centre, in white cursive handwriting, it said:

MADAM CRONE
the truth is in the cards…

'Fantastic!' she grumbled. 'Fan-bloody-tastic!' She kicked the ground with her boot but pocketed the card anyway.

She stared at the campsite, unsure what to make of it or what to do.

Alex stood a metre away from her, a thoughtful expression on his face, 'Do you believe in coincidences?'

Ruby scoffed. 'Nope.'

'Me neither.'

Ruby met his gaze; he wasn't that much taller than her— she couldn't help but notice how long his eyelashes were.

Eons passed.

Alex took a deep breath. 'Can you stop ignoring me now? Please,' he whispered.

Ruby's heart skittered around in her chest. Growing up in a boy-less household and going to a boy-less school meant that she didn't have the slightest inkling of what to do with the opposite sex. Years of watching Sarah with her various paramours had taught her to believe that she wasn't missing out on much. But there was something in the way he stared at her—an earnestness to his features that she couldn't quite resist.

What do I do? She thought manically. *Pat him on the head?* She could feel her face grow warm.

Alex shuffled his feet awkwardly. Around them the lampposts on the street flickered on, night had officially arrived.

She rolled her eyes. 'Fine, I will once again honour you with my company. Happy now?'

Alex Mason tilted his head to the left a little, a curious expression lighting up his features; bemusement and delight all rolled into one. 'Ecstatic,' he grinned.

Ruby glanced over her shoulder, hoping that he couldn't see the smile tugging at her lips.

Chapter Seventeen

A CINNAMON SONG

'I can't believe you've adopted that devil creature,' Ruby hissed.

It was lunchtime and the four of them were sitting at the back of the field far away from prying eyes and ears. Ruby had been both shocked and appalled to see Emily cradling the black cat in her arms like some adorable little baby, rather than the mangy, ugly-pet-of Satan that it actually was.

Emily shrugged and dotingly fed tuna into its mouth.

'What if it has fleas or something?' Sarah said, her nose crinkled up in obvious disgust.

'Screw fleas, what if it's trying to *kill* us?' Ruby demanded.

Emily watched them passively, the cat's furry face poked out from under her school jumper and gently licked her fingers; 'It's just a cat.'

'How do you know it's *just* a cat? That thing has been a serious bad omen for all of us!' Ruby gestured wildly at the four of them, then she turned to Harriett. 'You can't seriously be okay with this?'

Harriett stroked her plait. 'No, I'm not happy with it. But I do think it's better to know the whereabouts of the creature and what it's doing.'

Ruby sighed and pulled out a chunk of grass from the ground, if Sinclair was okay with it then that was the end of the discussion. The cat looked up from Emily's lap, its head turning to face Ruby, then it let out a slow, mocking purr.

Smug little shit-stain, Ruby thought.

'I'm more of a dog-person anyway,' she sneered. But the cat was no longer interested in her, more focused on eating tuna from Emily's outstretched palm.

'Let's get back to this Madam Crone business. Tell us again what happened.'

Ruby did, she told them about her dream, she told them about the Cornerhouse and the old woman, she told them about the caravans appearing from nowhere and she told them about the card the old lady had slipped into her hands.

She did not tell them why she had skipped school.

Nor did she tell them about Alex—although she was unsure why.

'Then she said, "come see me, and bring your friends with you,"' Ruby finished.

'And you think that definitely means us?' Harriett asked, for what seemed like the tenth time.

'Well, she said, "bring your friends" and in case you hadn't noticed I'm not exactly winning any popularity contests over here,' Ruby said.

'That's an understatement,' Sarah scoffed, not looking up from painting her nails.

'But what about this *Gwendolen's dog* business, what does that mean?' Ruby asked, ignoring her. It was the question that kept swirling through her head. She simply couldn't shake the notion that the name should *mean* something to her—though she couldn't for the life of her think what.

'Gwendolen...' repeated Harriett. 'It's strange, but I swear I've heard that name before.'

'Me too,' said Emily and Sarah at once.

Sarah finally put the nail varnish down and looked up.

The four of them eyed each other. The cat yawned.

'This is getting so weird,' Sarah murmured.

'*Getting* weird?' Ruby sniggered. 'We jumped ahead of weird when Sinclair found that skull in her rucksack. I hate to break it to you, but we're now knee deep in horror movie territory.' Ruby got out her fingers and started reeling things off; 'Shadow monsters, creepy cats, physic old ladies, dead boys and oh did I mention the random skull? Let's face it, all we're missing is a talking puppet and some red balloons.'

'You forgot Hayley's ghost,' Emily said matter-of-factly.

The effect of saying Hayley's name was instantaneous; Ruby turned to look at Harriett, Harriett froze, Sarah knocked over her nail varnish.

'Which is why we need answers,' Harriett said carefully, regaining composure. 'We need to go and speak to this Madam Crone.'

'Yes, because we should *definitely* do as the cryptic old psychic says,' Ruby said.

Harriett's face remained stern. 'I don't care how creepy she is. If she can make any sense of this nightmare we're living in, then I want to talk to her.'

Ruby had predicted as much, she rolled her head back. 'When do you want to go?'

'Tonight.'

Ruby bit her lip. After leaving the house the night before it had been a battle to even come to school this morning, her mother might have a fit if she disappeared for another evening in a row. Then again, it wasn't every day you got to visit a psychic and unravel the mysteries of a murderous Shadow.

Ruby grimaced. 'Okay fine, I'll go.'

The four girls remained sitting in their circle. Ruby swore that every time she saw her friends recently, they looked a little stranger to her. The same but different, somehow, they seemed *larger* and more *vivid* than anything around them. It was like living inside a black and white photograph where the only flecks of colour sat in front of her.

She went back to yanking out clumps of grass. She didn't want to see a psychic. She didn't want this *Madam Crone* to look into her eyes, read her like a book and pluck out her secrets for all her friends to see.

Her mind flashed to Timothy Small, and her hands shook the way they always did when she remembered him. With every passing day the image of him lying on his back, eyes open, became harder and harder to forget. She knew that she had to go, for him and for herself.

And maybe—just maybe—it would be worth it.

SCHOOL FINISHED, AND the four girls made their way through the pouring rain to the sea front. Their uniforms soaked through and their hair dripping wet. They stood facing a wild sea, the pier stood ghostly in the distance, its iron legs consumed by the waves. The caravans seemed so wildly out of place—colourful wooden toys that seemed in danger of being swept away at any given moment.

Music rang clearly through the downpour, a sweet tinkling song that cut through everything else.

Ruby could not help but think that there was a strange, fantastical atmosphere that surrounded the campsite. A whisper in the wind that told them to tread carefully.

The cat let out a strangled mewling sound as Emily cuddled it in her arms.

'So, are we going to venture inside this hell-hole or what?'

Harriett nodded vigorously, and Ruby recognised the hunger in her eyes—it was the same hunger that Harriett got every time she had an idea for a new project, every time she thought she was on the verge of discovering something new.

It was the same look she'd had when she had decided to put herself forward for Head Girl.

'Come on,' Harriett said. 'Let's go find Madam Crone.'

It was like walking into a very bright and very colourful dream. There was a sense of non-reality that surrounded them. There were about a dozen caravans in total, and horses loitered near almost every single one. Despite the rain, eccentric, marvellous clothes were hung out of every window and every caravan they passed was painted in vibrant colours; in reds, greens, purples and blues.

Each was decorated with its own unique design of swallows or roses or stars. Children played with their dogs, of which there were too many to count. As they ventured further, they found the source of the music: A man playing a guitar to a soft, lowly tune while a woman sung back to it gently, in a language that Ruby didn't know.

It was an assault on the senses, there was too much to take in, too much to see. The people themselves were as animated and interesting as their caravans, wearing top hats and blazers, long flowy skirts and old-style shawls. The adults were all adorned heavily with tattoos, while many of the children were covered head to toe in painted-on illustrations.

Rain spattered gently on the concrete beneath their feet. A calming, soft *pitter, patter, pitter, patter.*

They had reached what felt like the middle of the site, but there was no way to be sure. A group of children spotted them and ran past giggling.

'Maybe we should just ask where she is?' Sarah suggested.

It was then that the sound of a voice broke through all the noise and the confusion. Sweet and sugary—a cinnamon voice.

> *When the sun goes down in the night sky,*
> *When the trees grow down instead of up high,*
> *That's where you'll find me, that's where I'll be,*

Underneath the dirt in the hollow of a tree...

They turned around to see a small girl with bright red hair and a sun painted onto both cheeks. She was kneeling in the rain and singing to a dog that sat eagerly watching her, listening. Ruby looked to Harriett; her eyebrows raised.

'Because that's not creepy at all.'

'Come on,' Harriett said, grabbing her and Sarah's hands.

But Sarah did not seem keen to move. 'I don't know about this...this place gives me the shivers.'

The girl stopped singing abruptly when she spotted them, and her mouth broke open into a fervent smile. 'You're here!' She skipped toward them, the dog trotting closely by her side. 'We thought maybe you had gotten lost. Oh, she'll be so happy!'

With that she beckoned them forward with a tiny finger. Sarah's dark eyes narrowed.

'I don't like this,' she said. 'I don't like this at all.'

It didn't matter though, the four of them were already following her, how could they not? When Harriett's pale face was set with such determination—desperate to solve a mystery.

The girl led them to the smallest caravan of all—it was also, without a doubt, the oldest. It was painted a dark ebony green, but the paint was fading and peeling off. Purple drapes covered its door – but they were moth eaten and stained. The wood was chipped and decorated with yellow moons and stars and suns.

It was unusually beautiful. Old and broken, yet somehow perfect.

A woman stood out the front, her arms tattooed with illustrations of woods and wildflowers. Her skin was weathered and tanned from being outdoors so long. She held a jug full of water under her right arm. She also had red hair, and it occurred to Ruby that the singing girl was her daughter, she nodded approvingly when she saw them.

'Out fishing I see,' she said. Her voice was not cinnamon, it was deeper, smoother. It put Ruby in mind of dark, dark chocolate. The girl beamed and ran to her side, the dog—ever her companion—barked once and bounded up next to them.

'And what a good catch,' the lady said, eyeing the four of them up and down. 'She's inside. She's been expecting you,' she waved an arm graciously to the purple draped door and it was clear that they were meant to enter.

It was in that split second that Ruby thought she saw something strange about the mother and daughter pair. As though they were not two entities but one. A soul divided. Suddenly, she found herself agreeing with Sarah.

'Maybe we shouldn't—' she began, but Harriett stopped her.

'This is how we get answers,' Harriett said, and Ruby was surprised to see Emily nod forcefully in agreement.

'Can't you feel it?' Emily whispered. 'There's *truth* here.'

Ruby did feel something. Something pulling on the frayed and ragged edges of her being. Whatever it was, she didn't think it was truth.

She could see the curiosity in both Harriett and Emily's faces, the desperate *want* for answers. Ruby did not share Harriett's desire to make sense of the world, nor understand Emily's fascination with the campsite itself, but she couldn't deny the voice inside her that whispered; *Go. Go inside.*

Without another word Harriett and Emily climbed up the wooden steps and disappeared through the drapes, the god-awful cat still cocooned in Emily's arms. The ache in Ruby's stomach panged, but she ignored it. Together she and Sarah exchanged a dubious look, then trailed in after them, Harriett guiding the way as she always had.

Chapter Eighteen

FRUITCAKE WITH
A SIDE OF EXORCISM

It was deceptively bigger on the inside than it had looked outwardly. Wooden wagon wheels were mounted on the walls, while sage and rosemary herbs draped from the ceiling. Several candles burned on a table at the back of the room, on which there also stood an assortment of trinkets and pots filled with incense.

Thin smoky tendrils coiled through the air, carrying with it a lavender musk, a smell that was soothing to the point of sleep-inducing. A deep purple carpet lay across the floor, atop of which there lay scattered crystals and an odd-looking deck of cards. Huddled in the corner of the room there was a heaped pile of dirty rags.

The four girls simply stood there for a moment, clustered in the dark. The only sound was the sound of water dripping from their clothes and onto the wooden floor.

'I expected someone to be here...' Harriett murmured.

'But there's not, so can we go now?' Sarah said.

The bundle of rags began to move, and Sarah gave out a little shriek. In an instant, Ruby somehow found herself standing protectively in front of her friends. Her body prepared to shield them.

She almost laughed at herself, as if *she* could protect anyone.

The rags weren't rags at all, just some of the mustiest clothes to have ever existed. Slowly, an old woman pulled back the head scarf to reveal a thick head of the whitest, most brittle hair that Ruby had ever seen. Ruby instantly knew her to be the woman from the teashop, and yet she looked so much *older* here. A collection of bones held together by stretched out skin.

If Ruby had to guess right then, she would have said that the woman was in her hundreds—and she wore the line of every year upon her ancient face. Gradually the woman leaned forward over the carpet, craning over the deck of cards and crystals, her beady eyes glistening in the dark. She put Ruby in mind of a magpie, lording over her trinkets and jewellery.

'Madam Crone,' Harriett said, greeting the woman as though they had met countless times before.

The old woman smiled. 'Funny thing about magpies is that they're very smart. They're one of the only non-mammal species to recognise itself in a mirror. Did you know that?'

Ruby froze.

'Sit,' her voice was somehow sharp, rasping and clear all at once. Harriett and Emily immediately sat; Sarah followed suit after a second's hesitation, until only Ruby remained standing. There was silence and Ruby became suddenly very aware of her own heart slamming against her ribcage. Emily had said that there was truth here but looking into the old woman's eyes Ruby thought there might be something else as well.

'This was a mistake. We should go,' Ruby said.

Harriett's head spun around. 'Ruby!'

The old crone tilted her head back, pearl earrings hung from each ear, in the darkness of the wagon they seemed to gleam like two pale creamy moons. Again, Ruby was struck by just how white her hair was, though she had a sneaking suspicion that, once upon a time, it had been the same shade of red as the mother and daughter waiting outside.

'You poor, starving creature,' Madam Crone croaked. 'Must you run away from every problem that you cannot fight?'

The hairs on the back of Ruby's neck stood upright, and Madam Crone's smile widened revealing gaps of missing teeth. Cautiously, she sat herself on the musty purple rug next to Emily.

'Who are you?' Harriett asked, as soon as Ruby was sitting still. The old woman stretched out her fingers and picked up the deck of cards, she began to shuffle them leisurely with her long spindly fingers.

'I was a girl once, then I was a woman. Now I am a crone. It is the *proper* way of doing things. Don't you think?'

The four girls nodded, unsure of exactly what they were agreeing to. Ruby was fairly certain it was the *only* way of doing things.

'Now, who are you? That is the far more interesting question,' she gazed at each one of them in turn, but it didn't feel as though she was looking at them so much as *through* them. 'I look at you and I see old rivers and withered trees...' Madam Crone whispered.

Her eyes fixed on Harriett, and then she leaned forward quickly—too quickly for someone with such old bones—and licked Harriett's cheek.

Each of the girls began to shout but were cut off when the old woman sat back and held up a gnarled hand.

'Coffee and chocolate. Magic, grave-dirt and blood,' the Crone's eyes widened. 'What *are* you?'

There was such an intensity to her words, every syllable sounded heavy and coated with a deeper meaning. Then Madam's eyes landed on Sarah.

Sarah gawked at her, 'Erm... Well, my name's Sarah.'

'*Tsssk*. Name's mean nothing, and they mean less to you than most.'

It was then that Harriett leaned forward.

'Why did you want to see us? How did you even know we were here?'

'I was sitting outside this very wagon, in the fresh, fresh mountain air. And then I felt the pull, the need to go south. My kind has always followed the trail... We follow the stench of magic. And it led me straight to you.'

Harriett shook her head, disbelieving. 'Magic doesn't exist.'

The old Crone shrugged. 'Magic and miracles, enchantments, and curses. Different cultures and different religions have different names for it—but it all smells the same.' She turned to look at Emily. 'Wouldn't you agree?'

Ruby watched as Emily's eyes widened in confusion. 'I don't... I don't know what you mean.'

Madam Crone placed the deck of cards gently on the floor, she regarded Emily carefully and then she stood up. Or rather, she *unfurled,* like a baby deer learning how to stand. She seemed so fragile, as though a small gust of wind could topple her over.

The Crone wobbled about, her rags hanging off her as she meandered toward Emily. 'When we arrived here, I was almost certain we had the right place. Power lives here. It can feel it when the sea brushes against the shores, but mostly it lives in *your* skin.' The woman grinned at them, and then she scooped up the cat from Emily's arms. 'And this right here, proves to me that I am right.'

'Not that bloody cat again!' Ruby hissed.

Madam Crone knelt back to the floor holding the cat close to her, like a secret. 'Oh children, this is no cat,' she said, as though it were obvious.

'It looks like a cat,' Sarah said bluntly.

'If it's not a cat then what is it?' Harriett asked.

The woman held the creature so that her cheek was grazing its nose. 'I have no idea. But it's something *else*. Whatever it is though, it is old. Older than me I think, but not older than you.' She placed the creature on the floor beside her and it immediately sprinted back into Emily's lap, who ran a hand through its thick fur and narrowed her eyes at the Crone.

'That doesn't make any sense.'

Outside the rain continued to hammer on the wooden ceiling and a gust of wind blew the purple drapes open.

'I suppose it doesn't,' Madam Crone said, then she withdrew a plate of something clearly inedible from beneath the table. 'Would any of you girls care for some fruitcake?'

The four girls looked at one another and, in unison, replied, 'No.'

'Suit yourself.'

A minute or so passed and the four girls watched in silence as the old lady nibbled on a slice of fruitcake, crumbs and raisins spilled down her grubby cloak. All of them wanted to leave and yet none of them felt as though they could.

When she had finished, she dusted herself off and grimaced. 'You were wise not to eat that.'

'I'm sorry, but why are we here?' Sarah demanded, her voice reaching a higher pitch than usual, the tone she usually reserved for shop managers. 'Do you actually have anything useful for us? Or do you just enjoy wasting people's time?'

Madam Crone pursed her lips, she pursed them so tightly that they practically disappeared into the wrinkles on her face. 'My kind follows the trail of magic and when we find it, we endeavour to either protect it or destroy it, though in this case I fear we must leave it be. It is too tangled up in your lives and I find I cannot separate the living from the dead.'

'What does that mean?' Harriett whispered. 'Can you see the dead? Can you see my sister?'

Madam Crone went on, ignoring Harriett's question. 'Magic is unpredictable at best, dangerous at worst. And the four of you are positively drowning in it,' she sniffed. 'I have only two pieces of advice for you. Beware of the water and beware of your dreams. For that is where spirits and ghosts can breathe once more, that is where the barriers between the worlds are weakest.'

Ruby could feel the pain in her stomach rise, but worse was the feeling of dread that suddenly washed over her; 'What do you mean, "barriers between the worlds"?' she whispered.

Madam Crone fixed her beady eyes on Ruby and blinked. 'There are many, many worlds, girl. Separated by doors that have long since been locked. But in water and in our dreams those doors can be opened, if only briefly, by those determined enough to find a key.'

Ruby thought of her dream from a few nights before. She thought of the Faceless Man, and of the Shadow that had flown into her mouth. 'I saw my sister in a dream,' Harriett said, her voice clear. 'And now I see her when I'm awake. In mirrors and… and standing behind you right now.'

Ruby, Sarah, and Emily turned to face Harriett, stunned.

'She's here? Right now?' Sarah breathed, and they each stared at the spot behind Madam Crone's head which was hauntingly empty.

Madam Crone, on the other hand, did not seem particularly perturbed by this revelation. On the contrary, Ruby swore she could see her black eyes sparkle a little brighter and a smile play on the corners of her lips.

'What is she saying to you?' Madam Crone asked, her voice didn't seem quite as rasping now. Ruby thought she even looked a little younger.

Harriett looked nervously to Ruby, and somehow Ruby knew what was going to happen next. She was overcome with the sudden urge to run, to flee into the rain and fling herself into the sea.

'She isn't,' Harriett said. 'She's just pointing at Ruby.'

That was when Ruby felt it.

She could feel the Shadow's presence, hiding in her skin, buried in her veins. The pain in her belly bubbled; frothing and spitting. It had been there for almost two whole days. Living within her, watching the world through her eyes.... and she hadn't even noticed.

Now that she knew, the Shadow writhed inside her and screamed for control.

Madam Crone's bony hands grabbed at Ruby's wrists.

Harriett, Sarah and Emily all jumped up. Ruby wanted to jump with them, but she couldn't. She wanted to shout at them to *do something*, but her mouth wouldn't open, the words wouldn't come. Her lips were stitched together.

There was shouting. Harriett and Emily desperately tried to pull the Crone away from Ruby but their efforts were futile. The old woman's grip only tightened, the cat scarpered under the table to where the fruitcake had been, screeching and hissing in Ruby's direction.

'I see you spirit,' the old witch rasped, and she took the candle from the table. 'This may hurt a little.'

For a terrifying moment Ruby thought she was going to make her swallow the fire, what happened instead was only marginally less horrifying. Instead she rammed Ruby's open palm into the flame. Ruby screamed—and the scream echoed. The light of the candle seared through her, setting her entire body ablaze so that the Shadow had nowhere to hide.

The Crone was burning him out. She closed her eyes and smiled, 'Gotcha.'

Madam Crone pulled the Shadow from Ruby's being, the

way a fishing line pulls a fish from the stream. First, there was a tugging in the pit of her stomach, as though a hook had been lodged there and was being shook loose. And then, it sprung free.

The Shadow leapt from Ruby's mouth—the flickering orange light of the candles could no longer be seen; the room was covered in darkness.

Coldness swept over them.

There was only blackness. There was only the sound of their breathing. The Shadow slithered out of the caravan and light returned, the candles were bright once again.

Ruby keeled onto the floor.

Harriett bent down to see if she was alright, as Emily and Sarah gaped at the old Crone in shock.

Ruby couldn't take it all in. All she could focus on was the cold that seeped farther into the room and the sudden urge to be sick. She forced herself to focus on one of the incense sticks as it dwindled down to the nub.

Not here. Not now.

Madam Crone sat back down. Emily and Sarah glanced at one another and then all of them were sitting on the floor once more. Ruby swayed slightly. Trying to distract herself from the pain and nausea.

'The cat is old and yet it knows you. The Shadow is old and yet it knows you. It stands to reason that you are all connected. That you are also old,' the Crone said this all so nonchalantly. Then she picked up the deck of cards and shuffled them.

'We're not old!' Sarah insisted. 'Harriett, Ruby and I haven't even turned sixteen yet!'

The Crone smiled. 'Just because one thing is true does not make the other false.' She fanned the cards out across the floor in front of them. 'Pick one,' she demanded.

Harriett went first, she went for the card in the middle.

The one that found itself poking out a little farther than the rest. She held it up and Ruby could just see the image of a woman sitting on a throne, overlooking the sea. Underneath it read *Queen of Cups.*

The Crone smiled serenely. 'You will lead them,' she said.

Then she motioned to Sarah to do the same, hesitantly Sarah picked the card closest to her. A portrait of two naked figures—*Lovers.*

'You will betray them.'

Emily chose the third card without being prompted, she plucked one from the very end, tucked away and almost completely hidden. It also showed a woman, but with a crescent moon by her feet and a black and white pillar standing on either side of her—*High Priestess.*

Madam Crone nodded as though she had expected this all along. 'You will tell them all you know.'

Finally, she turned her bird-like face to Ruby. Ruby looked at the apprehensive faces of her friends and then back at Madam Crone. A part of her, the part that laughed at the sight of blood and burned for the thrill of a fight, wanted to tell her to shove the card where cards should never be shoved. She wanted to put her middle finger up at the room and leave.

Instead, she placed a hand around her own throat and thought of the way the old woman had reached into her being and pulled out a demon from inside. She knew it wasn't madness. She knew it was *magic.*

A prediction.

A promise.

Clutching her stomach with one hand she leaned forward and snatched up a card with the other. It was only after she held the card between her two fingers that she realised she'd chosen the spot next to where Harriett had picked hers. She turned it over in her hand.

It showed a knight astride a horse, sword raised against a

backdrop of stormy grey clouds. Unlike the others' cards, hers was facing upside down.

Knight of Swords.

She let out a sharp, short laugh and laid it so that the others could see. The Crone raised what was left of her eyebrows.

'And you will let them go,' she finished.

Ruby balled her hands into fists and felt the tarot card crumple against her skin.

'What does that mean?' Harriett asked.

But Ruby couldn't listen to the answer. She could feel the bile rising up, up, up in her throat and she could no longer push it down. In that moment it was all she could do to stand up and stagger her way out of the caravan and into the rain. She stumbled over the stones and as far away from the caravans as she could, until finally she collapsed onto the stony beach and stopped fighting.

In the distance she could once again hear the cinnamon-sweet voice of the singing girl.

When the moon swims down to the bottom of the deep,
When old ships soar in the white cloudy sea,
That's where you'll find me, that's where I'll be,
Singing with the birds, body-less and free.

Chapter Nineteen

AN ABSENCE OF MIRACLES

When they found her, she was sitting shaking next to a puddle of her own sick. She couldn't stand yet and she had made no effort to try.

'Did you bring my bag?' she asked sullenly.

The stones were wet and clammy, and the wind whipped at her face. Her head hadn't yet stopped spinning. Harriett passed the rucksack to Ruby in silence.

At least it had stopped raining.

Ruby rooted through the bag for one of her shakes and her bottle of water, all the while her friends watched her in silence.

And you will let them go...

'She was talking absolute crap.' Ruby held the bottle of water to her lips and rinsed it in her mouth before spitting it onto the stones. A futile attempt at washing away the aftertaste of vomit.

'Ruby, what's going on?' Harriett asked quietly.

'Isn't it obvious? She's ill!' Sarah exclaimed, then she turned to Ruby, clearly exasperated. 'You know, you could've just told us. We don't care if you take a few days off Ruby, you can just come back to school when you're better. It's no big deal.'

Ruby looked up at the sky, right then it was a swirling grey and white, an empty canvas ready to be painted black. How long had they been with the Crone? An hour maybe? It felt like so much longer. She could feel the prickle of tears in the corners of her eyes and blinked it away.

She would not cry.

She composed herself and looked back at her friends. Each of them was soaked, but there they were, still standing in the cold, salty air, waiting for her. The Cornerhouse behind them, tall and proud in the distance.

Ruby met Harriett's thoughtful gaze, Suddenly, Harriett's brows furrowed, then her eyes widened, her mouth falling open.

'You were missing all over summer,' Harriett whispered.

Ruby stayed silent.

'And… and I haven't seen you eat in weeks.'

Ruby stayed silent.

'And the school hasn't suspended you for truanting because… because you haven't been truanting, have you? You've been—'

'Sick,' Ruby finished for her.

There was no other explanation left to give, no excuses left to make. Ruby wasn't a liar by nature, she was merely a secretive thing. She would always rather help Harriett with a problem of hers, than admit to having problems of her own. But now she wanted it done. She took a deep breath.

'Last year, I started having some problems. We thought maybe I'd caught a stomach bug but then… then it didn't go away. I was diagnosed with Crohn's disease and… and I've been on meds for it ever since. Over the summer Mum took me to a hospital up in London for some more tests. They said there aren't any more drugs for me to try. It's shit, and it's incurable but that's life.'

'Croonies Disease? What is that?' Sarah asked, looking nervously to Harriett.

Ruby snorted. '*Crohn's.* It's an autoimmune disease. Basically, my body is rejecting food and kind of rotting on the inside. It's really painful and really fucking gross and I don't want to talk about it.'

And there it was.

Ruby Coleville, who prided herself on being a fighter and who had deliberately shaped herself into a demon of a girl, was sick. She had spent so much of her young life openly declaring war against the world, it seemed almost too deliciously ironic now that her body was waging a war against itself.

'Oh Ruby, I'm so sorry—' Harriett began.

'*Don't,*' said Ruby shortly. 'I'm tired of people being sorry. I'm tired of…' She paused. 'I'm just tired.'

'Why didn't you tell us?' Harriett asked. But Ruby knew what she really meant was, *"why didn't you tell me?"*

Ruby ran a hand through her hair and let out a slow, rattling breath. There were so many answers to that question and all of them at least partly true; she didn't want them to pity her, she didn't want to take away from Hayley's death, she didn't want to trouble Harriett, she didn't want to add to their ever-growing list of increasingly freaky troubles.

But it was more than that.

Ruby's friends were her world. Without them she was just another troubled girl with a mother who worked too much and a father that she'd never met. The three of them were the pillars of her childhood; all her happiest memories began and ended with them. Sleepovers at Emily's and tea-parties at Sarah's.

Midnight conversations with Harriett Sinclair.

She liked the way her friends thought of her. She liked the way they rolled their eyes at her, how they laughed at her jokes and how they never ever hesitated to call her on her crap. She didn't want them to tiptoe around her the way her mother did, to treat her as though she were so fragile that she might break.

So, she had clung to an idea the way a child might cling to their mother's skirt, the ludicrous idea that all monsters could be defeated. She had hoped and hoped that one day she would wake up and the hurt would be gone. She hoped that tomorrow would be different, or the tomorrow after that. Because it had to be, because she *needed* it to be. Yet every morning she would wake and be faced by the absence of miracles. For the hope to be swallowed up by the truth.

Because, if she was somehow magically cured then maybe—just maybe—her friends would never have to know, and it would be as though it had never happened at all.

But this is it. This is my life now.

'Because... because if you all knew then it would be real,' Ruby said finally. 'Because I didn't want you to have to deal my shit on top of everything else.'

Harriett knelt to Ruby's level, the stones clacking underneath her feet as she did, 'Ruby, we're your people, we *want* to go through the real stuff with you.'

'You should have said something,' Sarah agreed. 'We would have helped.'

'You don't need to worry about it,' Ruby said. 'This is the hand that I've been dealt. I'll deal with it.'

And then, as one, all three of them rolled their eyes.

Harriett tutted. 'One of these days Ruby all of those emotions you bottle up are going to spill out.'

'Or explode, more like,' said Sarah.

'Like a volcano,' finished Emily.

Ruby opened her mouth to argue but stopped abruptly. They hadn't gone anywhere. They knew the truth and the ground had not vanished beneath her feet.

'In the future you tell me when something's wrong. Okay?'

Ruby nodded, but this wasn't good enough for Sinclair.

'*Promise* me,' Harriett said earnestly.

Ruby closed her eyes and listened to the sound of the sea behind them. Gentle and rippling, a murmur in her ear.

Sometimes, when Sinclair spoke to her, Ruby felt the air tighten. As though the world was holding its breath simply waiting for her to obey. It was impossible to ignore a direct request from her. As impossible as staring into the sun or plucking a star from the heavens. Ruby had tried before and she had never *ever* succeeded. She could never decide if Sinclair was aware of the strange power she possessed, but she supposed it didn't matter in the end. Ruby had long since given up attempting to say no to her.

'I promise,' she said, and she opened her eyes. Then she clasped Sinclair's hand and let her pull her up from the ground. Together the four of them walked up the pebbled beach and away from the sea until they stood on the empty pavement opposite the Cornerhouse.

The caravans, the dogs and the horses had vanished from sight.

'They've gone already?' Harriett exclaimed.

'How did we not hear them leave?' Sarah asked.

Emily said, 'Maybe they were never really here.'

The thought was unsettling but short-lived. From the corner of her eye Ruby spotted something glinting on the pavement, it was the jug that the red-haired woman had been holding, only now it was empty of water.

She held it up for the rest to see. 'Oh, they were here alright.'

Harriett eyed it suspiciously. 'What do we think of it all? The connections between us, the cat and the Shadow?'

Ruby sure as hell didn't know. She was too tired, and the events of the afternoon were weighing on top of her.

'To be honest, I feel as though we'd already made that connection ourselves,' Harriett continued. 'I was hoping that she'd tell us exactly *what* that connection is.'

Emily frowned and scooped up the cat from the ground. 'She said that we were old. I thought that was the connection.'

Sarah let out a huff. 'I. Am. *Not*. Old.'

'Hmmm,' Harriett said, unconvinced. 'And what was all that stuff about water? *Where the spirits and ghosts can breathe once more.* That doesn't sound good.'

Ruby let out a cold laugh. 'Yeah. Especially when we're surrounded by the bloody stuff.'

They each turned around to face the ocean, in all its glorious vastness. Silence ebbed between them.

Finally, Ruby said what they were all thinking. 'If that's where the ghosts are coming from then we're all fucked.'

THE JOURNEY HOME was slow, and Ruby's breathing was still heavy and thin. She and Emily walked together, as they often did. Unlike Harriett and Sarah, they lived in the poorer side of Wooly's—the East Side. Where every other house seemed to have an old woman smoking a cigarette on a front porch, shouting obscenities at passing children.

'Put that thing on a leash!' screeched one such woman.

'It's not a dog Ms Pelkins,' Emily replied calmly.

The two continued walking, the cat trotting closely by Emily's side.

'Doesn't mean it shouldn't be on a leash,' Ruby grumbled. Her distrust of the creature had only increased since their visit to Madam Crone.

They reached the top of Ruby's road. Emily met her gaze. 'Do you need me to walk you to your door?'

Ruby raised an eyebrow. 'Why? Are you gonna try and kiss me goodnight?'

'*No,*' Emily said, blushing furiously. 'I just wondered if you needed help getting home.'

'Don't do that,' Ruby said. 'Don't treat me differently. I don't want no violins playing and I don't want no extra help. Not from anyone. Especially not you guys.'

Emily thought for a moment, then said, 'Being vulnerable isn't the same as being weak, Ruby. And being loved isn't giving power away.'

Ruby baulked, so surprised by the sudden earnestness of Emily's words that she couldn't think how to respond.

'I'll see you at school,' Emily said, smiling softly. 'If you turn up that is.'

Ruby grinned. 'Ouch! *Burn!*' Then she made a sizzling sound, just for good measure.

The two girls parted ways and Ruby slowly made her way down the street. She reached the end of the road and froze, scratched her head, and then turned around and made her way up the road again.

And then back again.

And then up again.

And then the impossible, ugly realisation hit her.

She couldn't remember which house was hers.

She knew she should be panicking, that this latest development should send her reeling. But she was just frustrated and angry and— more than anything—exhausted.

She leaned against the nearest lamppost and swore. Staring down the road, she silently prayed that it would all come back to her, and she would know which house was the one she grew up in. But they all looked alike, each as identical and unfamiliar as the next.

With every passing day Ruby's life was feeling more and more like some tripped out dream sequence where up was down, down was sideways and sideways was even more sideways. It was as though she no longer knew how to navigate her own life, her own *world.*

Swearing some more she retrieved her phone from her pocket and dialled.

'Mum? I'm gonna need you to come get me.'

Chapter Twenty

GWENDOLENS AND GRUDGES

Ruby awoke the next morning to the sound of her alarm blaring. She sat up, aching and bruised, to find her room in a state of chaotic disarray. She blinked, confused, then spotted the tarot card lying face up on the nightstand by her bed, and it all came flooding back.

Madam Crone. The Shadow in her mouth. The tarot reading. Her secret being exposed.

Forgetting what her damn house looked like.

Her mother had collected her from the end of the street, shaking with worry and fury. She mistakenly believed that Ruby had let herself get so ill to the point that she couldn't manage the final steps to the house. Ruby, unable to offer up any other explanation, was both infuriated by her mother's reaction and incensed that she had forgotten where she lived to begin with.

This had, naturally, culminated in a blazing row, after which Ruby had been ordered to bed.

In her anger and eagerness to prove to her mother that she was *not sleeping*, Ruby had blasted the music from her CD player as loud as she could and then proceeded to trash her room with the little energy she had left. Posters had been yanked from the walls, books had been thrown across the room and clothes had been strewn across the floor.

Somewhere along the line she had exhausted herself and fallen asleep. Though she could not remember when.

Her reality was such a strange place to live now.

She thought back to a time where it had just been her, her mum and her friends. She had been content then, and angry of course, but in a habitual, harmless kind of way.

The anger she breathed now was different. It scorched even her.

She missed being able to run. She missed being able to go to Charles Park and start a game of netball, football, *anything*, with the local kids there. She missed burning out her rage into the pavement when she ran. She missed feeling the sweet relief that came with releasing all her anger into sweat.

Now, she had all this restless energy cooped up inside her head and no place for her body to take it.

She could not help but repeating Madam Crone's words over and over in her mind: *You will lead them; You will betray them; You will tell them all you know; You will let them go.*

It was impossible. There were very few people that Ruby loved, but she loved Harriett, Sarah and Emily. They were sisters in everything but blood. Sisters in every way that mattered or was worth a damn. They sometimes squabbled and scrapped but they always, *always* had each other's backs.

As quietly as she could, she dressed herself for school and tiptoed down the stairs. She swiped a few shakes from the fridge and made a beeline for the front door, slamming it violently shut as she left.

RUBY WAS SITTING on top of a table, legs crossed and sipping one of her shakes. Sarah watched her intently, an earphone dangling from one ear, the sound of tinny music just about audible to the others.

'So, is that like, your *food* now?' she asked.

Ruby nodded. 'Yup.'

'Shhh!' Harriett hissed.

Ruby glanced around the library. Aside from the librarian, they were the only ones there, because no other self-respecting student would willingly sacrifice their lunch for more studying.

Of course, it wasn't exactly homework they were doing.

Harriett sighed and took a sip of her coffee. Technically they weren't allowed food or drink in the library, but the librarian didn't seem too keen to reprimand the school's golden girl.

'It's no use,' Harriett said, poring over her notes. 'I've searched, and searched, and I still can't find a Gwendolen that matches what we're looking for.'

Sarah continued to scroll through the music on her phone, without looking up she said; 'And what exactly are we looking for?'

Harriett frowned. 'Madam Crone said that we're connected to something old. So, I've been looking for historic Gwendolen's. But the most historic Gwendolen I've found is Gwendolen Fitzalan-Howard, a Duchess of Norfolk born in the late 19th century... And I don't know, it just doesn't feel right, plus it doesn't seem *old* enough.'

Emily, who had been doodling in the back of one of her sketchbooks, put her drawing to the side and picked up Harriett's list.

'Queen Gwendolen of the Britons. That sounds promising.'

Harriett shook her head so viscously that some of the hair from her plait fell loose. 'That's what I thought. But apparently, she never existed! She was made up by some British cleric in the early 11th century.'

Ruby took the list from Emily, Harriett's neat, wavy writing filled the page with names and dates and question marks, all written in orderly columns. She scanned the page and let out a loud laugh.

'Merlin's wife Gwendolen? Really?'

Harriett threw up her hands in anguish. 'I was getting desperate! Everywhere I look I meet more dead ends. I even tried searching for Madam Crone and do you know what I found on her?'

None of them answered, they all knew what it was she must have found.

'Nothing,' Harriett said bitterly. 'Absolutely nothing.'

The three of them glanced at each other, it was unlike Harriett to be so defeated. She believed in answers, she believed in finding answers or *making* them when no clear solution was possible.

Emily picked up one of the many books that stood piled up on the table, the books that Harriett had so meticulously chosen to help with their search. 'Then we keep looking.'

Ruby's gaze met Sarah's, whose expression perfectly echoed Ruby's own sentiments.

Neither one of them wanted to read those damn books.

Yet they both would. For Harriett.

Ruby glanced furtively at all the titles, which contained such gems as; *'Life After Life,' 'Religion and the Decline of Magic,' 'Life on Replay, Have You Been Here Before?'* and the infinitely more boring, *'Timeline of British History and its Peoples.'*

She downed the rest of her shake, picked up *'Life On Replay'* and in silence the four of them began to read.

For twenty solid minutes Ruby read. She read about precognition, the impossible foreknowledge of an event, and of retrocognition, the impossible knowledge of a past event. She read about the importance of dreams and the belief that birthmarks were relics from a former life. She read and read, and while most of it seemed like nonsense hooey, there was a part of her that tingled uncomfortably at the notion that maybe... just maybe... there was a kernel of truth hidden amongst it all. That somehow, they had all been here before.

The cat is old and yet it knows you, the Crone had said. *The Shadow is old and yet it knows you.*

Ruby slammed the book shut. 'I've gotta get some air.'

She stalked out of the library and into the corridor. She couldn't stand the stuffiness of the library and she wasn't one for sitting slouched over books for ages on end. Mostly she just needed to stretch her legs and splash some water on her face.

She wandered down the flight of stairs, her head still reeling, then made her way into the second-floor bathroom. Like all the bathrooms in St Catherine's it was a horrible shade of beige, complete with six stalls (only two of which were likely to have working locks) and a dirt-spattered mirror covering one wall.

Ruby examined her face in the mirror. She looked tired. No, she looked gaunt. And the roots of her dirty-blonde hair were beginning to poke through all the black.

She sighed and turned on the tap, closed her eyes and splashed the water onto her face. It trickled down her neck and into her shirt.

The door to the toilets swung open.

'I thought I saw you creep in here,' a voice drawled.

Ruby didn't need to see who it was to know who the voice belonged to. Sighing, she turned around and opened her eyes.

In front of her stood Sophie Grimely, Lacey Greenfield and some other lackey that Ruby didn't know the name of.

'Nice of you to come and say hello,' Ruby said calmly.

Sophie sniggered. 'Oh, I've been trying to see you for a while now, but you keep disappearing on *us*.'

Ruby took note of the deliberate emphasis on the word *us*. And she took notice of the violence plastered onto Sophie's face, and saw a hatred there that she recognised. It was the kind of violence that comes from not understanding why you're angry. The kind of hate that comes from pain.

This wasn't going to be a fight. This was going to be a beating.

She should have known Sophie would want to get back at her after their last fight. She should have known that wasn't the end of it.

When Ruby looked at Sophie, she saw a cartoon version of herself, a mirror highlighting all her worst attributes. And she had the sneaking suspicion that Sophie saw the same thing when she looked back at her.

They were the fatherless girls, the hungry ones, the girls who never knew better.

And they both hated it.

'Come for another thumping?' Ruby asked, knowing full well that the only way she'd win this fight was if she miraculously grew two more pairs of arms and legs.

Sophie grinned. *'Get her.'*

Then they did.

Chapter Twenty-One

SHARP KNIVES, SHARPER WORDS

She didn't even manage to get one punch in. The three of them lunged at her and soon she was curled up on the ground, feeling every kick vibrate though her. She could feel warm blood spurt out her nose; she could see it spray across the floor.

And then there was the nausea, the bile rising in her throat threatening to release. She could not let them see her weakness. They could never know. In the back of her brain she remembered something her mother had said to her years ago;

'Honey, there are some arseholes in this world, some'll hurt you, some'll break your heart. The trick is to never give them the satisfaction of seeing you bleed.'

Of all the things she had endured—of all the things she was still enduring. This would not be the thing to break her. She would not cry out; she would not whimper or beg for them to stop.

She would not be broken.

She was a warrior.

A goddamn warrior.

Sophie let out a cold, high-pitched laugh as she landed another swift kick to her abdomen. Ruby curled her hands into fists, she curled them up so hard she could feel her fingernails pierce the skin.

She was getting dizzy; her head was pounding, and darkness was threatening to envelop her. It was just as she stood at the edge of consciousness that an image gripped hold of her.

It was the image of herself, battle clad and withdrawing a blade from its sheath. She pictured her own hand reaching down and taking hold of the hilt, ornate and cold and deadly.

She did not move, her hands remained balled into fists, yet something heavy appeared there.

Without looking she knew instinctively what it was. She placed her hands carefully behind her back.

The pain evaporated. The knife was all that mattered, the knife was all that was real.

She rolled onto her back and flipped upwards onto her feet so quickly that the three girls staggered backwards in surprise. She held the dagger outward, it glinted dangerously under the fluorescent lights of the bathroom stalls.

'Shit,' whispered Lacey. 'Shit, shit, shit!'

She wanted to say something bold. Something terrifying that would make them all scarper. For as comfortable as the knife felt in her grip, she did not want to use it.

But she would, if she had to.

Sophie regarded her carefully, a dangerous gleam in her eye. 'You wouldn't dare, Coleville. You're too fucking soft.'

'What are you doing?' Lacey hissed. 'She's got a *knife*.'

It was so much more than just a knife. It was the power to take life or give it.

'She won't use it!' Sophie snorted. 'She don't want to disappoint *Saint* Sinclair, do you Rubes?'

There was something in the way Sophie said the words, the lingering way she dragged out the word *Saint*.

Ruby knew what people thought of her—smart kid, rough around the edges. But Ruby had long ago given up thinking she could ever be smooth.

Sinclair was different. Sinclair was kind and smart in ways that Ruby couldn't even fathom. She'd always known that she could never be like her, she could never achieve what Sinclair would doubtlessly achieve, and that was okay. Ruby didn't need to be like Harriett Sinclair, not when she could be dangerous instead.

'Take another step closer and I'll guess we'll find out,' she spat.

Sophie moved forwards and on instinct Ruby moved back. Sophie laughed again; Lacey laughed a little too—her confidence returning.

The third girl, the girl that Ruby didn't know, had clearly had enough. She raised her hands up in the air.

'You said nothin' about knives Soph!' and she sprinted from the room.

'Where'd you get that thing anyway?' Sophie asked, her brows creasing, then she shrugged. 'No matter, it'll be mine in a minute.'

She lunged forward.

Only this time Ruby was expecting it, a voice from deep within her screamed in rage and something inside her *shattered*. She lunged forward pressing Sophie against the wall. Vaguely she could hear Lacey scream, but the blood was rushing to her ears now. Sophie tried to push free but as she did Ruby lifted the dagger, flipping it over in her hand in an elaborate gesture, before throwing it into the air.

Sophie stopped breathing. Lacey stopped breathing.

The dagger fell, and Ruby caught it by its handle so that she was holding it a mere inch from Sophie's face.

She could feel words in her mouth, and she growled them out vehemently: *This blade begs for blood and I would gladly give it yours.*

Except they were not the words she spoke. Sophie's eyes widened in confusion and fear, for she had said something else, in a strange language that sounded guttural and rough.

'Sê blæd nîede heolfor yfel wordlung tôgife gieldan sê êower.'

She released Sophie from her grip, her heart was thumping loudly in her chest, and her mind was racing with words; ancient words, *forgotten* words.

The two girls sped away, the door swinging shut behind them, but Ruby did not notice.

She was too busy staring at herself in the mirror, at the horrific sight she made. A gaunt girl with jet black hair and blood smeared across her nose, mouth and chin. A girl with flecks of red decorating her collar and a purple bruise swelling up on her cheek. A girl clutching an ornate dagger fiercely in her hand.

She cleaned her face the best she could and rubbed a gentle finger over her nose. She thought it might be broken.

It didn't matter. Only one thing mattered now.

She stormed back up to the library and placed the blade on the table for them all to see. The girls each gasped in horror when they laid eyes on her.

'What happened to your face?'

'Are you okay?'

'Where did you get that?' Harriett breathed.

Ruby ignored all the questions; her mouth was burning. 'Aðollan êow oncunnan ma?'

Do you know me?

Harriett's eyes flashed and met hers, a fire burned there too. 'Efenwel swilce yfel oncunnan mîn selfe.'

As well as I know myself.

Sarah almost fell out of her chair and Emily closed her eyes. They had heard the words, and they understood what had been said.

Ruby collapsed into the chair nearest to her as all the aches and pains came crashing back.

Finally, finally, finally there was a sense of relief. A sense of relief that came with surrender.

They thought they knew themselves; they'd even thought they'd known each other but the truth was now impossibly, perfectly clear.

They didn't know anything.

Nothing at all.

Chapter Twenty-Two
A MORE DELICATE
TYPE OF STUPID

It came as a surprise to absolutely nobody when Ruby was pulled out of school. She was getting thinner by the day and bruises adorned her face and most of her body. Thankfully her nose wasn't broken, but they weren't the only injuries she had sustained.

'Have you burnt your hand?' her mother had exclaimed.

Ruby had almost forgotten about the moment Madam Crone had shoved her palm directly into scorching hot flame. Fortunately, she had the pinched and puckered red scar to forever remember it by.

So, she'd been confined to her room; her mother even took a few days off work to ensure she stayed there. The days that followed were a dreamy haze of pain medication and fitful bursts of sleep, hot water bottles and sweat.

Harriett visited her every day after school. She would bring school notes to her room and would try in vain to help her catch up with schoolwork. Sometimes Emily and Sarah were with her, sometimes they weren't.

A week into her inclusion and her mother was forced to go back to work.

It was a dull Tuesday morning and the rain pattered on the glass outside the widow. Her mum had propped up an old television on a chair in Ruby's room, an old DVD player sat underneath it and a pile of black and white movies sat on top of that.

'Right so I will be back at six o'clock,' her mother said.

'I know.'

'You have all the shakes you need downstairs.'

'I know.'

'Don't forget to take your tablets around midday.'

'Yes Mum.'

'And what are you categorically not allowed to do?'

Ruby buried herself further underneath the covers of her bed, pressing the side of her face fiercely into her pillow.

'Leave the house,' she grumbled.

Her mum kissed her lightly on the forehead, a waft of perfume and smoke drifting past her as she did. 'Good girl.'

Ruby waited until she heard the downstairs front door close before she swivelled herself out of bed, crouched onto her hands and knees and withdrew the blade from underneath her mattress. She had hidden it there at the first opportunity and had not had a chance to admire it since.

She hopped back onto the bed and held the blade flat in her palms. It had a gold handle wrought with green and red jewels, it twisted elaborately at the base of the hilt before tapering down into steel so clear and bright that it appeared almost like silver.

'Lufiendlic,' she whispered.

Beautiful.

The strangeness of the old language no longer bothered her. It tasted right on her tongue and the words fell out of her mouth as easily as any English words ever did.

Inside she felt a stirring, like the shaking of a baby bird's wings. During her fight with Sophie Grimely, a force inside her had awoken. A roaring that would not quieten.

She flipped the knife so that the blade balanced on the tip of her finger, before flicking her wrist into a quick, curled motion and catching the hilt of the dagger.

Ruby was having more and more moments like this. Moments where her body acted before her brain even registered what she was doing. It was unnerving. And exhilarating.

She sighed and held the dagger to her chest the way a child might cradle a favourite doll. She couldn't explain the reassurance that it gave her, the inexplicable rightness and comfort of it when she gripped it in her hand.

On her bedside table, her phone buzzed. Absent-mindedly she picked it up, expecting to see yet another message from her mother, or maybe Sinclair.

HEY RUBES, HOW ARE YOU? EXPERIENCED ANYTHING SUPERNATURAL LATELY? – AM

Ruby gaped at the message in shock. She glanced around her room, as though making sure nobody was there to see the moment she replied.

HEY WEIRDO, WHAT'S UP? – RC

She put the phone back on the table, eyeing it suspiciously until it vibrated again a few minutes later.

THE USUAL, JUST CONTEMPLATING THE INFINITE COMPLEXITIES OF THE UNIVERSE, WRAITHLIKE SHADOW MONSTERS INCLUDED.

– AM

She couldn't help it. She laughed; it was such an absurd message to send.

And it went on. For three days they messaged back and forth, until Friday lunchtime he'd rung her instead.

'Ruby?' he said. His voice soft, warm.

'That's me,' she whispered.

And then they were talking. Really talking.

He talked about his brother Max, and she told him about Harriett. She talked about all her favourite old movies and he told her that he collected maps. Maps of England, Scotland, and Europe. Maps so old that the names of cities and places had long since been changed.

'Why do you have so many?' she asked him, holding the phone closely to her bruised cheek.

'So that I can picture all the places I want to go,' he replied simply. 'I want to see *everything* once school is over. Don't you?'

In truth she had never really thought about what happened after she finished school. Sometimes she wondered *if* she ever would finish it.

Still, there were times when she pictured a river in her mind, wide and deep and still, surrounded by long green grass and tall spindly trees. She supposed it was a scene from a movie she had seen once, though she couldn't be entirely sure.

'My dad says if I pass my driver's test when I'm seventeen, he'll lend me his jeep so I can drive around Britain for a week. He doesn't think I can do it, but I'm going to be driving that car, just you wait.'

She believed him. 'Where would you go?' she asked him.

'Everywhere,' he breathed, and then he reeled off a list of all the things he wanted to do and see. He wanted to climb Ben Nevis, he wanted to explore the Lake District, he wanted to see Stonehenge and visit ruined old castles with histories too long and too grizzly to fathom.

'You could come with me,' he said.

It felt dangerous, the way he said that, like a promise he intended to keep. She wanted to let him believe it.

Because Ruby had told him everything—everything except that she would be having surgery soon and that she would be scarred and weak and recovering.

She didn't tell him because a tiny part of her suspected that he might *like* her.

And for reasons she didn't quite understand—she didn't want him to stop.

But in that moment, as she sat with her knees drawn up to her chest in the dim light of her small, dingy room, phone pressed to her ear as though it were a lifeline, she wanted to do something reckless.

Not her usual shout and spit-in-the-face-of-danger kind of reckless. What she craved was a softer, more delicate type of stupid.

'Do you want to meet me?' she asked abruptly.

She knew what his answer would be and yet she still felt a fluttering of nervousness in her chest.

'Yes.'

THE STREETLIGHTS SEEMED to wink at her as she made her way through the town. It was the beginning of November and the cold was biting. The sky was a brilliant white and the entire town appeared greyer than usual. Every few seconds clouds of breath would escape from her lips.

They met at the Neville.

The Neville was the derelict, out-of-use car park that local skater kids used to smoke and practice tricks. It was commonly thought of as an eye-sore by most of the town's inhabitants. Yet despite years of talk about tearing it down and replacing it with something useful, the Neville somehow remained.

Alex stood outside the side door entrance, posture perfect and clean-cut. He wore a long black coat over his uniform. His eyes lit up when he spotted her, then his brows knitted together as she drew closer.

'Oh my god. Are you alright?'

Ruby lifted a hand and rubbed her cheek, the bruise still panged at her touch, she shrugged.

'Oh this?' she asked, feigning surprise. 'This is nothing. You should see the other gal.'

'What happened?'

Ruby shrugged and moved past him, opening the door. 'Do you want to ask me questions or do you want to follow me into this crumbling, piss-filled building?'

Alex rubbed the back of his neck and regarded the door with open disdain. 'I don't get why you wanted to meet here.'

'If you stop gawking at my face for a second, maybe you'll find out.'

Cheeks reddening Alex followed Ruby into the stairwell. The smell of urine was overpowering, and the walls were almost black with grime. Alex coughed into his arm sleeve, the disdain on his face growing sharper by the second.

'This is disgusting.'

'C'mon!'

Together they made their way up the narrow staircase and up thirteen flights until they reached the very top and made their way onto the rooftop. The fresh air hit them with welcome relief, the faint scent of salt was carried on the back of the wind.

Ruby held out her arms wide and spun around slowly, enjoying the feel of the cold air between her fingers. Alex stood watching her curiously, as she then made her way to the rooftop's edge, where the wall came up to her waist.

'This is what I wanted to show you,' she said, beckoning him over.

From where they stood, they could see all of Woolington-on-Sea. The town stretched out beneath them, a landscape of rooftops and chimneys. They could see the tinted green domed roof of the Cornerhouse, they could see the fields that sat behind St Catherine's school and the field that belonged to St David's. They could even see the pier, which appeared more skeletal than usual, its iron legs half hidden by the white foam and mist of the sea.

'Pretty cool, huh?' Ruby said, and then she sat down and leant her back against the wall. Alex still stared out over the town.

'How come I didn't know about this?' he asked, leaning over the wall slightly. 'I can even see my house from here.'

Ruby shrugged. 'Not many people know about it, only the skater kids really.'

Alex looked at her quizzically. 'And you?'

'I used to be a bit of a skater,' Ruby smirked. 'But when my last skateboard broke, I couldn't afford a new one.'

Alex grinned and sat down opposite her, he crossed his legs and placed his hands on his knees.

'It's even prettier at night,' Ruby said, shaking off her bag and pulling out two bottles of water and a shake. She handed one of the bottles to Alex and popped a straw into the shake. She sipped it quietly, aware of him watching her.

'You're still not allowed any food?'

She shook her head. 'How come you skived off school anyway? You don't seem the type.'

Alex pushed his glasses up his nose. 'I didn't skive! I have Friday afternoons for free study.'

'And this is studying?' Ruby snorted.

Alex's cheeks flushed pink again, then he pointed at her. 'What about you! Aren't you supposed to be at school? You're not even in uniform!'

Ruby ran a hand through her hair. 'Because I'm not going to school anymore.'

Alex's mouth dropped open.

'I'm taking time off...indefinitely. Everyone knows now. My friends, the teachers... the whole school. I'm officially the sick kid.'

She met his gaze ferociously, daring him to pity her—hoping that he wouldn't.

'How did your friends take it?' he asked.

She let out a breath. 'I think Sinclair had suspected something for a while... Sarah was the most surprised.'

'How did you all meet?'

She frowned. 'I can't quite remember.'

She scrolled through the memories in her head. Did she know them before or after Sophie Grimely? She thought perhaps after. And yet it felt as though they'd always been there. Her earliest memories were of them sitting on the playground in first school, sharing lunch and practising hand clapping games.

'I think it must have been at first school. I've known them forever.'

'You always tell me about your friends but never your family. Why is that?'

Ruby shrugged. 'Cos there's not much to tell. I live with my Mum and we get by.'

When she had finished speaking Ruby reached into her bag and pulled out two little boxes, she could feel Alex's gaze as she opened her bottle of water and lined up the tablets in the palm of her hand. With one smooth motion she popped the pills into her mouth and then pressed the bottle to her lips. Alex tilted his head to the side.

'What's she like? Your mum, I mean.'

Ruby grinned her most dagger-like grin. 'She's a viper. She takes no shit, not from anyone.'

'Like you then?' Alex said, smiling.

Ruby nodded, 'Exactly like me.'

Alex returned her nod and leaned backwards, resting his hands on his knees. 'What about your Dad? What's he like?'

'I don't know. I never met him.'.

'What? *Never*?' he exclaimed.

'Well... When I was really young. He buggered off shortly after my first birthday, just up and left in the middle of the night. We never saw him after that.'

'I'm so sorry,' he whispered.

Ruby shrugged and grinned at him. 'Don't be. You can't miss what you never really had.'

'I suppose that's true.' He frowned. 'But just because you've never known something, doesn't mean you can't want it. I think... I think wanting is just missing something that you've never had.'

Ruby folded her arms; she wasn't sure exactly how true that statement was. 'Either way, I've never wanted to know him either.'

'Don't you ever wonder about him though?' Alex asked. 'The kind of person that he is?'

Ruby let out a loud, bark-like laugh. 'What is this, twenty questions? I don't think I've had to answer this many questions' even on exam papers!'

He blushed again. 'I just want to know you better. You're interesting to me. That's all.'

Ruby sighed and rolled her eyes. 'I guess I don't wonder what kind of man my Dad is because I already know. His actions have told me who he is,' she paused as an old phrase brushed the edges of her mind and danced on the tip of her tongue. She smiled softly to herself. 'Dôð môna canne sêon dôð môdsefa—*Only the stars can see the soul.*'

Alex blinked at her. 'What kind of language is that?'

'Ancient English,' she replied, without pausing to blink. She frowned. 'I think'

'Really?' He made a low whistling sound, impressed. 'Where on earth did you learn it?'

'Oh, it's just something I picked up,' she said, smirking.

He tossed his head back and laughed, it was such a warm sound; throaty and gruff. When he finished laughing, he simply looked at her—but it was the *way* he looked at her. His head tilted to the left, his lips curved into an earnest, open smile.

Damn that smile.

'You're incredible,' he said. He didn't say it as though it were a declaration, nor did he say it playfully or teasingly. He said it as though it was a fact, and when he said it, she almost believed him.

Something reckless.

Like… holding his hand. That felt reckless.

Slowly, tentatively, her fingers linked with his, Alex watched the movement with wide eyes, until finally he was looking at her. She stared at their hands, astounded at just how easy it was to touch him.

'What do you want from me?' Ruby asked after a moment.

Alex's eyes did not stray from her face, his eyes were so impossibly dark. 'I think you know.'

'I'm gaunt, I'm sickly and I'm mean,' Ruby said, a hint of warning in her voice.

His fingers gripped tighter around her own. 'You're wonderful and fierce and not nearly as mean as you think you are.'

Alex moved his head forward, then hesitated, before finally leaning in close to her. She let him. She could feel his warm breath against her cheek and could clearly see the rise and fall of his Adam's apple. His skin was so pale—almost as pale as her own. Slowly, she untangled their hands and lifted her index finger to trace the curve of his neck. Alex's breath hitched at her touch.

Her mother had once told her men were only useful for two things; *money and something you're not old enough to understand yet.*

She wondered if this was the beginning of understanding.

There was so much noise around her. The sound of blood rushing to her ears, the sound of her heart beating, the sound of cars rushing past on the streets below.

Then she kissed him—and the noise stopped.

It was skin against skin, breath mingling with breath. It was heat and taste and fingers tugging through hair. It was simply this; his lips against hers, soft and gentle and true.

It was too much.

It was not enough.

They pulled apart, but not so far that she couldn't still feel the warmth of his breath against her skin, nor see the flecks of black in his eyes.

'Alright,' she said.

Alex grinned and when he spoke his voice was deeper than usual. 'Alright.'

Chapter Twenty-Three

MAPS AND MURDEROUS THINGS

Ruby pulled at the frays of her sleeves and then ran a hand over her head. It was getting colder, and her teeth chattered against the wind.

Yet she didn't want to leave.

She tugged her jumper closer around her neck. She hadn't properly dressed for the weather. Black jeans, black shirt, and a black jumper decorated with holes. The only splash of colour was her cherry red doc martens. Sarah would have winced to see the drabness of the outfit she had put together; Ruby couldn't help but smirk at the thought.

'I've got something to show you,' Alex said, rummaging through his school bag. She peered into the satchel and almost snorted at how neatly organised it was, sectioned and labelled, everything in its proper place.

'I should really introduce you to Sinclair some time. She's uptight about all that organisational stuff too.'

Alex smiled softly. 'I'd be more than happy to meet your friends.' He leafed through one section of the bag until he pulled out one large folded paper. Carefully he unfolded it and slowly smoothed it out onto the ground. 'This is the route I'd like to take around England, see?'

The map was relatively new, but it was large. A large map of the United Kingdom sectioned into different colours accordingly. Purple for England, yellow for Wales and red for

Scotland, with dozens of lines highlighting different roads and rivers along the way. Ruby watched as Alex placed a finger on where they were at the bottom of the little island—smack-bam in the purple—and followed his movements as he traced his finger upward along the map.

'I was thinking of going to Bristol first, and then detouring through Cardiff before heading back toward Oxford. After that I was planning on going straight up...'

But Ruby wasn't listening anymore. Her eyes had zoomed in on a thin blue line labelled SEVERN that sat a little to the right of Wales and directly above Bristol. 'Alex, what's that?'

'Oh that? That's the River Severn. We could stop there if you'd like. It's the longest river in the UK. Supposed to be pretty impressive to look at.'

Ruby shook her head. The name was familiar and yet not all at the same time. Again, she had that feeling, the feeling of *knowing* something, but her mind was fuzzy. It was the mental equivalent of having an anagram in her brain. She knew the letters made sense, but she couldn't fit them together, couldn't arrange them in the right order. Yet the image alone of the river, the way it curved away from the land... She recognised the shape.

'It's important,' she said numbly.

'Really?' Alex asked, an edge of excitement in his voice. 'Is this to do with the Shadow thing?'

Ruby shrugged, the previous want to stay at the Neville had evaporated. Now she felt the urgency to *go*. To go quickly and hunt for answers. 'I don't know. Maybe,' she picked up the map. 'Can I borrow this?'

Alex nodded eagerly. 'Of course.'

Ruby shoved the map into her bag and stood up. There was a chill crawling down her spine, and she couldn't decide if it was from the weather of the sudden shift in her mind.

'Are we going?'

'I need to go show Sinclair,' she said.

Alex scrambled upward and dusted the front of his school-trousers down. 'Do you think she'll be back from school yet?'

Ruby nodded.

Together they walked back down the stairs and passed the grime-covered walls. Only now the stench and filthiness didn't bother her. Instead the pounding of her heart was growing more viscous, and it didn't feel so much as though they were walking away from something so much as *towards.*

'Hey, Rubes... Was that door here before?'

Ruby spun around and saw Alex standing opposite a door that most certainly hadn't been there before. It was so different to everything else in the dank, peeling walls of the Neville. Where all the other doors were a faded blue, this was a deep chestnut brown. Where all the other doors had broken silver handles, this had what looked like an old iron knocker, as well as twisted iron shapes that decorated it from top to bottom.

'Wait!' Ruby ordered—her voice sharp.

For Alex's hand had somehow found itself pressing against the wood of the door, his fingers splayed out. He looked at her and blinked.

'There's something in there,' he whispered.

Ruby could feel it too, a presence lingering behind the door calling out to them. Begging to be set free.

Her breathing was fast and heavy as she moved in front of Alex. There was a part of her that told her to keep walking, to turn around and not look back. But she had seen too many incredible things.

And there was a door. A tantalising, impossible door that could be the key to something. The key to *everything,* even.

There was no chance in hell that she wasn't opening it.

Hands shaking, she reached out and gave it a gentle push. It swung open the moment her fingertips pressed against the wood.

It was as though all the air had been sucked out from around her, their surroundings suddenly felt dry and a stale taste appeared on her tongue.

Instead of finding a room of empty car park spaces, they found themselves standing at the end of what appeared to be a vast stone hall. Immense and long with high ceilings and windows. The ceilings were tall – far taller than they should be. Logically Ruby knew none of it should fit into the space—and yet somehow it did. It was as if they had stepped into another world.

Or another world had leaked into theirs.

Light shone through the large stone windows, leaving stretches of yellow on the otherwise grey floor. It shone brightest in the middle of the hall.

In the centre there was a stone slab, and on the stone slab there lay a man.

He was a glorious creature.

Even Ruby could see that. He had thick brows and honey coloured skin. He had broad shoulders that were tightly fitted with dense, metal armour. A sword lay flat across his chest, a crown sat atop his head.

Alex let out a sharp exhale as they edged closer toward the figure. Their footsteps clanging against the stone floor.

'*What* is he?' he breathed.

Ruby stared down at the man. His face was impossibly familiar. His eyes were closed and yet she knew that if he were to open them, they would be burning amber.

'A king,' she said.

The words reverberated around them. A soft, soft echo, taunting her.

Long live the king.

Alex bent his head over the body.

'A king of what?' he murmured, his hand reaching out to examine the crown with the tip of his finger. Ruby frowned, in one of the puddles of light, something flickered.

'It's his…' Ruby whispered, her pulse quickening. 'The Shadow belongs to him.'

Suddenly, she could *smell* it. She remembered the scent from when they had stood outside Emily's house in the dead of night those many weeks ago.

It was the smell of dirt after rain. It was the putrid scent of decay.

Ruby grabbed Alex's hand. 'Run!' she screamed.

And they did.

It seeped out from the cracks in the floor and the walls. Vines of thick smoke—an impenetrable mist. As it gathered it grew larger and larger until it appeared to them like a storm. This time there was no semblance of a man in its form. Only darkness, large and black and shapeless. It rose above them, blotting out and consuming all the light until darkness was all that was left.

Together they ran. They ran down flights of stairs, Ruby's feet pounding against the concrete to the rhythm of her wildly beating heart. She ran faster than she ever had in her life and she knew, as they ran, that it was not fast enough. She could feel the black space behind them, so close that she knew it was only toying with them. It was erasing everything they touched.

They reached the exit, Alex stumbled, and she dragged him back up.

They were outside, and the sky was no longer grey.

It was no longer anything at all.

The Shadow was eating away at everything around them. Lampposts blinked out of view and the Neville itself seemed to have been swallowed by the darkness. The creature flooded out from the entrance door, spilling forward like a wave. A terrifying sea of black eager to drown them.

They continued to run, and though Ruby knew that she shouldn't, she looked back. And when she did, she saw that it was already on them.

She fell to the ground and was vaguely aware of Alex crashing down behind her.

She couldn't see.

There was only blackness. There was only Shadow.

It was as though the blackness was a fog and it was suffocating her, forcing itself down her lungs and clogging up her throat. Her breathing was turning into a strangled, wheezing rasp with every second that she fought for breath.

She couldn't die. Not here, not now.

In her head she could see an image of Harriett Sinclair waiting patiently for her. She needed to show her the map... she needed to...

She *needed* to *not* pass out.

In a panic she fumbled in the dark, she felt along the seams of her trousers for her boot and curved her fingers around the comforting hilt of the dagger. In a desperate rush she wriggled it free and threw her arm above her, plunging the blade into the blackness.

The blade shone. A gleaming sliver of silver that pierced the void. With all her might she dragged it through air; and let the light bleed through.

There was a scream. No—a *growl.* Deep and inhuman and guttural.

And it was in pain.

The intensity of the sound shocked her, she scrambled further back until she was pressing into Alex's chest.

The dagger still shone brightly, and it was growing brighter by the second. She could almost see the shape of the Neville in front of her now.

She gritted her teeth and held firmly onto the hilt of the dagger, keeping it held high she grunted; '*Piss off* already, will you?'

A hiss in her ear, a voice that was not Alex's.

Until we meet again, Gwendolen's dog...

Then the Shadow seemed to collect and fold in on itself, the blackness shrank and shrank, smaller and smaller until finally it had disappeared.

They were back in dreary old Woolington-on-Sea.

Ruby dropped the dagger and it clanged onto the pavement in front of her. She leaned her head back and found herself looking directly at Alex's chin. For a moment they both sat there.

'Well...' Alex said, his voice small and breathy. 'That certainly was an experience.'

Chapter Twenty-Four

A FEELING OF ENDING

The series of events that took Ruby from standing by Alex's side, to sitting in Harriett's room were a jangled-up, incoherent mess. From the moment the Shadow had vanished, she was lost. She went from standing outside the Neville to standing where she needed to be, with no recollection of how she got there, the journey she made or the people she may have passed.

The world vanished, blood pumped through her veins and then she breathed again. Suddenly, her friends were there, dressed in their uniform and watching her, bewildered.

She explained what had happened, or as much of it as she could, all the while pulling at her sleeve and tapping her foot.

'Can I see the dagger?' Emily asked when she was finished.

Ruby pulled the dagger from her boot and passed it to Emily, who held it carefully in front of her.

'I don't get it,' Sarah said, flicking her hair over her shoulder. 'It just looks like a knife.'

'I don't get it either,' Ruby said. 'But I think that man we found, that *king,* is who the Shadow belongs to. It's the only thing that makes sense.'

Harriett's eyes narrowed. '*We*?'

Ruby bit down on her lip. 'That's... not important right now. What's important is that we found the guy; the guy causing all this trouble!'

'You don't know that,' Harriett said, shaking her head.

Ruby ran a hand through her hair and scoffed. 'Yeah I'm pretty sure I do! You didn't see him; you weren't there. I'm telling you, it's him.'

Harriett sighed. 'I'm sure you're right Ruby. But what do we do about it? You almost died today; we can't go back there. Even if we did, what would we do? Or what if we go back and he's gone?'

Ruby could feel her mouth curling into a sneer and heat rush to her face. She knew Harriett was right, but that didn't stop the way her hands clenched into fists at the thought of doing nothing. She could feel the weight of the day's events pressing on top of her, she could feel the aching hunger and pain in her stomach and there was no relief to be had. So, she bit harder on her lip and stood still.

Sarah sat on Harriett's bed. 'What made you think he was a king?' she asked, her eyes wide with curiosity.

'Well the crown on his head was a dead give-away,' Ruby said drily.

'Oh,' Sarah paused. 'What did he look like?'

Ruby shrugged. 'Tall, broad, kind of scary looking.'

'Handsome?' Sarah asked.

'Jeez, Acton!' Ruby exclaimed, 'Is that all you can think about right now? Yeah I guess he wasn't the ugliest thing going but Jesus Christ...'

'Was he young? Did he look old?' Sarah frowned. 'What does he even want with us?'

'Hmmm well, maybe he's lonely and wants to go to the cinema with us,' Ruby said, her words dripping with sarcasm.

'Hey!' Sarah said, 'I'm just trying to make sense of it all.'

'And I'm forever grateful that you've put *all* your brain power on the case,' Ruby snapped.

Harriett held up her hand just as Sarah was about to snipe back.

'Ruby, the questions Sarah's asking are important. The more we know about him, the better equipped we are to deal with him. Although, I have no idea *how* we're going to do that...'

Emily passed the knife back to Ruby.

'What do you think?' Harriett asked, as Ruby tucked it back into her boot.

Emily idly twirled a strand of her curly hair around her finger. 'I think it's a dagger. And I think it doesn't belong here.'

'What do you mean?' Ruby asked, leaning forward.

Emily spread her hands out in front of her. 'I can't explain it. The Shadow, the cat, the skull, the dagger... Even *us.* There's a...' she trailed off, thinking. 'There's an energy that doesn't feel right.'

Sarah rolled her eyes. 'Em, c'mon don't scare us.'

Emily's face remained perfectly still; her expression placid. 'I'm not trying to. It's like there's a *scent*... I never noticed it before but after we visited Madam Crone, I started paying attention. And I... I don't think we belong here.'

Silence washed over them all, until finally Harriett clapped her hands together. 'Okay. We're not going to figure this all out tonight. How's this for a plan: Tomorrow, we walk past the Neville and see if anything has changed, then we head straight to the library for more research. Okay?'

Sarah shook her head. 'I can't tomorrow. I'm watching Anthony play football and then he's taking me out to lunch.'

Emily kept her eyes fixed on Harriett, Ruby smiled to herself. Apparently, even Emily could occasionally get annoyed with Princess Sarah.

'I'm in,' Emily said. 'Just text me the time.'

Ruby shrugged. 'I'm sure I'll wangle it.'

It wasn't a particularly good plan, but it was all they had.

Together Sarah and Emily said their goodbyes while Ruby and Harriett lingered behind. Harriett made her way over to her bedroom window and watched as Emily and Sarah made their way up the road and out of view.

The silence settled and rested on top of them, an invisible weight. Ruby wasn't sure what to say, where to begin.

Thankfully Harriett did.

'What was he like?' she asked quietly, she didn't look at Ruby instead she continued to stare out the window.

Ruby thought for a moment, there were a dozen words she could use to describe him; handsome, terrifying, strong... but only one word mattered.

'Familiar,' she said.

Harriett let out an unsteady breath. 'Of course. Everything seems familiar yet none of it makes a lick of sense,' Harriett paused. 'Are you okay though?' she asked, still not looking at her.

'I have something to tell you.'

Harriett's lip twitched. 'Is this about the *"we"* you were with?'

'Yes... and no,' Ruby said. 'I've been hanging out with a boy called Alex.'

'The one from the party?'

'Yeah... I'm sorry I didn't say anything.' Ruby paused. 'I just didn't want you to think I was being like Sarah.'

Harriett blinked. 'Why? What does Sarah do wrong?'

'Nothing, *I* know that,' Ruby said, but Harriett's gaze narrowed, and Ruby felt herself squirming underneath the scrutiny.

'I don't look down on Sarah for having boyfriends,' Harriett said simply.

'Neither do I!'

'You kind of do,' Harriett said. 'Your mum has always told you how worthless men are. So, you've always acted as though Sarah's stupid for liking boys.'

'What are you saying?'

'I'm saying you have daddy issues. But you already knew that.'

Ruby gaped at her. 'Fuck you, Sinclair.'

Harriett smiled, and despite everything, Ruby smiled too and then she laughed.

'God, why does this feel like the most normal conversation we've had in a long while?'

'Maybe because it is,' Harriett murmured.

Ruby shook her head as though trying to shake away the notion, then she bent down and rummaged through her bag. After a few seconds she pulled out the map that Alex gave her. It was all crumpled now, but she smoothed it out on the carpet anyway. Harriett knelt beside her.

'This is a map that Alex gave me. Take a good long look, does anything stick out to you?'

Ruby watched as Harriett's eyes scanned the page. Blonde strands of hair fell loosely in front of her face, then the skin between her eyebrows crinkled.

'You see it too?' Ruby whispered.

Harriett took the map from the floor and held it up to the light. 'That curve; is it a river?'

Ruby nodded. 'It's connected to us somehow, I'm sure of it.'

Harriett put the map back down and pinched the bridge of her nose. 'And I'm growing less and less sure of everything every day.'

They both stood up and it was Ruby's turn to stare out the window, her eyes fixing on a lamppost that flickered lazily outside the house. There was something else she needed to say, something she was almost embarrassed to admit.

Ruby ran a hand through her hair, trying to find the words... trying to find a way to explain. 'Today, there was a moment when the Shadow had me, where all I could think about was you.'

'Ruby...' Harriett began.

They faced each other. Two girls, their silhouettes framed by a window and their shadows resting on the floor. They looked so small with the whole town spread outside – waiting and watching.

'In that instant, Sinclair, in that split second where I believed myself to be on the brink of death, surrounded by darkness. My only thought, *my only thought* was to find you.'

Harriett swallowed but her lips were sealed shut.

Ruby continued; 'The other day, after we saw Madam Crone, I was walking home, and I suddenly couldn't remember where my house was. And I've been having those moments more and more... Sometimes, I don't even recognise my own mum. You've been having those moments too, haven't you?'

Still Harriett didn't say anything, but her silence was more than enough.

'And yet, I always know who you are,' Ruby said, voice trembling. 'You and Emily and Sarah—not always your names but who you *are.* And do you know why I think that is?'

Harriett was watching her so attentively now, her mouth barely moved when she whispered; 'No.'

'I think it's because we already know each other, from somewhere else, somehow. But my mum, Sophie Grimely, Alex... they're brand new. And that's why sometimes, I don't see them. It's like Em said, we're different.'

The two of them gazed at one another, Ruby's words filling the space between them. Ruby expected her to deny it, to call her crazy, but she didn't. Instead she sighed, and pulled her hair out from its side plait, letting her bright yellow hair fall over her shoulders.

'I don't know what to do Ruby. I don't know how to protect us from whatever this is.'

'C'mon Sinclair, I thought you understood,' Ruby said. 'Your job isn't to protect us, it's to lead us; *You will lead them, you will betray them, you will tell them all you know, and you will let them go.*'

Harriett blinked at her. 'We don't even know what that means.'

'Maybe not, but I think we're very close to finding out.'

Harriett slumped onto the bed and Ruby copied her, after a moment Harriett pulled out an ugly patchwork doll, absent-mindedly she began to squeeze it in her hands. Ruby glanced around the room, so much had happened in the past few weeks alone that it had been so easy to forget that Harriett was still dealing with the very fresh loss of her sister.

Without Emily and Sarah there to fill up the space, Hayley's absence was a lot more noticeable. The carpet where her bed had once been was so much lighter than the rest of the floor, a ghostly reminder that another person used to sleep there.

'Sinclair, are you okay?'

Harriett gave a painful smile. 'No. I miss Hayley.'

Without meaning to, Ruby's eyes glanced back to where Hayley's bed used to be. From beside her Harriett let out a long, shaky breath, Ruby didn't need to face her to know that she was holding back tears. She gazed at the floor; Harriett never liked people to see it when she cried.

'I feel like... I feel like if she were here, she would know what to do. She would have already figured it out.'

'That's impossible,' Ruby said, eyes still firmly fixed on the carpet. 'If you can't figure it out then no one can.'

'The worst part is that I know I'm close to an answer. But it feels so much *bigger* than me... Too big. Maddeningly, insanely big,' she let out another sigh and then shook her whole body as if to rid herself of the thought. 'How about you? Are you okay?'

Ruby finally lifted her head, ready to grin her most dagger-like of grins and say *never better* in a dry, sarcastic tone. But she found she couldn't. She thought about Hayley dying, and her own incurable illness. She thought of Timothy Small and how his heart had stopped beneath her touch. She thought of the Shadow and how it seemed to be nowhere and everywhere all at once, hidden in the darkest corners of the town and in the even darker cracks of her mind.

She met Harriett's eyes. 'No. I'm not. I feel like I'm on a sinking ship and no matter how many buckets of water I throw overboard, I'm still going to drown.'

Harriett reached across the bed and touched Ruby's shoulder.

'We will fix this,' she said quietly. 'We will find a way to fix all of this.'

The worst part was, Ruby kind of believed her.

She needed to leave, her mum was going to arrive home at any minute, but she found she couldn't. There was an emptiness to the room that Ruby felt only too strongly, she couldn't imagine what it had been doing to Harriett.

Besides, there was a feeling… a bone-deep feeling in the pit of her being that told her time was running out. That their world was changing.

She remembered a young girl, playing in a garden and wielding a stick instead of a sword.

'Harriett…' she whispered.

'Yes,' came the reply.

'I promise I'll never let anyone hurt you,' she whispered. But the promise didn't feel right, it didn't feel *enough*. 'I promise to follow you wherever you lead me… To ðætte môdgeðôht heonu dôð su.'

In this life, and the next.

Harriett's eyes widened and Ruby knew she felt it too. The familiar weight of the words, the eerie notion of having lived the conversation before. With every breath the feeling became more present, more powerful.

For a moment neither of them spoke, and the only sound was the sound of a clock ticking loudly on the wall.

Tick, tock.

Tick.

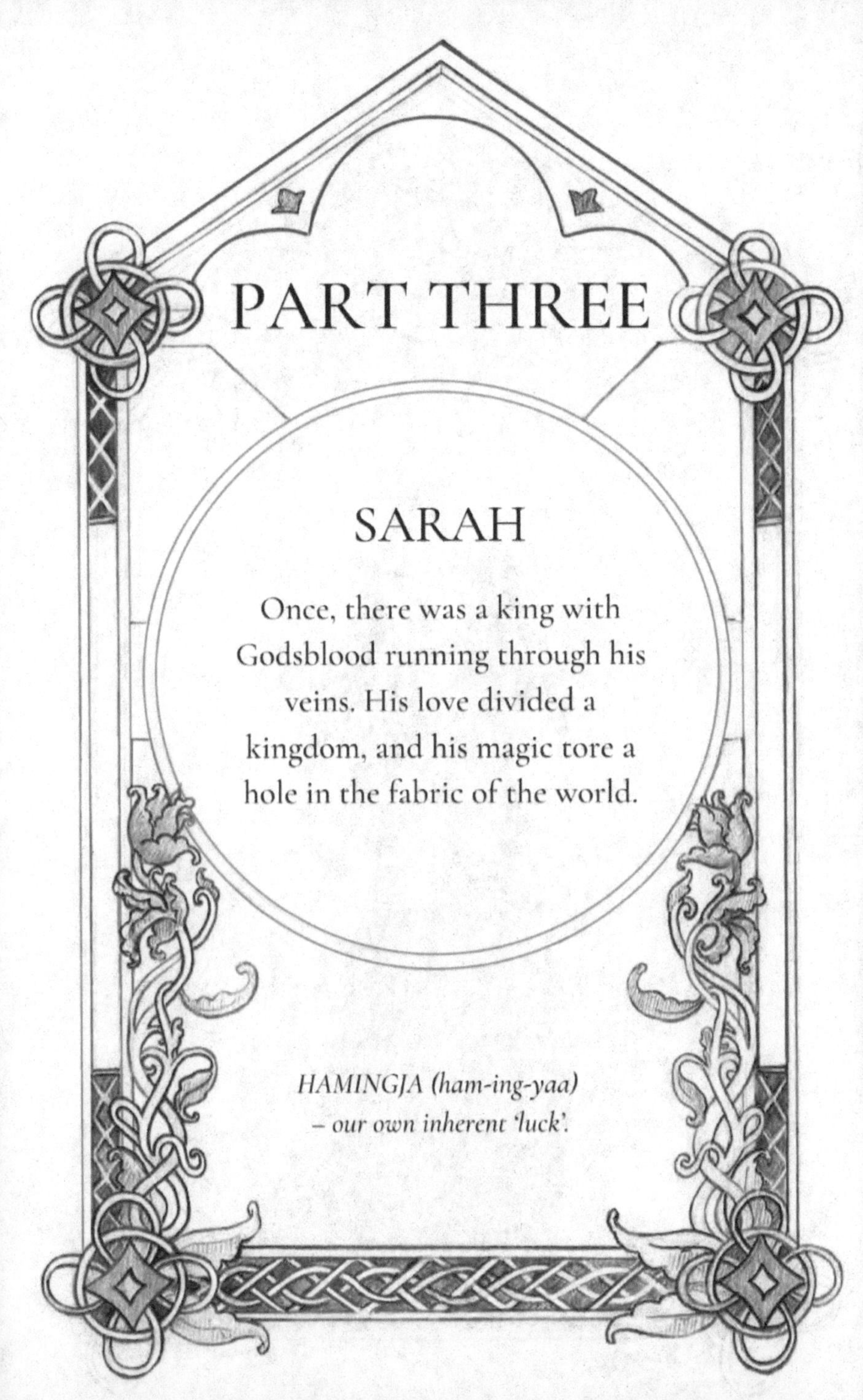

PART THREE

SARAH

Once, there was a king with Godsblood running through his veins. His love divided a kingdom, and his magic tore a hole in the fabric of the world.

HAMINGJA (ham-ing-yaa)
– our own inherent 'luck'.

Chapter Twenty-Five
A MISSING PIECE

Sarah Acton had never seen two people so inextricably in love as her parents. Theirs, she thought, was the kind of love that inspired the greatest ballads. Theirs was the kind of love that romantic films could only hope to imitate. Theirs was the kind of love... that eclipsed everything else.

Even her.

She did not mind. Or at least, she told herself that she didn't. After all, she was lucky. She always had money, as her parents always gave it to her. And she always had space, as they were rarely ever home. They were too wrapped up in each other to take much notice of her. Too busy loving being in love.

If she ever felt lonely, then she did not show it. It was a truth that she could not and would not admit. And yet... sometimes...

Sometimes, she could not help but feel as though some vital part of her was missing. As though there was a hole inside her chest just waiting to be filled.

She did *try* to fill it—god, did she try—with friends and music and boys and kisses. Yet the emptiness; that strange, aching, *hollowness* always remained.

Despite all this Sarah always believed with an absolute certainty, with a faith that bordered on delusional and a confidence that bordered on arrogance, that one day... one day she would be whole. She would find her happy ending.

Then the Shadow came.

ON THE NIGHT that they had seen Madam Crone, Sarah had arrived home, drenched from the rain, to a large and empty house. The house had two colour schemes; white, and even brighter white.

Her room was immaculate, thanks to the cleaner that came every day. It too was white and large, with a double bed that was positioned in the centre of the room, covered in pillows and soft toys. On the right-hand side there was a vanity table, paired with an ornate mirror and a lilac pouffe. The table itself was adorned with bottles of different perfumes, a jewellery box and make-up case. On the left-hand side of the room attached to a wardrobe there hung another full-length mirror. On the windowsill, next to a photo of Sarah and her friends, there sat some silver speakers.

Sarah had switched it on, as she always did. It didn't matter that she couldn't remember what was previously playing, she was always listening to something and it was always something good.

She had excellent taste, after all.

As the music gently trilled from the speakers Sarah had removed her wet school clothes and pulled on her pyjamas before sitting in front of the vanity table. Then she'd slowly rubbed off her make-up with the wipes she kept in her drawers.

The *Lovers* tarot card that had been given to her, she'd placed in the corner of her mirror.

When she was finally finished, she'd turned down the music and switched on the fairy lights that dangled above her bed. She'd taken off the pillows one by one and carefully placed them on the floor. Then she laid down and pulled the quilt up to her chest as the music continued to play.

Sarah had let the music wash over her. The sweet ringing pitch of the woman's voice matched flawlessly with the gentle clinking of the piano. She'd looked out across her room, taking in the little perfume bottles that glittered underneath the glow of fairy lights, then she cast her eyes over the mirrors and the pretty pillows and the pretty pouffe. Everything was still, and everything had its place.

It was serene and beautiful and peaceful.

Lonely.

Sarah had sighed, turned off the fairy lights, closed her eyes and dreamed.

SHE'D DREAMED OF shadows and skin. She could feel the touch of someone's breath against the back of her neck. The feeling was soothing and gentle. It sent small shivers of pleasure down her spine.

She could feel someone wrap a pair of warm arms around her and pull her close. She could smell the familiar scent of dirt... and rot, the too-sweet stench of apples left to decay in the sun. But she was not afraid. There were other scents as well, the intoxicating smell of spices and sweat.

Gradually the feeling of dreaming faded away, the blurred edges of sleep hardened as the world came back into view, until there was only the night. Sarah had frozen under her sheets and sat up abruptly. Hands shaking, she'd dragged the quilt away from her—but there was no one there. She felt her breaths slow and the panic leave her.

Then her bedroom window had opened, and the cold night air whisked through the room. Without thinking she'd jumped out of bed, ran towards the window and leaned outside into the wind. Orange leaves spilled through onto the floor, as a thin mist pooled out into the streets below. Above her a swarm of black blocked out the stars. Her breath hitched in her throat and yet still she did not feel fear, rather a soft swelling of excitement in her chest.

She could see, faintly, the outline of a hand. It reached out to her through the darkness, its long fingers desperately longing to caress her face. Some part of her—the sane part of her—understood that she should be afraid. And yet... there was fire singing underneath her skin. A desire to let herself be touched.

She'd felt something soft brush her cheek.

Gently, gently, gently, Sarah watched as the Shadow's hand traced the shape of her jawline, the arc of her cheek, the bridge of her nose.

And then a voice—clear and deep—a hiss on the wind.

Remember me... please...

Sarah still gripped onto the window. The voice had sounded mournful, aching with a hunger that Sarah not only recognised but matched with her own.

She'd looked out and down onto the road but there was no one there, no one watching her aside from the pale moon that hung eerily low in an inky night.

'Who are you?' she'd whispered.

But the Shadow had gone.

She did not know how long she stood there, gazing out at nothing. When she had finally pulled the window to a close, she'd felt sorry to do so.

She laid back in bed, turned over onto her side and started to hum.

Sarah had always loved music. Over the course of her young life she found she was always searching for the perfect song or the perfect playlist. Music to express everything she had ever wanted or ever felt. Rhythm and romance.

Excitement and thrills. Cheerful beats and dramatic melodies. Yet by far her favourite songs were ballads—the kind that promised happy endings.

Before sleep took her once more, she'd found herself rubbing the spot on her cheek where the Shadow had touched. Of one fact Sarah was certain, she did not know the current song that was playing, but the tune sounded all too familiar.

The missing piece inside her was slowly being filled.

Chapter Twenty-Six

THE BARRIER BETWEEN WORLDS

Sitting in Harriett's room, Sarah felt herself having to bite back her words. She wanted to attack Ruby with questions about what the sleeping king looked like and why they thought he might be there. She wanted to know more, more, more...

More about the *king*.

But of course, Ruby would much rather snipe and get *theatrical* about the whole thing.

When they finally left, the wind was a biting cold perfume of sea salt and damp grass. It was always damp in Woolys'.

She peeked backwards at Harriett's house. Harriett and Ruby were probably swapping secrets now and making plans *without* them. She and Emily were used to it, to watching the pair of them as though through an invisible sheet of glass, while they exchanged knowing glances and inside-jokes. An exclusive membership to a club that only the two of them belonged—Harriett Sinclair and Ruby Coleville; the superhero and her sidekick.

Girl Fight Club, indeed.

'What do you think they talk about? When we're not around, I mean.'

Emily met Sarah's eyes and she smiled softly. 'Everything, I imagine.'

The cat curled around Emily's ankle, taking Sarah by surprise. The creature followed Emily everywhere now, but so silently that it was easy to forget it was there at all. Sluggishly, the decrepit creature started to walk up the street. Without speaking, Sarah and Emily followed it, passing by Anthony's house and then turning the corner.

Try as she might, she could not shake the feeling of being touched by the Shadow.

'Have you named it yet?' Sarah asked, motioning to the cat.

'Yes,' Emily said, 'I've decided to name it *Cat*.'

Sarah scoffed. 'That's a bloody stupid name.'

Emily's smile widened. 'Funnily enough, that's exactly what Ruby said.'

They continued to walk in silence.

A thin layer of mist rain started to fall from the clouds. Sarah couldn't help but let out an irritated groan. She hadn't thought to bring a hat - her hair was going to get ruined.

'You know...' Emily began thoughtfully, a dreamy expression sweeping over her features. 'There is one thing we haven't tried.'

'Oh?'

Emily looked upward to the sky where the crescent moon hung low and sinister—a sharp white smile carved into the night.

'Water,' she said. *'For it is where the barrier between worlds is at its weakest.'*

Sarah regarded Emily carefully, her brown eyes were almost black in the dark and her frizzy hair swept untidily around her face. There was a smudge of ink on the corner of her top lip. Sarah sighed. Normally, she wouldn't want to go anywhere while it was raining. Normally, she would simply invite Emily back to her house for tea, they'd watch trashy television together then Emily would go home, and Sarah would fall asleep in her big empty house.

Normally.

The problem was that nothing *felt* normal anymore.

She followed Emily's gaze—even the stars looked different now. It was as though she was looking at a painting of the night instead of the night itself—and it was a painting she found somehow *lacking*. A pale imitation of something far more brilliant. She closed her eyes and felt the cool wet of the rain soak into her skin.

'We could go to the sea,' she said after a while.

Emily raised her eyebrows. 'Now?'

'Why not? I've got nowhere better to be, have you?'

Emily remained silent but Sarah knew that for all of Emily's silence, she would follow.

She always did.

THEY WOUND THROUGH the wide streets of Woolington-on-Sea, passing by the various red-brick houses and grey fences. They walked through the twisted alley ways that took them through the parks and into the town. The town itself was ghostly, not a soul wandered through the streets and every door was closed. The lampposts shone orange light onto darkened shop windows and the rain continued to steadily fall.

Sarah briefly wondered what they must look like. Two schoolgirls, still in uniform, wandering through the rain with a cat trotting obediently by their side. When she was struck by the notion that she simply didn't care.

For she was alive, vibrant and the night was calling to her.

Sarah, Emily and the cat passed through the town in minutes, until they stood on the promenade facing a black and glittering sea.

If they were to walk further to the left and down, they

would reach the Cornerhouse and find that empty too. But they didn't. They walked straight forward, onto the stones and toward the iron pier, where even late in the evening the sign for the Arcade flashed bright red.

'So, what do we do now?' Sarah asked, realising that she hadn't thought her plan through. But then, thinking things through wasn't exactly her forte. Spending time with Harriett Sinclair meant getting used to somebody else doing most of the thinking for you.

Most. Not all.

'I don't know,' Emily said.

The rain was slowing, and the waves were lapping gently against the shore. Emily stood at the exact point where the tide stopped, if she moved forward by even an inch then her school shoes would be soaked. The cat now sat perched on her shoulders, its furry face brushing against Emily's cheek. It almost looked as though it were whispering in her ear, and maybe it was. Sarah was beginning to think that anything was possible nowadays.

Emily knelt to the water and placed her fingertips into the sea, the cat jumped off her shoulders.

'The barrier between worlds...' she whispered under her breath. Then she stood up and started to peel off her clothes.

'What the hell, Emily!' Sarah exclaimed.

'I'm going for a swim,' she said.

'But it's bloody freezing out there!'

Emily stood in front of her, now wearing only her underwear. The dreamy expression had completely vanished. She was determined. 'Do you want to find out about the Shadow or not?'

Sarah did. She had never wanted anything more. She rolled her eyes, pulled her hair into a ponytail and began to strip, placing her school bag and clothes next to Emily's on the stony beach. Emily looked away.

When she was done Emily held out her hand, still not looking at her. 'Together?'

Without hesitation, Sarah took it. 'Together.'

Then they ran into the sea, into icy and salty water, into the murky unknown. The cold was instantaneous, and goose bumps spread across Sarah's skin. She let out a shriek and watched as her breath turned to smoke in the night air.

The cat stood on the shore, watching them with bemused eyes.

'Coward,' Sarah hissed, through chattering teeth.

They swam further and further, still holding onto each other's hands until their feet could no longer touch the ocean floor.

The rain stopped and everything was still.

It was so dark that it was impossible to tell where the sky ended and where the sea began. And yet there they were, the two of them floating in the middle of it all, two lone stars in an otherwise empty universe.

Emily's hand slipped out of her grip.

'Emily!' Sarah called. 'Emily!'

But there was no answer, only the sound of sloshing water. Emily was gone, almost as though she had never been there at all. In a panic Sarah swam toward the direction of the shore, but no matter how far she swam it did not get any nearer. Frantically she paddled on the spot, her head tossing from right to left as she continued to try and find Emily across the waves.

'Emily! EMILY!'

Silence.

Sea, sky, stars.

And then... in the distance, a speck of white, drawing closer and closer.

'Hello?' Sarah practically screamed the words and yet no sound escaped her lips. She tried again, but again her voice made no sound. Like Emily, it too had been snatched away. She waved her arms above her head, signalling with all her might, until finally in one last distressed attempt to be seen she threw herself upwards only to come crashing into the water mere seconds later.

Salt filled her mouth and nostrils, her eyes stung from keeping them open and she could see the murky emptiness of the ocean. The fathomless, never-ending black.

When she arose, the white speck was no longer a speck and she could see it for what it really was—a boat.

The little boat floated no more than a few metres away from her and standing inside it was a woman. The woman was draped in a white dress, her skin was bronze, and her hair hung wild and greasy around her face, yet there was something proud and graceful in the way she stood.

Two men in armour accompanied her, one sat in the front while the other guarded her back.

That was when Sarah noticed the rope.

It was wrapped tightly around the woman's waist and wrist and ankles and bound together with rocks. Her dress, Sarah now saw, was muddied and torn in places. Not really a dress at all.

The woman was a prisoner.

Yet she did not seem afraid. Instead there was only a grim resignation—red eyes and a distant, vacant stare.

For the first time since crashing into the sea, Sarah could not feel the cold, it was as though the water that flowed between her fingers and toes had turned to silk. She found herself fully captivated by the scene unfolding in front of her.

There was something about the woman, something in the way she moved that Sarah thought eerily familiar...

The men stood up, the boat swayed slightly, and they made to grab hold of the woman. Forcefully, she shook her head so that her hair, matted and dirty as it was, flicked over her shoulder.

'Allow me the dignity of walking to my death like a lady and not a prisoner,' Sarah heard her say.

Her voice reverberated through the air, clear as a bell. Her accent was thick and heavy, and it took Sarah a moment to realise that she hadn't spoken in English but in the strange, ancient language that was buried somewhere in her mind.

The two men regarded each other, unsure.

'Where else can I go?' the woman asked.

They did not try to take hold of her again.

The woman looked out across the sea and Sarah thought that the woman was seeing something entirely different. She was squinting, as though trying to block out the sun, her eyes seemed to be scanning for something, though Sarah was at a loss as to what.

And then the woman saw *her*.

From across the water their gazes met and something inside Sarah *sang*.

The woman was beautiful. She flaunted high cheekbones and heavy-lidded eyes and a smile that could bring a thousand men to their knees.

But it was more than that. It was not mere beauty alone that held Sarah in the woman's thrall. It was the fact that in that moment, suspended in the water in a place that was most definitely *not* Woolington-on-Sea but rather somewhere *else* entirely. Sarah found she was certain of one impossible thing.

The woman on the boat neither looked nor sounded like Sarah, and yet Sarah was convinced they were one and the same. That she was looking into a mirror; and had found another version of herself.

The woman smiled a knowing smile, a secret for them both to share.

'*We fers mêtan tîmlic,*' she whispered.

Until we meet again.

And then, without looking at the men behind her or hesitating for even a second, the woman in the boat leaped forward and plunged into the depths of the sea.

Chapter Twenty-Seven
A KISS GOODBYE

Sarah couldn't breathe.

The instant the woman had been swallowed by the waves, so had she. It was as though she had been pulled into the ocean by a force stronger than gravity. Sarah was trapped. She was being pulled deeper and deeper into the ocean, unable to move her arms or her legs, it was as though they too had been bound by rope and stones. She flailed around miserably, wildly thrashing as water filled her nose, her throat, her *lungs.*

Her vision was growing cloudier and cloudier, until even the darkness no longer seemed in focus. Yet still she kept her eyes wide open, ignoring the sting of the salty water as it pressed against her vision.

It was a rather beautiful way to die, she thought. Not too messy. She could be like that painting their history teacher always banged on about, the one with the woman dying in the river...

Her eyes were closing now, and the cold didn't feel so cold anymore.

What was its name? She really ought to remember, Emily was painting a version of it as her final art project...

Everything was slowing, slowing, down. She could no longer hear the water anymore, or maybe she hadn't heard it since she first saw the woman on the boat.

It was a funny sounding name, she knew that much, hard to say. Maybe it was Greek?

Her eyes shut as one final bubble parted from her lips.

...

...

...

The cold rushed back into her and the sound of crashing waves surrounded her. She could feel the attack of wind and rain on her bare skin as a pair of small hands dragged her across stones.

'Sarah? Sarah!'

She knew that voice.

Sarah tilted her head to the side and spluttered out what felt like half the contents of the sea. Her eyes itched as she opened them, but when she did, she found she was back. Back in Woolington-on-Sea, back on the shore, back to herself...

Emily stood over her. Her hair was clinging to her face and she was shivering like mad, but her eyes didn't so much as blink as she stared down at Sarah.

'Are you okay?' Emily asked, her voice sounded strained—nervous.

'Yeah, yeah I'm fine,' Sarah said. In fact, she was *better* than fine. If her body was a house, then it was as though all the lights had finally been switched on.

Emily let out a long, long sigh of relief. Her breathing was shaky, and she was looking up at the sky as if giving it her thanks. Sarah could see raindrops spattered across her face, and maybe a few tears as well.

A few minutes passed and then she reverted her gaze back to where Sarah was now sitting.

'What the hell happened out there?'

Sarah raised an eyebrow. 'Isn't it obvious? I almost drowned.'

Emily crouched down so that their faces were level. 'Almost? *Almost?* I thought you were dead! Sarah, do you even know how long you've been under for?'

Sarah shook her head.

'You were gone for almost an hour.'

Sarah tried not to let the surprise show on her face. An hour? It didn't feel nearly that long.

'After we got separated, I saw you start to head toward the shore and then you just *vanished.* I tried to find you in the sea, but I couldn't, then I went to the shore to see if you were there, but you weren't. I even tried calling the police, but it was like something static was blocking my calls! I was just about to run into town to find someone when Cat started screeching at the water and I spotted you.'

Sarah didn't know what to say. Emily didn't normally speak in such long sentences, and it was as though the energy of doing so had worn her out. She slouched forward and the cat rubbed itself against her shin comfortingly.

'Were you really going to run into town in your underwear?' Sarah asked.

'It was the least of my worries,' Emily said.

Sarah grinned. 'You know, that might just be the sweetest thing anyone has ever done for me.'

Even in the dark, Sarah knew that Emily would be blushing. After a few moments Emily spoke again.

'Where did you go?'

'Nowhere,' Sarah replied quickly—too quickly.

Emily simply looked at her.

'You saw where I went,' Sarah said, putting on her best exasperated tone. 'Carried away with the sea, to get seaweed in my hair no doubt,' she ran a hand through the tangled mess of her hair and sighed.

'I couldn't see you anywhere.'

'Yeah because it's *dark*,' Sarah exclaimed. 'Look it doesn't matter that you couldn't find me Em, really it doesn't. You tried your best and I'm fine, see?'

Emily once again said nothing, she merely regarded her with a closed expression. It was evident that she didn't believe a single word that had left Sarah's lips.

'Come on,' Sarah said, standing up and stretching. Her skin felt horrible and grimy, and her teeth were starting to chatter. 'Let's go home.'

They walked in a stony silence until they reached the end of Pavilion Road, the road where they had to part ways and walk in opposite directions. Sarah's thoughts had been full and fuzzy since leaving the beach. She couldn't stop picturing the woman's smile, the secret that somehow belonged to them both. The secret that Sarah was so tantalisingly close to unlocking.

'Something's about to happen, isn't it?' Emily whispered, turning to face her.

Sarah flicked her hair over her shoulder. 'What do you mean?'

Emily shrugged. 'I can just feel it. Can't you?'

Sarah could. 'Not really, no.'

Emily let out a disgruntled scoff.

They both remained still, standing at the end of the road, neither of them willing to take the first step.

'Did you see anything in the water?' Sarah asked after a few minutes had passed.

'No,' Emily said. 'But the moment before you disappeared, I thought I could hear voices.'

'What were they saying?' Sarah breathed.

'I don't know,' Emily said unfeelingly. 'I didn't get to find out because then you proceeded to drown for the next *forty-five* minutes.'

Sarah didn't have a response for that, and she wasn't about to offer up the truth now.

'I'll see you later,' Emily said, then she turned on her heel.

Sarah watched her go. She couldn't bring herself to feel guilty, not when she wasn't sure what had happened to her. Besides, she had never been one to offer up all her secrets and woes on a plate. That had never been her, that had always been *them.* Harriett and Ruby and sometimes... even Emily.

Just as Emily was about to turn the corner Sarah had a sudden thought. 'Emily, wait!'

Emily paused, Cat on her shoulder, bag on her back. She did not turn around, she simply waited for what was next.

'What's the name of that painting you're doing? The one with the woman in the river.'

There was a pause, and for a split, brief second it seemed like Emily might not answer her. That she might simply ignore her and walk away.

At the very least she was considering it.

Sarah watched as Emily's shoulders slumped ever so slightly. 'Ophelia,' she called, her back still facing her, then she left.

ALL SARAH HAD ever wanted was to be happy. She didn't have clever, ambitious dreams like Harriett, she didn't want to fight the world like Ruby, nor heal it like Emily. Her dream was different and that's what made it hers.

She had one simple wish: To love and be loved in return.

She didn't think that made her a bad person. She didn't think that wanting love was silly or selfish.

As she walked home, she could feel the reality of that dream more than ever before. She was hungry for it, hungry for the love that she knew was waiting for her.

Abruptly, her feet changed direction and within five minutes she was once again walking down Romulus Road—

Harriett's road. Only this time she stopped outside Anthony's house. Her phone was still in her bag, dangerously low on battery but enough to make a phone call.

When he answered, his voice was groggy and coated with sleep. *"Ello?"*

'Come down, I'm outside.'

'Sarah? Jesus Christ, it's one o'clock in the morning!'

'I know,' she said, although she hadn't. 'Come down.'

Eventually the door opened, and he stood before her, his perfectly blonde hair mussed and his blue eyes half-open, wearing only boxer shorts and a white t-shirt.

'Fucking hell, Sarah!' he exclaimed. 'You look like a drowned rat!'

She supposed she did. Her hair was soaking, and her uniform was completely drenched.

He was staring at her and she was staring at him, and she realised just how much she *liked* Anthony. He was sweet and kind and pretty.

Oh, so very pretty.

She kissed him then. Her cold hands went to his warm cheeks, her chapped lips met his warm mouth. One kiss slid into another, and then another, and another...

Out of all the boys she had ever kissed, Anthony was by far the best at it. He did this wonderful thing with his tongue where he would gently press it into her mouth before pulling slowly away.

He did so then.

'Ok-ay,' he murmured, then he swallowed. 'What was that for?'

It was at that moment she knew; she knew why she had pitched up outside his house and why she had wanted to kiss him.

Because she liked Anthony, she liked him a lot.

But she didn't love him.

She was saying goodbye.

'Please remember me, exactly as I am,' she whispered. 'Promise?'

Anthony frowned. 'What do you mean, babe? I'm seeing you in the morning.'

Sarah looked at him for what felt like the last time. The night was reflected in his eyes. 'No,' she said sadly. 'You won't.'

Chapter Twenty-Eight

MAN IN THE MIRROR

When she arrived home it was, as she expected, empty. Although, her parents had left her a crisp fifty-pound note on the mantelpiece, presumably to order dinner.

It was far too late for dinner now.

Her muscles ached and her uniform clung to her body, yet every single part of her was thrumming. The night was not over yet.

Sarah took off all her damp clothing and showered, rinsing herself clean with hot, practically scalding water. When she finally went to her room, she was dressed in her purple nightgown, her now-clean hair pulled up into a high ponytail. Excitement and eagerness overwhelmed her, she plucked the tarot card from the vanity table and flung open her bedroom windows.

'I'm ready,' she whispered to the wind. 'I'm ready to remember you now.'

She turned on her music, sat on the bed and waited. The *Lovers* card cupped in her palm.

For weeks, strange and horrible events had been taking place, yet nothing bad had specifically happened to *her*. Around her? Yes. To her? No. She had not found skulls in her rucksack or knives in her hands. She had not been endlessly followed by an ugly, filthy cat. She hadn't even had any of the nightmares that plagued her friends so relentlessly. Not of faceless men or red rivers or ghastly castles.

Her friends were being haunted... but she was being *claimed.*

Something floated through the window, drifting slowly through the air until it landed on the bed, near where she was sitting.

It was a flower; small and yellow with petals that curved upwards in the shape of a cup. Gently, Sarah scooped up the flower so that it nestled in her palm. It felt as soft as satin.

She remained sitting on the bed, her heart racing and her hand outstretched with the yellow flower in her palm. Something brushed against her head, light and soft. She was about to reach for it, when more sauntered down through the air, landing right in front of her. Yellow flowers, identical to the one she held in her palm, just as small and just as pretty.

Then another fell, and then another, and another.

All around her the tiny flowers were falling through the air like snow. Until soon her bed and floor were sprinkled with them. She tilted her head backwards and watched in wonder as they appeared from nowhere, popping into existence, only to fall to the floor.

Laughing, she jumped up to grab them.

From across the room something flickered in the smooth surface of the mirror. Sarah stopped. Through the storm of yellow flowers, she could see a shape inside the mirror's surface. She edged closer. When she stared into the mirror, she did not see her own reflection gazing back.

It was a man.

No, not a man - a *king*. His face filled the mirror and she could see the beginnings of broad shoulders. His head titled upward; their eyes met.

'*Estildris...*'

The sound of his voice cut through the music, through the

magic of the flowers, a deep sombre growl. Sarah could hear her own heartbeat pounding in her ears, she edged even closer, entranced and unable to look away.

He was olive skinned, with eyes of burning amber, his hair so dark it was almost black, and plaited into intricate braids that framed the square of his face. Yet it was his lips that held her attention the most—full and round and parted just ever-so-slightly. She could not stop staring at them.

'*Estildris*,' he said again.

He reached out his hand so that it protruded from the surface of the mirror, his long fingers grasping the sides of the frame, ready to pull himself free.

Sarah was vaguely aware that anyone else would be running at this point, or screaming, or doing *something*. But Sarah only stood there and watched as the man in the mirror clawed his way out until he was standing right in front of her, smack bang in the middle of her bedroom carpet.

The flowers stopped falling.

He was tall, so very tall. He filled the room, not only with his height but with his mere presence. Everything seemed duller by comparison, as though he was made of such a brilliant light that it cast a shadow over everything else.

It took several moments for Sarah to take in the full reality of him. He wore armour, spattered with something that looked suspiciously like blood, and a deep purple cape that had been torn in half.

On his head there sat a crown like none she had ever seen before in either movies or museums. It was thick gold and encrusted with more than a dozen gems of various colours and sizes. Briefly she wondered how heavy it was, sitting there atop his head.

The man gazed down at her, his eyes looking through her and into something hidden.

'Estildris,' he said the word carefully, as though wrapping

his tongue around each syllable.

Eh-still-drisss.

'My name is Sarah,' she said, gripping the corners of her nightgown. Again, she knew she should be running away, that she should be terrified and sprinting to get out of the house.

She stayed.

The crowned man gazed down at her and she saw pity in those fearsome, amber eyes.

'In this life you are young,' he said throatily, kneeling in front of her. There was barely any space between them. He was so close that she could count his eyelashes if she wanted to. 'But I know that you are strong. No matter where I am, no matter how far apart we are... we will make each other whole again.'

Sarah gripped the corners of her nightie even tighter.

'You know me, Estildris,' he whispered. 'You know where I am.'

'No...' Sarah said quietly. 'I don't. Tell me,' she was unsurprised when the words that left her lips were of that other-worldly tongue.

Slowly, the crowned man reached out his wide hands and cupped her face. His skin was cold and yet his touch was burning.

'Our love has transcended the stars, the oceans, the skies, even time itself. For you I have bent the rules of the universe so far as to almost break them. For you I have hungered and waited and lived and died and searched. For you, for you, for you, I have become monstrous.'

It was everything she had ever wanted to hear and more. A king on his knees in front of her, surrounded by a blanket of flowers. She believed him. She believed in the truth of his words and the earnestness in his eyes and the feel of his skin against hers.

We will make each other whole again.

The missing piece.

She knew what was going to happen next. Slowly the king rose from the ground so that he towered over her once more. His eyes never leaving hers, not even for a moment. He placed one long finger under her chin and tilted her head up to face his.

The edges of her world were crumbling, and she wondered what would happen if the ground beneath her feet were to disappear completely.

She ached to find out.

Sarah let the kiss happen. His mouth met hers, his tongue traced her bottom lip, she felt his hands clutch at her waist and pull her into him. It was hungry and fierce and urgent.

It was also familiar.

Sarah had always loved fairy tales; she had always believed in the power of a kiss. Yet this felt like all her favourite bedtime stories rolled into one and then twisted into something new.

The kiss went on, fiercer and deeper, all consuming. She was the sun; he was the moon—and he was eclipsing her.

Time stopped and the air was growing thinner.

Sarah found herself filled with a sense of knowing and at the same time, *un*-knowing.

She could feel her mind slipping away from her body, deeper and deeper into the kiss, until it was all that was left. And then...and then there was not even that, only darkness and the sensation of being rocked to sleep.

It was 3:46 am.

Chapter Twenty-Nine

A SKY ON FIRE

*O*nce, there lived a king with magic in his veins. He was the son of a tyrant, the grandson of emperors, and the descendant of gods.

Even in his own time, Locrinus was a myth walking among men, inspiring terror and awe in equal measure. Whispers of his deeds spread across both land and sea. It was said that he had battled the King of Goliaths and won. It was rumoured that he had swum with Sirens and lived. There were even tales that he could converse with spirits from other realms...

Yet, of all the stories told, it was the tale of the stolen princess that lingered the longest. It was said that he loved her.

It was said that it was his love that killed him.

Lorcrinus had been a myth amongst men, then he was just a myth, and then eventually... he was not even that. Time took his legend and buried it deep, until even his name was lost.

The world still knew of him though. All the swirling masses and colours of the universe felt his presence—even in death. For that's where his soul was hiding; floating in the spaces between time, hidden in the emptiness that bridged the stars.

It was said that on the eve of King Locrinus' birth, the moon bled red. Yet it was his death that forged a crack in the world.

SHE HAD BEEN *stolen.*

She had been stolen as though she were merely some sought after piece of jewellery or gold, and then she had been treated as such.

Stashed away at the bottom of a ship the Lady Estildris had lived as both prized possession and prisoner. She hadn't seen the light of the sun nor the glimmer of stars in so long, and she had no recollection of what it was like to stand on solid ground. All the days had melted into one impossible night.

Fortunately, her dungeon was draped in a splendour of finery, and filled with other precious and valuable, stolen things. It was this alone that made her captivity bearable. Better a gilded cage than iron bars.

It was a cold, wintery morning, on the coast of Albany, that Estildris' life changed again. It was underneath a sky of fire and ash that she found herself stolen once more...

THE DOOR OPENED, *but it was not one of the Huns who opened it. It was a woman—though the strangest woman that Estildris had ever seen. She wore armour, and her long hair had been fashioned into a warrior's braid.*

The lady's eyes fell to the sword that rested on one hip, and the dagger that rested on the other. Of all this it was the woman's size that seemed impossible. She was taller than most men, and though slim, she seemed muscular too. When the tall woman saw Estildris her eyes widened, then her eyes landed on the chests of gold that were stacked behind her.

When the woman stepped into the room, the Lady Estildris lurched backwards. The woman smiled, and that alone was a terrifying sight to behold—it was as though the shape of a smile had been carved into her face. She marched forward, picked up one of the chests and slung it over one shoulder. The chests were heavy, Estildris knew this having tried to pick up one herself, yet the tall woman carried it with apparent ease. With her remaining hand the tall woman grabbed hold of the princess's wrist and pulled her out of the room.

Estildris did not fight back. She did not scream, she simply allowed herself to be led through the belly of the ship and up onto the deck. When the doors were opened, the light was too bright and it took some moments before she could adjust to the outside. Finally she could take in the scene. And when she did, she felt a thrill of excitement at what she saw.

The sky was on fire.

It was a churning, chaotic mix of smoke and ash.

Across the shore ships were burning, and the heat of the flames was carried on the back of a cold, icy wind. Men were screaming and Estildris watched as the Humber's warriors were slaughtered one by one.

The tall woman dragged Estildris across the deck of the ship and down onto land. The moment their feet touched the ground they were met by two men who wore the same chainmail as the woman.

The same thick armour and purple shields.

One was stocky and broad and fair-haired, while the other was tall, lean and brunette with a large, crooked nose. They looked at Estildris questioningly before turning to the warrior-woman, who started speaking rapidly in a language that Estildris immediately recognised. It was the Old Tongue, the language of the Britons. Estildris was immediately relieved to be hearing a language that she understood after months of listening to the Huns bark at her in their foreign speech.

The tall woman dumped the chest onto the ground, so that it split open and dozens of gold and silver coins spilled out.

She did not release her grip.

'There's more on the ship,' the woman said, her voice uncannily like a growl. 'On the bottom deck, where I found this one.'

'What shall we do with her?' the blonde man said, looking at Estildris with mild curiosity. His voice was soft, and his eyes were kind. Estildris felt a glimmer of hope. 'Who is she?'

The dark-haired man spat onto the sand. 'Who cares? Just kill her. The king would want her dead.'

The hope was extinguished and immediately replaced by panic. Had she been released from her cage only to be slaughtered like a dog?

The woman shook her head fiercely, the fire from the ships casting an eerie glow over her features, highlighting a collection of fine scars that Estildris hadn't noticed before.

'No,' she snapped. 'She was being kept in a locked room with treasure. Could be that she's valuable somehow. Besides, the queen would want her kept alive.'

The brunette man spat again. 'Have it your way,' then he sauntered off to another nearby ship, walking casually past a group of men engaged in a vicious brawl.

The blonde man let out a sigh. 'Algar won't forgive you for that, Augusta,' he said. 'He'll tell the king what you said.'

Augusta smiled another ruthless smile. 'Let him. Stinkin' no good piss-weasel.'

The blonde man laughed and then went about the business of using a piece of ship-rope to bind Estildris' hands, narrowing his eyes at her as he did.

'Are you sure Gwendolen will want this one? It might be hard to bring her back against the king's wishes.'

'You let me worry about that, Osric,' Augusta said sternly, and then in an even lower voice she said; 'And you shouldn't be *speaking so casually about Her Majesty. Remember, we're her subjects—not her friends.'*

Osric's pale face flushed red as he fastened the final knot into Estildris' binds. Then he moved away and the three of them regarded the scene.

Some of the ships had all but sunk into the sea now, while others still burned brightly. Estildris' ship—her prison—was the only one that remained. The shore was littered with the corpses of Humber's men, their swords gleaming like jewels underneath the glare of fire. The sand was spattered with blood. Estildris had never seen so much death before.

She could not bring herself to be sad about it.

'What now?' asked Osric.

Estildris watched as the tall woman stared out at the sea and into the flames, her black eyes glinting malevolently.

'Get some men, grab the rest of the treasure and then set the damn thing ablaze,' Augusta replied, motioning to the ship. 'Let's go home.'

Chapter Thirty

BELONGING

Augusta was of an unsettling nature. She growled rather than spoke, sneered instead of smiled and—most infuriatingly of all—refused to answer any of Estildris' many, many questions. The tall woman's silence was impregnable, even as they rode the same horse, Augusta managed to ignore the lady's presence.

They rode through the day, marching in a long solemn line. All the men from the shore and all the treasure too. Estildris tried counting their number, though she found her attempts ultimately fruitless as men would ride ahead to chat with another warrior before falling to the back once more. She figured that there were at least a hundred.

A hundred men who took the Humber's ships and turned them to ash.

The horses took them further inland until the sound of the sea was nothing but a distant memory. They passed through thick woodlands and barren fields. When they had left the shore, it had been the early hours of the morning, but now night was drawing in and there was no sign of them stopping for rest.

'Where are we going?' Estildris asked, though she did not expect an answer. She thought it was at least good practice to speak in the language of the Britons. She had learnt the language at a young age, when some warriors of Briton had held court with her father for months on end. Though she was

out of practice, her accent was thick, and her tongue could not quite wrap itself around the strange 'w' sounds.

'Keep quiet,' Augusta hissed. 'Do you want to draw even more attention to yourself?'

Estildris felt her body go rigid. It hadn't occurred to her that the tall woman might be protecting her.

'No,' she whispered.

'Then keep your mouth shut, and I might be able to get you to the queen in one piece.' Augusta did not so much as glance in her direction, she remained facing forward so that the only view Estildris had was of her back and the matted blonde braid that dangled against her armour.

Not another word passed from her lips.

It was as the moon was rising into an empty black sky that Estildris' question was answered. The horses marched through the last few metres of woodland and into a vast, open field. It was an assault on the senses, smoke from campfires filled the nostrils, while the sound of men laughing, and cheering filled the air.

The horses came to a stop and Augusta swung off with apparent ease before hoisting Estildris down after. The men all dispersed to either tie up the horses or join the revellers. It was clear to Estildris that while this was a war camp, it was also a celebration.

Buckets of ale littered the grass while big chunks of meat were being roasted on open fires. Augusta pulled Estildris roughly past crowds of men and into one of the tents that clustered the edge of the field. It was smaller than the rest, and shabbier too.

Once they were inside Augusta sat down and rubbed her hands over her face as Estildris regarded the dingy surroundings. Weapons were stockpiled in one corner while a pile of rags sat in the other, in what Estildris supposed *constituted a bed. All of this led Estildris to a simple and obvious conclusion: Augusta was not respected.*

But then, what respectable woman would wish to live a warrior's life?

Estildris looked at the woman as she pulled off her leather boots, scars lined her face and hands, and there were large grey bags that circled her deep-set eyes.

Augusta took off the first layer of armour, revealing pale and purpled arms. She let out a groan as she dropped that to the ground too.

'Why are you helping me?' Estildris asked.

The woman regarded her, as though surprised to see her standing there, then she frowned. 'Would you rather I didn't?'

'No,' Estildris said. 'I'm grateful. But I have nothing to give you.'

Augusta let out a harsh laugh. 'Am I asking you for anything?'

Estildris couldn't think of what to say, yet her mouth hung open as if waiting to catch some words, the way a frog might catch a fly. Augusta laughed again.

'The queen suspected that Humber might be holding some prisoners. She told me that if there was anyone needing saving, to save them.'

Estildris thought back to what the brutish man had said on the beach; 'The king would want her dead'.

'And you always do as the queen says, even if it goes against the king?'

Augusta didn't even blink when she answered. 'Always.' It was almost a soft snarl, the way she said it, and there was an intensity to her stare, a devotion that Estildris had never seen before – not even in her father's men.

She shivered.

'We have a problem,' a voice said. The tent opened and the blonde man—Osric—poked his head through.

'What?' Augusta demanded.

'Algar's on his way, the king wants to see her.'

Augusta swore and then stood up so that she was facing Estildris. 'How long?'

'Minutes. I ran ahead to warn you.'

Estildris felt her pulse quicken. Even a brute like Augusta couldn't fight the hundreds of soldiers that lay mere feet outside the tent.

'Listen to me,' Augusta said quietly. 'Locrinus is vicious, ruthless and strong. He's also clever when he wants to be, you're clearly noble and he has his pride. Play to it, and maybe you'll live.'

Osric opened the tent wider. 'I see him.'

Augusta patted Estildris on the shoulder and gave something that was a close approximation of a smile. 'Let's hope you don't die then.'

Algar's voice cooed from through the fabric. 'Come out dog. The king wants to see your new toy.'

Augusta's lips curled up into a sneer as she took Estildris' wrist and pulled her outside.

Directly in front of them stood Algar, with a small group of soldiers. Unlike the revellers they all still wore their armour and shields. They looked rather menacing, standing there with their swords and staring at them with such intent.

Apparently, Augusta disagreed.

'Look at you,' she snarled. 'Bringing an entire cohort to collect one noble girl, tell me Algar, are you that frightened of me?'

Algar scoffed. 'The men wanted to see the woman you snatched dog, that's all, I told them she was quite the beauty. What do you think lads, do you agree?'

Augusta's eyes narrowed in disgust. Estildris however forced herself to stand a little taller, she was no stranger to men's advances, though her title at home had always protected *her. She had always been proud to be handsome. Her beauty had been worth almost as much to her as her crown. Now, standing in a field amongst an army of men, she wondered whether her looks were an asset or a shortcoming.*

Do you want to draw even more attention to yourself?

The men beside Algar grunted their agreement, and Estildris found herself suddenly wishing that she had large warts on her nose.

'If you dare touch her I—' Augusta began, but her words were cut short.

'Relax, dog,' Algar laughed. 'The king wants to see her. And until he has, no harm will come to her. I give you my word.'

It was Augusta's turn to laugh. 'Your word means less to me than the shit that comes out of my horse's arse.'

The sneers on the men around Algar faltered, and from beside her Estildris could feel the other warrior, Osric, go still.

Algar's eyes darkened as he regarded Augusta carefully. 'One day, I'm going to have the immense pleasure of removing your head from your body.'

Augusta raised an eyebrow, and then pulled back her mouth into that menacing, leering smile. 'Or maybe I'll have the pleasure of removing something far less precious from you.' Her eyes flickered meaningfully to below his waist, and Osric started to laugh.

Algar's cheeks flushed red, then his eyes darted to Osric. 'Careful cousin, you spend enough time with this embarrassment, and you'll become one yourself.'

Osric's laughter stopped though the smile did not quite leave his face.

'Come, woman,' Algar ordered, beckoning to Estildris. 'It's time to meet the king.'

As A_{LGAR AND} *his men led her through the camp Estildris was keenly aware of the eyes of the warriors' following her. She was not sure if it was because of curiosity, or simply that she was a woman, or a prisoner, or if it was because she was, as Algar said, quite the beauty. Whatever the reason, she could feel their stares on her skin, and it felt as though she was being branded.*

'What is the king like?' Estildris asked. Hoping against all hope that he might give her some information she could use. Some tiny morsel that might save her.

Algar scoffed. 'What did Gwendolen's pet tell you?'

Estildris thought back to the tall woman's words and thought that in this instance a half-truth was her best weapon. 'She told me that he was vicious, and clever and strong.'

Algar looked thoughtful as they passed a crowd of men waving purple flags and cheering.

'The king is all that,' he conceded. 'But he is also much, much more. Locrinus and his brothers, they are the descendants of gods.'

There was a strange relish in his voice as he spoke, and his eyes gleamed proudly.

Estildris didn't slow her pace, merely kept in step beside Algar as the rest of his men walked both in front and behind them. In her mind she carefully crafted a reply.

'But Sir, how is such a great thing possible?'

'Locrinus is the first son of King Brutus. Surely, you have heard of him?'

Estildris had.

'I thought...' she whispered. 'I thought Brutus was a myth?'

Algar scoffed again, but didn't deign to answer, and so Estildris had no choice but to follow him in silence.

Yes, Estrildis had heard of Brutus of Troy. Her father loved to regale her with tales about him. He was the great grandson of the Greek Goddess, Aphrodite, or so it was said. It was foretold by a magician that he would kill both of his parents and then he disappeared when the prediction came to pass.

'Brutus of Troy,' her father had once said. 'Was the greatest conqueror to have ever lived—that is, if he ever existed at all.'

She felt a pang in her chest at remembering her father's voice and the words of her own language being spoken to her.

It occurred to her, as she continued to march forward, that she would never hear the tongue of her people spoken aloud by anyone that was not herself, ever again.

'We're here.'

Estildris was snapped unceremoniously out of her reverie only to find that the sounds of the campsite had greatly diminished, and that the lights from the fires were mere dots to her now. Instead, she stood by a river and a canopy of trees. The water shimmered gently, and the branches swayed softly in the night breeze.

'His Majesty is waiting for you.'

The king stood by the river, cutting a sharp shape into the night. A broad figure—tall and brooding against the starlight. Estildris moved slowly toward him, she heard the rustling of branches behind her which signalled the departure of Algar and his men.

The king did not look at her nor acknowledge her presence in any way. His eyes were fixed on the smooth surface of the river, staring at it with such vehement hatred that his mere gaze threatened to set the water alight.

'Did you know the Humber well?' he asked after some time passed, though still he did not look at her. His voice was deep and smooth and Estildris found herself taken aback by its song-like quality.

'As well as any prisoner knows their jailor,' Estildris replied.

The king nodded thoughtfully. 'Humber murdered my brother, then I murdered him in return. That's justice, isn't it?'

Estildris didn't say anything. There was nothing that she could say.

Locrinus sighed. 'It doesn't feel like enough. I could kill him a hundred times over and still it would not be enough.'

In all the time that they had been speaking, Locrinus had not pulled his gaze from the water. Estildris followed his gaze, the river seemed so still, so peaceful. Yet she knew that Humber's body lay hidden deep within its depths.

Drowned—a traitor's death.

'I would help you,' she whispered, thinking of all the months she had spent locked away in that dark solitary room.

It was then that the king finally turned to face her and when he did Estildris felt the breath leave her body.

He was beautiful, in a way that she hadn't thought men could be. His jawline was strong and his cheekbones sharp and his lips were full. His dark hair was pulled back into a warrior braid and yet on one side his hair had been shaved into a strange, intricate pattern.

He was younger than she expected, perhaps only five summers older than herself. And unlike many of his soldiers he did not have a beard, only a soft stubble that seemed to highlight his features rather than diminish them. Yet it was his eyes that held her in place—they burned the colour of molten amber.

The colour of fire.

Locrinus and his brothers, they are the descendants of gods. Estildris believed it.

Locrinus took a strand of Estildris' hair and gently wound it around his finger.

'I heard a sad story,' he said softly. 'The story of a stolen princess who was to be ransomed back to her father for a heavy weight of gold. Her father loved her dearly, and most certainly would've paid the price...but he died before any ransom could

be made, and her brothers did not want her. Does any of this sound at all familiar to you?'

'Yes.'

She had never been told exactly what happened. Though it hadn't been hard for her to piece together the truth. Her father, who had loved her above all his children, had been old and frail when she was taken and there had never been much affection between her and her brothers. She doubted that they would have paid any price at all to see her returned. She watched entranced as the king continued to play with her hair.

'I think... I think Humber intended to sell me off into a marriage eventually, or perhaps... keep me for himself.'

Locrinus nodded thoughtfully, his stare now lingering on her face. 'And did he? Keep you for himself?'

Estildris straightened and made sure that her eyes did not so much as blink when she answered. 'No. He did not.'

The corner of his mouth twitched into a faint flicker of a smile. She wondered if that pleased him, and then wondered what she could do with that information.

'You are indeed lovely,' the king sighed. Then he released the strand of hair that he had been holding. 'Some of the men think you brought bad luck down on the men that kept you, and that you carry bad luck still. They say I should kill you. What do you think?'

Estildris paused. She was no simpleton, she knew that she was being tested, and that her fate might depend on her answer.

'I would make a beautiful corpse, your Majesty. But I would make a far more exquisite companion.'

The king raised his eyebrows in surprise and this time Estildris did not imagine the smile that passed across his face.

'My queen will be pleased. She has a soft spot for outcasts, oddities and broken things.' There was a faint bitterness in his

voice now when he spoke. He made to brush past her but paused as their arms touched.

There was a shift, an energy that hummed between them. Their eyes met and Estildris' heart went still. It was as though a match had been struck.

She was suddenly overwhelmed with the urge to reach up and press her hand against his cheek, to feel his skin beneath hers. She could see her own want reflected in the king's face.

And she was thankful for her beauty. Thankful that it had given this opportunity to be noticed—to be saved.

She removed her arm carefully, then looked modestly to the ground, she allowed her hair to drape down, covering her face in an artful display of supposed bashfulness.

Estildris had never been bashful nor shy, not for one day in her life. Though she had perfected the act so well as to almost convince herself.

The king knelt to the ground and plucked a single, yellow flower from the grass. When he stood, he slowly brushed her hair behind her ear, and carefully tucked the flower there. After a few moments, he finally removed his hand, but he did this even more slowly, letting his finger trace the shape of her chin. His gaze never left her face, his eyes continued to burn. She could hear her own breaths, shallow and heavy.

'You will be one of my wife's ladies, but make no mistake princess,' he paused, as though to make his intent perfectly clear. 'You belong to me now.'

Estildris allowed herself to smile as sweetly and as innocently as she could.

'Of course, your Majesty.'

She had done it. She was alive—alive—and she was going to court. Her skin singed with the perfectness of it, her soul brimmed with the joy of knowing, for the first time in a long time, exactly what she was walking into.

For Lady Estildris knew that court was a game. After all, she had grown up in the thick of it back home. In this new land she was nothing more than a pawn, a colourful piece handed down from one person to the next. But she was beginning to learn who the players were now, and she was beginning to learn the rules. She had the advantage; they didn't see her as a threat. How could they? She was just a lost girl in the company of warriors and kings and queens.

But she could be a player—she could be dangerous too.

She could even hold the heart of a king in her hands.

Chapter Thirty-One

GWENDOLEN'S LADIES

*I*t had been three summers since the Lady Estildris had first been found, weak and cowering in the depths of the Humber's ship. Three summers since she had found herself living alongside the Britons, walking their earth, eating their food and breathing their air. It was colder here than it was in Germania, colder and harsher and far less kind.

But there were similarities, the ground was as fertile, the woods were beautiful too in their own twisted, ancient way. But above all, their gods were the same.

She stood in the clearing of the weoh: The hallowed space where the trees reached highest toward the gods, the place where even the birds and the creatures of the forest dare not tread for fear of waking the spirits that slumbered there.

In her hands she held the limp carcass of a chicken, she had killed the creature herself earlier that very morning. It had been a gruesome task but a necessary one - she needed wisdom now more than ever.

The weoh was made into the shape of a circle and seven stones marked it. On four of the stones there were symbols carved deep into the rock, a symbol for each of the main gods.

Woden, King of the gods and leader of the wild hunt.

Thunor, God of thunder and ruler of the skies.

Tiw, God of warfare and battle.

Frige, Goddess of love.

Estildris moved into the centre where the altar was placed plainly under the morning sky. She could feel the twigs and leaves crack and crunch beneath her feet. Winter had set in and the leaves on the trees burned red and brown. Golden light poked through the branches, leaving tiny flecks of sun dancing on the woodland floor.

She slapped the chicken onto the slab and blood trickled out onto the stone. 'Gods, I offer this sacrifice so that you may hear me and guide me in my path.' Her voice was soft; a whisper, a prayer. The air was fresh and smelt like grass and lavender. She knelt onto the ground and lay her hands out flat into the earth, allowing all the dirt to scoop up underneath her fingernails. 'Oh goddess, lend me your wisdom and show me the way forward. Tiw give me the strength to keep the path.'

Two birds flew across the empty sky, mere silhouettes against a wintery backdrop.

"Tis a sign from Frige,' a voice said from amongst the trees.

Estildris spun her head to look behind her.

'Thea,' she said, 'I did not expect anyone else to be here this early.'

'I am always here,' Thea said, she stood leaning against a tree, a black cat yawned beside her feet. 'The bones do not clear themselves.'

Estildris glanced around the altar. Aside from her own sacrifice it was bare, she smiled. 'It never occurred to me before that the weoh needed cleaning.'

Thea wandered over to Thunor's Stone, her tunic was plain and dyed to a deep blue, around her neck dangled the teeth of animals and an amulet made of pure amethyst. Thea placed a hand on the stone's surface, her fingers were painted black with runes on top of runes.

'Have you found your guidance?' she asked.

Estildris looked back to the sky where the birds had now disappeared, snatched away by an invisible hand. 'Perhaps. The sign was unclear.'

Thea gave a wry smile. 'Was the sign unclear or is it your head that is clouded?'

Estildris chuckled. 'The gods work in mysterious ways.'

'That they do,' Thea murmured.

Estildris stood and wiped the leaves from her tunic. 'How come the preparations for Modraniht?'

'Is that why you worship? You are fearful of what the night might bring?'

Estildris felt her heart jump. Yes. I am afraid of what I might do. 'No. It's just... I know how important it is to the queen.'

Thea nodded. 'It is Madden's fourth Modraniht. She wants him to enjoy it.'

Estildris felt her heart skip once more. 'I'm sure it will be.'

Thea stared at her for a moment, her skin was the palest pink, and her hair shaved close to her head. She often stared at Estildris with such an intensity that Estildrissometimes supposed the woman could see into her head.

'We should go,' Thea said. 'The queen wishes all her ladies to be with her by midday.'

'I have not forgotten, Witch.'

Thea laughed, and lifted her face to the sky, after a moment the laughter died on her lips, her eyes froze and for a moment the woods itself held its breath. She closed her eyes.

'What is it?' Estildris demanded. 'What do you see?'

Thea's eyes opened once more; her irises were pinpricks.

'Change,' she whispered, the cat at her feet purred.

Change.

'Let's head back,' Thea said abruptly.

Estildris looked to the chicken carcass that still lay across the alter. 'Shall we take it with us?'

Thea shook her head. 'No, let the gods enjoy it a little while longer.'

The two women left the weoh and walked back toward Wighus Hall. Estildris' heart was pounding. Tonight would be the night, tonight she had to make her decision, and then everything would change.

AS THEY EXITED *the forest the trees began to thin and Estildris was able to lay her eyes on her home once more. Wighus Hall was always a terrible and glorious sight to behold. Estildris' reaction to the castle was the same as when she had first seen it: A cold shiver followed by awe. It was grim and bleak, made up of large grey stone and covered in dark green moss. But it was the towers that entranced her, tall and spindly, dozens and dozens of them sitting on top of one another, the turrets almost touching the clouds. Estildris' own room was in one of the towers west of the building, overlooking the stables and the forest.*

'Where are we going?' Estildris asked, upon noticing that they were steering away from the main gate and toward the stables.

'To retrieve one of our party,' Thea replied simply.

Estildris paused and let out a startled gasp. 'So, it's true? She really does sleep with the dogs.'

Thea merely shrugged. 'Augusta will only sleep in the castle if the queen asks it of her. She does not like to feel trapped.'

Estildris wrinkled her nose in disgust. She liked Augusta, or rather she tried to like her. She was thankful to her, certainly, for choosing to save her on the ship when she could have easily let her die. But there was something in the tall woman that the Lady Estildris simply did not understand—a wicked glint in the warrior's eye that suggested when given the option between safety and chaos, she would always choose chaos.

They reached the stables and found her in the nearest stall slumped atop the hay, her long limbs stretched out lazily, four large grey dogs slept around her, one was curled up next to her head, another tucked under her arm, while the other two slept either side of her feet. The warrior looked content. Peaceful even.

As Estildris and the witch drew nearer the dogs' ears began to twitch, a few of them even opened their eyes to regard them. Thea must have visited Augusta before though, for none of the dogs made to move. They simply watched them through heavy-lidded eyes.

Thea bent down and picked up a long straw of hay. She leaned over the dogs and brushed the tip of the straw across the bridge of Augusta's nose. The tall woman's hand moved to swat the annoyance away, once, twice... and then she awoke startled.

'Can't you wake me up like a normal person?' Augusta demanded through a large yawn.

'Normal people sleep in the castle,' Estildris said.

Augusta grinned sharply. 'Look who it is! The little princess.'

Estildris ignored the mocking tone and instead regarded the dogs. They were all stretching now, their long tails wagging, watching Augusta expectantly for scraps of food or attention. Augusta stood and patted each of the dogs on the head. She was wearing farming clothes; rough shirts made of harsh wool and loose trousers that belonged on men.

'Come,' Thea said. 'We don't wish to be late.'

Obediently Augusta nodded and stripped herself of her clothes and changed into the newly polished armour that was stacked in the corner of the hut. She fed the dogs, scattering raw lumps of meat into the hay from a nearby bucket, and then *placed another bucket full of water in the corner of the stables before leaving.*

'Will they be okay to hunt later?' Thea asked.

'Yes,' said Augusta, a hint of pride in her voice. 'You'll find no better hunting dogs than mine.'

Estildris couldn't help it, she clucked her tongue. 'I still can't believe you'd rather keep company with dogs than people.'

Augusta didn't look at her when answering. 'Dogs are honest, people lie.'

Estildris couldn't argue with that. She lied every day.

Together the three women made their way across the yard and to the gates where two soldiers stood, they were waved through immediately, though Estildris could not help but notice their wary and distrustful stares.

Many people still did not understand it—Estildris did not fully understand it herself—Why the three of them were held in the queen's utmost confidence; the witch, the warrior and the foreign princess.

When Estildris had been brought before the queen she had expected to beg for a place, for her life. Yet, Gwendolen had taken her into her confidence and told her that she was to be welcomed.

Gwendolen had kept to her word. Augusta, Thea and Estildris were the three that the queen had chosen. Her ladies, and they were always by the queen's side. Thea offered council, Augusta offered protection, and Estildris offered news of ongoings in the castle.

They were her servants.

And...impossibly...her friends.

They climbed the stairs, winding their way to the queen's chambers. Gwendolen liked their gatherings to be as private as possible. Her rooms were situated in the highest tower in the south of the building, they were grand and wide and— conveniently—half a castle away from her husband. They reached her rooms and there she was; calm and collected, sitting on a large chair with her son, Madden, playing with some string on her lap.

She was comely, with wild red hair and freckles that dusted her face, she had deep brown eyes and a wide, welcoming mouth. Madden, however, took after his father entirely. Dark hair and eyes that burned like fire.

It made Estildris' heart ache.

'Your Majesty,' Augusta said bowing, Estildris and Thea curtsied.

Gwendolen smiled briefly. 'My ladies. How are we today?'

'Well. And you?'

'I wish I could say the same,' Gwendolen said, she ran a hand over Madden's head as he proudly held up the piece of string, now a mess of knots. 'Brutus is dying.'

Estildris let out a gasp, but neither Augusta nor Thea seemed surprised. Felix Brutus had many names, each inspiring more awe than the next; Brutus of Troy, the Conqueror King, Brutus the Godsblood. He was a man who had lived his life and gone on to live several more. People had often guessed at how old the Great King was, though no one knew for certain. Gwendolen's own father, Corineus, supposed that he was two hundred when the two men had met. Yet Corineus had still died before him.

'I do not think he will live to see the next summer,' Gwendolen said. 'Whatever power that was keeping him alive... seems to be dwindling.'

'I'm sorry for your loss,' Estildris said.

Gwendolen grimaced. 'It is not my loss we should be mourning. His death is not why I called you here.'

'I thought you called us to prepare for the Modraniht?' Estildris whispered.

Gwendolen shook her head. 'That's what I need you to say when you leave here,' she took a deep breath. 'When Brutus dies, Locrinus will no longer have a reason to stay married to me, with both our father's dead there is no bargain left to uphold. I think he will want me gone as soon as possible. But while my father may be dead, his people are not, they will revolt. There will be war.'

It was no secret that there was little love between the king and his queen. They had been fond of each other, once, a long time ago. Though that time had long since passed. Madden was all they shared now. Sometimes Estildris wondered how they had even brought him into this world. So distant were they in both body and spirit.

'What of Madden?' Augusta asked, her voice once again taking on a deep, feral growl.

'Locrinus will want him,' Gwendolen said simply. 'He is the heir. But he is my son, and by the gods I swear he shall not have him. Not without me standing by his side. I believe... I believe he has already started making plans to remove me.'

Estildris' eyes widened; she could feel a flush of heat beneath her cheeks. 'That can't be possible,' she said quickly. 'What makes you think that?'

Gwendolen didn't look at her, instead her eyes were boring into Augusta. 'Osric tells me that Algar has been disappearing for days at a time. Is this true?'

'Yes, Your Majesty. We think he's recruiting for the king's army.'

Gwendolen stood, lifting Madden on to the floor where he continued to play happily with the string. 'Then we must start to do the same,' she murmured.

'The same?' Estildris repeated. 'You can't be planning on waging a war!'

'No,' Gwendolen said calmly. 'I plan on winning one.'

Estildris gaped at her, then looked to Augusta and Thea. Augusta had a steely glint in her eye and her jaw was set as though ready for a fight, while Thea looked supremely unperturbed by the news. Only Estildris was aghast. Only Estildris was afraid.

Gwendolen was a solemn creature by nature, she was sincere in her kindness and serious in everything else. She believed to be queen was a privilege as well as a task. Her marriage to the king had unified the lands, and she intended to keep them unified for as long as she lived.

'Don't worry, my friend,' Gwendolen said. 'There will be no battle tonight. Tonight, we feast and drink. And when the time does come to fight, I know where you each will stand'

'In this life and the next,' Augusta whispered ferociously.

'In this life and the next,' said Thea.

'In this life and the next,' said Estildris, but the words burned her throat and the lie felt hot on her tongue.

One more promise she would have to break.

Chapter Thirty-Two

MIDNIGHT MODRANIHT

Woods and open fields, stars and night and campfires, laughter, food and love.

This was the Modraniht: The Mother's Night.

It was a night of celebration, to thank the past year and greet the new. There was singing and dancing, as men and women drank and offered sacrifices to the gods. It was Estildris' third Modraniht in Loegria, though she had attended many at home in Germania. It was much the same, people dressed in their finery, townsfolk and castle-folk alike dancing under a sparkling night as the fires crackled.

Estildris sat on a log next to one of the smaller fires with Thea and watched as Gwendolen showed Madden the crows' feet that hung from the nearest tree. They had been placed there earlier in the day, to ward off any evil spirit that might be tempted by the festivities. Together they watched as farmers brought in animals to be sacrificed to the gods, and animals that were to be cooked on the fire. She spotted Algar and Osric sharing a drink together, no doubt using Modraniht to lessen the rivalry between them. Some couples had retreated to the bushes, to whisper and worship the gods in other ways.

Thea had worn a deep purple tunic to match the amethyst around her neck and had painted the rune for Modraniht on her cheek. She stared into the crowd intently.

'What are you searching for?' Estildris asked.

'To see if any of the folk have come to play,' she answered.

Estildris chortled. 'I doubt any of the fae will be here.'

Thea raised an eyebrow. 'Do not be so sure.'

It was Estildris' turn to look sceptical. It was said that the folk came out at night and disappeared at dawn, preferring the woods and wilder places.

'Have you ever seen one?'

'Once,' Thea said. 'When I was a child.'

She spoke with a tone that invited no follow up question and Estildris wondered, not for the first time, where Thea the Witch had come from. Everyone knew the tale of how Augusta had arrived, she'd rode to the castle holding the head of a man named Eadwulf, a warrior who had been raiding on Locrinus' land. She had asked to be accepted into the king's service, but he had denied her.

The queen however, had welcomed her with open arms and Augusta had served her faithfully ever since. Thea however... Thea had by all accounts, simply appeared. No one knew when she had arrived or where she had arrived from.

Estildris gave an involuntary shiver and then abruptly changed the subject. 'Where is Gwendolen's pet tonight?'

Thea tutted at the use of the warrior's nickname. 'Augusta is out hunting; the kitchens will need to be restocked by morning.'

Estildris nodded and the two women fell silent. She had just reverted her gaze back to watching Gwendolen playing with her son, when a small girl tugged on her skirt. Estildris looked to her, alarmed, and the young girl pressed something small and soft into her palm.

'By the river,' she whispered, and then she scarpered off.

Her skin humming, Estildris glanced around and saw that Algar had disappeared too, Osric was sitting with a different soldier now. She unfurled her fingers to see a little yellow flower sitting in her palm.

It was his flower.

His summoning.

'Do you know what the common folk call that flower?' Thea asked softly, peering over her shoulder.

Estildris had the sudden urge to throw it away, but what would be the point? She had seen it now. She shook her head.

'See how like gold its petals are? See how they curl into a crown?' Thea almost murmured the words as she ran a delicate finger over one of the petals. 'They call these flowers the kingcup.'

Thea looked up and their eyes met. Estildris' breathing quickened and she felt the cold wind of winter a little more keenly.

'I need to go get some water,' Estildris said, unable to stand the tension any longer. 'Do you want anything?'

Thea shook her head and Estildris turned on her heel and left.

She walked past the revellers and soldiers, past many a fire and dance until she reached the woods. The woods that her kept her secret for over three years now. She took a deep, icy breath and stepped into the shadow of the trees and kept walking until Wighus Hall and its festivities were nothing but a faint noise behind her. She wound herself through the twisted trees and scraggly overgrowth, it was dark, but her feet knew the way. It was a path that had been made for her after all.

She felt almost as though she were fae herself, a creature of the night, tempted by the promise of something beautiful.

When she reached the clearing, she saw him standing by the river. It was a different river to the one that they had first met at, it was a river with no name, but it felt as though it were theirs, as though they had claimed it.

He stood with his hands behind his back, poised and looking up at the sky. Somehow the starlight seemed to touch him, illuminate him even.

All the secrecy and all the lies were made meaningless in the moments that she found him waiting for her.

For her, for her, for her.

The king looked over his shoulder and their eyes met.

'Algar,' he said. 'You may leave us.'

There was a rustle from further along the clearing, and then silence.

They were alone.

When they kissed it was like tasting sweetness and sin all at once. It was excitement and tenderness, it was forbidden and traitorous and she always, always wanted more.

She pulled apart from him. 'My Lord,' she said.

He smiled at her. 'My Lady.'

She took a deep breath. This was the moment; this was what she had been praying for in the weoh early that morning. Her future depended on what happened next.

'Locrinus, my love,' her voice sounded timid, even to her. She hoped she wasn't overdoing it. 'I have some news for you.'

The king raised an eyebrow mischievously. 'Oh?'

She had to get this right. Locrinus liked her strong but gentle, she needed to be sure of herself yet vulnerable enough that he'd want to protect her. She looked to the ground, then up at him.

'I didn't want to say anything until I was certain. But I'm certain now,' she spoke the words in a rush and then paused as though searching for the next sentence. 'I carry your child.'

She had played the scene over and over in her mind the past few days. How to tell him and how he would react. She expected shock, she expected to have to coo him into calmness but as she watched him, she was astonished to see his face crack into a glorious smile.

'Thank the gods, this is good news!' he exclaimed in a breath. 'How far along?'

'Two moons,' she gushed. This was playing out better than

she ever hoped to dream. 'Are you happy my king? Tell me you're pleased.'

'I'm pleased,' he whispered, and then he pulled her to his chest. His arms wrapped around her; his lips pressed against her head.

Minutes passed and they stayed that way.

'Do you have a plan for what happens next?' Estildris asked, when she couldn't hold the question back any longer.

'What would you have me do, my love?'

'You have one of two choices, Your Majesty,' Estildris said, pulling away slightly. 'My king...'

Locrinus bent his head low so that it was touching hers.

'Tell me,' he said quietly, the smile still on his lips.

Estildris let out a shaky breath. This was the moment that she had wanted and feared. This was the moment when she had to make a choice between king or queen.

Although, if she was being truthful with herself, it was a choice she had made years ago. His answer was all that mattered now.

'You can send me away. Somewhere where we can't be found, somewhere where the child and I will be safe. And you can forget—' she paused.

Locrinus stared at her, unblinking. His face a mask of stone. 'And the other choice?'

Estildris forced herself to look into his eyes, to let herself be uncowed. 'Make me your queen,' she breathed.

Locrinus' eyes bored brightly into hers, but his expression did not change.

'Why do you think I have been raising my army?' he asked her quietly, dangerously. 'What do you think I intend to do once my father passed?'

Estildris' breath hitched in her throat. 'You mean you always planned...?'

Locrinus grinned and held her chin in his hands. 'You are my woman, and soon everyone will know it. Gwendolen can go back to Cornwall; she has served her purpose and she will be kept well enough. But I cannot bear to see her miserable face here any longer. I want you.'

A pang of guilt flooded through her at the same time she felt a thrill run across her spine. He wanted her. She would be queen; her child recognised.

And Gwendolen... Gwendolen could go back to her people. She preferred it there anyway; Hadn't she always said she wished to return? If anything, this could be the best outcome, for all of them.

She thought back to Madden playing with his piece of string.

'What about Madden?' she asked. 'What happens to him?'

Locrinus looked at her, his eyes narrowing. 'He is my son. He stays with me.'

Estildris could feel her heart beating faster again. 'Gwendolen will not let you take him. She knows you're planning something. She will fight.'

Locrinus let out a rich, warm laugh. 'She is as likely to lead an army as I am to sew a dress.' He placed a hand on her stomach. 'Don't worry, my love, all will be well. Your only concern is with keeping the babe safe and healthy. Can you do that?'

She beamed at him. 'Of course.'

AFTER THEY PARTED, *she wandered back through the crowds of people until she found the main pyre where Brutus sat in a chair, his withered body rigid and his golden eyes staring blankly into the flames. He had been cocooned in blankets, and yet he still shivered.*

Estildris could not believe how much the old man had aged in the span of just a few short months. Less than a year ago he could stand and walk and laugh. He had appeared old but not ancient, and there had still been something of a strength to him. Now, it seemed all the years had caught up to him all at once, and they were weighing him down.

She bent down and placed a hand on his.

'Whatever magic is keeping you here,' she whispered. 'Let it go. Locrinus and Camber can rule these lands without you, you raised them well.'

For a brief second, his eyes flickered from the fire to look at her. Then his gaze went back to the flames and it was as though he hadn't seen her at all.

She stood up and regarded him more carefully. His skin was still bronzed though covered in wrinkles, his silver hair hung long and loose over his shoulders, and his beard was thick and wiry. He wore no crown on his head, having passed his lands to his three sons, Locrinus, Camber and Albanactus, many years before.

He was just an old man, if there was anything of the gods in him still, it was only in his eyes.

'It is sad to see him like this, is it not?'a voice said behind her.

Estildris turned around to see Gwendolen standing there, Madden resting sleepily on her hip.

'Yes,' Estildris replied. 'Yes, it is.'

'He seems to have aged fifty years in the space of three. And yet he stayed the same for so long, I think a part of us all believed he would live forever. He has outlived so many.'

Estildris nodded thoughtfully. 'He outlived your father, did he not?'

Gwendolen smiled ruefully. 'Yes, and all three of his own wives. People kept ageing but Brutus stayed the same, until he did not.'

'Do you miss him?' Estildris asked. 'Your father.'

'Yes,' Gwendolen said. 'Do you miss yours?'

'Dreadfully,' Estildris said. 'I miss how he used to tell me stories. He would be so envious if he knew I had met the great and terrible Brutus.'

Gwendolen smiled softly. 'I miss seeing my father in his hall at Cornwall. His men loved him dearly. I used to think I would be happy, if I could marry a man that inspired the same trust... the same love.'

The words hung in the air, but it was the words that the queen didn't say that held Estildris in place. That she had married such a man, and that she was not happy.

Gwendolen smoothed over the hair on Madden's head and made to walk away.

The question left Estildris' lips before her mind was aware of what she was asking. 'Did you ever love him?'

Gwendolen turned to face her, a curious expression on her face. 'I liked him for a long while. But did I love him?' She paused thoughtfully. 'No. I do not suppose I did. Goodnight Lady Estildris.'

Estildris watched as the queen and her son made their way back to the castle. 'I'm sorry,' she whispered into the wind, to Gwendolen's distant figure. 'I really, really am.'

And a big part of her wasn't lying.

Chapter Thirty-Three
A WITCH'S PROMISE

LOEGRIA (England) 1014 BC

The hardest part of keeping a secret is knowing that at any point it can be revealed. Estildris knew that she was running out of time. The secret she was keeping could not and would not be hidden for much longer. Her belly was starting to swell, and soon, no number of layers and oversized tunics would be able to hide the truth.

Still, Brutus would not die.

She almost dared asking Locrinus to break his oath while his father was still breathing. But she knew he would not. Brutus and Corineus had arranged Locrinus and Gwendolen's marriage between them, and it was only when they both passed that their arrangement could end.

It was a morbid thing, to pray for someone else's death. Estildris tried not to ponder on the matter too much, and instead started confining herself to her own chambers, feigning sickness and weak spirit.

Locrinus would visit her every night, as the sun began to set. He would bring her hot rolls and warm milk, sweet apples and juicy plums. He would kiss her on the head and promise her such wonderful things: one day he would show her the caves where water spirit's lived; one day he would bring her dresses woven out of spider's-silk, one day he would place a crown of roses and thistles atop her head and the people would love her for it.

Then he would leave, and she would be alone.

ESTILDRIS WATCHED AS *the door swung to a close and lay back on her bed.*

She felt the same pang of disappointment every time Locrinus left, the same desperate want for him to stay. She knew it was foolish, she knew that they dare not be open. Not yet.

The scent of him always lingered behind though, sweet and musky, sweat and brimstone.

There was a knock on the door, eagerly the lady sat up. 'Come in!'

The door creaked open and the witch stepped inside. Estildris pulled the blanket around her and smiled as brightly as she could.

'Thea! I was not expecting you.'

Thea walked past Estildris so that she stood looking out of the window. It was as though she could not bring herself to look Estildris in the eye. She had new runes painted on her forehead, though Estildris did not know what they meant. Her hair had grown since she had last seen her, no doubt she would shave it again soon.

'You cannot feign sickness forever, Lady,' she said, calmly. 'The queen will soon find out.'

A lump rose in Estildris' throat and a coldness spread across her chest.

'What...' She paused mid-sentence, blinking rapidly. She wanted to appear confused, she needed her illusion of innocence to remain intact. She frowned, as though puzzled. 'Thea, I don't understand,' she said. 'Are you upset with me?'

At this, Thea spun around. Estildris had never seen the witch angry before, but it was a rather terrifying sight. Her nostrils flared and her grey eyes seemed to hold a storm inside them.

'Yes, I am! The queen welcomed you into her court and this is how you repay her?' She glanced at the door, ensuring that no one was listening before lowering her voice to a whisper. 'Did you really think you could become mistress to the king and have nobody know about it?'

Mistress.

Oh, how she hated that word. Hadn't she promised herself to Locrinus before even meeting the queen? Was she not a princess in her own right? As far as she was concerned, mistress was a title that belonged to somebody else.

And still... she felt as though a large rock had been lifted from her chest. For years, she had walked these halls with a secret pressing against her heart, now she could breathe.

'When a king wants you, you daren't deny him,' she said carefully, but even as the words left her lips, she knew that Thea would not be satisfied. Thea, who had the singular talent of looking at Estildris and tugging every stray thought from her head.

'Did he find you, or did you seek him?' the witch asked, an icy tone to her voice.

Estildris found she did not have the nerve or the desire to lie. 'Both.'

Thea closed her eyes and leaned her head back, a small sigh escaping her lips. The cat, which Estildris hadn't even noticed come in, let out a small hiss from behind her skirts.

'How long until the babe is born?' she asked, her eyes still closed.

'Am I really showing that badly?'

Thea opened her eyes, and Estildris knew she was not imagining the disappointment in them. 'I have known for a while now.'

Estildris let out a disbelieving laugh. 'How?'

Thea scooped up the cat from the floor and scratched the top of its head. 'I told you that day in the weoh, I sensed it around you. Change.'

Estildris allowed the information to sink in. 'You really are a witch.'

The smallest of smiles tickled at the corner of Thea's mouth. 'So-they-say. How much longer do you think you have?'

Estildris let the blanket fall away. 'Five moons, at most.'

Thea nodded slowly while the cat watched her unblinkingly with its bright blue eyes. 'Then you have five moons to get away.'

Estildris tilted her head to the side. 'And you'll give me those five moons, will you? You won't tell Gwendolen?'

Thea put the cat gently back on the floor and made her way back towards the door. In the corner of the room the candles were beginning to wilt and the night crept further in.

'I won't tell her. But if she asks me directly, I will not lie.'

Estildris bit her lip thoughtfully. She had no intention of leaving, but five moons of silence was an offer she couldn't refuse.

'Promise?'

Thea looked away from her and said in a voice so quiet that Estildris could barely hear; 'I promise.'

She opened the door and was just about to leave when Estildris stood up. 'Wait!'

She waltzed over to the witch's side so that they stood level with one another. She regarded Thea carefully; her round pale face and watery grey eyes, the runes that were painted onto her head and cheeks, the mousy-brown hair that was cut so short she appeared almost boy-like.

'Why are you helping me?'

Thea stared back at her, her face and runes illuminated orange from the candlelight. The intensity of her gaze forceful *enough for Estildris to take a step back.*

'I think you know,' Thea whispered.

And Estildris, who had spent her entire life performing to one man or another, who knew how to use her face like a painting and her body like an instrument, who knew exactly how to interpret another person's movements and how to exercise her own, was startled to discover that she did.

Chapter Thirty-Four

A PROMISE MADE
IS A PROMISE KEPT

'*It won't be long now.' Gwendolen's voice was sure and crisp. From her position behind the door, Estildris held her breath and waited. She had been summoned, ordered by the queen's messenger to make her way to Gwendolen's chambers. She knew why.*

Her condition was no longer a secret, and the rumours were spreading like wildfire. She had considered not answering the queen's summons. Of ignoring it and taking refuge with the king, putting a stop to the rumours for good. But even as she had toyed with the idea, she'd felt a stab of guilt.

This was a conversation that could no longer be avoided—she owed Gwendolen at least this small courtesy.

Yet, when she found herself standing outside Gwendolen's chambers, she could see not one, but two figures through the crack in the door: Gwendolen and her pet knight, Augusta.

For a terrifying moment Estildris wondered whether Gwendolen had called for her only to have her executed on the spot. Augusta would undoubtedly do it, had she not once told her that she would do anything for her queen?

So, she hid behind the door, frozen in fear, and listened intently.

Augusta's rough voice carried across the room, though Estildris could only see her back. 'Your Majesty?'

'Brutus' death. Thea told me it would happen before sunrise.'

Estildris could just about see Gwendolen's outline, sitting on a large chair in the corner of the room.

'Thea is rarely ever wrong,' Augusta said. 'Locrinus will not waste time in trying to remove you, and then—'

Gwendolen made a gesture that Estildris could not quite see. A few moments passed before she spoke again.

'You have always been loyal to me Augusta. It pains me to ask you to push your loyalty further.'

'Anything,' Augusta said, and her voice was so low and so smooth that Estildris found herself pressing her ear against the door.

'I need a warrior to lead my army. I can think of no one I trust more than you.'

'I would be honoured, Your Majesty,' Augusta said, and indeed it sounded as though her voice might crack from strain of emotion. 'But the men, they will not follow a woman.'

'They will follow me.'

'You're their queen. I'm just... they think of me as an abomination.'

There was silence again, and so Estildris peered back through the crack in the door to witness the moment that Gwendolen cupped Augusta's face in her hands.

'Augusta,' she whispered. 'You are my sword.'

Slowly, uncertainly, Augusta bent down on one knee, and plunged her sword into the stone floor in front of her, then she curled her hand around the blade and tightened her grip.

Blood squeezed from between her fingers and trickled down the silver edge of the blade, but if she felt any pain, she did not show it.

'I, Augusta of Blackhedge, promise to be true and faithful to you, Queen Gwendolen of Loegria, Daughter of Corineus and Ruler of the Britons,' she said. The growl had gone from her voice and instead there was a strangled waver to her words. Estildris suspected that the tall woman might be crying.

'I promise to love all which you love and shun all that you shun, according to the law of the gods and the order of the world. Nor will I ever with Will or action, through word or deed, do anything which is unpleasing to you. I swear to let no harm befall you while you are under my protection, and to follow you wherever you may lead me... In this life and the next.'

Gwendolen nodded and lifted the bloodied sword from the ground and lifted it so that it rested delicately on Augusta's shoulder.

'I, Gwendolen of Cornwall, accept your pledge and promise that you will always have my confidence. That I shall ask nothing of you that is unworthy or deemed evil in the eyes of the gods. You submit yourself to me and I will strive every day to be worthy of that honour.   This I swear by all the gods that ever were or ever will be,' Gwendolen paused, as though certain that she was missing something. Then she smiled wryly. 'You may rise.'

Augusta did.

'I have said the words, but I would like you to know that you are not just my warrior. You are also my friend.'

And then, to Estildris' disbelief, Gwendolen hugged her. It was a brief hug, lasting barely more than a moment, but Estildris knew exactly how much the gesture was worth and was certain that Augusta did too. A coldness washed over Estildris' skin and there was a gnawing in her heart. An ache that whispered of jealousy and regret.

Augusta shoved her sword gracelessly back into its sheath. 'What happens next?'

Gwendolen sat back into her chair so that she was once again directly facing the door.

'I'm not sure, but I rather think we should find out. Augusta, would you do me the favour of opening the door and asking

Estildris exactly what she thought she was accomplishing when she started lying with my husband?'

Augusta spun around before Estildris had fully digested the words that had been said. The warrior's expression had twisted into something malicious and horrible, Estildris jumped back from the door just as Augusta wrenched it open.

She could see the room in full light now, it had a large table pushed to the side, a grand tapestry that hung at the back of the room, a spinning wheel, one long window and a chair so large that it almost constituted a throne.

Estildris let her eyes rest on Gwendolen as she walked further into the room. She could feel the burning of both their stares as she made her way to the centre. She stood there silently, wishing that she'd worn something looser, something that might better hide the now obvious bulge of her belly.

'How long have you known?' Estildris finally asked when the quiet became too much.

'Always,' Gwendolen replied, leaning backwards in her chair. 'Since you first arrived here. I mistakenly thought that once you came to know me, you might reconsider your intentions.'

Estildris looked from Augusta to Gwendolen. It was clear what Augusta thought of her, disdain distorted every part of her scarred face, her lips so thin and pulled so far back into a sneer that they had almost disappeared completely. Yet Gwendolen... Gwendolen showed no hatred. Only hurt.

Estildris didn't know what she could say. Explanations were worthless, and her apologies insincere.

'Perhaps you underestimated me,' she finally said. From behind Gwendolen, Augusta let out a snort of disgust.

Gwendolen ran a hand over the ends of her red hair, her expression thoughtful.

'Or perhaps I overestimated you. For a while there, I truly believed we were friends.'

Estildris opened her mouth, closed it again and then bit her lip. Her palms were sweating, and she was finding it increasingly difficult to look the queen in the eye. She had never found it within her to hate Gwendolen, though she'd known that it would make her deceit much easier. Gwendolen had made the hours when Locrinus had not been there bearable. She had given her a place, given her friends, had made the castle her home. And to repay her kindness, Estildris had torn it all down.

'We were,' she said quietly.

Gwendolen nodded slowly and delicately brushed a finger under one of her eyes. She sat up a little straighter.

'A pity then, that it must come to this.'

'It doesn't have to,' Estildris said. 'Locrinus doesn't wish for war, you will have everything you could possibly ask for in Cornwall.'

Gwendolen laughed bitterly. 'Everything except my son.'

Estildris didn't argue. Locrinus would keep Madden, he was his heir, his eldest son. If Gwendolen was going to return to her father's people, she would be doing so alone.

'I am sorry,' Estildris whispered.

But whatever melancholy the queen had been feeling only moments before had now evaporated. Estildris looked up at the queen and saw only steely determination.

'I wish to make something very clear to you, Lady Estildris. I no longer care for you, and I certainly do not care for him; the only life that I care for is my child's.'

'What are you saying?' Estildris said slowly.

'I will have the rivers run red and turn this castle to ruin, before I let that man steal my child from me. There cannot be two queens sitting on one throne,' Gwendolen took a deep breath before continuing. 'So, there is only one way that this can end, in either my death or yours. The witch seems to think it will be soon.' She spoke so calmly, so simply.

In truth, Estildris had never even considered that she might die, the notion seemed absurd to her. 'I don't understand, why are you telling me this?' Estildris asked, her voice softer now, less certain.

Gwendolen stared directly at her, fierce and unblinking. 'I want to ensure that in the event of my passing, that my son lives and is cared for. That you will not belittle him in favour of your own. In return I make the same promise to you. That if I am to live your child will be kept safe and cared for. A mother's promise if you will, from one mother to another.'

Estildris did not think anything was likely to happen to Madden in the event of Gwendolen's death. But then, she had never truly thought that Gwendolen would be killed, she hadn't truly believed that the young queen would choose to fight.

And if Estildris were to die... No, it was ludicrous. She had survived too much to be killed now, besides, she had the love of a king on her side.

Still, Gwendolen had been good to her. She could at least assure her that Madden would be looked after. She could give her that gift.

Estildris nodded. 'That seems... fair.'

Gwendolen let out a short, quick breath of relief and Estildris suddenly realised how desperate Gwendolen had been for that answer.

The queen straightened her back, and all expression was wiped from her face once more. 'Then we have an agreement,' she said.

'We do.'

Gwendolen paused and rubbed a hand over her face. Estildris could see that the young queen was tired, yet still she remained composed, her thin silver crown sat perfectly atop her head and not a hair out of place. She narrowed her eyes at Estildris, as though deciding something. 'Answer me honestly,' Gwendolen said quietly. 'Do you love him?'

The question startled Estildris. She wondered if maybe it were a test, and then decided that it didn't matter. She thought back to when she had first met the king all those years ago at the edge of a river in Albany. She thought of yellow flowers and midnight kisses, of his deep booming laugh and the child growing inside her.

'Yes,' she answered.

'Well, at least that is something,' Gwendolen murmured, she turned to Augusta. 'Get her out of my sight.'

'With pleasure,' she snarled, and then Augusta took Estildris roughly by the arm and hauled her out of the room.

IN THE EARLY *hours of the morning before the sun had dragged itself into the sky, the great King Brutus took his last, tired breath. Gwendolen did not wait for the morning birds to sing their first song before she fled. Underneath the cover of darkness, she abandoned both the castle and its king, but she did not go alone. Her son, Madden, was with her, as well as several warriors of notoriety.*

The brute Augusta and the golden-haired Osric were but a few of the carefully chosen that Gwendolen had whisked away.

Thea the Witch had also disappeared, and in the days that followed it was Thea's absence that was found most disconcerting. There were whispers that Thea was using magic to support Gwendolen's cause and that she had been instrumental in Brutus' death. It was rumoured that she had cast a terrible curse on the king and his new queen. It was said that when Thea left the castle, she had taken the God's and their favour with her.

Chapter Thirty-Five

A THREAT TO ALL THE WORLDS

Rain slapped against the castle's walls. The sound echoed through corridors and water leaked in drops from cracks in the ceilings.

Estildris sat at the far end of the Great Hall, there was a puddle on the floor a few feet to the side of the throne, and she watched as droplet after droplet landed into it, causing small ripples to spill out. In the centre of the room, Locrinus' council spoke in deep and urgent tones.

'Gwendolen has raised quite an army. She has all her father's people on her side, and some of our own have even defected,' a voice said.

'What right does she have?' Locrinus growled. 'This was always my land. It was never hers to claim!'

'She fights for her son's throne. She claims that he will be usurped if you are to have another son.'

Estildris did not pull her gaze away from the puddle of water. She knew that the council would be stealing glances at her, even as they spoke. Her stomach was so very round now, and the babe moved as though agitated inside her. She was running out of time.

'I feel as though I should warn you, your Highness,' Algar's voice was a loud rasp that carried across the room. 'Gwendolen's people have been roaming across the borderlands, spreading rumours about our new queen.'

At this Estildris finally turned her gaze to the men. There were twelve of them, in armour and sitting at a long, rectangular wooden table. Locrinus sat at the head of the table, while Algar sat to his right. There were other familiar faces, though Estildris had not heeded much attention to them before and did not know their names.

'What kind of rumours?' Estildris asked, her voice ice.

Algar looked up at her, and then nervously back to the king who, after a pause, nodded for him to continue.

'They have been saying that you were with child when Gwendolen was still queen. That your marriage angers the gods and your child has no claim to the throne.'

Estildris blinked rapidly.

In other words, Gwendolen was claiming her child to be a bastard.

Estildris regained her composure and smiled sweetly. 'Of course, my child will not be king. Madden is the eldest. Madden is the heir.'

Locrinus' eyes met hers and he smiled. 'Gwendolen is just trying to stir up as much trouble as she can before the battle. It is a strategy, that is all.'

An older man who sat halfway down the table let out a scoff. 'As a strategy it is excellent. More and more men are joining her army every day,' he shot Estildris a filthy stare. 'My Lord, if you were to just accept Gwendolen back, this could all be forgotten. There would be no war, and Madden could return to his rightful place by your side.'

Locrinus did not spare a glance to the man. 'I am aware of your opinion Cuthbert.' He looked to Algar. 'How far is she from our border?'

'Less than two days away,' the warrior replied quickly. 'Perhaps sooner, if the rain slows.'

'Then we must meet her by the river, before she crosses,' Locrinus said.

Cuthbert leaned forward in his seat. 'This is ridiculous! Her Majesty is a reasonable woman, I'm sure if you were to speak with her—'

At this Locrinus stood up, the fire that always simmered behind his eyes was now scorching. He turned his gaze on Cuthbert and the old man seemed to shrink in size beneath his stare.

'There is but one queen, and her name is Estildris.' His voice was so deep and powerful, that Estildris felt the air quiver with his rage.

Locrinus and his brothers, they are descendants of gods...

She smiled to herself as Cuthbert began to whimper and mumble his apologies. Locrinus ignored him once more and instead turned to Algar.

'Ready the men and horses, we leave before night falls. If the woman wants a battle, then by gods we shall give her one.'

Algar, Cuthbert and the rest of the council bowed, then they were gone.

Estildris waited until she was certain they were alone to make her way to Locrinus. She stood in front of him and placed her hands on either side of his face.

'You cannot fight,' she whispered. 'We finally have each other. I'm not ready to lose you just yet.'

The king remained stoic, unchangeable. 'I must. You know I must.'

'You mustn't do anything. Who makes the rules if not you?'

Locrinus let out a mirthless laugh. 'What kind of king cowers behind the walls of his castle? What kind of king will not fight for his own throne?'

She remained standing straight. 'Better a cowardly king, than a dead one.'

Locrinus sighed and pulled her close; one hand tangled in her hair, the other wrapped fiercely around her waist. 'I have to go.'

Estildris lifted her head and brushed her lips against his, then in a moment of desperation she bit down on his bottom lip. Locrinus let out a soft groan into her mouth and she bit down harder, until she tasted the warm salt of his blood on the tip of her tongue.

'Promise you will come back to me,' she murmured, her head swimming.

'I promise,' he said in a low voice, his lips pressed against her neck.

Estildris shook her head and let out a small laugh. 'I need more convincing than that.'

Locrinus pulled away from her so that they were facing one another.

'I promise you,' he whispered, and she felt the warmth of his breath on her face, 'that I will travel across all the realms and all the worlds to come back to you. If all the worlds were to be destroyed, I would build a new one, just so that our souls could meet again. And if Gwendolen is to be the destruction to our happiness, then I will come back for her too.'

It was only words. But words said with intensity, honesty and violence; a silent weight upon each syllable. It was not only a promise, but a threat he intended to keep. Estildris looked into his eyes, into the golden fire that burned there. Locrinus' eyes were the only part of him that hinted at his heritage, a constant reminder that Godsblood ran through his veins. Blood that was now smeared at the corner of his mouth.

She felt as though something in the air had shifted in that single moment; an agreement with the universe had been struck.

His sombre expression melted away and he smiled at her. 'Satisfied?'

Estildris tilted her head back and smiled. 'Only barely.'

He lifted her chin further up and pressed his mouth softly against her neck.

'Return to me,' she breathed, both a demand and a plea.

'I will.'

And she was released from his grip, suddenly and unceremoniously. Her last image of him was of his shadow leaving the room.

That night, as Locrinus went to war, their child was born.

Chapter Thirty-Six

A BEAUTIFUL DAY
FOR DROWNING

It was said that he died by the river, by Augusta's blade. Others say he was drowned in it; the tall woman having pushed him under.

Some stories claimed that she strangled him with his own crown. Estildris heard every grim story of how her king had died, had been told every gruesome version and only two details ever stayed the same: That Locrinus, son of a Conqueror and descendant of gods, was dead, and that Gwendolen's pet, Augusta the she-wolf, as they were now calling her, had taken his life.

Taken *his life.*

As though it had been there for the taking, easily grasped. When really, she had stolen it. Snatched it away like some hungry, bloodthirsty beast. Leaving Estildris without her love, her daughter without a father, and the country without its king.

Estildris paced her old chamber, the irony of being returned to her old quarters was not lost on her. She thought that Gwendolen had done it deliberately, to put her back in her rightful place, to remind Estildris of her betrayal. It did once occur to her that Gwendolen had placed her there rather than the dungeons for her own comfort, but she had quickly cast the thought aside.

Estildris had never been able to hate Gwendolen before, but she hated her now. She hated her with such a passion that she found there was not enough venom in the word alone. It was hatred larger than the word could ever describe, it consumed her, ate at her soul.

She screamed into the room, releasing as much rage, and bitterness as she could into the emptiness. As if hearing her shriek, the door opened.

'Gwendolen did warn you,' Thea whispered sadly. Her small frame filled only but a portion of the doorway.

It did not escape her notice that Thea held a child in her arms, and yet Estildris' eyes went past Thea and her daughter and straight to the lean, tall figure lingering behind her.

'How dare you,' she hissed. 'How dare you bring her near me.'

'I was not permitted to come alone,' Thea said calmly.

Estildris regarded Thea and Augusta carefully. To her satisfaction they both appeared tired. Augusta's neck and face were covered with bruises and slashes, and even Thea had a deep cut that ran across her left eyebrow, Estildris suspected that it might even scar. But as Estildris stared at them, she noticed the tall woman staring back.

'How can you look at me?' Estildris spat at Augusta. 'How can you face me? You ugly creature, you unnatural thing!' She wished for her words to be like knives and cut the warrior deep. Yet Augusta merely stood there, her expression indifferent.

'How could you do it?' she asked finally. 'He was your king.'

The merest flicker of anger passed across the warrior's face. 'And Gwendolen is my queen.' She spoke the words softly, no trace of the usual growl in her voice. 'The true queen.'

Estildris fell to the floor, exhausted. 'Get her out of here,' she said to Thea.

Thea nodded to Augusta. The warrior narrowed her eyes.

'I'll be on the other side of the door.'

As soon as it was closed Thea stepped further inside, the black cat that was like her shadow creeping close to her feet. Estildris reached urgently for her child. The feel of her against her breast was simultaneously the greatest happiness she had ever felt and the worst sorrow. To hold her one last time, she knew, was an act of mercy, but it would never, ever be long enough.

She pressed her nose to her tiny head and breathed in her smell. The scent of your own child's head, she thought, was the scent of love.

'Habren is a lovely name,' Thea said, after what seemed like hours. Estildris sniffed. It was a lovely name, a name her child would not get to keep.

'What will happen to her?' she finally asked.

Thea crouched down beside her, there was pity in her eyes but when she spoke her voice was emotionless.

'Queen Gwendolen has found a suitable family for her close to the Northern border of Loegria. They are wealthy and unable to have children of their own. She will live a good life there.'

Estildris nodded, a tear falling onto Habren's blanket.

'The princess will have to be believed to be dead,' Thea went on. 'The queen has arranged it so that a stillborn from the village will be drowned in her place. No one will look for her, she will be safe.'

Estildris nodded again; it was all she could manage. She was grateful, despite herself, for the promise she and Gwendolen had made to one another only a few short months before. If people believed Habren dead then no one would ever look for her, she would never be used as a pawn against her brother. She would be safe.

'No one can ever know,' she agreed.

Thea's lip tightened. 'There is one other detail,' she said slowly. 'Gwendolen plans on naming the river after Habren.'

Estildris let out a cold laugh. She had to marvel at the calculating mind of the woman. The river would act as both a statement and a warning. By naming it after Habren, the river would serve as a constant reminder to the people of Loegria that the princess was dead, and that only one true heir survived.

Estildris closed her eyes and pressed her lips against her daughter's head. All the while Thea watched her unblinkingly, then she looked to the door and turned back to face her.

'Is there anything else I should know?' Thea asked quietly, so quietly that Estildris almost did not hear.

Estildris frowned, puzzled.

Thea's voice went even lower. 'I was there the moment the king's soul left his body, and do you know what I sensed?'

Estildris frowned and shook her head.

'Magic,' she said, her voice caressing the word as though it were made of honey. Beside her, the cat purred, and Estildris had the bizarre notion that the cat understood exactly what Thea had said. 'You wouldn't happen to know anything about that, would you?'

Estildris thought back to the last words Locrinus had spoken to her, and how impossible his promise had been. But then, he himself had been impossible.

'No,' she lied.

Thea's eyes narrowed and Estildris once again had the unsettling feeling that the witch already knew exactly what Locrinus had said.

A harsh knock on the door pulled her from her thoughts.

Thea stood up. 'It is time.'

Estildris pulled Habren close to her, and knew no matter how long or close she held her, it would never be long enough to say goodbye.

'I love you so much.'

But Habren would never know that, she would never know

her mother or who she was. She would be a different person, with a different family, living a different life.

'You are a princess,' Estildris murmured, her vision blurring. 'You are my princess.'

She watched as Thea took her child from her arms, her fingertips brushed Habren's blanket for the last time and it felt like.... It felt like breaking.

She was finally broken.

EAGER EYES WATCHED *in silence as she was led to the edge of the riverbank, the sun was beaming, and the water was still. It felt like a mockery to die on a day such as this.*

Hundreds of Gwendolen's people had come to witness the death of the false queen, ripped from all her splendour. She wore a plain white tunic and it itched dreadfully in the summer heat. She wished that they would have let her wear her green robes from her homeland. She wished they would let her wear anything that had a little more pride.

She was led slowly through the crowds, some hissed at her, others called her names, but she paid them no mind. She had eyes only for Gwendolen.

The queen sat on a makeshift throne above the crowds, the warrior and the witch by her side. She noted with a vindictive pleasure that Gwendolen looked tired. Her pale skin paler, and if Estildris was not mistaken, she even appeared a little thinner. It was satisfying to know that this war had taken its toll on the queen as well.

Estidlris knew that Habren's supposed 'death' had been the day before, and that the same vultures who were here for her had watched the show. But she knew the truth, she had watched from her chamber window as Thea and Augusta had handed the princess over to her new family.

It seemed that Gwendolen was a woman of her word.

It was a strange and twisted feeling, Estildris thought, to feel grateful to the person who had ripped your dreams apart.

The two executioners pushed her through the final part of the crowd until they reached a boat where, with as much grace and poise as she could muster, Estildris stepped inside.

The boat was pushed into the river and the three of them drifted out.

She closed her eyes and felt the warmth on her face, birds chirped and there was a gentle swaying as soft splashes of water lapped at the side of the boat. When she opened her eyes, they were in the middle of the river, and she could more clearly see the green trees and bushes that decorated the riverbank— it truly was a beautiful day.

One of the men tied her hands together, while the other tied her feet, attached to the rope wrapped around her feet were three rather large rocks. Her heart beat faster.

She turned to the man standing to the right of her. 'Allow me the dignity of walking to my death like a lady and not a prisoner.'

The men looked at each other suspiciously.

'Where else could I go?' Estildris asked.

Cautiously the two men released her from their hold. Estildris looked at the queen one final time.

She gazed out to the crowd again, intent on making them feel something, anything as they watched her. Yet, her eyes only saw one face; the face of a girl. She floated in the middle of the river, staring up at the boat, her eyes wide with awe and confusion. She was handsome, Estildris thought, with thick brown hair and wide brown eyes not entirely dissimilar to her own.

Estildris quickly glanced around, but it appeared as though no one else could see her. For a moment, Estildris thought she was seeing a vision of Habren, a prophecy of her daughter's future, but then Locrinus' voice came to her; 'If all the worlds were to be destroyed, I would build a new one, just so that our souls could meet again.'

She smiled and understood.

'Until we meet again,' she whispered, and then she stepped off the boat and into the water.

She almost looked like a bird taking flight the way she launched herself forward, elegant and purposeful. But then she hit the water so unceremoniously that the illusion shattered. She disappeared completely, until the only evidence that she had ever been there at all were the ripples in the water and the cheers from the crowd.

Water filled her mouth, it rushed down her throat and into her lungs—she was suffocating, and yet she did not struggle. She remained oh so still and allowed herself to sink like any ordinary stone.

The Lady Estildris closed her eyes until there was nothing, only darkness pressing against her. Darkness and death.

It would all be over soon.

HER EYES OPENED, the light flooded in and she was awake— awake and alive.

Chapter Thirty-Seven
THERE AND BACK AGAIN

It took several moments for Sarah to understand where she was.

Sitting up she rubbed her head gingerly; she must have collapsed onto the floor after the kiss.

The *kiss*. She could still feel it lingering on her tongue.

Locrinus had gone, and it occurred to Sarah that he had never truly been there at all. Outside it still looked like the earliest hours of morning, Sarah grappled to her feet and made her way over to the mirror and her bedroom clock.

3:55 am.

Her entire body was shaking. She felt... out of place. As though she were wearing a dress that was two sizes too small. The world didn't *fit* her anymore. Her life had been carved into the wrong shape.

She looked down at her hands and found they did not look like her own.

All these years she had lived oblivious, unaware that tucked inside her soul there was another part of her lying dormant. All her life she had been sleeping, like a princess from every fairy-tale she had ever loved, just waiting, waiting, waiting to be kissed awake.

A piece of folded paper with secrets written on the inside—she had finally been opened.

Not possible. She told herself.

Then again, wasn't *life* impossible?

She knew it then; in her heart, in her soul, in whatever it was inside her that looked up at the stars and saw a different sky.

She might dress in a school uniform but once upon a time she had worn a *crown.*

Jolting her out of her reverie her phone rang from her bedside table, she marched over to it and saw Harriett's name flash upon the screen. She did not move to answer it, instead she watched it ring and ring and ring until the ringing stopped.

From outside her window, Sarah could hear the faint wailing of a siren. She made her way to the window and pulled it shut.

Until we meet again.

THE SATURDAY MORNING that followed was perfect in its Autumn-ness. Red leaves decorated the pavements of Woolington-on-Sea, the wind swept through the branches and the sky was white instead of grey. There was to be no sign of rain until later that afternoon, and so collectively all the dog-walkers in town decided to wrap themselves up in their coats and scarves and take their various hounds out while the going was good.

It was on this perfect Saturday morning that the police arrived on Sarah's doorstep.

By noon, everyone in the town knew that Sarah Acton had been the last person to see Anthony Goldsmith alive. Sarah's parents had been informed and as a result they had to cut their weekend trip short, though they wouldn't make it back until the early evening. The police left, unable to interrogate her formally without her guardian's present.

And so, Sarah was trapped alone with her thoughts. She kept picturing Anthony lying in his bedroom... eyes open, cold and still and dead.

There was a faint stabbing pain in her chest that told her of her hurt. Yet, more than grief, more than shock, more than sorrow... more than anything else, she felt guilty. Because her mind kept flickering back to *him*, like a playlist with only one song. Her mind kept repeating the memory of the king who had promised her the world.

Yesterday Anthony's death would have broken her. Yesterday Anthony's death would have had her sobbing and confused and grieving.

But that was yesterday, and she had been a different person then.

She was still standing on her doorstep when her phone flashed in her hand.

I'M SO SORRY TO HEAR ABOUT ANTHONY.
MEET US IN THE ART BLOCK. – HS

So, with no parents to stop her, and absolutely nothing left to lose. Sarah did.

IT WAS ALWAYS eerie to enter the school on the weekend, when there were no students or teachers in sight, only empty classrooms and clean whiteboards. Year Eleven students were sometimes allowed access to classrooms outside school hours, all it required was a polite word with the right teacher; A talent Harriett had acquired and started abusing when she was in Year Nine.

Sarah made her way across the field and round the back of the red-bricked Watts Building until she reached the Art

Block. The door was already unlocked and open, so she walked inside and down the corridor toward the only room with a light on.

And there they all were.

Harriett sat perched on the end of a table, her back straight and poised. As always, she looked as though she were running a campaign for tidiest teenager of the year; she wore a maroon jumper over a white button-up shirt, dark blue jeans and a pair of white trainers that didn't seem to have a speck of dirt on them.

Meanwhile, Emily sat hunched over a canvas, a paintbrush perched behind her ear. She was also wearing a knitted jumper, but hers was cream and baggy and so long that it almost covered her skirt. She was also wearing a pair of strangely patterned woolly tights. Cat was lying on her lap and there was blue paint smeared across her chin.

Then there was Ruby, who paced restlessly behind them both. Dressed in a zombie Minnie Mouse jumper and the grubbiest pair of torn jeans Sarah had ever set eyes on. She really did look so thin now, the jeans hung loosely around her legs, while her cheekbones poked out a little more prominently from her pale face. A face still decorated with small purple bruises.

They all froze when Sarah walked in. Where Harriett was neat, Sarah was fashionable. She had worn her favourite pale denim trousers, a pale pink jumper, a long white coat and a grey scarf with grey lace up boots to match. She'd even made the effort to tie her thick hair up into a twisty bun, and to put on the smallest amount of make-up.

Sarah couldn't help but notice these small details about the four of them now. How even when it came to the simplest of choices, they were fundamentally different.

'How are you feeling?' Harriett asked tentatively.

'Anthony's dead. How'd you think I'm feeling?' Sarah said coldly.

Harriett and Ruby exchanged a wary glance. Emily closed her eyes, leaned her head back and stroked the back of Cat's ears. It was a gesture that was so entirely Thea that it took Sarah a moment to remember where she was and who exactly she was with.

'You all remember, don't you?' she whispered. 'You have your memories back.'

They each nodded.

'It was fucking weird, man,' Ruby said. 'I went to bed as myself and when I woke up, I was this whole different person. Well, not different 'cos I'm the same but, like, *more* of the same.'

Harriett ran a hand over her side-plait, she was looking away from them, her expression vacant.

'It felt like being ripped apart,' she said hoarsely. 'And then being put back together all wrong.'

Sarah was trying to listen to them, but all she could focus on was the anger bubbling up inside her. 'That's all very interesting,' Sarah said icily. 'But isn't there anything you'd like to say to me?'

'No,' Ruby said flatly, running a hand through her hair. 'You haven't done anything yet.'

'Yet,' Sarah repeated. *Yet.* As though there was no doubt at all that she would. She stood a little straighter, lifting her chin proudly.

'You *killed* me,' she practically spat. '*You* should be apologising *to me*.'

Ruby rolled her eyes. 'It was quite literally thousands of years ago. Get over it.'

Sarah could feel her own face flush hot with rage, she could feel her cheeks burning red. She didn't think she had ever been this angry before. She could still feel the freezing water of the river filling up her lungs. Harriett buried her head deep in her hands.

'I died!' Sarah shouted.

Ruby let out a bark of a laugh and then smiled her knife-like smile. Again, Sarah found herself taken aback by the moment. It was like looking into a distorted mirror, Ruby's face was completely different to that of the tall black-eyed warrior. Yet, everything about the way she curled her top lip into that sharp-edged grin was identical to Augusta. Sarah found she almost couldn't separate the person she was looking at to the image in her mind.

'We all died, Sarah. What makes your death so special?'

'You know exactly what I'm talking about,' she hissed.

Ruby strode across the room so that Sarah was only a foot away from her.

'No, I really don't. Because if I remember correctly, you weren't exactly innocent in all this.' Her voice grew louder. 'I rescued you on that ship! Sinclair let you live in her castle knowing the entire time exactly what you were up to. Now you expect me to waltz up to you and say; "Hey Acton, remember that time a thousand years or so ago when I killed your stupid, traitorous arse and your stupid, traitorous king? Well, that was my bad. Sorry!"'

Sarah had never so badly wanted to throttle someone. 'It wasn't a thousand years ago!' she yelled. 'It was yesterday.'

'No, we only *remembered* yesterday,' Ruby said. 'It was a gazillion years ago in a different time, when we were different people.'

Sarah opened her mouth to argue but Harriett stood up. 'Enough!'

And it was.

Ruby shrugged and walked back over to the other side of the room.

'I'm not going to argue about this,' Harriett said. She

turned to Sarah, her plait was hanging a little looser than usual as though she had done it in a rush, and there were small bags hanging under her eyes. 'Ruby can't apologise for what happened at the river because it wasn't her idea. It was mine. So, if you want an apology for that, I will give it. Sarah, I am so sorry about what you went through, I can't even imagine…' she trailed off, her eyes watering. 'I can't imagine how you're feeling. But we can't afford to do this now, we've got to work together and come up with a plan. Anthony is dead. Timothy is dead. Hayley… Hayley is gone. Who knows how many more people he's going to murder?'

He's. Sarah noticed the way Harriett brushed over saying his name, the way she avoided Sarah's gaze when she spoke of him.

'He won't kill anyone else,' Emily whispered.

They all turned to look at her, dumbfounded. Emily did not tear her gaze away from the canvas in front of her.

'Magic, it has rules. The king… the Shadow, his magic is bound by the same pattern. Three is the most magically powerful number. For example, the Holy Trinity; father, son, spirit. Or the Triple Goddess; maiden, mother, *crone*,' Emily emphasised the word *crone*. 'When we talk about time, we talk about the past, present, future. When we talk about the world we talk about land, sea, sky. Three deaths for one life.'

Sarah knew immediately by the stunned silence that she was not alone in her confusion.

'Walters, you might suddenly understand all this magic stuff, but we don't,' Ruby said. 'You gotta explain.'

Emily frowned, puzzled. 'I thought I did. Ruby, you found his body, right? So, we can assume he's trying to return to his physical form. To do that he needs to enact a ritual, a sacrifice. Blood for blood. What I'm saying is that he's already killed three people, he doesn't need to kill anyone else.'

Emily let out a long breath, and Sarah thought that

perhaps she had exhausted herself from having to speak for so long.

Harriett was gaping at Emily and wearing the expression of someone who was about to be violently sick. 'So, what you're telling me is that Hayley... Hayley died for *him* to *live*?'

Emily didn't say anything. She didn't need to.

Harriett shot each of them a horrified glance. Her skin was pale, and her eyes were red from tears she would not let spill. She stood up straight. 'I have to go.'

Ruby watched her leave, then swore aggressively the moment she was out of sight. 'So, are you saying he's already awake?' she asked, turning to Emily.

Emily cast a furtive glance at Sarah and then shrugged. 'I don't know. Maybe. It depends what the last part of the ritual was.'

Sarah's mind flashed to the yellow flowers falling like snow in her bedroom.

We will make each other whole again.

Ruby swore once more. 'Okay, okay. We can fix this. I've still got the dagger. All we need to do is get Harriett, go to the Neville, and get this over with.'

At first Sarah didn't fully register what Ruby had said, she was still reeling from all the memories still swirling around her head. 'Wait. What do we need to get over with?'

Ruby gaped at her as though she was some sort of deranged lunatic. 'Isn't it obvious? We need to get rid of your Shadow King.'

Sarah couldn't believe it. She couldn't believe what she was hearing. 'You're going to... you're going to kill him again?' The words came out strangled and wrong, as though they had fought their way out.

'No, actually I was planning on inviting him to the cinema and giving him some popcorn,' Ruby said, her words pure venom. 'Of course, I'm going to kill him! Or at least give it my best damn try and with any luck, this time it'll stick.'

'You can't!'

Ruby looked at her, her menacing stare softened, and Sarah did not think she mistook the sympathy in her eyes. 'We have to... I'm sorry.'

Sarah picked up the bottle of blue paint that sat to the left of Emily and launched it across the room where it hit the side of Ruby's face. Ruby rubbed the spot where the paint hit, her expression darkening.

'No, you're not!' Sarah shrieked. 'You're not sorry! All you want to do is destroy everything around you. That's all you're good at! That's all you've ever been good at.'

Ruby breathed heavily, her nostrils flaring, and then she ran a thin white hand through her soot-black hair. She had stopped pacing now, instead she was forcing herself to stand perfectly still. For a moment Sarah thought Ruby was going to march over and punch her. Then Ruby's shoulders slumped, and she shoved her hands into her jean pockets. Ruby looked Sarah directly in the face.

'Fine. I'm not sorry,' she said spitefully. Then she went to the door and said to Emily; 'I'm going to find Harriett, answer your phone when I ring.'

The door slammed shut behind her.

The entire time Emily had sat rigid and quiet, as though she could become invisible by sheer force of will alone.

'You have to help me. You have to help me stop them.'

Emily sighed. 'I can't.'

Sarah threw her hands up in despair, but the cogs in her mind were spinning.

'Locrinus brought me back, I don't know how, but he did,' she spoke slowly. 'But everything else... must have been *you. You* must have been the one to bring us all back together.'

Emily didn't say anything, the cat on her lap let out a soft purr.

'Why then?' Sarah demanded. 'Why did you do it if not to save him?'

Emily pulled the paintbrush from behind her ear and dipped it into the palette beside her, then in one smooth motion she wiped the brush against the canvas. It was only now that Sarah truly looked at the painting. It was a woman, lying in the water with a crown of thistles and roses perched upon her head. Her skin was bronze, and her thick hair was splayed out behind her like angel's wings.

The likeness was incredible.

Estildris as Ophelia.

Emily looked up from the canvas and into Sarah's face.

'I think you know,' she whispered.

Chapter Thirty-Eight

KISSED AWAKE

Locrinus had been right about one thing: She *did* know where he was. But so did the others, and she didn't want to risk them getting there first.

When she left Emily, she ran. She ran out of the school, through the grey town centre all the way to the Neville.

When she reached it, Sarah was almost unsurprised to find that the Neville no longer *looked* like the Neville anymore, instead it looked like... Wighus Hall.

Or rather, a collection of parts of it. Haphazardly stuck together, as if built by someone who had once seen an image of a castle a long time ago and had only used what they could remember. There were towers protruding from odd angles and large oak doors where before there had only been cracked walls.

It was a monster of a building. And she was heading straight inside it.

She told herself she only wanted to look at him. She only wanted to confirm her suspicions. Yet with every step up the strange structure that was a twisted mixture of both castle and car park, she found it harder to feed herself the lie.

Because there were two lives trapped within her one soul. Memories upon memories pressed against each other, fighting for room to be seen. Too much sand in one hourglass, too many grains pressed together. Unable to move, staying completely still.

A part of her, the younger part, the life that was wholly and truly Sarah, thought of laughing with her friends, hot chocolate at midnight and a cupcake for every birthday. She thought of parties, bubbly drinks and the occasional Sunday dinner with her parents.

But her first life, the life that had been cut away from her for so long, burned hot inside her. Like a volcano once lying dormant, it had now exploded—flashes of memory assaulted her in waves over, and over again; Habren. The river. The king. Habren. The river. The king.

She had been a mother once, briefly. The thought both terrified and thrilled her.

As she climbed the steps, she found herself being led by some invisible strength, as though the king's hand was guiding her. His soul whispering to hers, instructing her where to go.

She reached the fourth floor and grimaced when she realised that she needn't climb any higher. The door was as Ruby described, deep dark wood and twisted iron. She hesitated, her phone burned in her pocket, connecting her to her friends.

She went through anyway and saw not empty car spaces but a hall, vast and long with high ceilings and windows that could not possibly have fit, but somehow did.

In the middle of it all, was the king. He lay placed on a pedestal in the centre of the room. A sword balanced on his chest and a crown on his head. He looked exactly as he did in her memories.

Ferocious and beautiful.

Sarah crept forward until she hovered over him.

His eyes were closed and not a breath left his lips. She found herself staring at his lashes, so long and dark and thick.

He was every handsome prince that she could have possibly conjured when she was young and playing with dolls in her room. His face was a strange, entrancing mixture of fine lines and a strong jaw.

A whispering voice inside told her that he was hers. That he belonged to her, and she to him.

When Sarah was a child, she and the others used to play fairy tales, and she had always loved the simple elegance of the stories. Heroes and villains and happy endings.

He did not look like a villain to her.

Once upon a time, there was a princess who was awoken by true love's kiss. Once upon a time, there was a princess who was rescued from a tower by a handsome prince. Once upon a time, there was a girl who was drawn to the sleeping body of an 11th Century King.

She never expected to find herself living out a story.

Something was inside her, screaming at her, pulling her apart. She loved this man. Or at least, Estildris did.

She clasped her hands over Locrinus' and allowed the tears to spill freely.

The two lives that rested inside Sarah's mind were desperately fighting for control. Memories battled memories; emotions swallowed emotions. Love and hatred and fear and passion all blended together into one chaotic, turbulent mess as Sarah tried to control her tears and remember herself; who *she* was, what *she* wanted.

Finally, the stronger feeling won.

Sarah stood on the stone floor, reached into her pocket and pulled out her phone. It looked so alien here, in this seemingly grand and old place. Slowly, her hands shaking, she typed out two words, knowing that once she'd sent the message there was no way to bring it back. She took a deep shuddering breath and clicked send.

Then she leaned down and kissed the king awake.

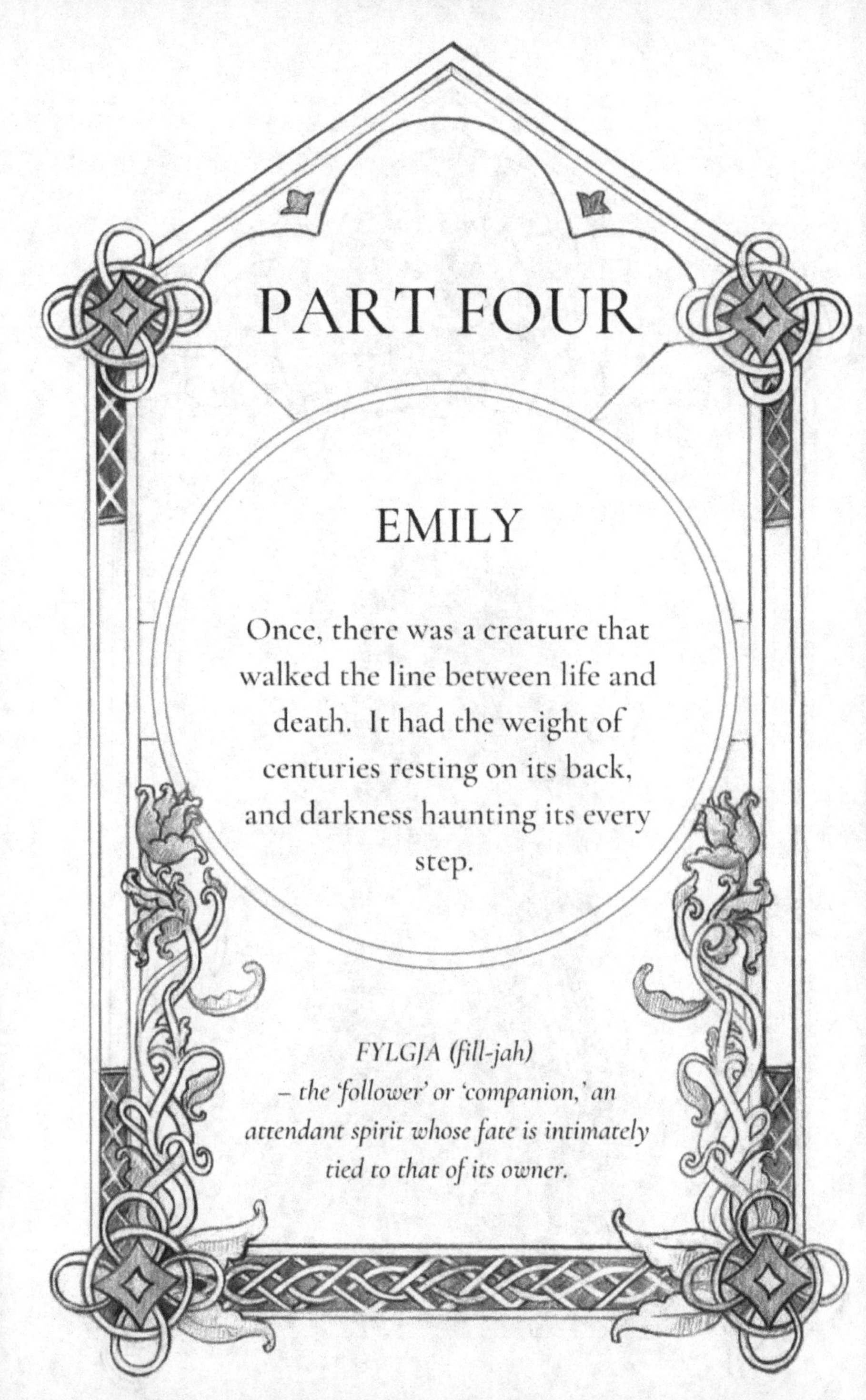

PART FOUR

EMILY

Once, there was a creature that walked the line between life and death. It had the weight of centuries resting on its back, and darkness haunting its every step.

FYLGJA (fill-jah)
– the 'follower' or 'companion,' an attendant spirit whose fate is intimately tied to that of its owner.

Chapter Thirty-Nine
TRUTHS UNTOLD

Emily Walters had always known that she was a witch. Or rather, that she had descended from a long line of witches. Her father would often make jokes at her mother's expense.

'She bewitched me; you know,' he once chuckled whilst making stew. 'It was the eyes, grey like the storm.'

To which her mother had tapped the back of his hand with a wooden spoon. 'You're burning the onions,' then she'd kissed his cheek and laughed.

Freya Walters had skin as pale as milk and eyes that were indeed as grey as a winter storm. Freya came from a long line of Irish Travellers. Her grandmother, Emily's great grandmother, had been one of the first to settle, but many of their traditions had remained. And this, more than anything, was why the Walter's household was filled with good luck charms.

A horseshoe hung over both the front and back door to ward off any evil spirits. Sage, heather and lavender could often be found hanging in their kitchen; lavender for calm, heather for luck, and sage for protection. When Freya cooked, she would always throw just a pinch of salt over her shoulder and every winter she would watch the flames in the fireplace carefully, to see if any embers spat onto the ground.

'If they do, it means good fortune is coming our way,' she would tell her children.

Freya Walters never gave gifts with sharp edges, she always cut a cross into any bread she was baking, and she made sure to step over cracks in the pavement.

However, the most peculiar of all Freya Walter's traditions was this; every night when she wasn't working, she would take an empty walnut shell from out the kitchen cupboard and pour a teaspoon of cream into it, then she would place the walnut shell outside.

'Why do you do that?' Emily had once asked, when she was very little.

'To make friends with the Fae,' her mother had said, locking the kitchen door. 'My Ma always did it. She believed that if you're good to the Fae, then they'll be good to you.'

'Do you believe?'

Her mother had looked thoughtful for a moment. 'I've never thought not to. And I would rather that the little folk didn't steal my keys.' She'd winked at her then and kissed her on the cheek.

Chadwick Walters did decidedly not believe. But he delighted in his wife's quirks and never complained that the house always stank of incense or that salt could always be found on the kitchen floor. Emily's father had dark skin and dark eyes and a smile so brilliant that when he smiled, other people couldn't help but smile with him. He was also descended from travellers of a sort.

His Grandparents, Emily's great Grandparents, had come over from Jamaica in the Windrush after the second world war. At first, they had lived in London, then Devon, and then Sheffield. After that, they just kept on making their way further and further south. Emily's own father had lived all across the United Kingdom, making his art and working in galleries, that is until he found Freya, and together they found

Woolington-on-Sea.

'Exploring and travelling, it's in your blood,' he often said to Emily and her siblings. 'The sea and the open road calls to you.'

At the time Emily had thought her father had just been talking sentimental nonsense. Spewing the kind of inspirational drivel that parents so often feel the need to fill up their children with.

Now, though... Now, she wasn't so sure.

Some*thing* was calling her.

AFTER SARAH HAD left, Emily had carefully rolled up her painting and made her way slowly through the streets of Wooly's. Her feet dragged and time crawled.

The world was different now, seen through some sort of lopsided kaleidoscope.

A broken mirror split in two, with a different reality on either side.

It had been strange seeing them standing in the art room, they had all looked eerily out of place. Emily had kept getting distracted by their faces. When she looked at Ruby, she saw Augusta. When Harriett spoke, she heard Gwendolen's voice. And when Sarah moved, it was with Estildris' grace.

When she arrived home, she received another text from Ruby, letting her know that she still hadn't been able to track Harriett down.

Emily wasn't sure what would happen when she did.

She put her keys on the side and made her way into the living room. Chadwick Walters had been doing commissions from home lately, so it seemed that there was always easels and paint in the living room now. He stood at his canvas, painting the background of what Emily knew would no doubt be a landscape piece, while *Homes Under the Hammer* played on the TV in the background.

'Where's Mum?' she asked.

Chadwick turned around. 'Hello to you too, wonderful daughter of mine! She picked up an extra shift at the hospital. She won't be back until late.'

Emily plonked her bag onto the floor. 'Okay.'

Her father regarded her carefully and wiped the ends of his brush before resting them back on his palette.

'And why do you look so much like Atlas, on a day as beautiful as this?' he asked.

Emily sat down on the sofa and frowned. 'The weight of the sky on my shoulders?'

Her father grinned. 'I can never catch you out.'

Emily couldn't help it, she smiled, but then she caught herself smiling and felt guilty. Ruby still hadn't found Harriett; Sarah was distraught and confused...

And it was all Emily's fault.

'Is that a painting I see in your hand?' he asked, reaching for it. 'May I see what my protegee has created this time?'

Absent-mindedly Emily passed the canvas over to her father and allowed herself to fall further backwards into the sofa. There was suddenly a loud thudding from upstairs followed by the girlish shrieks of her sisters and her brother's high-pitched wail.

Normally, she would go up the stairs to see what was wrong. Instead she remained seated.

'Petal, this is beautiful,' her father said. 'It's colourful but not loud and the linework is damn near perfect, it only needs a little bit more shading, that's all. It's a modern depiction of Ophelia, right?'

Emily nodded.

Her father raised his eyebrows at her, impressed. 'You've outdone yourself petal, really you have,' he held up the canvas higher, inspecting the woman's face a little more carefully. 'Did you use a model as a reference? She's beautiful, whoever she is.'

'No, I didn't use a reference,' Emily mumbled.

Although, that wasn't strictly true. When she began the painting, she knew exactly what she wanted the finished result to be.

Ophelia, draped in white surrounded by water, flowers and reeds, her face staring upwards out of the canvas as if judging the viewer. Emily herself had been impressed when the image of the woman, golden skinned and glorious, had appeared effortlessly and fully formed onto the page. It was only now that she realised she hadn't been painting from her imagination at all, but from a memory.

It was her best piece.

And now it horrified her.

She closed her eyes, she wished Cat was beside her, but she wouldn't be able to let him into the house until later, until after both her parents were asleep.

'Emily, are you sure you're okay?'

She opened her eyes and looked up to see her father watching her curiously. He was still holding the wretched painting in his hands.

She shook her head. 'Dad... I did something terrible.'

Her father carefully placed the painting down onto the floor and sat down beside her on the sofa, he wrapped an arm around her as she started to feel the tears slide steadily down her cheeks.

'Sweetheart, it's okay, I'm sure whatever it is we can work it out. I'm sure it's not that bad.'

Emily shook her head again. Now her father seemed truly concerned. 'Tell me what happened. Tell me what's wrong.'

Emily rubbed her eyes with her sleeve. 'I can't...'

He wouldn't believe her, even if she did.

Chapter Forty

CATS AND CURSES,
SOULS AND SECRETS

Emily Walters had lived her relatively short life feeling uncomfortable. A misshapen piece to a puzzle she didn't fully understand. At home she was the eldest of five siblings; she took on the role of the quiet one, the one they "didn't have to worry about." And in a town of approximately twenty thousand predominantly white people, Emily was one of the hundred that was mixed-race.

She grew accustomed to avoiding people's stares and ignoring strange and absurd questions like, for instance, how her mother was white. Over the years Emily learned the art of melting into the background, and how to use her silence as an impenetrable armour. At school she became so inconspicuous it was a miracle that she didn't disappear entirely. Harriett had always noticed her though, and so she'd had friends.

Yet, still the world didn't feel right.

The world was smudged, and nothing ever made sense to her. She believed in nothing except the truth of her own name, and sometimes even that didn't fit.

When Ruby finally messaged her, Emily had stopped crying. Her father had given up trying to coax out of her what was wrong and, though with misgivings, had conceded into letting her go out to see her friends. When she closed her front door, she turned to see Cat sitting at the end of her front garden. He yawned at her, revealing all his tiny, dangerous teeth. Emily grimaced.

'Come on, let's go and face what we did.'

Yes, Emily Walters had lived her relatively short life feeling uncomfortable. But Thea had lived hers dancing on a knife's edge, until eventually she'd tripped and carved herself in two.

THE CUNNING FOLK believed in gods, not God. They did not think the world, in all its complex beauty, could have been made by one single entity. Just as they did not believe that a person was but one entity; singular, and utterly unremarkable.

They believed instead that the self was divided into four separate parts, each beautiful and ethereal: *Hamr,* the physical form, the vessel with which a person experiences the world around them; *Hugr,* the spirit inside, the essence of a person's personality and feeling; *Hamingja,* the individual luck or fortune that a person carries within themselves.

Thea had missed her people, the Cunning Folk were fortune tellers, healers and charmers. She had missed their warmth and their magic, their herbs and their spells. Sometimes, in the dark velvet of night, she thought she heard wooden wheels and she let herself imagine going home.

But she had been tasked, she who could see the essence of magic, she who had been gifted by the gods themselves, and she would not let them down.

She was to keep the gods and their magic alive through the crown.

She had not anticipated a war. She had not anticipated so many things.

Thea of the Cunning Folk had not expected to be so wholly trusted by the queen, she did not realise that by becoming Gwendolen's friend she had inadvertently chosen a side to fight on. Yet she had, and she could not bring herself to regret the choice.

On the eve of battle Thea had blessed Augusta's blade, and then she'd watched as the warrior plunged it through the king's neck. At dusk, beneath a shining red moon, Thea saw the king fall to his knees, she saw the exact moment that a smile formed on his lips.

She felt the shift in the earth, the wrongness of the moment.

The king had been killed—yet he did not die. King Locrinus of the Britons had a knife driven deep into his neck, and though his heart stopped beating, the most important part of him still gripped the mortal world.

His soul.

His *hugr*.

When the king's last breath left his body, his soul left with it. His soul—a swirling furious mixture of passion and love, hatred and fire—clung to the fibres of the universe and seeped its way inside. Lingering between life and death, refusing to move on.

A Shadow stalked the battlefield, and Thea knew what it was waiting for—what it wanted.

She should have told Gwendolen then; she should have warned her. But Thea the Witch had a secret, and she saw an opportunity for a different soul to be saved.

THEA HAD CLOSED her eyes when the Lady Estildris leapt into the river, but she heard the slap that her body made when it hit the water. An awful sound that reverberated through the air and sent a wave of cheers through the crowd.

Thea did not cheer. She could not bear to think of Estildris' *hamr* trapped beneath the water, her *hugr* bound by the ropes and stones that Thea herself had spelled.

And so, late that night, Thea carried her secret down to the River Habren, cupping it gingerly in her hands the way you would any treasured thing. The cat, ever her companion, padded the ground softly beside her.

She found the air to be thick with magic, but it was not a magic she had ever sensed before. It was not the magic found in plants and animals, or the magic that rested inside a person's faith. It was a curse—dark and dense and heavy. She found she could barely breathe due to the sheer power of it.

And there *it* was.

The Shadow loomed over the water, consuming everything. It blotted out the stars and swallowed the moon, giving a new, deeper meaning to the darkness of night.

Now, the Shadow took the form of a man wearing a crown, and in its crudely made arms it held the limp body of a princess. The vision of them both together was striking and unnatural and somehow *right*. As if the two of them were fated to be together—in life, death and everything after. Thea watched as the Shadow, oblivious to her presence, lifted one of its mist-like hands, reached into Estildris' lifeless chest and gathered up her soul in its unearthly fingers.

Thea understood then; she did not know how, but Locrinus had somehow fastened them together. The king and his princess, their *hugrs* were bound to the mortal world and together they would start an unmaking.

Thea had hoped that the Shadow would save Estildris' soul from the depths of the water, and once it had done so she could banish it.

Now she realised, she could not destroy one without the other.

In that moment, seeing Estildris dangling lifeless in the arms of a dead king, her *hugr* being ripped from her body—being *saved*—the secret that Thea had worked so hard to bury deep, burst free.

The fourth and final part of self was stranger and more elusive. A slither of humanity encased within a creature, separate but one in the same. Most lived their entire lives without catching even a glimpse of their *fylgja*.

Thea was not most people.

The cat leapt through the air, graceful and predatory with claws unsheathed. It was both animal and spirit, it passed through the Shadow and landed hissing in the water with Estildris' *hugr* caught like a mouse caged between its fangs.

Thea could not stop the king's curse, but she could slow it down.

Cats and curses.

Souls and secrets.

This was the language that Thea spoke. The twisted thread that connected magic and men.

For every spell cast the Old Gods required a sacrifice be it with blood or soul, and that night on the riverbed, her knees and hands covered in mud, Thea sacrificed the most important part of herself. The *fylgja* that followed her wherever she went. The part of herself that rested inside the animal, her own magic sheathed in a feline form.

She could not give the *fylgia's* death to the gods, so she gave them even more. She gave them its *life*.

Her life.

Using her *flygia* as a vessel, Thea called out to the Old Gods, *her* gods. *Woden, Thunor, Frige* and *Tiw*. She begged with all four aspects of her being for them to keep Estildris and her queen safe, not knowing that another soul had trapped itself into the bargain.

I swear to let no harm befall you... to follow you wherever you lead me... In this life and the next.

And so, she bound the four of them together tightly, but not neatly. Like necklaces tangled together in the bottom of a jewellery box, they were wound together so taut that it was impossible to tell where one chain ended, and another began.

The cat was to become both a protector and a curse. It would hold the Shadow at bay, keeping the spirit of the king from fulfilling his promise. And when finally, it could not keep him from this world any longer, only then would it release the *hugrs* of the women it kept from between its teeth.

A queen.

A warrior.

A lover.

A witch.

It would feed them to the bodies of babe's whose own souls would be too young and too weak to fight the spirits away. It would be a repossession, a reincarnation—an eviction of the cruellest kind. But so strong and dark was Thea's love that she did not care.

The Shadow let out an unearthly shriek, its form twisting and writhing before melting into the night sky. To hide in the stretches of space that lingered between the world and nothing, to sleep wrapped in its own darkness and to feed off its own hunger until it was powerful enough to slither free.

Thea remained crouched in the mud, the cat still hissing and spitting as it made its way slowly back to her, inside its frail body it held two *hugrs*. And it was destined to hold two more.

Chapter Forty-One
THE GRAVEYARD

Emily could picture it so clearly. Cat, *her* Cat, roaming the earth decade after decade keeping the spirit of a king at bay. It was no wonder the creature looked so wretched now. She could picture in horrifying detail the moment that the *fylgja* pressed its whiskered mouth against the mouths of children, tearing their new spirits away and replacing them with their own ancient wills.

She hoped their *hugrs* were at peace. She prayed that their effervescence to the next realm had been a smooth one.

EMILY MET RUBY at the iron gates.

'Are you sure she's in there?' Emily asked.

Ruby nodded. 'I've searched everywhere else she's likely to go. And this makes sense considering...well, y'know.'

Emily did know. She nodded sombrely, Ruby nodded in return, and then she pushed the gates open with a loud, scraping creak.

The graveyard was still. Cat sauntered ahead of them, weaving its way between the headstones, jumping from place to place. Emily pulled her scarf tighter around her neck, beside her Ruby was clutching at her stomach, her face scrunched up in a wince.

'Are you okay?' Emily asked.

Ruby nodded. 'Oh, don't mind me. I'm just casually dying over here.'

Emily frowned, the few trees around them in the graveyard were bare, while the leaves beneath their feet were an orange mush. 'Aren't we all?'

Ruby appraised her, an impressed smirk creeping across her face. 'Touché, Walters,' she pointed ahead to a large oak tree. 'I think it's just over there.'

It still sometimes surprised Emily that Woolington's Cemetery was this large. Filled with this many dead.

Now though, she could feel them.

She could feel the magic around them, from the love that was imbued into each headstone, and the way the grass grew so green because of the *hamrs* that fed the earth.

She shivered.

Together they made their way through the gravestones until they passed the oak tree, where they found a shadowy figure knelt in front of a large slab of stone. They stood behind her, each unsure of what to say.

It was Harriett who spoke first.

'Strange, isn't it?' she whispered. 'That this is all that's left of her: A piece of granite and a carefully mowed patch of grass.'

Emily looked to Ruby, whose eyes had widened in some sort of stunned panic. 'This isn't all that's left of her,' Emily said quietly. 'You and your family, your memories of her... that is what's left.'

Harriett let out a laugh—a cold, harsh sound. 'My memories... my memories are a joke. They aren't even mine.'

'Of course, they're yours,' Ruby snapped. 'We're still us.'

Harriett ignored her, then tilted her head back so that she was gazing upwards. Above them the sky was blushing softly, and together they watched as a flock of birds swirled through the air, black flecks on a pink canvas.

It was just the three of them and Cat, alone in the graveyard.

Ruby sat down on one side of Harriett while Emily sat on the other. They each faced the headstone.

Hayley Catherine Sinclair
03.01.2001 – 12.08.2018
Loving daughter, sister, friend
Always a light, always loved, forever missed.

'I didn't feel like I could come here before,' Harriett said after a long while. 'It was as if coming here made it true. Made it permanent. I didn't want... I didn't want it to be permanent.'

Emily could hear the crack in Harriett's voice. She heard it, and she could feel it too. She knew it was a crack that had appeared the moment Hayley had died, and despite all Harriett's best efforts, it had been growing since.

Emily did not know how to smooth it over.

Neither Ruby nor Emily looked to their friend, for they both knew how she hated to be seen crying. Instead, Ruby wrapped an arm around her shoulder, while Emily placed a gentle hand on her knee.

For a while the three of them just sat there, silently facing the headstone while Cat slowly circled around them, a sinister black figure slinking between the gravestones.

Harriett wiped her eyes and shook her head. 'I knew I had to come here today. I had to face this...after all. It's my fault she's here,' Harriett turned to look at Emily. 'Isn't it?'

Emily rubbed her temple, there was so much running through her head, she could barely sort one *thought— memory—feeling*—from the next.

The morning that Thea had banished the Shadow, she'd

had no choice but to tell Gwendolen of the curse she had enacted, the curse she had cast to prevent another from taking place. Only at that point neither curse had been completed. The Shadow hadn't found Gwendolen for its revenge, and Cat had only captured two souls instead of four, the full sacrifice had not yet been made—Thea's protection had not yet properly taken hold.

Gwendolen had had a choice to make. She could not allow Loegria to be ruled by a child, and yet she could not allow the Shadow to break free from its make-shift prison. In the end, it was Augusta who took the choice into her own, bloodied hands.

The warrior seized the blade with which she had murdered the king and promptly turned it on herself. The third soul had been caught.

And so, the protection held.

Gwendolen ruled for another eleven years and then, when Madden was but fifteen years of age, when the spell could be kept back no longer, she'd abdicated the throne to him.

Queen Gwendolen and her witch disappeared.

Ruby lifted a hand to her neck and rubbed it self-consciously.

Harriett stared at her hands, revulsion in her gaze. 'This body, this life, it's *stolen*,' her head snapped up suddenly. 'Did you know? Did you know that it would happen like this?'

Emily closed her eyes.

Harriett scoffed. 'I've thought about it a lot today. If Cat had chosen some other child as the vessel, then I would not have been Hayley's sister, she would not have been in any danger, and she would not be dead now.'

'You can't blame yourself! You had no—' Ruby began, but Harriett cut her off.

'Madam Crone said it, you both heard it. Magic is heavy around us, it's part of our skin, and traces of it rub off onto the people we're close too. The Shadow—' Harriett hesitated. 'I mean, *Locrinus*, could sense it. Hayley and Anthony... they must have reeked of it.'

Ruby shook her head. 'But what about Timothy? None of us even knew him!'

Emily watched as Harriett turned to Ruby, a grim expression on her face. 'And who was Timothy standing next to when he was murdered?'

Ruby's eyebrows deepened into a frown. 'Then why didn't he just kill us already? He's had plenty of opportunities.'

Harriett sighed. 'Thea's curse, her *protection*. He didn't kill us because he couldn't. He wasn't strong enough then.' She fixed her eyes firmly on the headstone in front of her. 'That's why the knife appeared to you, Ruby. That's why even when he was inside you, he couldn't cause you harm. He's been toying with us, making us afraid. And now we really should be afraid because now he's back...'

Harriett didn't bother to finish the rest of her sentence. They all knew what she had been going to say.

Now he can.

Ruby's mouth fell open and Emily too, remained silent.

Harriett sighed and started smoothing out the grass in front of her. 'My head is so full... I can barely make sense of anything. I feel like I'm going a little mad.'

Emily felt the same way. She could not yet discern where Thea's memories ended and where Emily's began, and she wasn't entirely convinced that there was a difference. After all, weren't they one and the same?

One soul. Two separate lives.

Harriett leaned forward and placed a hand on Hayley's gravestone in a soft, wordless goodbye.

'Who *are* we?' she whispered. 'If not our memories of what we've done and what we've been through?'

Emily did not know the answer, she wasn't even sure if it

was a question that Harriett was asking them or asking herself.

Harriett stared at Hayley's gravestone, her green eyes gleaming black in the twilight. 'I'm not going to sit around and wait to be haunted by darkness any longer. Harriett Sinclair's sister, *my* sister, is dead and it's our fault. I don't care that we don't have an army, I don't care that I no longer wear a crown. As of right now, we're at war.'

She stood up so that she looked down on them.

Ruby also arose, slowly, a sharp dark silhouette even against the night sky, and as Emily looked at them both she once again had the jarring notion of having lived the moment before. Only now she could see the memory playing out in her head and she knew which words were going to be spoken next. Harriett's lips twitched and Emily knew that she was remembering the same thing.

'What are you saying, Your Majesty?' Ruby asked. Even through the sarcastic tone with which Ruby said the words, Emily could still hear Augusta's deep guttural growl.

Harriett did not smile, nor did she seem particularly scared. Instead, she looked on into the distance with a serene, decided expression on her face.

'Yfel hêrespel âwierdan a gûðweard.'

We shall kill the king.

Then, one by one, each of their phones went off.

Chapter Forty-Two
YOU JUMP, I JUMP, JACK

They had each read the message, and they had each chosen not to say a word about it. None of them needed to ask what Sarah was sorry for. They already knew.

She had left them, abandoned them in favour of her king.

In silence they made their way out of the graveyard and through the streets of Woolington-on-Sea. Each of them knew the direction in which they were heading, though none of them bothered to say it aloud.

After they had been walking for about ten minutes. Emily stopped in her tracks.

When she had awoken with Thea's memories, another part of her had awoken too. The part of her that could see and smell magic. She could see the marks of it on her and her friend's skin. The runes that no one else could see, the ones that said; ᛒ for *berkana*, growth, rebirth, renewal. ᚺ for *hagalaz*, disruption, chaos, change.

And right now, Woolington was positively drowning in the stuff.

She could see the lines it made in the air, like heat rising off a pavement. The sickly-sweet poisonous scent of it, intoxicating and dangerous.

Locrinus' curse weaved through the town like a thin layer of smoke, ready to transform everything it touched. A part of her longed for her own magic to return. *truly* return.

In front of her Harriett and Ruby had stopped too, a quizzical expression written on both of their faces. At first Emily thought that they could see the curse too, but that wasn't it at all... It was that the *sound* had been sucked from the town. There was no whooshing of cars, no chatter of people. Emily scanned the street around them.

There was no one there.

'Let's get to the main road,' Harriett said.

Together the three of them sprinted up the street and around the corner.

The air was murky with a heavy, dense fog.

'Holy shit,' Ruby breathed.

Cars had stopped in the middle of the road, their drivers sitting frozen and asleep. At the bus stop people stood waiting for buses with their eyes firmly shut.

'Come on,' said Harriett, her eyes narrowed. 'Let's hurry.'

Emily did not know what she had expected when they arrived at the Neville.

She did not imagine a demented, nightmare-version of Wighus Hall, but that was what they found. It was as though the building had been stretched, made taller and more ominous. Graffiti still decorated the walls and there were large gaps from where the car parks multiple levels used to be seen.

'I, for one, vote that we *don't* go inside,' Ruby said, cutting through the astonished silence. 'This place might as well have the words "*Murder Castle*" spray-painted on the front door in blood.'

Harriett nodded thoughtfully. 'Oddly graphic, but yes, it might as well have.'

'Sarah's inside,' Emily said quietly.

Harriett turned to look at her, her face was grave. 'I know.'

'Are we not going to save her?' Emily asked.

Harriett stared up at the side of the building. 'Do you really think she wants saving?'

'Fucking leave her there,' Ruby snarled to Emily, and then she pointed to the building with a thin, accusatory finger. 'She chose *him*. Over literally *everyone* else. Just like last time.'

Emily shook her head. It didn't feel like last time. In their previous lives there had been months—years even—of deception and trickery. This had happened too quickly, maybe even Sarah herself didn't understand the choice she had made.

Emily could feel the thread of her pulse beat faster. 'We don't have to make the same mistakes twice.'

'Why not?' Harriett demanded. 'Sarah obviously did.'

For once, Emily flinched from Harriett's gaze. She had a way of pulling the truth out of someone, Emily was not yet ready for her truth to be revealed.

'Back then you said you didn't want to have to kill her,' Emily murmured. 'And today you apologised.'

Ruby threw her hands up wildly, Harriett looked as though she could cry.

'That's right, I did both those things. I never wanted to sentence her to death. I had to, to do otherwise would have made me seem weak to lords who preferred having a king over a queen.' Harriett's mind seemed somewhere else now. Her eyes were downcast, and her cheeks were shining red. 'Back then, I tried to spare her, offered her my friendship, protected her when my guard thought it easier to get rid of her. And she spat it all in my face. She would have been happy to let me die, if only she were to be queen.'

Silence hung between them, and Emily knew not to argue against what had been said. Most of it was true, after all. Only,

Emily didn't think Estildris would have been happy upon Gwendolen's death.

'But you're not like her,' Emily finally said.

'You're damn right I'm not!' Harriett shouted, and both Emily and Ruby were so surprised that they each took a step back. Harriett's eyes were wide, and she was breathing heavily. 'I don't lie to my friends! I don't sneak around keeping secrets. And I would *never* betray you like this.' She reached into her pocket, withdrew her phone and waved it violently in the air. '"*I'm sorry*"?' She let out a bitter laugh that sounded so unlike her that Emily couldn't help but wince. 'Well, I truly hope she is. Because in going back to him she has essentially agreed to let us die. For him to kill us.'

Harriett shoved her phone back in her pocket and turned to look at Ruby. 'What do you think we should do?'

Ruby glanced from Harriett to Emily and then back again. She ran a hand over her arm and then through her hair.

'I don't think we should go in. It's his territory, and only gods know what he's got waiting for us. We need to be smart about this. One wrong move and the whole of Woolington disappears and becomes the perfect setting for a BBC period-drama.'

Harriett bit her lip. 'I agree. But we have got to do something.'

Emily thought to the moment in the sea, where Sarah vanished beneath the waves and then reappeared almost an hour later. Where had she travelled to?

'Beware of water... for its where the barrier between worlds is at its weakest,' Emily said slowly. She walked toward the building and pressed her ear to the wall.

Nothing. No hum and no vibrations.

'The magic isn't coming from here. It's just where his curse is manifesting.'

Ruby frowned. 'Then where is it coming from?'

Emily couldn't help it, she smiled. 'The River Habren is where this all began. And where do all rivers go?'

Ruby swore viscously, but there was a glint in her eye, the kind of gleam that told Emily she was gearing up for a fight.

Harriett did not share the same enthusiasm; her own face was blank when she finally met Emily's gaze. 'The sea.'

THEY STOOD AT the front of the pier.

The light from the lampposts shone a dim yellow, while the sign that read 'PIER AMUSEMENTS' glowed a bright crimson, though the 'P' from pier and both the 'Es' in amusement seemed to be broken, the lights flickering on and off, on and off.

The sea was eerily quiet, there was no crashing of waves against the piers iron legs, only the occasional gurgle of water. The ocean was black—as black as the sky—it was as though they were looking into an abyss.

They stood at the end of the pier.

Even at this time of night, the pier reminded Emily of sitting on a bench with her family, eating fish and chips, watching the windfarm on the horizon. She could practically taste the salt and vinegar on her tongue.

In a line the three girls climbed over the iron railing, so that they stood perched on the edge, facing the vast, empty sea. The stars hung low in front of them, and they seemed almost close enough to touch. As though all they had to do was reach forward, and *grab*.

Emily held firmly onto the bars behind her, the ice-cold metal oddly comforting beneath her skin.

'Are you certain about this?' Harriett asked.

'Yes and no,' Emily replied.

It was a long, long way down, she thought.

'So, where do we think this will take us?' Ruby called from a little further along the line. 'If this works.'

Emily took a deep breath, inhaling the cold, sea-salt air. 'He's using the water as an anchor. The same way we used Cat. So, in theory, it should take us to where he's been hiding all these years. A place between life and death.'

Emily could almost feel Harriett's frown. 'Limbo?'

Emily thought for a moment. 'Yes and no.'

Water was a powerful source; it could both give life and take it away. It was the world's veins—the world's blood. Spirits could either flow through it or be trapped by it. Somehow Locrinus had used it as his own personal passageway, his own special door taking him from one realm to the next.

But that was the thing about doors, once one had been opened just about anyone could walk through.

Emily had a suspicion that they weren't the first to have discovered it.

'Are you ready?' Harriett asked them, looking from one to the other, loose strands of hair whipping around her face.

Ruby leaned forward, so that she dangled at an angle in the air, her arms the only thing holding her back. Her smile was wide and wild.

'You jump, I jump, Jack.'

Emily's heart panged, but she nodded all the same.

Magic, intangible and unknowable as it was, always had a certain pattern to it. Life born from life, death into death, blood for blood. Emily knew in her gut that any curse which began with a murder must end with one too. Only she was not certain whose murder it was that had set the ball in motion, Locrinus' or Estildris', so she did not know whose murder would put it right.

She could only close her eyes and hope. And hope. And hope.

Harriett took a deep breath and bent her knees. 'One…two…three!'

And then, holding tightly to each other's hands, with Cat beside them, they jumped.

Chapter Forty-Three

THROUGH THE DOOR

When they had been younger, they had all used to play make-believe in Emily's garden. They would dress up in costumes and use bamboo sticks as brooms. The knotted old tree at the back of the garden served as a portal, or a tree house, or a haunted forest or pretty much anything that their young minds could conjure up.

Emily remembered them playing the summer days leading up to their final year in middle school. They were eleven years old, and Sarah was the lost princess, Ruby was her prince, and Harriett and Emily were the goblins who wanted to steal her for themselves. Ruby had knocked Emily's bamboo stick forcefully out of her hand.

'You can't do that!' Harriett had said, even back then she was their unspoken leader.

'Why not?' Ruby had argued, 'I'm the prince, I have to protect the princess from the goblins!'

Emily remembered feeling a twinge of something twisty in her stomach.

Sarah and Ruby escaped the clutches of the goblins, but the goblins found a magic tree and decided that they did not need the princess after all. At the end the four of them drank lemonade in Emily's living room, princess, prince and goblins all equal at last.

That had been the day that Sarah gave them each a gift.

'You know we'll have to stop playing these silly games soon,' she had said, matter-of-factly.

Harriett had frowned, back then she had not mastered her signature side-braid, so instead her blonde hair fell in ratty curls over her shoulders and in front of her eyes.

'Why would we do that?'

'Because we'll be grown up of course.'

'Hayley says we should do what we want to do, and not what society tells us,' Harriett said knowledgeably.

Ruby had laughed. Back then her hair had been dirty-blonde instead of black and her smile had been nowhere near as sharp. 'I'll stop playing these stupid games when they start being boring as well as stupid.'

Sarah had rolled her eyes, then pulled out her rucksack. 'I got you all something from Turkey.' She withdrew four small paper white bags, handing one to each of them. Emily's fingers brushed Sarah's ever-so briefly when she went to take the parcel. 'They're friendship bracelets. Mine's pink, see? Emily's purple, Ruby's blue and Harriett's green. That way, even when we stop playing pretend, we'll still have these bracelets.'

Emily eagerly put the bracelet on, a purple string decorated with four silver beads. She vowed to never lose it.

'You're so weird, Sarah. We're never going to stop playing together,' Ruby had said, but she'd put the bracelet on anyway.

Sarah crossed her arms huffily. Out of the four of them, she was the only one who hadn't changed. Her olive-skin was still smooth and golden, her hair still thick and brown. She had only grown taller really, taller and more beautiful.

'What about when we start getting boyfriends?' she had demanded.

Little Ruby had laughed again. 'Boys are stupid.'

Harriett looked thoughtful; the bracelet tied tightly around her wrist. 'I think we can have boyfriends and still stay friends.'

Sarah had turned to her then, her tiny face scrunched up and determined. 'What do you think Emily?'

But Emily could not think of what to say, so she'd simply shrugged instead.

That was the first time Emily had ever pictured herself kissing her... and over the years that image had never faded. The *wanting* had never stopped.

Sometimes, she felt the need and the want and the hunger so keenly and so hard that it filled her up and up like a balloon to the point of bursting.

But no matter how much she yearned, or how badly she wanted, she knew she was not entitled to the kiss – or to her.

Just because we want something, does not mean that we deserve it.

Emily did *not* deserve it.

AS THEY PLUMMETED through the water, Emily could not help but remember that moment in her living room. As they sank deeper into the icy cold, she clung to the memory as fiercely as she clung onto Harriett's hand.

The weight of the water seemed to be crushing them. Pushing them deeper and deeper, yet they never touched the ocean floor.

Emily wondered briefly whether she had made a mistake. Maybe they hadn't found a door after all, maybe they were simply going to drown.

And then she felt it: The tug of magic and the whisper of spirits.

There were so *many* of them.

She opened her eyes, but all she could see was black.

The spirits called for Thea the Witch and her spells. They wanted to be released, they wanted to be set free.

Suddenly, it felt as though she was being pulled upwards, as though there was a current and they were being dragged along with it.

Harriett's hand gripped more tightly to her own, as they rose up, up, up through the water.

The darkness was fading, she could see a light through the endless waves. She saw a light, and it was *red*.

They could breathe again.

They were no longer in the sea. They were in a river, long and winding and scarlet. The sky above them was pink and even the trees seemed to have a soft crimson hue. Harriett gasped from beside her.

It wasn't night here.

It wasn't *anything* here.

It just was.

Emily looked to the shore where Cat was waiting for them. His fur was soaked through, he looked even more skeletal than ever, his round eyes seemingly too big for his head. He hissed at them and Emily knew he was urging them to hurry up.

It was only as Emily reached the shore that she realised someone *else* was waiting for them. As she pulled herself up onto the riverbed, she heard a collective gasp from both Harriett and Ruby. She rolled over onto her side and watched as a familiar figure knelt in front of Harriett's damp and dishevelled form.

'Finally! I was wondering if you were ever going to turn up.'

Hayley Sinclair looked almost exactly as she did in life, her blonde hair was immaculately in place, her daisy dress had not a single wrinkle, yet there was a sadness in her eyes that starkly contrasted with the smile on her face.

Harriett let out a strangled sob as she scrambled up from the ground and threw her arms around the ghost of her sister.

Emily and Ruby remained sitting awkwardly on the ground, looking to each other rather than the two sisters in front of them. Yet Emily could still hear Harriett's words, breathless and high-pitched.

'I'm sorry. I'm so, so sorry. I didn't mean for anything... I didn't want...'

Hayley gently caressed the back of Harriett's head. 'Hattie, it's okay! I know, I know.'

After a few moments Harriett finally managed to pull herself back. And when she did there was confusion knitted in her brows.

'How is this possible? How are you here?' Harriett looked to the bleeding sky and the rose-coloured grass. 'What *is* this place?'

'It's the River Habren and Wighus Hall,' Emily said. 'Or at least, it's the River Habren and Wighus Hall as Locrinus envisions it.'

Ruby snorted. 'Blood red and depressing as hell.'

Harriett nodded slowly, already turning her attention back to her sister. She ran a hand through the ends of Hayley's hair. 'How are *you* here though?'

Hayley frowned. 'I'm not... I'm not completely sure. When I died, I could feel a *hatred*, and somehow, I knew that it was aimed at you. When I left my body behind, I followed it and I landed here. And then I couldn't figure out how to leave. Not properly anyway.'

Hayley stood up from the ground and pulled Harriett with her so that they were all standing. She held Harriett's hand and took a step back to look at her.

'How did I not notice it before?' she mused. 'What an ancient soul you are.'

Harriett's skin paled and she let her hand drop from the ghost's grip. 'I'm sorry.'

Hayley shrugged. 'You didn't know.'

Emily turned away from the scene, her own skin was flushing hot and she could not bear to look upon the tragedy she had created. Instead she scanned the horizon. The river twisted and bent the same way she remembered it to, and the trees were exactly where they used to be.

It almost felt like home. Almost.

Magic pulsed through every inch of this place. Magic that Emily knew she could touch and pull apart and bend. The magic used to fashion the landscape was powerful but crude. It was like drawing over an oil painting with a permanent marker, effective, but if you squinted you could still see the original work.

And the original work was horrifying.

It was an empty space filled with both awake and sleeping ghosts. A pretty picture painted with the memories of all the soldiers that had once fought by a river. It was a void, with nothing but souls floating around inside it. Emily wasn't surprised that Hayley had found herself trapped here. She was being anchored, alongside all the other spirits that were not allowed to fade into the next realm.

In fact, the longer Emily looked at it, the more terrified she became. Because the only part of the landscape that was real, that was *solid*, was the grand and glorious Wighus Hall that sat ominous and looming in the distance.

And with every second it was looking more and more like a derelict car park.

'Mirror magic,' she breathed. That was why she hadn't been able to feel the hum of magic from the Neville in Woolington, because the Neville was only half there.

Ruby appeared beside her. 'What? What's going on?'

Emily pointed to the castle. 'That fake Wighus Hall is mirroring the *real* Neville car park. Eventually the car park will be here and Wighus Hall will be in Woolington, as real as it ever was. Locrinus will be completely free of this place.'

Despite the desperate thudding of her heart Emily's words left her lips smoothly, her voice so very calm. As though having a king from the Middle Ages walk around 21st Century Britain wasn't a cause for concern.

Harriett and Hayley were both standing beside them now, Emily wasn't sure how long they had been listening.

'What happens if we're still here when the transformation is complete?' Harriett asked.

Emily answered with a dark, sombre look.

Ruby let out a short, wicked laugh. 'Well guys, I hope you like the colour red.'

Harriett bit her lip and shook her head. 'No. He won't want to end it that way. He'll want to be here to lord his victory over me, he'll want to see the look on my face when he's won...' She frowned and turned back to the river. 'Hayley says he's gathered an army. I think he wants to beat me on the battlefield.'

'No offence Sinclair, but that's not going to be hard to do. There's three of us and one ghost, no offence Hayley.'

Hayley smiled. 'His army is made of ghosts too. I might be more useful than you think.'

Ruby's mouth dropped open and faced Emily. 'Yeah, what is with that? How come Sinclair can touch Hayley here?'

This time it was Harriett who answered. 'It's because this place both exists and doesn't, so we're both here and not here. The rules aren't the same. Right?'

Emily nodded. 'We still have to be careful though. If we die here, we die everywhere.'

'Which brings me back to my original point: What the hell are we going to do against an army?' Ruby demanded.

Harriett met Emily's eyes. 'Hayley says there are other ghosts trapped here.'

A wordless exchange passed between them, after which Emily walked forward three steps, crouched down and plunged her arm into the water. 'I guess it's time to wake the dead.'

Chapter Forty-Four

HARRIETT'S ARMY

The water was ice on her skin. Emily closed her eyes and sent her magic, what little power she had, into the opening. Because that's what it was; it was no more a river than she was just an ordinary girl. It might have looked like the River Habren, but she knew it for what it was—a split leading to another place. Somewhere *in-between.*

Though the spirits were sleeping she could still hear their voices, and it didn't take long for one voice to ring loudly in her mind. A soul that shouted for her, one that kept pushing its way through the rabble, desperate to get away from the Shadow's grip. She could sense its panic, its fear, its *love* and she caught him, like a fish in a net. He was mist at first, an impression vanishing between her fingers like smoke.

Then there was the smoothness of skin. Or perhaps only the *memory* of skin, Emily couldn't quite be sure. She grappled harder and harder until her hands clasped around a wrist, and then an arm.

Eagerly the spirit held on and Emily pulled, and pulled until her hand was free from the water and a man came with it. He fell inelegantly into the grass, his blonde hair plastered to his face, his arms and legs flailing as he grew slowly accustomed to his body once more. She knew him for who he was immediately. He was the man who would die for the love of his queen.

After a moment he grew still, then he slowly sat up, his gaze falling on Harriett. When he saw her his body tensed and his eyes grew wide with wonder, and suddenly he was in front of her. His hands placed on either side of Harriett's cheeks; his forehead pressed against hers.

He kissed her. It was the kiss of someone who expected to be kissed back, as though they had kissed a hundred times before. Harriett did not pull away.

'Mîn cyninge,' Osric whispered, awestruck.

My queen.

Because of course he recognised them for who they really were.

Harriett's face was pale. Paler than the luminous skin of the man that stood in front of her.

Ruby looked from Osric to Harriett and back again, realisation dawning. Silence washed over them until finally it seemed that Ruby could take it no more.

'What's wrong Sinclair? You look like you've seen a ghost.' She eyed Osric warily, her voice dripping with sarcasm.

Osric did not seem to understand the remark, and Emily almost wanted to laugh, because he *didn't* understand. Instead, he turned to Emily, and said in the Old Tongue.

'There are others.'

But he'd needn't have bothered telling her, for Emily could hear them, the faint voices of the soldiers that she knew so very long ago...

She rolled up her sleeves, plunged her hands into the river, and got to work.

THE NIGHT CAME, or rather an imitation of it. It did not come gradually, but like the flick of a switch. Until, suddenly, they sat underneath a black sky that was a few shades too dark, and a crimson moon that glowed a few shades too brightly. In front of them there were the luminous but not-quite translucent bodies of soldiers loitering amongst the grass.

Thirty-three. Emily had counted them, thirty-one soldiers and two teenage boys. Like Hayley's spirit, Timothy Small and Anthony Goldsmith had found their spirits drawn to the web of Locrinus' magic. Now they stood, awkward and gangly in comparison to the other ghosts.

She sighed, Locrinus had managed to summon an army of hundreds, and she had barely managed thirty-three. She had called their names into the abyss and for the most part, the souls had answered. Until she ran out of both names to call and strength to pull the spirits free. Her body was weak and her *hugr* faint. By taking from the makeshift world around them it had taken from her in return.

'We're not going to win, are we?' Ruby grunted, collapsing beside her.

Emily scanned her eyes across the meagre crowd. 'It does seem unlikely.'

Ruby leaned back and sighed, though she did not seem too anxious. Emily could see that her eyes were focused on Osric, Hayley and Harriett, their heads bent together deep in conversation.

'Did you know about that?' Ruby demanded.

Emily did not need to ask what she meant. Osric's nearness to Harriett was a strange sight to behold. 'Yes. It happened after you died.'

'Ah,' Ruby said. 'Of course, *after* I died. How silly of me.'

They both smiled. It really was absurd when they said it aloud, after a moment Ruby sighed. 'He always was too familiar with her. I should've known that he was in love.'

Emily lifted her shoulders in the smallest of shrugs. 'It worked in her favour: with Osric by her side she let the lords believe that perhaps it was *him* leading her. It reassured them to think that their young queen was being guided by a warrior's hand.'

Ruby snorted. 'Grouchy old bastards. If *I* had been that warrior, it would have been a whole other story.' She paused, thoughtful. 'Did she love him?'

The two of them looked over to where Harriett was standing, Emily thought she looked the happiest she had been in a long time, with the ghosts of Hayley and Osric standing on her either side. Yet Emily found herself unsure of how to answer. 'She was fond of him. She trusted him completely...' She trailed off.

Ruby grinned wolfishly. 'I know what you mean. Our Harriett ain't really built like that.'

The two of them looked over at their little army camp. Soldiers were dotted around crude fires, catching up as though they had been on holiday instead of being dead for hundreds of years.

'I never asked you where you came from... *Before*, I mean,' Ruby said abruptly.

'That's because you never cared to know,' Emily replied.

'That's 'cos I feared the answer back then.'

Emily smiled. 'And now?'

'I'm not going to lie, the air of mystery has somewhat evaporated.' Ruby took out her blade and planted it into the deep red grass. 'Come on, tell me the story of Thea. How did one of the last true witches of Loegria wind up having the ear of a queen?'

'It's a short enough tale,' Emily said with a gentle sigh. 'I sought her out. My people had grand ideas of bringing true magic back into the world. The crown seemed a good way to do that.'

Back then magic hummed in the air, but with every passing day another note would go missing. Her people

314

feared the day that there would be no notes left. Thea had simply wanted to bring the music back.

'I found myself bitterly disappointed.'

'Disappointed?' Ruby repeated. 'By Gwendolen?'

'Yes,' Emily whispered. 'She was *strong*, smart and practical; she was focused on how to rule, how to bring people together—she wasn't the least bit interested in anything I had to say about religion or magic. But she was someone worth following, so I followed.'

Ruby nodded, following Gwendolen was something that came easily to her—like breathing. 'We all did.'

Emily barely heard her; she was too busy rifling through old memories in her head. Thea had long ago failed in her quest to save magic, and when she had endeavoured to use her own magic to keep both the queen *and* the king's mistress safe—she had failed at that too. Now here she was, in a different body with a different name, about to fail all over again.

It was too pathetic, her eyes stung with the futility of it all.

Ruby cast a curious glance at her. 'There's something that still doesn't make sense to me: Why *us*?'

Emily knew what she meant. Cat had held their souls for centuries, but had chosen them, these *bodies* as their new skins.

Emily pulled at the grass. 'Before Thea went to Gwendolen, she had a family... A sister.'

'Oh?' Ruby leaned forward, listening.

Emily could remember Thea's sister's voice more clearly than she could remember her face. When she pictured her family now, she pictured the Walters, of all the younger siblings that looked up to her. But when she closed her eyes, she could hear a different sister's song.

When the moon swims down to the bottom of the deep... that's where I'll be, singing with the birds, body-less and free...

'Did you know that my mother—Emily's mother—supposedly comes from a long line of witches?'

Ruby's eyebrows shot up. 'No way!'

Emily felt the corner of her lips twitch. 'Thea's sister's name was Freya.'

Ruby let out a cackle, and Emily knew she had made the connection, that Emily's own mother was named Freya, too.

'Are you seriously trying to tell me that *you* are related to *you*? That's insane!'

Emily laughed and went back to pulling at the grass.

'Blood is a powerful thing,' she said quietly. 'And magic works in patterns, in circles. The Shadow drifted south to the sea, and without knowing it Thea's bloodline unwittingly followed the trail. And all the while there was Cat, the curse, tethered to it all.' Emily dropped the strands of grass to the floor, her mind picturing it. Cat yawned in front of her, stretching out and then laying on the ground.

'I imagine that when it became clear the Shadow was close to breaking free, Cat released Thea's *hugr* into a child of Thea's blood, and had no choice but to release the others as well.'

'Huh... nice to know the rest of us were so carefully handpicked,' Ruby mused, pulling the dagger back out of the ground and examining its hilt.

Emily's gaze drifted to Wighus Hall. It seemed a little smaller than it had hours before. Or had it been minutes? It was impossible to tell.

'I hate her,' Ruby said after a moment had passed, her voice soft and venomous. 'And yet I want her here safe with us, all at the same time. Crazy, right?'

Emily's skin tingled cold. 'Her place is with him. It always was.'

She'd been stupid to think that that would ever change, no matter how many curses she cast.

'How could she do this to us, though?' Ruby said. 'What about us? I mean, shouldn't who we are *now* be more important than who we were before?'

Emily's head shot up and she regarded Ruby carefully, her hard face was suddenly thoughtful and earnest. Emily was struck by the thought that Ruby was rather like a Russian doll, occasionally breaking open to reveal a different aspect of herself.

'And who are we now?' Emily whispered.

Ruby shrugged. 'Just four ordinary girls.'

Emily shook her head. 'We were never ordinary.'

'For a while there we were. I wasn't a warrior. You weren't a witch. Sarah wasn't some king's mistress and Harriett *definitely* wasn't a queen. We were all just friends.'

Emily gazed out at all the flickering campfires; day could come at any moment, rendering them all useless. She rubbed a hand across her wrist, feeling the comfort of the thread that was tied there.

We were all just friends.

'Well, well, well, if it isn't the famous, she-wolf,' a man's voice crooned.

Emily and Ruby both looked up, to see a lean figure sitting atop a horse, his dark eyes glinting malevolently.

Ruby leaned back onto her elbows in a deliberate show of nonchalance, she smiled lazily. 'Well, well, well, if it isn't the king's favourite errand boy. Tell me, has death cured you of being such an unbearable kiss-ass?'

Emily couldn't help but smile. Even in the Old Tongue, Ruby was quick to find inventive ways to insult people.

Algar let out a hiss between his teeth. 'Your new body doesn't suit you, *Dog*,' he spat. 'It's such a weak and fragile thing, I doubt you can even hold a sword.'

Ruby's eyes flashed and her grin grew even wider. 'Why don't you give me yours and we'll find out?'

Algar laughed. 'Nice try, *little girl*. I'm here to take you to the king. He wants to speak to the false queen one last time, before the sun rises.'

At this Ruby finally stood up, all her lazy, loose movements had vanished and suddenly she was a warrior, her back straight and her dagger held out before her. Though her bruised face and zombie Minnie-Mouse jumper somewhat softened the effect.

'Like hell you are,' she sneered.

However, in the time that they had been speaking, Emily had noticed what Ruby had not, that Harriett, Hayley and Osric had made their way over to them. It was now that Harriett moved forward so that she stood by Ruby's side.

'Lead the way.' When Harriett spoke, it was with the clear surety of Gwendolen's voice.

Ruby's dagger dropped to her side.

Chapter Forty-Five

ESTILDRIS RETURNS

They were a strange, mismatched motley crew. Algar took the lead, his grey horse trotting at a slow, even pace while Harriett, Ruby, Emily, Hayley and Osric marched behind him. Harriett had ordered the rest of her ghosts to stay by the riverbed, which Ruby thought was a colossally bad idea.

'What if he tries to kill us?' she seethed. 'We're waltzing in completely undefended!'

'We're in his terrain, if he wanted to kill us, we'd already be dead,' Harriett replied.

To which Ruby was silent.

It was true that Emily was also uneasy with walking woefully under-prepared into what felt so obviously to be a trap. Yet, Harriett had made up her mind and it seemed futile to try and change it.

'We have much to discuss, my *husband* and I,' she said, grimly.

The further they walked, the less *red* everything became, the closer they drew to the castle the more colour seemed to seep into the landscape around them. Until finally they were standing in front of the gates.

It was eerie to see the world they once walked with brand new eyes. To walk through trees that were identical to those that had once hosted the *Modraniht.* To stand in front of a castle that had once been their home. Memories and nostalgia, this was what this place was. A reminder of lives lived and lost. A bittersweet taste of wine that they could no longer drink.

'Walters...' Ruby whispered from behind her. 'Is this place exactly the same as we left it?'

Emily nodded. 'Everything but the castle itself.'

Ruby let out a sharp sigh of relief.

Algar turned to grin at them. 'Welcome home.' The acid tone of his voice said to the contrary.

The gates swung open and Wighus Hall enveloped them all.

It was the scent of smoke and spices, of fresh grass and summer sun.

The castle stood half-formed before them. Ivory grew where it once had thousands of years before, the oak gates were just as strong, just as intimidating. The windows were long and thin, and the turrets towered toward the pink sky.

And then there was the graffiti that decorated the walls, stolen from a different time and a different place. There was *glass* glittering amongst the stone, and there were bricks in the same smooth grey colour that belonged to Woolington-on-Sea.

It was Thea's home and Emily's nightmare all at once.

She heard Ruby swear from beside her, while Harriett's face was set into a fierce determined expression. Emily looked around, and it took a moment to realise what she was looking for.

Sarah. She was looking for Sarah's reaction to the large castle-car park monstrosity that stood before them.

But of course, Sarah was already inside.

'Come on,' Harriett said stiffly. 'Let's get this over with.'

She took a step forward, and obediently they all followed her. Even Algar jumped down from his horse and made his way inside.

Ruby met Emily's gaze; her hand still clasped firmly around her dagger. 'Hâlettan dôð a gûðweard.'

All hail the king.

Emily did not know what to expect when they were finally placed before the king. She had not wanted to imagine Sarah standing lovingly by her king's side, her back turned against them.

Yet, when she saw the two of them together, the hurt was nothing compared to the overwhelming *foolishness* she felt.

The hall alone seemed untouched by change. It was as long and wide as she remembered, and torches burned brightly along the walls illuminating the cobbled stones.

It held five long tables, four stood at the front of the hall, each heavily laden with food and warriors, all of whom stared at them as they entered, none trying to hide the curiosity in their eyes. The fifth table was positioned at the back of the room, larger and heaped with just as much food as the rest. It was positioned on a dais, so that the occupants looked down over them all.

What a sight they were, King Locrinus and his chosen queen.

They sat in high wooden thrones, adorned with golden leaves and ripe berries. Locrinus' mouth curled into an open smile when he saw them. Just as strong and just as intimidating as he had ever been in life; broad shoulders and burning eyes. His crown was a crude thing, heavy gold and large, roughly cut gems the size of golf balls encrusted haphazardly along its rim. With a jolt Emily realised that he was not wearing his armour, but instead donned a black tunic and a deep purple cloak.

He was not yet dressed for war.

By his side was Sarah, though not a Sarah any of them recognised. The girl who sat on the throne beside the king looked more like a young woman. Her dark hair plaited into two thick braids and threaded with strings of gold and small yellow flowers. Her crown was thinner, more delicate, and sat atop a turquoise lace headdress that perfectly matched the deep green of her dress.

The young queen regarded each of them with a cool indifference, her brown eyes showing no hint of the girl who had dragged them all to a party only a few weeks before.

The Lady Estildris had returned, and she finally had her king.

Looking at them, it was impossible to think that they had ever been apart. The king placed his hand over hers on the table's surface, and that small gesture said so many things.

Look at us together.

Look how well we fit.

Look at what is mine.

A silence penetrated the room broken only by the king's soft laugh; 'Do you remember me now? Gwendolen of Cornwall.'

Emily winced. His voice was as deep and as powerful as it was in her memories, only now it was also smooth and rich and coated with magic. Unlike Osric and Algar, the king spoke his words in clear, clipped English.

Harriett raised her head and smiled genially. 'A little too well, perhaps.'

Locrinus' smile did not falter, though the mirth in his eyes flickered. 'Please, sit.'

He motioned behind them, where wooden chairs were now prepared for them. Emily did not know how or when they had appeared.

In unison they all sat, Emily and Hayley on one side of Harriett, Ruby and Osric on the other.

'I suppose you know why I have summoned you,' Locrinus said, raising his goblet and taking a swig.

'I imagine for the same reason that I came,' Harriett answered.

Emily leaned backwards in her seat as Ruby did the same. Their eyes met and an understanding passed between the pair. *This is not a conversation meant for us.* Ruby grimaced and turned her attention back to the dais, Emily followed suit and found her gaze locking with Sarah's. She must have seen their little exchange, Emily wondered how it felt for her to see their group from the outside. Sarah flushed and turned her head to the king.

Locrinus' eyes burned in Harriett's direction, and for a moment Emily imagined that they had changed colour completely.

'Yes. I imagine you have noticed his absence by now.'

Harriett tilted her chin upwards. 'Truthfully, I did not look for him. I figured you would have found him by now and if you hadn't... Well, I didn't want to disturb his soul for this.' Her voice wavered slightly as she waved a hand over the hall.

Locrinus leaned forward on his throne. 'I found him. But his soul did not wish to come to me. You did an excellent job in poisoning him against me.'

Harriett sighed. 'I did no such thing. In fact, I never spoke of you. Once you'd died it was as though you never existed.'

Locrinus went rigid. 'Madden was my son. *Mine.* He should have learnt how to rule from *me.*'

Harriett crossed her legs. It was incredible that, even in a room of such splendour, with warriors in their armour and Locrinus in his crown, she still seemed to hold control in her blue jeans and white trainers. She did not blink when she met the king's gaze.

'He was my son too. And I assure you he did not lack for education.'

Locrinus slammed his goblet onto the wooden table. 'You always were too smart for your own good.'

Harriett smiled. 'At last, we can agree on something.'

From beside her, Ruby let out a snort and for the first time since Harriett had entered the room, Locrinus shifted his gaze.

'You are not quite as fearsome in that new body of yours, *Dog*,' Locrinus hissed. 'I wonder if you are of any use to Gwendolen at all.'

Ruby simply tilted her head to the side and smiled, flashing her teeth in a dangerous grin. Then the king focused his gaze on Osric and Hayley in turn. A flicker of what may have been confusion passed over his features when he took in the ghost of Hayley Sinclair, but it vanished when he laid his eyes on Emily.

'I suppose it is you that I should thank,' he said, smirking. 'If it were not for that night by the river, we may not all be here now. Tell me, what were you thinking? I have had many years to wonder... and still I do not know.'

Emily looked to the ground.

After a few moments the king leaned back in his chair, apparently unconcerned by the lack of an answer.

'It has been a long time since we have all sat together in a room like this,' Locrinus said. He was speaking in the Old Tongue now, a language everyone but Hayley could understand. 'I did not originally wish to call you here. I would much rather have slaughtered you all the moment you drifted onto the riverbed, but the Lady Estildris wanted to ask you a question and in exchange we would offer you some mercy.'

'What question?' Harriett asked.

At the same time Ruby said; 'What kind of mercy?'

Locrinus picked up an apple from the table and examined it. 'You need not all die, though undoubtedly you each deserve it. In exchange for answering my Lady's question truthfully, there will be no battle. Only Gwendolen's life needs to be taken.' He smiled at them, it was both a handsome and horrible thing. 'Gwendolen, and only her.'

In a flash Ruby and Osric were on their feet, each positioned themselves in front of Harriett's chair while Hayley, confused, placed her hand on Harriett's shoulder.

'Death has made you delusional,' Ruby sneered.

Locrinus raised an eyebrow but kept his eyes firmly fixed on the spot where Harriett sat. Once again, Emily found her gaze drifting to Sarah. There was a coldness in her expression that Emily did not recognise.

Harriett pushed Ruby and Osric to the side gently but remained sitting in her chair.

'How?' she asked.

'You can't be serious?' Ruby interjected.

Harriett ignored her. 'How would you kill me?'

Locrinus turned to Sarah, his hand still locked firmly with hers.

'Drowning,' Sarah said, and there was no falter in her voice. Nothing to suggest that she was anything apart from calm. Meanwhile, Emily could feel her own heart quicken in her chest.

How had it come to this?

'No,' Harriett said clearly. 'I will not agree. Firstly, because I know you, husband of mine, and there is nothing to stop you from killing everyone after I'm dead. Secondly, because I do not wish any harm to come to Woolington. And thirdly, because this body was not meant to be mine. It was stolen for me. I wish to treat Harriett Sinclair's life as the gift that it is, and I do not intend on chucking it into the bottom of a river any time soon.'

Neither Locrinus nor Sarah seemed particularly shocked by this answer. Sarah picked up her own goblet and swallowed the contents whole.

'However, I will answer your question. Since we've made the journey here.'

For the first time since arriving, Emily watched as Harriett turned her attention to their friend.

'Come on, Sarah,' she whispered. 'What do you want to know?'

Sarah lifted a jewelled hand to her face and then, as though with extreme effort, raised her chin so that her eyes met Harriett's.

'What was Habren's name?' she asked, so quietly that if it were not for the silence that echoed in the room, they could not possibly have heard her. 'What was the name given to her by the family that raised her?'

Emily heard the deep sigh that escaped Harriett's lips.

'I don't know,' Harriett said honestly. 'I thought it best to leave them in peace and keep her as far away from court as possible. I thought the less was known of her the better, so I never asked.'

Sarah let out a sound that was somewhere between a laugh and a sob, and Locrinus wrapped an arm around her. Sarah buried her head into his shoulder. Harriett frowned in confusion, but Emily understood what Harriett did not.

'You couldn't find her soul, could you?' Emily whispered. 'Not without her name.'

'No,' Locrinus hissed. 'For centuries I searched for Habren, unable to find her and unsure why I couldn't. Estildris made it clear to me why: that name belonged to a river, not to the girl who lived with my blood in her veins!'

'I'm sorry,' Harriett said, it sounded like she meant it.

This did not seem to be the response that Locrinus was expecting. His nostrils flared and his eyes burned.

'You will be,' he spat. 'You have until dawn. Now, *get out.*'

The force of his voice echoed through the room like thunder and the heavy oak doors flew open at his command.

One by one, the five of them stood. Osric took hold of Harriett's arm and pulled her from the room. Ruby trailed after them, her eyes surveying the crowd, watching for any sudden movement or attack.

Until it was only Emily left behind, watching as Locrinus and Sarah comforted one another.

'Don't worry, my love,' he murmured, his long fingers trailing the shape of her cheek. 'We shall truly live again soon.'

Chapter Forty-Six

CLANG. CLANG. CLANG.

The night lingered like smoke; everything remained frozen in place, exactly how they had left it hours ago.

Emily positioned herself to the left of Harriett as they sat circled around a campfire. Osric sat to her right, a space which Ruby usually occupied.

'Where's Ruby?' Emily whispered.

Harriett cast her eyes downward. 'She said she had to check something.'

'And you let her go?'

'I can't always be the one to stop her. Besides, it seemed like something that she needed to do.' Her eyes turned to swim over her ghost army. 'Doesn't it seem cruel, to keep them here to fight all over again?'

Emily pursed her lips. If Harriett was looking for fairness, she would be searching for a good long while. Locrinus had built the foundations of his in-between world on spilt blood and bad memories, Emily was not convinced that anything true or good could grow there.

'They are honoured to serve you even in death, my queen,' Osric said, his voice low, eyes searching her face.

Gods, Emily thought, *the way he stares at her...*

'Last time we fought him we had numbers,' Harriett said. 'We had a plan.'

Emily remembered. Before, Gwendolen had known that Locrinus was a brutal and efficient warrior, she had also known that he would underestimate her.

When the king met the young queen on the battlefield next to the river—the river that would soon take the name of Habren—he had found a small army and laughed. The battle had commenced and just as the king's victory seemed imminent, Gwendolen's true army arose. It came from behind him and to the side of him, trapping his troops and pushing them to the river's edge. Finally, Augusta brought the battle to an end when she took the king's life.

The same plan would not work again, they did not have the numbers nor the element of surprise.

Osric knelt in front of Harriett. 'What do you need Gwendolen? Tell me, and I will make it so.'

Harriett looked over her meagre troop, her hand running over her plait.

'I need an *advantage*,' she whispered, then her eyes landed on Emily. 'When will dawn come?'

Emily glanced up to the sky. 'Time doesn't exist here. Dawn will come when he wants it to.'

'It must take an awful lot of his power to hold everything here...' Harriett mused, and Emily recognised the spark in her eyes. The glimmer of an idea.

'Yes, I imagine it does, and concentration too,' Emily said.

Harriett nodded slowly, the faint traces of a smile playing on her lips. Then abruptly she stood and waited until she was certain that every face was looking at hers. Timothy Small's round face stood out from the crowd.

'I did not wish this for you all,' Harriett said, her voice crystalline. She did not shout, yet every soul hung on her every word. 'But here you stand, dragged here by the hatred of a king and the desperateness of a queen. For that I am truly sorry.'

The warriors cast each other confused glances. Queens did not apologise, least of all to the men that followed them.

Harriett stood a little straighter, from behind her Emily saw Osric beam softly, his gaze cast at the ground. All attention was now on their little circle and the fire that blazed before them.

'If it were up to me, I would let your souls go. I would let you find peace,' Harriett stated, her voice wavering slightly. Emily knew the earnestness of Harriett's words, but a part of her questioned how much of it was a performance. A queen rallying the troops to her side.

Silence followed, so that the only sound was the sound of the river, its waters flowing smoothly, the trickling of water piercing the night's darkness.

'But I can't,' Harriett continued. 'I can't let you go, no matter how much I might want to. So instead I must ask one more thing of you,' she paused, her green eyes burning furiously into the crowd of warriors that watched her. 'I ask you to win.'

The confusion broke, to be replaced with low murmuring grunts of approval.

Osric started slamming his sword against his shield.

Clang. Clang. Clang.

'No, I *command* you to win.'

Clang. Clang. Clang. More soldiers joined the noise, raising their swords and beating them on their shields.

'This is not a war; this is already a victory!

Clang. Clang. Clang.

'Losing is simply not an option!' Harriett called, her voice louder.

Clang. Clang. Clang.

Now the noise was deafening, every warrior was clanging their sword. 'Can you do that?' Harriett shouted.

Clang. CLANG. CLANG!

'CANNE ÊOW WINNAN?' Harriett yelled, her voice somehow carrying over the noise and chaos. The clanging stopped, to be replaced by the deep thundering cheers of her small army, as they raised imagined goblets and cheered for battle.

Hayley and Osric both moved to Harriett's side and Emily watched as they each took their turns to embrace her.

'I had no idea our Sinclair had such a flare for the dramatics,' a voice said from behind Emily.

Emily resisted rolling her eyes; she did not even turn to see who it was. 'Where have you been, Ruby?'

Emily could practically hear Ruby's shrug. 'I had to fetch something that belonged to me.'

At this Emily turned around, and there, Ruby stood, wearing chainmail that was three sizes too big for her and scratching the ear of one of four large, grey hounds.

Emily's mouth dropped open. 'How is this possible?'

Ruby grinned. 'It was just like you said, everything here is exactly as it was. My old armour was stashed in the stables, along with my faithful hounds. It was as if they were waiting for me.'

Emily let out a breath. 'You're lucky you didn't get caught.'

Ruby barked a laugh. 'Luck had bugger all to do with it.' She ran a hand through her hair and crouched down onto the ground, taking it in turn to pet each of the dogs as they panted and wagged their tails for her. Her sharp features were somewhat softened as she let one of the dogs playfully nip her hand.

Emily hadn't seen Ruby so happy nor so relaxed since— Since she couldn't remember when.

That's when she realised—Ruby had not clutched her stomach or winced in pain once since arriving on the riverbed.

'You know it's not real, don't you?' Emily said quietly after a few moments had passed. 'How you feel here... none of it.'

Ruby wrapped a hand self-consciously around her waist and focused her gaze on the dog that was now licking her palm.

'I know,' she murmured, not looking up.

Emily nodded. 'Okay. Please don't forget it.'

'You two!' Harriett called from the fire. 'Get over here, we have work to do.'

Obediently Ruby rose and Emily followed until a circle had again been formed around the campfire. Harriett and her ghost-sister, Osric the blonde-haired warrior, Ruby and Emily. It was not quite the war-council that Gwendolen had once assembled all those many years ago. Yet it was all they had, and it would have to do.

Underneath the inky black sky and the glow of the crimson moon, Harriett told them of her plan and together they ironed out the details. They spoke deep into the night until the sky bled red and the water in the river stopped gurgling.

Until silence descended upon them all.

Chapter Forty-Seven

BÆRNAN

The night disappeared and the sky glowed red once more. Two black birds flitted across the horizon and Emily could not help but follow the path they made, rooted to the spot, as a memory rose to the surface, unbidden and unwanted.

'Have you found your guidance?' she asked.

'Perhaps. The sign was unclear...'

'Was the sign unclear or is it your head that is clouded?'

The Lady Estildris laughed. 'The gods work in mysterious ways.'

Emily blinked and the birds disappeared.

She sighed. Even now, she longed to bring Sarah back to them, to pull her away from the king's side. But just like the two birds in the sky, they always followed each other.

She thought of Woolington-on-Sea, a cursed town now smothered with sleep, and shook the thought away.

'This is crazy,' Timothy said from beside her.

Emily didn't even look at him. She had been given a job to do, a job that *only* she could do. Yet turning her back on the battle still felt wrong to her, and it felt even stranger to have Timothy and Anthony by her side.

'They won't be of any use to us in battle,' Harriett had explained. 'But they could be of use to you, as look-outs.'

But every time she looked at Timothy, Emily saw his death. She could picture the moment the Shadow spilled from his mouth, and the small bubble of blood at the corner of his lip. Every time she looked at him a voice whispered; *He's dead because of you.*

Timothy's spirit, however, did not seem the slightest bit bothered at being dead. In fact, he rather seemed to be enjoying himself.

'This place is crazy. I've never seen anything like it. How 'bout you Ant?'

Anthony shrugged. Sarah's ex-boyfriend was having a harder time mustering up enthusiasm for their surroundings and their task. Emily could hardly blame him.

The moment the sky had changed they had made their way across the field to Wighus Hall, keeping to the ground and as out of sight as possible. Now, the three of them stood in the woods that surrounded the castle. Watching and waiting as the last of Locrinus' army marched toward the river.

'If he's smart, he will want to leave a few men to guard the castle,' Harriett had said. *'I doubt he'll be so arrogant as to leave Wighus Hall completely unguarded. Can you handle that on your own?'*

'Yes,' Emily had answered truthfully.

In Woolington, there was little to no magic for Emily to draw on. Here, *everything* was magic, she could practically breathe it in.

Harriett had been right; the king hadn't left Wighus Hall completely unguarded. However, he clearly hadn't felt the need to leave it with much protection, judging by the two warriors that had alone been left to guard the gate.

'Okay,' Timothy whispered. 'What do we do now? Do we kill them?'

Anthony snorted. 'They're already dead, idiot.'

Emily suppressed a smile. She couldn't kill them, or even force their spirits to return to the void. If she did, Locrinus might *feel* their absence the moment she cut their strings, just as Emily would notice if any of her ghosts were severed loose from her. Even now she could feel the weight of them all, each of them a link in a chain that she was holding on to.

Besides, Harriett had made it clear that Locrinus was not to know that Emily was at the castle.

'If he has any reason to turn back—any at all—then we have lost.'

Jaw set, Emily walked toward the two soldiers, found a thin thread of magic and pulled.

'Nihtslæp.'

The two men dropped to the ground like stones.

'What did you say to them?' Timothy gasped.

'Sleep,' Emily answered, and she opened the gate.

THE CASTLE WAS unnervingly empty, and barely resembling a castle anymore. There were hardly any signs of the grand stones and turrets that made up Wighus Hall. Instead, it was all open space, dreary and grey, with white paint lining the floors and graffiti covering the walls. One piece of graffiti stood out, written in a garish orange and in handwriting she recognised.

Sophie Grimely is an intolerable fuckwit.

Emily let out a *tssk* sound and wondered how long-ago Ruby had written that.

Then panic began to froth and bubble inside her. If the car park was what now stood here, then what was standing in Woolington?

Locrinus' make-believe world wouldn't be make-believe for much longer.

Emily closed her eyes, running a hand over the wall, feeling for the vibrations of magic, allowing it to pull her in and show her where she needed to go.

'Come on,' she urged, picking up her pace. 'We need to hurry.'

She ran across the parking-lot and up several flights of stairs, Timothy and Anthony following close behind, until they reached the grand hall—the throne room—and she stopped.

It was still a throne room.

For now.

Cursing herself, she wondered how she had not thought of it immediately. When the king had first willed this place into being, of course this room would have been what he created first. It was the room that held the most power for him in life, the room that was most intricately tied to the crown. It was where his curse had first started to manifest.

Emily ran a hand through her hair.

'*Destroy it,*' Harriett's voice whispered in her ear. '*Destroy it all.*'

'Destroy it...' Emily repeated, more to herself than anyone else. 'Yes, but how?'

She crouched onto her knees and pressed her ear to the floor. She had once described magic to be like music, and now she found herself listening for a rhythm she could interrupt.

'We're not going to beat him,' Anthony said sullenly. 'We're all going to die here... Well, I'm going to *stay* dead here.'

Emily looked up at him, she had never much liked Anthony in life, but he seemed a pale imitation of the lively, obnoxious boy she remembered.

Timothy edged forwards. 'What is this place? It looks like the Neville, but it feels... It feels like something *else.*'

Emily's heart skidded in her chest. She stood up, she had

to find a way to end this and fast. 'It's a mirror,' she said. 'A mirror to our world. It's where he's focused most of his will, most of his magic. This is the place that connects the land he's made to the land we live in.'

'How do you break it?' Anthony asked, his blue eyes somehow dark. 'How do you break the mirror?'

Emily's eyes roved around the hall, lingering on Sarah's throne perhaps a few seconds too long. Then she made her way to the left-hand side of the room so that she stood facing the wall. She was all too aware of Timothy and Anthony's gaze following her, she had never before been the focus of so much attention.

Then she felt it, the pull.

There.

'King Locrinus used magic to tether us all here, to this place... to this *void*. But behind this colourful exterior, the darkness still lingers,' she motioned across the hall.

Anthony frowned but didn't speak.

'What does the darkness fear?' Emily asked them.

Timothy looked to Anthony and then back to her. 'I don't know. What?'

Emily took an unlit torch from off the stone wall and held it in front of her.

'Light,' she said simply.

Then, without looking to see their reactions, she strode over to Locrinus' throne, lifted the torch to her mouth and whispered; 'Bærnan.'

Burn.

Chapter Forty-Eight

A BALANCING ACT

It was a mournful sight, to watch as the fire licked at the stone walls, to witness as it ate its way through the grey brick so that segments of the building fell gracelessly into the ground.

When they had sat around the campfire making their plans and discussing their strategies, Harriett had remarked that there were only two ways in and out of Locrinus' world; the castle and the sea.

'Water is where the barrier between worlds is at its weakest. That's what Madam Crone said, right?' Harriett had asked.

'Right,' Emily had replied.

'So then how come Sarah is here too? She didn't come by the sea, did she?'

Emily had thought about it. 'No. But the car park and the castle are linked. Locrinus connected them, Sarah must have come through the car park—the castle, I mean.'

'But the spell isn't complete, is it?' Harriett's words tumbled over one another in their rush to get out. 'So, he's still using magic to tie the worlds together?'

Emily had agreed. 'He must be.'

'And he's using magic to keep his army here.'

Emily had agreed once more.

'And he's using magic to keep all of this exactly how he wants it,' Ruby's gestures were wild.

At this Harriett's eyes had gleamed. 'But it's not exactly how he wants it! How can it be when you found your armour, Ruby? Or how Hayley, Timothy and Anthony are roaming around here of their own free will? Don't you see? His power can only stretch so far, he can only focus on so much at once! Things have slipped through the cracks.'

It was Osric who finally asked; 'Do you have an idea, my queen?'

Harriett had turned to Ruby then. 'How do you win a fight, Ruby?'

Then Ruby's mouth had curled into her crescent moon smile. 'Hit them where they least expect it.'

THE LAST OF the Neville crumbled into the dirt, a charred and blackened mess.

Emily wiped her eyes with the back of her hand, then she turned her back on the scene.

Locrinus had expected Gwendolen to focus all her attention on her army, on the battle to come. After all, that was where he was focusing his. But he had underestimated her, just as he had done all those thousands of years ago. Once again, he had assumed that because he was powerful, that meant she was powerless.

He was wrong.

The Shadow King had spent centuries growing his strength, collecting memories and souls, building a land in his image and forging a path to link his in-between world to the one of the living.

But it was *too* much power, or at least too much concentrated in one place. In one fell swoop Emily had turned it to ash. She had ripped a hole in the landscape and now the void was leaking back in. She did not know if the king had the magic to stitch it back together while fighting a battle at the same time.

As they had sat around the campfire, plotting their next moves, Harriett had asked them one simple question; *How much control does the king truly have?*

Emily supposed they were about to find out.

IT DID NOT take them long before they could hear the desperate clanging of metal against metal.

The battle had begun.

Soldiers were clashing against soldiers in front of the river's edge. Roars and screams filled the air, the horrible squelching of weapons piercing armour. Blood spattered across the grass.

Only it wasn't blood. Not really.

For every time a ghost was struck it would drop to the floor in a perfect imitation of death—only to shakily stand back up again in moments. Emily watched as Osric went flying into the river, only to scramble his way back out again.

Ruby pulled him free of the water and together they went racing back into the fray, her four hounds tearing through the battle after her; snapping and gnawing their way through Locrinus' men. Emily realised with a jolt that if Ruby were to sink to the ground, she would not get back up again. Her eyes scanned the crowd and she saw Harriett, tiny and almost frail, hidden by a small huddle of soldiers.

'Did it work?' Timothy asked from beside her. 'Did we break it?'

Emily's heart pounded viciously against her ribcage. She wasn't sure. There were too many threads of magic, and she couldn't separate one from the other.

Her eyes continued to roam the crowd until she found him, though it did not take long. The king seemed even larger now than he did in life, his very presence magnified, his aura an overwhelming, powerful thing. He stood atop a large boulder in blood-spattered armour, staring down across the pandemonium, his mouth set into a thin grimace. But it was his eyes that held her attention, his eyes that were *burning*— and not the golden fire she was used to, the gold that had once marked him as Godsblood. They were burning like coals; they were burning *black*.

Emily squinted but even from where she stood, there was no mistaking the pain and concentration on his face.

'Yes...' she whispered. 'Yes, I think it did.'

Relief crashed over her; Harriett had been right! The king simply could not hold all his warrior's souls and sew the fabric of his world back together at the same time. *Something had to give.*

Emily watched, triumphant, as a slew of the king's men fell and, instead of getting back up, they *seeped* into the ground. Disappearing back into the void, waiting to be called upon once more.

More fell, and then more, until the numbers were—not quite even—but close... Close enough to stand a chance.

'Let's go,' Timothy said, gesturing for her to move forward.

Emily knew that she should. She knew that she needed to find her place by Harriett's side, where she could be protected. She knew that if she were to fall, Harriett's army would fall with her, she knew all of this and yet she remained rooted to the spot.

By her side Anthony had also frozen, and Emily knew why.

On the other side of the battle, draped in an emerald green gown and with a crown perched delicately upon her head, was Sarah.

She was breath-taking.

Emily was not sure where she had come from, only that she now dismounted from her horse and took her place by the side of her king. She did not seem all that concerned by the battle, in fact she didn't seem to notice it at all. All Sarah could see—all she had ever seen—was him.

'Sod this,' Anthony said, marching forward.

'Where are you going?' Timothy called, panicked.

Anthony looked over his shoulder, his pretty face all twisted with anger. 'Apparently we died for that bastard. I want him to regret ever laying a finger on me.'

For a moment Timothy was hesitant, he glanced from Emily to Anthony and then back again.

'I'm sorry,' he said, and then he made to follow him.

Emily knew that it was irrational, she knew that he was dead already and yet still she reached out a hand for him.

'Wait!' she said. 'Are you a fighter?'

Timothy smiled, and it was such an easy-going smile that she regretted never having seen the real one.

'No. But then, I was never a lot of things.'

Emily dropped her hand and she let them go. Like Hayley, they were both still in the clothes they had died in. For Anthony that meant a pair of boxers and a white vest; for Timothy it was the jeans and shirt he'd worn to the party. They both looked so woefully out of place. Yet, neither of them hesitated. Anthony was tall and sinewy while Timothy was short and runty, but they both threw themselves into the battle, and soon Emily could see neither of them.

For a moment she just stood there. Watching the mayhem unfold. Watching the blur of silver as swords clashed against one another, as ghosts fell and rose. It was a fight without end.

In front of her there was only death and blood, death and blood, over and over again. Behind her there was the charred ruins of a castle-car-park-curse, and the emptiness being kept at bay.

Emily knew what she was supposed to do next.

Instead, she crouched down low and skirted her way along the edge of the battle. There was no point in lying to herself, she knew where she intended to go.

Ruby had said that they were all just friends. And that's what Emily wanted to remind Sarah of now. She didn't want to think of castles and curses, kings and queens. She wanted to remember sleepovers and cupcakes, dressing up and staying late after school. She wanted to tell her that it didn't matter who they were then, when who they were now was so much more important. She wanted to tell her she loved her with or without a crown. But above all she wanted to save her from making the same mistake twice, she wanted to save her body as well as her spirit this time. She wanted to save it all.

She ached, and she wanted.

Yet all she could do was hold out the frayed friendship bracelet as though it was so much more than a few beads held together by purple string—-and to her it was.

'Sarah?' Emily pleaded quietly, so quietly that there was no way she could possibly hear her.

And yet, impossibly, she turned around.

Chapter Forty-Nine
LETTING GO

'Sarah?'

When she turned around her expression was empty of surprise, anguish or pain. Anarchy reigned around her and yet Sarah was somehow separate from it. She and her king, alone together.

'Emily.'

Her heart turned to stone in her chest. It wasn't what Sarah had said that made her insides twist—it was the way that she said it, as if Emily's name had died in her mouth.

'I know you don't want to do this,' she said, holding out the bracelet in front of her. Sarah did not even look at it.

Locrinus stood statuesque by Sarah's side. He did not move, his gaze still trained attentively on the battle, a puppeteer pulling his strings.

'You have no idea what I want,' Sarah murmured.

'How can you say that?' Emily said quietly. 'I *know* you. You're the girl who wanted to have her first kiss at the exact stroke of midnight. You want romance and sunsets and love. Look around you Sarah, this is not that.'

Sarah blinked; the sereneness of her expression unmoved. Behind her Emily caught a glimpse of Ruby making her way forcefully through the battlefield. Blood was spattered across her face, blood that could only be her own.

Something tugged at Emily's insides, panic and fear and a cold, terrifying *knowing*.

'We're your friends!' Emily pleaded.

Sarah's nostrils flared. 'Friends don't watch friends *drown*.'

'I never wanted you to—I tried to stop it, I tried to warn you!'

Sarah said nothing.

Emily's eyes flickered back to the battle, Ruby wasn't far away now, they were running out of time. She took a deep breath and the words poured out of her.

'Sarah, it doesn't matter who he was to you back then, what matters is who we are now. We're your friends and we love you. Don't waste this life over something that ended so long ago.'

Sarah took a step closer to her, so that she was standing mere inches away. Emily could see every strand of hair, every eyelash, and the tears that were beginning to flood in her eyes.

'He loves me. He fought death to be with me.'

Ruby was running closer and closer. Her sword swinging through the air like a deadly promise, the dagger glinting at her belt. Emily knew what would happen next, she fell to her knees and the bracelet landed in the mud.

She bit back the urge to scream, to curl up inside herself and disappear. She stared up at Sarah, and saw Estildris; powerful, determined, unquenchable. She took a deep, shaky breath. The time for secrets had long since passed.

'I love you,' she whispered. '*I* love you. I twisted the fabric of time so that I could be with you. I watched you die, and I traded my own soul to bring us all back. *I love you.*'

Ruby was so close now that Locrinus had noticed her, Algar charged in front of the king, sword raised and poised for Ruby, but Osric's ghost met with it instead. Ruby dropped her sword on the ground and pulled the dagger from its sheath.

The dagger that Thea had blessed, all those years ago.

The mask of calm on Sarah's face broke, only to be replaced seconds later.

She shook her head. 'I won't leave him. Not again.'

There was no time left. Emily grabbed Sarah's hands and pulled her hard enough so that she fell to her knees on the ground in front of her.

'Close your eyes,' she said. Then, without waiting to see if Sarah had followed her instruction, Emily pulled her fiercely and tightly into her arms. It felt like a hug, it may have even looked like one– but it was a shield.

She was shielding Sarah from what was about to happen.

Ruby carved her way through the dead soldiers until she reached the king. He stood looking down at her, but somehow Ruby did not seem beneath him in any way.

Then something odd happened, her vision splintered into two, Emily saw the scene in double. Ruby and Augusta, as one ferocious, feral being. When Ruby spoke, she heard both of their voices.

'Your Majesty,' Ruby said, a grin on Augusta's face.

Then it happened, exactly as it had once before.

The king laughed and raised his sword, bringing it down in a vicious stroke. Ruby rolled out the way, it was graceless but fast, the speed with which she moved was almost jarring. Locrinus didn't falter though, he lifted the sword once more and brought it down again, this time Ruby was not quite quick enough, and the blade caught her left shoulder as she crashed into the ground.

She let out a strangled hissing sound as the king raised his sword a third time, but before he could swing, Ruby lurched forward, her arm flicking out in a smooth curved motion, slicing into the king's leg, he buckled down with a roar and as he fell, Ruby kicked the sword out of his grip.

The king was on his knees, his eyes still like coal, but all around them the magic flickered. The ghosts of his army seemed a little less solid, a little more ghostlike. The sky burned less brightly.

Harriett and Hayley and Osric cut their way easily through the crowds.

Locrinus was losing control.

Slowly Ruby stood, a terrible smile on her lips, blood coating her teeth and dripping from her mouth.

Sarah shook in Emily's arms struggling to get free, but Emily only held her tighter. 'Not yet,' she breathed. 'Not yet.'

Ruby's hands tightened around the hilt of the dagger, and then without grace or ceremony, she plunged the blade into his neck.

Emily knew what Augusta had said next, thousands of years ago.

Timme ðolian ðone as gûðweard.

Long live the king.

Only Ruby didn't speak those words.

'Just fucking *die* this time,' she sneered, and then she pulled the dagger ruthlessly out of his neck, only to shove it right back in.

But he didn't. He didn't just die.

Instead, the king stared up at Ruby, his black eyes pouring out what looked like oil, and then, with a cold bitter laugh, he opened his mouth and the Shadow spilled out of it.

Ruby staggered backwards as the dagger and the king's body fell into the grass.

The Shadow wound its way through the air, growing larger and larger until it filled up the sky.

Ruby made for Harriett and stood in front of her, a pitiful human shield. At the same time Sarah broke free from Emily's grip.

As the Shadow consumed the sky Emily's thoughts were racing. In front of her Sarah crawled her way over to the king's body and flung her arms across his chest. And then it occurred to Emily just how stupid they had all been.

They couldn't simply *kill* Locrinus. Killing Locrinus was the act that had triggered his curse in the first place. By killing him, they were simply re-setting the spell.

Cold dread shot up her spine. She did not want to find herself wearing a different body and standing on this same, ghostly spot another thousand years from now.

From over the top of Locrinus' body, Emily's eyes found Harriett's, and she knew that Harriett also understood.

Sarah.

Estildris.

She was what kept him tethered to them. Emily was at a loss as to how, just as Thea had been confused all those years ago. But now she needed to understand. They needed to reverse it.

A strange rasping filled the air and the water in the river was rising. The strange make-believe land was disappearing, soon it would be nothing, the perfect place for a Shadow to hide, a void in which a Shadow could grow strong.

Soon they would all be dead.

Cat appeared beside her, baring his teeth, preparing to take their souls into his mouth once more. Cat alone could escape. Her *fylgja*, who had wandered between the worlds so often that it now belonged to none.

Harriett knelt by Sarah's side. 'We cannot let more people die because of us.'

Sarah looked up, her eyes and cheeks were red, and her fingers were digging into the king's armour.

'You killed him,' she said, her voice empty. 'You killed him again.'

Harriett nodded pitifully. 'Yes. I'm sorry that he's dead,

and I'm sorry that I never recognised just how much you loved him. I never meant for any of this to happen.'

Sarah looked up, the Shadow had now grown so big that it had taken up the sky, or perhaps it now was the sky. It was hard to tell.

'He'll come back for me,' Sarah whispered. 'He promised to always come back.'

Emily hurried to kneel beside Sarah. 'Was it a blood-oath? Did he swear it in blood?' she asked hurriedly.

But Sarah didn't seem to be listening to her, she had buried her head in his chest.

Above them the Shadow let out a deafening roar as darkness swallowed the horizon.

Emily gave Sarah's shoulder a hard, hard shake. 'Sarah, when he promised, did he bleed? *Did he bleed?*'

At this Sarah glanced up again, she gaped at Emily, her mouth hanging open, confusion sweeping across her face and then— understanding.

'It was only a drop...'

But apparently only a drop of Godsblood was needed.

Once, long ago, Thea had tied four souls together by sacrificing a piece of her own. Once, long ago, Locrinus bound his soul to his lover's with blood, and only with blood could it be unbound.

Magic on top of magic.

Souls on top of souls.

Locrinus the king and Thea the Witch had shared not even a sentence in life and yet in death... It was a marvel to look at the mess that they had made.

Emily looked to Harriett, a wordless exchange passing between them.

'Ruby, clean your blade,' Harriett said.

Time was running out; the land was shrinking all around them. All the ghosts but two had returned to the river, to either effervesce or wait until they were called upon again.

'Sarah, listen to me. You need to sever the tie. You need to make a different promise.'

'No!' Sarah cried, and she really was crying now. Her chest heaved with sobs and there was a string of saliva hanging from her mouth. 'We said we'd make each other whole, we said—we said we'd be together forever.'

Harriett took hold of Sarah's shoulders, forcing Sarah to meet her eyes. Emily turned away. It hurt to watch this. Everything hurt.

'Look around you!' she heard Harriett implore. '*This* is what forever looks like. Us, in this horrid place, watching him die over, and over again.'

Emily turned back around to see Ruby handing Sarah the blade.

'Let him go,' Ruby said. 'Let him be at peace. It's what I'd want.'

Sarah's jewelled fingers curled slowly around the hilt of the dagger. 'I don't want to be alone,' she said, and her voice sounded so small.

Harriett was trying not to cry now, her voice shook as she spoke. 'You're not alone. We're here, for as long as you want us.'

Sarah looked up at the Shadow, the rasping was so loud now, and nearly everything around them was black. The river was no longer seen, only heard.

Sarah pressed the tip of her ring finger to the blade, a bead of bright red blood seeped out, dripped down her finger, and fell onto the dead king's cheek like rain.

'I promise to love you until the day I die. I promise to never forget you. I promise to find you in this place when my body... when this body turns to dust.' Her voice wobbled, and she stared into his face. 'I promise to leave you now, I promise to let you go.'

The rasping around them grew deeper, louder, more harrowing.

A howl of pain.

'Let me go,' Sarah whispered.

And then he did.

The Shadow shrank and shrank and shrank. Sarah scrambled backwards as the king's body turned to dust and was swept away by a non-existent wind.

Remember me...

Sarah grabbed hold of Emily's arm and instinctively Emily hugged her. Around them the in-between world was shifting. Where the Shadow had been only moments before there was now only water, the river was expanding, growing wider and bigger until it wasn't a river at all. There were sounds—too many sounds—the whispers of thousands of souls finally finding peace.

Osric and Hayley both stood staring at Harriett. They were speaking, but Emily couldn't make out the words they were saying.

And just like that they were gone. Taken by the waves.

Sarah let out a shrill, piercing sob, and Emily pulled her up from the ground.

The tiny patch of grass that the four of them were standing on was shrinking with every second. A spray of cold water hissed and crashed over them; the taste of salt now filled the air.

Emily looked over Sarah's shoulder to see Harriett and Ruby watching her.

'Ready?' Harriett said.

Emily nodded. Gently, she pushed Sarah away from her and lifted her chin so that they were facing one another.

'Hold your breath,' Emily said.

Then she let the waves take them.

Chapter Fifty

DRIFT

Memories and experiences, thoughts and feelings: These were the things that made up a soul.

Intangible, invisible things, but as real as a breath of wind touching your cheek.

As the darkness enveloped them and the cold seeped into Emily's bones. She thought she saw it all a little more clearly now.

Their essences, their *hugrs,* had been reshaped and moulded into something new. Yet, the ingredients of who they were had remained the same.

Warmth and compassion.

Ferocity and loyalty.

Stillness and calm.

And love... Always love.

The magic was melting away, it was sliding off her like snow from a rooftop. Through the haze of murky water Emily saw the rune marks peel away from her skin, she felt the threads of rope—the curse that bound them all together—snap.

Suddenly she was adrift.

Alone.

Alive... Alive... Alive...

PART FIVE

HARRIETT
AGAIN

Once, there was a girl with the
future at her feet.
No shadows on her back.

Endung
– An ending of sorts.

Chapter Fifty-One

WASHED ASHORE

'**I**'m sorry,' Harriett said.

It was all she could think to say as the world ended around them, as the final two ghosts remained.

Hayley, still wearing the blue daisy dress she'd worn that fateful night. Osric, her would-be lover, a man from another time and another life. Harriett knew there was never going to be enough time to tell them both all she felt.

Hayley simply smiled at her in that maddening almost-but-not-quite patronising way of hers. 'For what?'

The sound of water grew louder around them.

'For everything,' she said, voice cracking. 'For your death… for not being who you thought I was…'

Her sister took hold of her wrist, her touch porcelain cold.

'Don't be…' She was still smiling, and there was so much love in that smile that it made Harriett's heart ache. 'You were exactly who I needed you to be. You were my sister.'

Hayley's ghost did not let go of her wrist as Harriett turned her gaze to Osric.

Gwendolen's Osric… *Her* Osric.

The warrior who had fought for her in life and then in death. Osric, who loved his queen so fiercely, all the while knowing that the love she felt for him in return was but thin smoke compared to his vibrant flames; and had happily accepted it all the same.

She met his eyes. 'Yfel sorig.' *I'm sorry.*

Osric raised his eyebrow. 'Tima cyinge nateshwon sprintan sorig.'

A queen does not apologise.

The tiny patch of land was getting smaller with every blink, and even as she stood talking to them, she could feel their spirit's melting away.

'Yfel frêogan êow.'

And it was true. She loved them. Harriett's love for her sister was unwavering. And Gwendolen loved Osric in the only way she knew how.

Osric smiled. 'Yfel tôcnâwan, yfel freogan eow min cyninge... synnes'

I know, and I love my queen... for always.

Harriett felt her throat go dry and her eyes sting.

'Fall in love with the world for me,' Hayley whispered—then she'd let go of her arm.

Together the warrior and Hayley Sinclair fell backwards into the water, sinking into its depths and disappearing entirely—gone. Harriett knew she would never see them again.

Not in this lifetime.

Eyes prickling, she turned to face the others. Emily and Sarah stood huddled next to each other, while Ruby perched on the edge of the shrinking piece of land, peering curiously into the black ocean deep that surrounded them.

'Ready?' Harriett asked.

Emily nodded and took Sarah's hand. 'Hold your breath,' Harriett heard her say. Then they, too, vanished beneath the water.

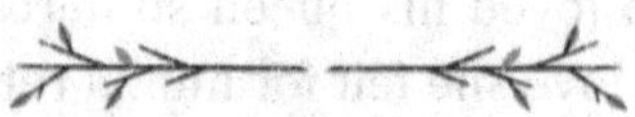

Now, it was just the two of them.

Sometimes it felt as though it was always just the two of them.

'Are you ready?' Harriett asked again, but Ruby did not pull her gaze from the water.

'No,' she said simply. 'I think I'm going to die here, Sinclair.'

Everything was black now. Harriett could only hear the rippling of the sea and *feel* it lapping at her trainers. Ruby's armour glimmered in the dark, her pale skin now white as paper.

'Don't you remember what the old Crone said?' Ruby whispered. '*You will let them go.* This is it; this is the moment.'

Harriett shook her head, as if to shake away the thought. 'No. It's not.'

'I can feel it. The pain returning... we've been under too long. My body can't handle it... this... *this* is it.'

Harriett took a step closer, partly because she needed to be closer to her friend, partly because there was barely a metre of land left to stand on.

'You're wrong.'

Ruby let out a cold, sharp laugh. 'It's an incurable disease. *Incurable*, Sinclair. Even if it's not a death sentence, it's a life sentence—a whole life of doctors' appointments, drugs and surgeries. They're just going to keep cutting away at me until there's nothing left.'

Ruby made a soft, gasping sound and Harriett realised with a jolt that she was crying. She had never seen Ruby cry before. She turned to face her, and sure enough, tear tracks streaked down Ruby's dirt and blood-spattered face.

When Ruby spoke, her voice was barely more than a whisper. 'I don't want to spend my life broken.'

Harriett placed her hands gently on Ruby's shoulders and shook her. 'You're not broken.'

Ruby tilted her head to the side, and black strands of hair fell in front of her eyes. 'I feel like I am. Every day is just pain and exhaustion and more pain. Wouldn't it be easier, wouldn't it be nicer, to just stay here? To let go?'

You will lead them, you will betray them, you will tell them all you know... And you will let them go.

'No!' Harriett said.

The tethers to this world were fading... she felt as though she were sinking. Yet, Ruby was solid, unmovable.

'No, you don't get to leave. I need you; Emily and Sarah need you; your mum *needs* you. If you give up now you don't just give up on yourself, you give up on everyone else.'

She dug her fingers in harder, she could feel herself slipping, slipping, slipping away and still Ruby was like a tree rooted in this land of make-believe.

'Please, Ruby, I've already lost one sister, I can't lose another...' her throat was raw. 'You said you'd be there for me, always. You promised.'

Ruby shook her head. 'I can't, I can't do it anymore; Harriett I'm tired.'

Harriett felt her skin turn to ice - Ruby had called her by her name, something else that Ruby never, ever did.

'You are not broken,' Harriett said fiercely. 'You. Are. *Not*. Broken.'

Yet even as she said the words, she wasn't sure if they were true. After all, weren't they all a little broken?

Harriett herself felt divided. Mostly though, she just *felt*. She felt so fiercely and so powerfully that she thought she might keel over from it.

Love for a sister.

Love for a son.

Love for her friends—twisted fractured creatures that they were.

It was too much love. It was too much pain. It was too much, too much, too much.

And then, beneath it all, *anger*.

Harriett straightened her back. 'Give up if you want, Coleville. But you're wrong if you think for even a second that *I'm* giving up on *you.*'

Without pausing to think, Harriett threw herself at Ruby, circling her arms around her and dragging her down into the depths below.

WHEN THEY BROKE the surface, the sky was bruised pink, and for a terrifying second Harriett thought she was still in the river. It was only when she saw Emily's form on the stony beach that she let out a sob of relief.

'Harriett!' Emily called, wading out into the water to meet them.

'See Ruby?' Harriett said. 'We're back!'

Only, Ruby wasn't answering. Frantically Harriett swam forward, desperately trying to keep Ruby's head above the water. Ruby's eyes were closed, and Harriett was all too aware of the trail of crimson that was being left in their wake.

She could feel the stones beneath her shoes. Grappling, she hoisted Ruby's limp form so that she was half carrying, half dragging her to the shore.

Emily reached them and when she saw Ruby her eyes went wide with panic. 'What's—?'

'Just help me!' Harriett shouted.

Emily didn't need to be told twice, she grabbed hold of Ruby's feet and together they carried her onto the beach and laid her down. Harriett pressed her head down to Ruby's chest, her heart was still beating, though it was faint and slow.

'She's not waking up,' Harriett breathed. 'Why isn't she waking up?'

Emily opened her mouth, closed it then said, in a dazed voice; 'She's bleeding...'

She was right. The armour that Ruby had worn by the river had vanished, replaced by the zombie Minnie Mouse hoodie once again, and there...all down her left shoulder, leaking through the jumper, was blood. Lots of it.

Where the king had stabbed her.

Harriett ripped off her own jumper and pressed it as hard as she could against the wound.

'Call an ambulance!' she shouted to Emily, not removing her hands.

It was only then that she spotted Sarah. Sitting on her knees a little further along the shore, the motionless body of a black cat by her side. She was watching them with wide eyes, her mouth hanging open.

'I can't!' Emily said, voice shaking. 'My phone—it's dead!'

Harriett shook her head. This all felt too sickeningly familiar.

'Then go find someone! GO!' she half-shrieked. Her heart was beating too fast and her mind was racing ahead of it.

She couldn't think.

She watched as Emily scrambled up the pebbled shore and disappeared, running to find help in whatever form it came.

Harriett pushed the jumper harder into Ruby's shoulder, she was shaking and whether it was from fear or from the aching cold of the wind, she couldn't be sure. From across the empty beach her eyes met with Sarah's once more.

Sarah was just as soaked through as the rest of them, her white coat no longer white and her long hair plastered to her face. She looked at Harriett, blinked once, then stood up and walked away.

No. Harriett couldn't believe it. Any second now, Sarah was going to come back for them.

'Stay with me, Ruby,' she whispered.

Any minute now.

'I order you...'

Any moment.

'To stay with me.'

She heard it then, as she stared at the empty spot where Sarah had been, the high-pitched wail of sirens. Harriett tilted her head back to the now-blue sky and cried.

Chapter Fifty-Two

AFTERMATH

Harriett was a diligent student. The problem was that, no matter how much she studied, there was no lesson for how to deal with somebody else's pain.

It had been a week since Harriett had pulled Ruby unconscious onto the stony shore of Woolington-on-Sea's beach. A week since Ruby had been rushed to hospital, half-drowned and bleeding from a stab-wound that neither Harriett nor Emily could explain. A week since Janice Coleville had arrived distraught and manic by her daughter's hospital bed.

A week since Harriett and Emily had watched from the back of the ambulance, as the doctors had injected her with who-knows-what and asked them question after question. A week since Ruby had been wheeled into surgery and wheeled out again half a colon lighter and a scar zigzagging across her stomach.

Harriett pursed her lips and stirred the coffee in front of her, on the other side of the table, Alex took a sip of his own drink and pulled a face.

'How can you drink this stuff?' he asked.

Harriett arranged her expression into the vague approximation of a smile. 'How can you not?'

He let out a soft laugh and took another sip. They were sitting in the hospital coffee shop; Alex visited every day straight after school and only left when the nurses kicked him out. Harriett, for her part, came whenever she could. When she wasn't by Ruby's bed, she spent her time loitering outside Sarah's house with Emily, trying to coax her into talking to them.

She never did.

'It's four o'clock,' Alex said, jumping up. 'We can go in now.'

Harriett smiled and followed Alex's lead down the hall and up the seven flights of stairs.

They walked into the room to find Janice Coleville already there. Visiting hours weren't supposed to start until four, but none of the nurses seemed to have mustered the courage to tell Ms Coleville this. Harriett couldn't really blame them.

'Alex!' Janice said warmly as they entered the room, followed by a stiff, 'Harriett.'

Harriett felt a pang. Ms Coleville had always liked her before, but ever since she hadn't been able to give a satisfactory reason as to why the four of them had been swimming in the ocean in the early hours of dawn, she had been decidedly cold toward her.

The two sat down on the opposite side of the bed. Ruby had an entire table filled with cards and shakes. Her black hair was noticeably greasy because she hadn't been able to have a proper shower since arriving. She was gaunter than ever, with deep purple rings under her eyes so colourful that they could have been painted on. But it was the tubes hooked up to her hands and arms that Harriett found most unnerving—she had to force her gaze away from them.

'Hey guys,' Ruby said, adjusting the bed remote so that she was sitting up, wincing as she did. From the stitches in her arm or the stitches that ran along her stomach, Harriett couldn't be sure. 'No Emily today?'

'Not today,' Harriett said. 'How are you holding up?'

Ruby grinned. 'I actually took a little turn around the ward this morning. It took five minutes to take five steps but... that's progress for you.'

Harriett forced herself to smile. The doctors had said that it would take three to six months for Ruby to fully recover. She still couldn't hold down food, and whenever she stood it took the wind right out of her, but she was determined to walk. Determined to get out of the hospital bed.

'She's doing so well!' Ms Coleville exclaimed proudly. 'My girl's so brave.'

'Mum...' Ruby groaned, her face flushing red.

'No, she's right,' Alex said. 'You're doing amazing—you're amazing,' he grinned at her and Ruby bit her lip.

Harriett found herself increasingly impressed by Alex. Never once did he treat Ruby as though she was sick, never once did he treat her as though she were something fragile. He didn't yet know the full truth of the soul that lay cocooned inside a schoolgirl's heart—nor did he know the events that had led to Ruby lying in a hospital bed. But Harriett could see how badly Ruby wanted to tell him.

Harriett rather thought that Ruby was falling in love with him.

And she had no idea what to do with *that.*

'Strongest person I know,' Harriett agreed. Ruby pulled her gaze away from Alex and their eyes locked.

Harriett's mind flashed to the moment when it had been just the two of them on that tiny spit of land... and how she had thrown them both into the water.

At that moment Ms Coleville yawned and Ruby turned to her. 'Mum, why don't you go home and get some rest? You need sleep.'

Ms Coleville eyed Harriett darkly. 'I'd much rather stay here—'

'I know, but Alex and Sinclair are here. Plus, I'd really like it if you could get me a change of clothes, these hospital gowns are driving me insane.'

Ruby had tried this tactic of getting her mother to leave more than once and it always failed, but this time Janice really did seem to be considering it. Maybe she really was that tired, or maybe it was because Ruby was staring at her so pleadingly. Ms Coleville regarded Ruby carefully.

'Okay, I will leave the three of you alone for an hour or so. I'm going to get you some stuff, get myself a coffee and then I'm coming right back, do you hear?'

They all agreed, and Ms Coleville bent down to kiss her daughter on the cheek before sweeping out of the room, leaving only a perfume cloud behind her. As soon as the sound of her heels had click-clacked out of earshot Ruby focused her ice-blue eyes on Harriett.

'You were right to bring me back,' she said. 'I know what you're like, you're feeling guilty—but you shouldn't. If I had stayed there... I wouldn't have anything; I wouldn't *be* anything.' She motioned down at herself and the tubes in her arms. 'This was always going to happen, Sinclair; it was only a matter of time.'

Harriett leaned forward and did the only thing she could think of, she grabbed hold of Ruby's hand. 'I'm so glad you're alright.'

Ruby let out a bark of laughter, followed by another wince. 'Oh, I'm dandy, picture of health me.'

Alex cleared his throat, his brow furrowed in confusion.

Ruby looked to Harriett imploringly.

Harriett grimaced; it was her feeling that no-one but the four of them should know. It was their secret, *their* pasts. In telling Alex this truth they were letting him into their world, once he knew this part of them, he couldn't then un-know it, no matter where the rest of his life might take him. And that terrified her, but it clearly did not terrify Ruby.

'Okay.'

Ruby let out a sigh of relief and began to tell Alex the tale of a king called Brutus who had once had three sons. She spun the legend of a young wise queen and a cunning Germanic princess, of Augusta the she-wolf and Thea the Witch, and when Ruby grew tired and out of breath Harriett carried the story for her.

She spoke of a cat that stole four souls into its mouth and a Shadow that loitered in-between everything and nothing, hungering for a body of its own and the love of a woman who had long since been lost.

Between them they cobbled together the story of their lives, of four girls who had lived before and who were once more living again in a dreary English town that sat by a pebbled beach and a perpetually grey sea.

It sounded too fantastical, and maybe it was.

They sat huddled around Ruby's hospital bed, using one of Alex's maps to circle the places from their tale; the spot where the battle at River Severn had originally taken place, the land where Wighus Hall had once stood, the route Locrinus' men had taken through Albany and Cambria to get home.

Together the three of them talked at length about old Briton, Ruby and Harriett taking it in turns to speak out words in Old English while Alex hastily wrote them down in one of his many, many notebooks. Then eventually Ruby, bleary eyed and smiling, fell asleep.

Chapter Fifty-Three

BORROWED SHOES

After, Harriett wound her way through the streets of Woolington-on- Sea.

Winter had arrived and the branches on the trees looked like bony arms, bare and withered. It felt as though Woolington-on-Sea was preparing to hibernate, preparing to sleep off the events of the summer and maybe forget it entirely. Forget about the deaths of Hayley Sinclair, Timothy Small and Anthony Goldsmith. And maybe, just maybe, forget about the mystery that surrounded four rather odd St Catherine's girls.

Harriett pulled her school coat around herself; the bitter cold had turned her cheeks numb but she barely noticed, her brain was on autopilot and she just kept walking.

When she reached the Neville, she found that somebody else was already there.

'I keep coming back here too,' Harriett said. Emily turned around to face her, showing no surprise at Harriett's appearance.

'I can't help it,' Emily murmured. Then reverted her gaze back to the blackened ruin, cradling a white bundle in her arms.

The ambulance that had fetched Ruby hadn't been the only sirens to wail the morning they had washed ashore. The

Neville car park had burned to the ground, from a fire that no one could explain.

'Are you worried that some of the magic still lingers?' Harriett asked, standing beside her.

'No,' she said simply. 'The fire burnt it all away.'

Harriett didn't think she misheard the longing in Emily's voice. The white bundle in Emily's arms rustled slightly and Emily lifted the blanket away to reveal a tiny black kitten with glowing blue eyes.

Harriett froze. 'Is that...?' She trailed off, unsure of exactly what she was trying to ask. She had seen Thea's cat lying lifeless on the beach and hadn't given much more thought to it.

'After Cat died... after everything that happened that day... I went home and there he was, waiting for me on my garden fence.'

Harriett's heart beat a little faster, panic beginning to rise. 'What does it mean? Will the Shadow return—?'

Emily shook her head. 'No...it's nothing like that... Cat was a part of my soul, what's left of my magic is tied to him... and although he died when the curse ended...'

'You're still alive,' Harriett said slowly.

'I'm still alive,' she breathed. 'So, he couldn't stay dead for long, he had to find his way back.'

The kitten mewed and poked out its tiny pink tongue.

They stood in silence for a moment. Harriett buried her hands in her coat pockets, rubbing her fingers together for warmth. 'Have you managed to speak to her?' she didn't bother clarifying who.

Emily grimaced. 'She's ignoring my calls, my texts... I've seen her hanging out with Lacey Greenfield.'

Harriett raised an eyebrow, Sarah must be desperate to spend time with Lacey, a girl she had once described as being as interesting as a patch of dry dirt. 'I can't believe she hasn't even visited Ruby...' Harriett said.

'It's hard for her.'

Harriett bit her lip, considering her next words carefully. 'Yes... but it's hard for Ruby too, don't you think?'

Emily's expression didn't change. 'How is she holding up?'

'She's thin and tired, but she's getting there.' She paused. 'She missed you today.'

'I miss her too,' Emily whispered, and then she wrapped the kitten back up in the blanket. 'I guess we're all a little lost right now.'

It was true.

They each felt it. A duality of sorts. An *otherness*, a feeling of belonging and yearning all at once.

'It's like stepping into somebody else's shoes,' Emily muttered after a moment. 'They fit but they're not comfortable. Maybe we'll get used to them.'

'Or...?' Harriett prompted.

Emily simply shrugged and turned away. 'Or maybe we won't.'

Harriett watched her leave. Since everything that had happened, Harriett had found herself acting the only way she knew how; burying herself in work and timetables and revision. Lingering after classes and occupying the library during lunch breaks. Only, she wasn't sure if it was *her* anymore.

Emily was even quieter than usual, and she carried the silence with her, people stopped talking as she approached. It was as though she cast a spell with every footstep, rendering passers-by speechless.

Meanwhile Sarah put in considerable effort to avoiding them both, as though they were a plague that she might contract from standing too close.

Harriett sighed, and her breath turned to mist in the night air.

There was nothing much she could do. They were all grieving, and Harriett was well acquainted with grief—enough to know that it wasn't something that could be cured, but rather something they had to simply live through. She and her friends were grieving the lives that they had lived all those thousands of years ago, grieving for all the things they could never have again.

Magic, strength, love...

But it was more than that, they were also grieving the lives they had *now*. The innocence that they had each lost. Before they had just been schoolgirls... Now, she wasn't sure what they were. Their lives in Wooly's had been so irrevocably changed and Harriett knew they would keep on changing.

She rubbed the back of her hand across her eyes, wiping away a stray tear. Somewhere in the distance an owl hooted.

Chapter Fifty-Four

ANCIENT SOULS
AND SCHOOLGIRL HEARTS

'It's decided then, *Roman Holiday* is the movie of choice,' Alex said, holding up the disc for all to see.

In the three weeks that Ruby had been home, there hadn't been one night where her friends hadn't come over. Harriett positioned herself so that she sat in the alcove of Ruby's bedroom window.

'Tell me again, what is with all the black and white films?' Harriett asked.

'It's the sound, it's so crackly' Ruby explained. Alex inserted a disc into the television Ms Coleville had propped haphazardly on the chair opposite Ruby's bed.

Alex flopped down onto the bed next to Ruby and placed his arm around her shoulder. Harriett averted her gaze. He was constantly finding innocent little ways to touch Ruby and every time he did Harriett's mind flew to faint memories of a soldier passing by a queen.

She found herself doing that a lot, comparing moments from one life to moments in another. Moments that she had experienced in one life but not yet experienced in this.

The sound of violins blared from the TV and the coal-black kitten playing by Emily's feet let out a high-pitched hiss.

Emily had named the creature Whisper, and indeed it did seem to whisper secrets that only Emily could hear. As they all settled down to watch the film the creature hopped nimbly onto Emily's shoulder and curled up into a ball in the crook of her neck.

The four of them watched the film in relative silence, the only exception being the sound of Ruby shovelling handfuls of marshmallows into her face. Now that she could eat proper food again, all decorum had been thrown out of the window. Knives and forks only slowed her down as far as she was concerned.

Together they watched as Princess Ann posed as a commoner so that she could enjoy a fun-filled day in Rome with the handsome Joe Bradley.

The four of them sat cosy and warm in Ruby's box-like room as rain hammered on the walls outside. Halfway through, Emily went downstairs to fetch hot chocolate and soon the smell of it smothered the air. It was the perfect lazy Sunday.

'This is a cheesy film, Ruby,' Harriett said, curling her fingers around the steaming hot mug.

'C'mon, it's a classic!' Ruby argued, pointing to the screen. 'Audrey Hepburn is a frickin' icon! Tell her I'm right Em.'

'She's an icon...' Emily said slowly, 'but I've got to side with Harriett. This could be the cheesiest film I've ever seen.'

Ruby flung a cushion at Emily's head then winced at the effort. Emily blinked slowly, frazzled, and suddenly they were all laughing. It had been so long since they had laughed together, that it seemed once they started, they couldn't stop.

It was in that bubble of laughter, that a fifth figure silently entered the room and the bubble popped.

'Your mum let me in, I hope you don't mind.'

Ruby shot up from her slouched position and immediately grunted in pain from the effort. Alex rested his arms around her shoulders, keeping her still and calm.

'What are you doing here?' Ruby demanded.

Sarah stood in the doorframe; she almost appeared to be pinned there, unable to move forward. Harriett cast her gaze to Emily, who seemed fixed in her place on the floor, her hands clenched into anxious fists.

'I needed to see you all,' she said quietly. 'I'm sorry I didn't visit you in hospital, Ruby, but I'm glad you're alright...really, I am.'

Even from where she sat, she could smell Sarah's sweet vanilla perfume. Harriett wanted to stand up and hug her, but she felt that there was an invisible barrier between them all, and she was afraid to cross it. It was then, as Sarah stood frozen in the doorframe, that Harriett knew she was leaving.

'The three of you have been such an important part of my life—lives even—and you will always, always be important to me...' Sarah paused and finally seemed to notice Alex sitting awkwardly by Ruby's side. 'Except you. I don't really know you.'

Alex waved his hand nervously; but Sarah ignored him. Instead, she fixed her brown eyes on the wall behind Ruby's head.

'I spoke to my parents, and they agree that after everything that's happened, I could do with a fresh start, so... they pulled some strings and I'm finishing my exams in London. I'm going to live with my aunt.'

Sarah still didn't look at any of them in the eye, instead shifting her focus to one of the posters hanging behind Ruby's bed. 'I think it's for the best.'

'But what about the four of us?' Harriett asked. 'What about Girl Fight club?'

'It's done,' Sarah said. 'I love you all and I know you love me too. But there's a part of each of us that's always going to kind of hate each other from now on.'

Harriett wanted to deny it, but there was a small morsel of truth in her words. Sometimes when she looked at Sarah, she saw a woman from another time—stealing her family and her crown.

'We'll get over it, just give us time,' Harriett said.

Sarah let out a tiny little laugh. 'Haven't we had enough time? Decades and decades of it?'

'Not really. Not time together. Don't we deserve that?' She turned to Ruby for assistance but of course Ruby said nothing. Harriett supposed that was the nicest thing Ruby *could* say.

'I never hated you,' Emily breathed. 'I only ever loved you.'

The room stilled.

Harriett had not heard what Emily said to Sarah the moments before Locrinus died but she'd had her suspicions. How she wished then that the world would open beneath her and suck her into the ground. She didn't want to watch the moment that Emily served her heart up on a plate only for Sarah to shove it right back.

'That's true,' Sarah said softly. 'You only ever loved me.'

From her bag Sarah withdrew the dagger and placed it delicately at the foot of Ruby's bed.

'I took this when he died, I thought it would help me keep my promise to him. But now I think the best way to remember him... is to just remember *him* and forget everything *else*,' she looked meaningfully at them. 'I need to find out who I am, without you three.'

She turned to leave but lingered a moment longer, her long willowy silhouette could have belonged to anyone. Estildris or Sarah... or some new person that Harriett did not yet know. She turned her head to the side so that they could just about see her lips move. 'Message me every now-and-then will you? Keep me up to date about the big things.'

'I will,' Harriett promised.

Then she left and Emily ran after her.

The door to Ruby's room slammed and there was the sound of footsteps thudding down the stairs.

'What does she mean?' Ruby asked, slicing through the silence.

Harriett thought she knew. Every day, Harriett woke up and her entire being went to war with itself. Memories tripped over memories in eagerness to be seen and felt and *there*.

The problem was simple, and it was this; they each possessed one soul that had lived two different lives.

They were faced with the age-old question.

Who am I?

Before, Harriett used to think she knew. Or at least that one day she *would* know. That one day she would know in her mind, in her bones and in her soul who she was, what she was capable of and what kind of life she should lead.

But all that had been wiped away like chalk from a blackboard.

What were they now?

A queen without her kingdom. A warrior without a blade. A witch without her powers. And a princess without her king.

Four schoolgirls and a bunch of shared secrets.

Then, against all reason, she looked out the window.

Two young girls stood outside. One solemn and earnest, the other taciturn and decided.

She watched as Sarah placed something small in Emily's hand, she watched as Sarah gave Emily the swiftest of kisses on the cheek, and she watched as Sarah walked away.

For a moment, Emily stood on the pavement motionless with her kitten by her feet, rain cascading down on her. Then, abruptly, she chased Sarah down the street, the kitten hurrying swiftly along beside her, until all three of them had turned the corner and disappeared out of sight.

For the life of her, Harriett couldn't think straight, so she just stared at the empty patch of pavement that lay at the bottom of the road, staring as a thousand tiny droplets spattered onto the cold, grey surface.

The sound of the TV blared.

Harriett forced herself to stare at the screen. It was one of the final scenes, where Princess Anne and Joe Bradley say their final farewell, knowing that in doing so they will never be together again.

Harriett closed her eyes.

Then the music played.

Chapter Fifty-Five

ALL THE TIME IN THE WORLD

September 2019 (9 months later...)

It was the end of summer and the sky was a patchwork quilt of whites and blues.

The car hummed beneath them, and Harriett watched as the houses of her street flashed by in a haze of red and grey. They flew past the block of flats that now stood where the Neville had once been, and past the stony beach until the dreary town of Woolington-on-Sea disappeared from beneath the car's tyres and they were driving along smooth open tarmac. She held a cup of hot coffee in one hand, and there was a suspiciously heavy bag at her feet.

It was almost a year since Sarah had left. Almost a year since Ruby had been rushed to hospital. Almost a year since they had been haunted by the Shadow of a dead king.

Everything had changed since then, yet nothing had. Sarah had gone; they had not seen her since that rainy December day in Ruby's house. Sometimes her absence was so palpable that Harriett was overcome by the longing to have her with them again. Other times, it was as though she had never been there at all.

Harriett found herself looking at life in terms of before and after. The *before* being back when it was still the four of them, together and whole and un-haunted. The *after* was the now, this strange yet familiar place where her reality seemed to be.

She was a girl who'd been poked full of holes and she felt each as deeply as the last. So many aspects of her life had been sliced away; Hayley, Sarah… the person she used to be.

Each day she took on the mammoth task of hastily stitching herself back together into a person that was recognisable for the world outside. She thought she understood her mother a bit better, how easy it was to become a ghost wrapped inside the shell of a person.

Then, something odd happened.

Just as she was growing accustomed to the sensation of being a phantom version of herself, the holes in her person began to fill and the rough edges of her being began to smooth themselves out.

She couldn't pinpoint exactly when the healing began but she knew the moment that she first recognised it. It had been a Saturday; the sun had been peeking out through the trees and the house had been calm and still.

She'd rolled out of bed and walked across her bedroom floor and for the first time since Hayley's death—she hadn't stopped to look at the empty space where Hayley's bed had once been. When she'd got downstairs her mother had been laughing, her brother had been eating breakfast and her father had been the one to tell the joke.

Hayley's photographs had reappeared on the walls as though they had never been taken down.

It was as if overnight their fractured family had been sewn back together. It wasn't the same, it could never ever be the same… But it resembled a family again.

Harriett had asked her mother what had helped her heal, what had inspired her to put the pictures back. Her mother had only smiled sadly.

'Oh honey...' her mother had said sweetly. 'Sometimes, we don't get closure; sometimes, we don't get to decide how we get better, sometimes the only thing we get is time.'

Time.

Harriett had plenty of that.

Chapter Fifty-Six

ALL THAT SHAPES US

I t was almost exactly as she remembered it.

The River Severn stretched ahead of them, its water still as glass and its surface winking in the sun as if hinting at all the secrets held in its depths. The trees were a little taller now and there was a village in the distance that had not been there before but mostly it had remained unchanged. Untouched by time.

Ruby walked forward, twigs snapping beneath her footsteps. 'This is so weird,' she breathed.

Harriett rummaged through her bag and withdrew the skull that had been hidden in the back of her wardrobe for so very long. At the same time, Emily opened the boot of Alex's car and pulled out a grubby white bundle. Harriett grimaced, she did not want to think too long or too hard about what was wrapped inside it, or how Emily had kept it hidden over the past few months.

After a brief pause, Ruby reluctantly bent over and pulled out the dagger tucked inside her boot.

They fanned out, Ruby and Alex wandering to the right, Emily and Whisper to the left while Harriett made a path straight down the middle. She could hear Ruby pointing out places to Alex, recounting what had once occurred there. She drowned the voices out, her feet pulling her toward a slight bend in the river, where the grass thinned until there was only wet mud and rocks.

She could feel a lump form in her throat, her mouth felt dry. She could see it all so clearly in her mind's eye. The trees had been smaller, the bushes less wild and there had been a wooden jetty that jutted out halfway into the water that had long since ceased to exist.

This had been the exact spot all those years ago where Lady Estildris had been sentenced to die.

Her hand trembled as she bent down to run her fingers through the sloppy dirt. It scraped up beneath her nails, but she didn't care. It was as if, by remembering her—remembering *Estildris*—she was closer to Sarah.

'I miss her too,' Ruby said, sneaking up behind her.

Harriett stood up slowly and brushed the dirt from her hands. 'I thought you said you couldn't care less about her.'

Ruby ran a hand through her hair, it had grown past her shoulders but was still dyed to the colour of charcoal. 'I lied. Sometimes it's easier to be angry than to be hurt.'

Harriett looked out over the river. 'Do you know what Severn means, when it's translated from Old Welsh?'

'Nope. But I'm sure you're going to tell me.'

'It means Habren,' Harriett said bitterly.

Ruby let out a low, impressed whistle. For the most part, it seemed as though time had forgotten about Queen Gwendolen and her short rule over England. Her marriage to Locrinus, her fight for Madden's throne, had all but been erased from history and translated into myth. It was a cruel joke that the river's name, despite being carried through centuries and being passed through a dozen different tongues, had somehow stayed the same.

Emily appeared next to them, she nodded approvingly when she recognised where they stood.

'This is the place.'

Harriett looked at Ruby and Emily. Each of them represented a duality, a *hugr* that had been pulled from time and a *hugr* that had been lost. Then there was Alex, standing in the distance waiting for them. He was brand new; his soul a shiny new coin that had not yet been corroded by rust nor tampered with by witchcraft.

She sometimes found herself wondering what Harriett Sinclair would have been like, had Gwendolen's essence not evicted the original occupant so violently. She knew that the other version of Harriett would not be standing at the edge of a muddy river right now, the weight of a skull resting heavily in her palm.

She supposed it didn't matter now. For better or for worse she was the one standing there, in Harriett Sinclair's clothes, in Harriett Sinclair's skin, in Harriett Sinclair's life.

There was nothing left to do but live it, and she intended to do so with ferocity and hunger.

Fall in love with the world for me.

Together they waded into the river, Whisper stood at the very brink of the edge, his blue eyes following them carefully. Alex stood even further back, as though afraid of interrupting the moment. Harriett wondered at how strange the scene must look to him.

Three girls standing in a river. One holding a skull, one holding a dead cat, the other a dagger.

It sounded like the beginning of a story and she supposed in a way it was, but in many ways... it was the end.

Harriett took a deep breath, nodded and as one they each let their burdens go.

The skull and dagger dropped into the waters with a satisfying *plop*, sinking into the muddy depths and out of sight instantly. The white bundle floated for a moment and then slowly, slowly, the water began to cover it. Until finally the river swallowed that as well.

The water flowed in a steady stream and the world went quiet.

Emily closed her eyes. 'Hêore thither endian.'

Here it ends.

Ruby coughed into her arm. 'I... I know it feels like everything is ending... But no matter how far we drift apart; we'll always find our way back to each other.'

Both Harriett and Emily gazed at Ruby, each of them waist-high in the water.

Harriett frowned. 'Why do you think that?'

Ruby shrugged, rolling her shoulders back in a slow, languid movement. 'I'm not sure... Maybe because we grew up together? Or maybe because we're all made from the same crazy, nightmarish stuff...' She paused, and then let out a deep, throaty chuckle. 'Or maybe because we're soulmates, in the truest sense of the word.'

Harriett felt the corner of her lips tug upward. 'Soulmates?'

Ruby grinned.

'All of us?' Emily whispered. 'Even Sarah?'

The grin vanished and Ruby's nose crinkled before smoothing out again. 'Even Sarah.'

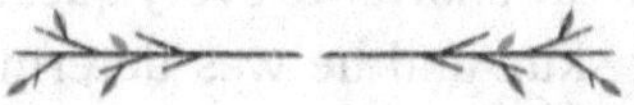

AFTER, THEY SAT a little further away from the water, a picnic laid out before them in the tall, wild grass. They watched as fisherman came and went, trying their luck in the River's unyielding waters. There seemed to be an unspoken agreement between them that they would not discuss the past.

'I'm going to find Madam Crone,' Emily said, feeding a piece of ham to Whisper. 'I feel like our paths need to cross again.'

'Do you still feel it?' Alex asked eagerly, 'Magic?'

Emily looked upwards, her deep brown eyes roving the heavens. 'Sort of. I feel a hum in the earth sometimes. Or I catch whiffs of it.'

Alex frowned. 'Whiffs of it?'

Ruby rolled her eyes and grinned. 'Don't bother trying to get much more out of her.'

'I take it I'm not the only one going travelling?' Emily asked, raising her eyebrows.

Ruby smirked and twined her fingers together with Alex's. 'We're going to explore England before my next fencing tournament.'

When she had recovered from surgery Ruby had argued bloody murder with her mother to let her try out for the regional fencing team. Harriett suspected that Ms Coleville only agreed to it thinking that Ruby would be considered too weak to participate. She could only imagine the shock on Ms Coleville's face when they informed her that her daughter was 'ruthlessly talented.'

'Her coach thinks Ruby's got a real shot of getting a medal in the under 18s championship,' Alex said, beaming at her. The way he stared at Ruby sometimes was almost indecent. As though she had the answer to every question he'd ever had etched upon her skin, and he was determined to read her forever.

'How about you, Sinclair? You can't tell me that you haven't got any big plans.'

Harriett smiled softly. 'I'd like to travel too. But first I think I'm going to go to college, then university and then, maybe… into politics.'

Emily, Ruby and Alex all smiled at that.

'Planning on ruling England again?' Ruby joked.

Harriett laughed. 'Not quite. But I'd like to try and do some good while I'm here… this time around.'

Sometimes, she heard a little voice in her head. One that crept into the crevices of her mind telling her that she could do more—that she could *be* more. That voice, she knew, belonged to Gwendolen.

The sun started to sink in the sky and the moon rose to meet it. They both hung there suspended for a while, leaning close to each other as though sharing a glorious secret.

Sitting there with the river sprawled out behind them, Harriett couldn't help but feel as though she was letting go of something intrinsic to her, something so deeply woven into the fabric of her being that she didn't quite know how to untie it. Her chest tightened and her breath hitched in her throat.

No longer a schoolgirl, no longer a queen.

Emily fixed her with an inscrutable gaze and took hold of Harriett's hand. 'It's important to remember who we used to be, and it's important to think of who we will become,' she said, as though reading her thoughts. 'But what truly matters most, from one breath to the next, is who we are *now*.'

She was right.

Because Harriett was all the experiences that had ever shaped her. She couldn't go through life trying to find herself because who she was, was constantly changing. Harriett Sinclair had been a student and a queen, kind and ferocious, merciful but deadly. Now, she had a whole new future ahead of her, all she had to do was grasp it.

The sky was now a curtain of purple, embroidered with starlight. Harriett ran a hand over Whisper's soft, fluffy head and smiled.

Who was she?

Harriett Sinclair was someone who endeavoured to fall in love with the world.

She was a bright girl—and she was also a queen.

For where was it written that she could only ever be one thing at once?

DEAR S, TODAY WE WENT TO THE RIVER SEVERN AND DROPPED THAT THING YOU GAVE RUBY RIGHT INTO THE SPOT WHERE IT ALL BEGAN. IT FELT STRANGE TO KEEP HOLD OF IT FOR SO LONG. I'M NOT SURE IF THIS COUNTS AS A BIG THING... BUT IT FELT LIKE IT. I WISH YOU'D BEEN THERE. UNTIL WE MEET AGAIN.

—HS

AUTHOR'S NOTE

> "Locrine deserted Gwendolen and raised Estrildis to be Queen. Gwendolen thereupon, being beyond measure indignant, went into Cornwall, and gathering together all the youth of that kingdom, began to harass Locrine by leading forays into his land. At last, after both had mustered their armies, a battle was fought on the river Stour, and Locrine, smitten by an arrow, lost his life and all the joys thereof. Whereupon Gwendolen laid hold on the helm of state, maddened by the same revengeful fury as her father, insomuch as that she bade Estrildis and Sabrina her daughter be flung into the river that now called Severn, issuing an edict throughout all Britain that the river should be called by the damsel's name."

Taken from *The History of the Kings of Britain* by Geoffrey of Monmouth, translated by Sebastian Evans.

I first had the idea for *Patchwork Girls* when I was working as a temp in a call centre. I knew I wanted to write a story based around female friendship and the pangs of growing up, but I had no clue as to what the plot should be. I'm not sure exactly when, but an idea came to me of four friends who have been reincarnated, destined to betray each other again and again until finally the curse is broken.

Of course, at this point I had no idea who they would be reincarnated from, or why they would continue to betray each other. And so began a hunt for female figures from history. At first, I was searching for inspiration, an idea of how far back in history I could go, until finally something caught my eye.

The tale comes from the famous book *The History of the Kings of Britain* by Geoffrey of Monmouth, most well-known for *Arthur of Briton* and *The Prophecies of Merlin*. Yet the story that attracted me was barely three pages long. The myth begins with Brutus travelling to Britain, naming it after himself, and then dividing it between his sons. It then ends with his eldest son murdered after causing a war focused around his two queens.

What fascinated me is that, according to Geoffrey, Gwendolen was the first Queen of the Britons, and yet so few people have heard of her. It made me wonder at who Gwendolen and Estildris could have been and whether their tale could be the focus of mine.

Through plotting and writing, my initial idea for the novel shifted, and the result is what you now hold in your hand.

I have, admittedly, played around with the timeline and settings of the myth, though I don't feel too guilty! The joy of mythology is to see how it changes over time. Despite my meddling, many of the details remain true to the original story. Indeed, the River Severn is still named after Estildris' daughter to this very day. Severn in Welsh is Hafren (or Sabre, Sabren, or Sabrina) and in Old Welsh it is Habren. Estildris was supposedly rescued from Humber King of the Huns and Locrinus did supposedly fall in love with her at first sight. It is also true that, in the original myth, Brutus was the son of a Goddess, though it is unclear whether it was believed his sons carried any god-like power themselves.

Ultimately, my story is far removed from the original tale. Thea and Augusta are my own creations, and Locrinus' curse is entirely my own invention. I wanted to weave a tale where the main characters are haunted by a shared past. I wanted to write a novel that focused on the beautiful and complex nature of female friendships. I wanted to show how as we grow up, our identities become an ever-changing thing.

I hope that Geoffrey doesn't mind that I used one of his stories to do it.

ACKNOWLEDGEMENTS

It takes a lot of work to write a book. It takes a lot of daydreaming, plotting, staring at a computer screen, crying over spongecakes and, y'know, actual *writing*.

For the most part, writing a novel is a lonesome adventure where the author gets to decide on the players, the stakes, and the outcome. We are captains of our own ships, deciding exactly which rocks to crash into.

But while the writing of a novel is a lonesome task, that does not mean I have ever been *alone*.

First, I must give my truest thanks to Xyvah, who made me think that not only was it possible to release *Patchwork Girls* in printed form, but then went on to *prove* that it could be done. Without her, quite simply, this book would not exist.

Second, a huge thanks to my Mum for always, always believing in me and for feeding the little book monster that she helped to nourish and grow. Mum, without your constant encouragement and book-giving skills, I may have become interested in netball or swimming instead, and that's just ridiculous. You are, and will always be, the little very, very LOUD voice in my head propelling me forward, pushing me to do and be better. You are crazy-amazing. Cramazing, if you will.

To my Dad, who has always taught me the importance of thinking BIG and then—if at all possible—even BIGGER. I hope you enjoy this book and proudly show it to all your friends down the club, and don't worry, I endeavour to make my next novel roughly the size of a Yellow Pages.

To Ryan, Kenny, and Andrea for always being there and

supporting me no matter what.

To Tasha, April, Jobie, Grace, Charlotte, Becky, Vikki, Jodie, Jema, Holly, and Katie G. You make up my world and helped me shape this one. My real-life patchwork girls.

To my October Deadliners, who reignited my passion for writing. Xyvah, Ezgi, Ekene, Tal and Hannah. I hope we continue to share our scribblings with each other in the years to come.

Finally, this book is for my husband, Shane. Thank you for being there through every beautiful high and devastating low, thank you for loving me when I've not been so loveable and for patiently waiting while this writing malarkey kicks off. Your support means more to me than I will ever be able to put efficiently into words. You are my rock, my muse, my best friend and without you this book most definitely would not exist. I love you.

And to you dear reader, for reading this book and getting to the end! I hope you enjoyed reading it as much as I enjoyed writing it.